IN

THE

WRONG

HANDS

a crime novel by

PORTER EIDAM

To my mother, whose faith was unwavering.
To my father, who taught me the importance of language.
To my wife, who inspires me twenty-four-seven.
To my stepkids, their partners, and their children, who stand as
assurance that all will be well.

A BRAIN EXERCISE

Saturday

1. Cardinal Romero Catholic High School
Potterford, Pennsylvania

"Wrath," said the bishop.

Philip's sides still hurt from 20 minutes of suppressing an overwhelming urge to giggle. Drawing unwanted attention to himself was not part of the plan, such as it was. Regardless, laughing at children … never good form. He couldn't even pinpoint what was giggle-worthy. It wasn't the white robes. The "hands in prayer" thing was a little hokey, but it showed conviction. He was a huge, dedicated fan of conviction. Perhaps it was the variety of casual footwear, frayed jeans and tie-dyed leggings peeking from beneath the robes. Or rather, the juxtaposition of the hands and the feet … the conviction and the lack of effort. He wished for someone to fart.

Please, someone, anyone! I can laugh at a fart. Everyone laughs at farts.

The term for what he'd witnessed eluded him. He could remember "Confirmation." That's what the children had walked *to*. But what was the walking part called? Philip was not Catholic.

"Greed," the bishop continued.

Asshole.

To the congregation's right was a massive mural of Cardinal Romero. St. Aloysius RCC hadn't yet broken ground on the new church, so Mass was held in the Cardinal Romero High School gymnasium. At least Philip thought it was a gymnasium. It could have been one of those all-purpose rooms he had lunch in as a kid.

What do they call them nowadays? Gymacafetoriums or some dumb-ass thing?

"Be very careful of these two Deadly Sins, children."

Two Deadly Sins? What happened to the other five?!

"One sin begets another."

Come on! These kids have sacrificed their dignity and a perfectly good Saturday evening just to make their parents happy. Give them their money's worth for fuck's sake!

"They work in tandem. That means they kind of piggy-back."

Condescending prick. Whatever. If I was caught serving booze to a bunch of 14-year-old girls, they'd send me to jail!

Another giggle crept into his throat. He squashed it quickly with a quiet, phlegm-laced cough (a side-effect of his smoking).
"That's a pretty cool back pack; I wish I had that back pack."

That's envy, not greed you idiot.

"We all have these thoughts."

What's interesting is I'm probably going to remember more of this sermon than anyone else in here. Wait, is it a sermon or a homily? Oh ... that's right ... I don't care.

The part of Mass that irritated Philip the most was the taking of Communion. He wasn't one to be self-conscious, but watching everyone else get in line and do their thing while he remained sitting in the congregation like a leper gave him the willies. In truth, he probably could have gotten away with joining in. It was a fairly simple process. Walk up to the guy with the wafers. Look at him placidly as he says, "the body of Christ." Say "amen." Receive the wafer orally. Cross yourself as you walk away. Piece of cake. Sure, he could have done it, but no one in the room wanted him to, so he didn't.
He respected their religion just enough to not participate.

Fucking Communion.

It was maybe 20 minutes off.

He fished about the room going from face to face giving everyone a back-story. One guy bred ferrets. Another had herpes. A girl across the aisle saw every *Twilight* film 12 times. When he got sick of that, he started imagining people naked. Then he glazed over and lost a couple of minutes.

"Everyone, please stand and let us all accept these young people into our congregation."

Whoah! That's it? Did I fall asleep? Did I sleep through Communion?

He checked his own face for drool. No, to his dismay, he had *not* missed Communion, although he had no idea what or whom he'd been looking at for the past however long it was. He hoped he hadn't been staring. He knew it was unreasonable to believe no one would remember him once the investigation started. Still, he didn't want to do anything overly memorable, like get into a subconscious staring contest with one of the altar boys.

After a few hymns, some readings, some prayers, a collection, a round of "Peace Be With You," and one taking of Communion, the Mass ended.

Philip stood and stretched.

Whoops!

Another half an inch and his jacket might have come up over his belt. That wouldn't have been good.

He yawned and looked around. Everyone was so shitting happy. Why was everyone so shitting happy? A 13-year-old boy, who had to be 6-foot-3, got a strangling hug from (presumably) his grandmother who looked as if she had already gone through a box and a half of tissues. Of all the things this boy would do in his life...high school, college, medical school...even if he found a cure for cancer...this would be the moment that made his grandmother the happiest. He was on the fast-track to heaven now.

Maybe, dream of dreams, he will become a priest. Doesn't that absolve every one of his blood-relations of all sin? Maybe not. Whatever. The question is moot. He's going to play for the NBA and contract a disfiguring STD.

He continued to distract and amuse himself with inner-monologue all the while remaining conscious of the 9-millimeter pistol stuck down the back of his jeans.

He eyeballed his target. Maybe this wasn't the day.

Ah well.

Bishop What's-his-face was surrounded by parents looking for photo ops for their children. Philip wasn't into the idea of collateral damage, and he certainly wasn't going to run the risk of hurting any kids. It was time to go. He had a steak dinner waiting for him at Applebee's.

Next time.

He turned and weaved his way into the exodus. The flow took him right past where the Bishop was appeasing his adoring fans. That's when he heard it. The (presumed) grandmother he noted earlier had engaged the Bishop in conversation. She was trying to be nice and suck up to God at the same time. The result was quite the opposite on both counts, but it wasn't her fault.

"Your Grace, why don't you come by for dinner while you're in town? We'd love to have you."

"Thank you very much, Constance, but Father Pascucci and I have some talking to do, so we'll just be grabbing dinner at Sullivan's, and then I'll be heading back to the hotel."

"Oh, well that's good. I hope they at least put you up somewhere nice."

"The Marriott actually. Not bad at all."

Of all the things for Bishop Whatzitz to bring up in conversation...his dinner plans and his hotel arrangements...while Philip was five feet away.

Bingo

Some would have called it fate; others would have called it coincidence; still others, like Philip…divine intervention.

He smiled to himself and looked to the heavens by way of the Gymacafetorium ceiling.

Thank you, man. You rock!

Sullivan's made a steak you could cut with a fork. They also had the best selection of single malt scotches west of the Delaware River. Fine dining. Sloooow dining. This meant Philip had time to eat. He had been looking forward to a steak all day but went off the idea when he found out Bishop Blah-blah was probably getting one too. He ordered a turkey burger off of the new Applebee's menu, and it was delicious. Afterward, he stopped at his girlfriend's place, just like he knew he would (he wasn't getting any that night, and he didn't much care). Once his business was done there, he headed for the Marriott.

It took 10 minutes to get to the 4th Street Exit. Philip tittered intermittently and uncontrollably the entire drive as if he was on his way to get ice cream.

Not a bad idea. Later perhaps.

The sun was down, but not far down. The hotel sign threw a dull glow over one of Potterford's more irritating intersections. Philip looked up and sighed indifferently at the red light that normally would have sent him into a psychological tailspin.

*Not tonight. Not even **you** can ruin my mood tonight.*

His thoughts shifted to parking. The spot had to be somewhere close, dark, and away from any kind of surveillance camera. He was going to be seen at the Marriott. He knew that. It didn't matter.

45 seconds passed, and he stepped on the gas.

Soooooo, where-oh-where to park. Yesss! There we go!

A slight squeal of the tires, a little bounce of the shock-absorbers, and the car was nestled in the perfect place, just as happily as Philip. Whistling

"Onward Christian Soldiers," he retrieved the gun from his glove compartment, shoved it into his pocket, and walked.

It was early autumn of 2015. That time of year, the days were still warm, but it got chilly in a hurry when the sun went down.

The Marriott was close. The hotel itself was quite nice; the area around it, not so much. At evening, however, covered in shallow moonlight, Philip found the whole scene downright soothing. He reached for his smokes.

"Dammit."

He'd left them in the car. Wanting not to take his eyes off the hotel, he considered getting a pack at a nearby BP.

"No ... trying to avoid security cameras. Remember, ya moron?"

There was a bench across the street from the Marriott that gave a clear view of all the vehicles going into and out of the lot. He sat with a jolly bounce, causing his ill-fitted trench coat to spread and drape over the edge. He slung his right foot onto his left knee and started to contemplate what make/model of car he should be looking for.

It's a shame the Pope doesn't loan his out. That would be easy to spot.

No kids, so no minivan. No wife, so no SUV. No point in having a sports car if you weren't looking to get laid. He figured he was looking for a 4-door sedan. It would be a modest color...maybe 3 years old. An hour hadn't gone by before a forest green Chevy Malibu pulled in with vestments hanging in the window. Philip was either on a serious roll or had missed his calling.

He pulled his hood over his head and walked leisurely toward the Malibu. He saw the Bishop get out of the car and start up the sidewalk to the hotel's side entrance. No snazzy greeting; no theatrics. Philip came up behind the Bishop. The Bishop turned around simply to acknowledge the sound of footsteps on the pavement. The shot rang out; the body hit the ground before the echo died down. Philip never broke his stride. He took his planned route back to his car, got in, backed out of his parking space, drove down 4th street for 6 blocks, and got into the drive-thru line at the Dairy Queen.

2. Headed West on 4th Street

Potterford, Pennsylvania straddled the Schuylkill River roughly 35 miles northwest of Philadelphia. The town was just big enough, populated enough, and laced with just enough crime for the local police department to have its own detective squad. The crew stayed busy with only four badges, and no specialized divisions, but still, it was Potterford. Most of their cases involved burglary, armed robbery, fraud, assault (mostly domestic), or drugs. Murder was rare. High-profile murder was unheard-of.

"I'm telling you Jaime, it's weird."

Sergeants Lynch and Gomez had just pulled their jackets on and were on their way to clock out when the call came in.

James Alan Lynch and Ernesto Juan Mateo Gomez worked well together. They compensated each other's lack of brain function in their respective right and left hemispheres.

With a Bachelor's degree in Software Engineering under his belt, Lynch had an overactive, sometimes oppressive, talent for deductive reasoning and problem solving. He went straight from college to an entry level position with a company that specialized in VPN technology for law enforcement.

He spent a year beta testing in the field and discovering his new passion. To him at least, the leap made sense.

He was at the dinner table with his mother, father, and younger sister when he announced his decision to change careers. He stood and revealed it proudly, as if he were coming out of the closet…which his parents (both mathematicians) probably would have preferred. His father made a solitary comment and never brought it up again.

"Full scholarship to Drexel. Could be worse…you could have gone Ivy League. Then you'd have wasted *my* money instead of the school's."

Gomez was from the asshole of North Philly and spent most of his young life working his way out. Along the way, he'd developed a deft gift of gab along with a keen understanding of human nature. Like his partner, his choice to go to the police academy was an easy one.

Their relationship on the job was simple, elegant, and followed suit with their personalities. Lynch usually led things in the field while Gomez conducted the station interviews. In the interims, they found ways to keep each other, and those who happened to be in their proximity, amused. It

11

had been suggested more than once that they start either some sort of self-help discussion-based webcast, or a Vaudeville act.

If you were a perp in the back seat of Lynch's car, the only consolation you had after having your nose broken was getting to listen to your captors' banter.

They were finishing up a conversation they'd started at the station, when the Marriott came into view.

Lynch drove; Gomez talked.

"It's like this. I saw a dead bird in the station parking lot the other day. It was flat…you know…run-over. The thing is, it affected me, hombre. I started thinking about what a miserable waste of life it was. I wanted to undo it somehow, like obsessively…"

He laughed to himself.

"…seriously a freakin' bird! Then it got worse. I started thinking about sitting in a traffic jam and all the anonymous faces I see in other cars slowly passing me on the right and left and how each of those faces is attached to a life just as important as mine. And then I started thinking about all the mosquitoes I swatted and ants I've stepped on and how I can't begin to understand their sense of self-importance."

"And you say this is new?"

"No, the bird just woke it up. It's happened before…bunch o' times."

"Really? Do you remember the first?"

Gomez answered with neither apology nor melancholy.

"Yes, I do, and that's the whole thing, Jaime. It started when my mom died last year."

Lynch had no response. He offered a front-facing, sympathetic smile that he knew Gomez didn't want or need. Gomez reached in his collar with his left index finger and pulled out a few inches of a thin, gold chain. He didn't expose the simple crucifix at the end of it. His partner knew it was there.

"You know where my head's at. I believe mi madre esta con Dios…"

He crossed himself and kissed his own right thumb as he tucked the chain back into his collar.

"…but, just as a brain exercise, what if body and soul have some sort of symbiotic relationship? What if the soul needs a body the same way a parasite needs a host? Like when a body dies, the soul leaves it and attaches itself to the closest healthy body it can find?"

Lynch took a moment of surprised silence before responding. Ernie's topics of conversation were rarely so elevated.

"What's got you thinking this?"

"Like I said, I didn't used to be this way. I never cared about things like dead birds and the consciousness of insects...but my mother did. I told you I was the only one in the room with her when she died, didn't I?"

"Yes, you did. So, you think your mother's soul...*attached*...to you somehow?"

"Attached? I wouldn't use the word 'attached,' but check this out. All the time, you hear people talk about sensing the dead, being spoken to by the dead, being influenced by the dead. What if our loved ones literally become a part of us when they die?"

They were stopped at a traffic light. The crime scene was two blocks away.

"But you said they just attach themselves to the nearest healthy body. Does that mean surgeons and EMTs are walking around with dozens of souls? I don't even know what the word would be...'inside' them?"

Gomez took a moment.

"Good point. Maybe it's not enough for the body to be healthy. Maybe the host needs to be suitable. That would make sense. It follows that loved ones would make the best hosts. It would also explain hauntings."

"Hauntings?"

"Yeah, like a haunted house. A ghost could be...you know...a soul that hasn't found a suitable body, so it's floating around until it does."

"Nah, I don't buy it."

Gomez shrugged and looked out the window at the person in the car next to them. The light turned green, and both cars eased forward.

"Suit yourself Jaime. Like I said, it's just a brain exercise."

"But...what you're saying could also explain schizophrenia."

Gomez grinned.

"Como es que?"

"Let's say I give your brain exercise some hypothetical merit. Maybe souls mess up sometimes. Like they enter unsuitable hosts and get rejected. That might explain dual personalities. When it's really bad, it turns violent and gets mistaken for..."

"Demonic possession?"

Lynch smiled forward again.

13

"I dunno, maybe."

Gomez held up his fist for Lynch to bump.

"That's what I'm talking about, hombre."

Lynch looked down at his partner's fist, then back at the road.

"You know I'm not bumping that, right?"

"Pendejo! Anyway, I digress."

"Ah, that's right."

"What was I talking about before I got on this topic?"

Lynch pulled into the Marriott parking lot.

"Neckties, I think."

A single shot was heard by several guests at the Marriott. The security guard, who had been flirting with the desk clerk instead of monitoring surveillance, waddled out to the parking lot to investigate. After emptying his stomach onto the concrete, he called the police. That was an hour ago. In a fit of panic and having seen the victim's collar, the guard also called St. Aloysius RCC. No one answered, so unable to think straight, he left a message. When he hung up, he squeezed his rosary, sped through a breathy "Our Father," and murmured "It's what God would want."

The crime scene officer's name was Kelly Truesdell.

"Hey, fellas."

Lynch dug for his pad and pen while Ernie met with forensics by the body.

"Evenin', Kelly. Priest?"

"Bishop."

"Oh boy. Please tell me this one got caught with his pants up."

"Pants are up, Jim."

"Witnesses?"

"No eyewitnesses, but a couple guests heard the shot and…"

"Shot? As in singular?"

"Yup, just one shot as far as we know."

"Who's on this? State? County? Fed?"

"No one yet. Just you guys."

Over Truesdell's shoulder, Lynch got his first look at Father Leonardo Pascucci. He had arrived a good 20 minutes before Lynch and Gomez. The priest was pulling what appeared to be a receipt out of his wallet to show Truesdell's partner. Lynch could see it quivering in the shadow of the squad car's head lights.

"Who's that guy?"

"Now, that *is* a priest."

"What's he doing here?"

"You'd have to ask Brian. The security guy called Saint Al's when he found the body. Left a message. That's all I know."

"Left a message? Christ!"

"Seriously?"

Lynch put on the necessary gear as to not contaminate the scene, and walked over to Doc Callahan while Gomez did likewise and disappeared into the hotel. The sheet-covered body lay close.

"Hiya, Doc. How we lookin'?"

"Clean shot to the front of the head. Looks like he pivoted on his left foot right before it happened. Never saw it coming."

"Yay."

"Yeah, Jim. Sorry. I'm afraid the 'how' is going to be easier than the 'why' and 'who' on this one."

Ernie called over from the side entrance.

"Looks like we have a couple cameras, partner!"

"Well, that's good news. Kelly! Where's the guard? The one that found the body?"

"Inside with the medic."

Ernie headed for the lobby while Lynch and Callahan knelt by the body of Bishop Ryan. The doctor pulled the sheet back. The bullet hole was small. The gun couldn't have been larger than a ten-millimeter. The shot was deliberate but probably not the result of a professional hit. Assassins run silent. Anyone with a game system knows this. Lynch jotted down a few more minor observations before Callahan replaced the sheet. Ernie returned.

"We got lucky on the surveillance. Well…sorta lucky. Want to take a look?"

"I do."

"Sorta lucky" was an apt description. After viewing the material twice, Lynch left the security room and reluctantly returned to the parking lot. There was someone he needed to talk to.

"Father Pascucci?"

The priest nodded wearily.

15

"I'm Sergeant Lynch. I'm sorry you had to find out about this the way you did. Has anyone gotten you anything to drink? There's a soda machine…"

"Thank you, Sergeant. I'm fine. Do you know anything yet?"

"I'm afraid I just got here."

"Of course. I'm sorry. I suppose this is when I'm supposed to say 'who would do something like this', but when, statistically, every fifth person you meet thinks you're a charlatan or a child molester …"

The statement abutted self-pity which the good priest detested, but he'd been bottling it for an hour.

"One of the officers took your statement, right?"

"Yes. I told him everything I could think of. I didn't know Bishop Ryan very well."

"Maybe you can help us then."

"Sure. Anything"

Father Leo was a fourth generation Italian-American in his mid-50s. He was a tall man in good shape with a full head of peppered grey hair and straight white teeth. When he was younger, he wore his nationality on his sleeve. Not so much anymore. He didn't really have to since the other two priests in his parish were Irish.

"One of the security cameras caught the shooting. If you're up for it, you might…"

"I am."

"I'm sorry?"

"Up for it. I'm okay. I'll look."

For Lynch, this was a first. Not the response itself, but the quickness of it.

"Okay then. Follow me."

Father Pascucci was asked three times if he was ready to see the tape. When Lynch and everyone else involved was assured, the security guard was asked to push [PLAY]. The priest squinted slightly as the dark colored Malibu came into view. Bishop Ryan exited the car, put his hands on his hips, and stretched his back. Then he went to the back seat to get his briefcase and vestments. He fiddled with them for a bit and realized that he didn't have enough hands to take everything in at once, so he closed the door. He was rummaging for his key card, so he could get in the side entrance of the hotel when…

"Pause it, Henry."

Lynch had the tape stopped just as a figure in a black trench coat over a lighter colored hoodie came into frame.

"Father Pascucci, we don't have the gear here to enhance the picture, but does this mean anything to you?"

The priest squinted tighter and leaned in to see what Lynch was pointing at. The killer's trench coat had some sort of symbol on the back. It was white, about 8 inches in diameter, and right between the shoulder blades.

"I don't know the symbol specifically, but it's probably Satanic or, at least, Pagan."

"Really?"

The priest stood straight.

"I know of a group of young people that hang around the church's neighborhood now and then. I don't know much about them. They keep in the shadows mostly as far as I can tell, but they all wear those jackets."

"A Satanist group you say?"

"I never heard them say it, but they act like it. It's doubtful that they really know what they are. Troubled, yes, but if that is one of them, it's strange. They've never been in the church. I don't know how they'd even recognize Bishop Ryan."

"But the jacket makes you think he's one of the kids from this group you're talking about?"

Father Pascucci chose his words carefully, realizing his answer could sic the police on an innocent.

"Maybe. A lot of kids in town dress that way, and a lot of them brand themselves with symbols they don't understand."

"Does this crew have a name?"

"I once heard them refer to themselves as 'The Unjudged,' but I don't know if that's what they call themselves or how they describe themselves. Both maybe?"

Lynch jotted "Unjudged" in his note pad with a snort of disgust. The word wasn't even grammatically correct.

The priest was skirting the truth. St. Al's last encounter with the "Unjudged" was more specific and complicated than he let on. As much as he wanted to help, it was important that he not be stuck at the hotel all night answering a hundred follow-up questions.

17

Lynch spoke.

"We've got one more…"

Henry cued up a second recording. It showed Philip entering the property from the street and walking across the parking lot. The shadow from the hoodie and the woeful quality of the recording left only the tip of his nose visible to the naked eye.

"We're going to do our best to scrub it out, but quite frankly, this gear is older than the building …"

Everyone was thinking the same thing.

At least the rates are reasonable.

Lynch asked his next question almost apologetically.

"Does *anything* look familiar to you? His gait? The shape of his head? Anything?"

The priest gave the image honest scrutiny before giving his defeated reply.

"No, not a thing."

Lynch stopped the tape with a satisfied nod.

"Thank you, Father. Here's my card. Give me a call if you remember anything else. I will probably be in touch over the next couple of days. Is it okay to phone the church?"

"Yes. Of course."

"Well, again, thanks. And Father…please, for the sake of the investigation, don't discuss anything you've seen tonight with anyone. If you want me to elaborate…"

"No. That's okay. I completely understand."

Father Pascucci would never take the Lord's name in vain, but old habits die hard. He came from a family of South Philly butchers. He also believed that God tells us what's offensive; not the other way around. Hence his muttering as he backed his car out of the hotel parking spot.

"Don't discuss this with any one? Are you fucking kidding me?"

3. Potterford Police Station

"Back off will ya Reilly! You know the smell of your tea makes me sick."

18

"Whatcha lookin' at, Jim?"

"Just some stuff on Bishop Ryan."

Top priority was tracking down the Unjudged. Step one was finding a legible version of the symbol on the killer's trench coat. The capture from the video tape wasn't clear enough to flash around the St. Al's neighborhood. This left Lynch and Gomez at their computers browsing pages and pages of Satanist rhetoric. Lynch had also opened a magazine article about the victim. He knew next to nothing about the man.

Sergeant Kevin Reilly leaned over Lynch's shoulder purposely positioning his cup by his fellow detective's face.

"Don't even tell me another cocksucker is coming after the diocese with this molestation bullshit! I've had it up to my..."

"No, Reilly. No one is accusing him of anything. He was killed tonight."

"He...he what?"

Lynch realized what he just said and, more importantly, to whom. If anyone in the squad was going to be affected by the night's events, it was Kevin Reilly. Lynch turned around and quickly tried to backpedal.

"I'm sorry, Kevin. I shouldn't have just blurted it out like that. Where have you been, man? The call came in two hours ago."

Reilly squeezed the handle of his cup and stared at an invisible spot on Lynch's desk as his face turned a few shades pinker. There was no mistaking when his Irish blood was boiling.

"I've been down in records since five o 'clock trying to close the goddam Del Rey case. Sons of bitches! Are the Feds in on this?"

"I think the Chief has been on the phone with them, but we haven't heard anything yet..."

Lynch looked toward his boss's office.

"...I dunno. It's weird"

"You keep me in the loop on this, Jim!"

Reilly put his cup down, muttered something about "lost time", and headed for the foyer. He needed some air.

"You hear me? In the loop!"

The previous two years had been rough ones for the Philadelphia Archdiocese. Three priests in their parishes were accused of child molestation. None were prosecuted, but there was plenty of damage done. Everyone with any kind of authority in the Archdiocese was replaced.

Archbishop Fellini was brought in to spearhead the effort to get things back in order. Sitting at his right hand was his pit bull, Bishop Ryan. The two of them were revered in the community with movie star status. Whatever they were doing, it seemed to be working. The centerpiece of the morale-building portion of the effort was the construction of the new St. Aloysius Church in Potterford. It aptly represented how the Catholic community in that part of the state had blossomed and thusly outgrown the old parish on Prospect Street. It was to be a beautiful building in every aspect with a comfortable seating capacity of 900. On Christmas and Easter, 1500.

"Ha! Jaime, I found it. Come take a look."

Lynch moved Reilly's cup off of his desk, and took a look at Gomez's monitor. He felt lousy about his accidental terseness, but there was no way he was spending the rest of his tour smelling mint tea.

"Are you sure?"

"Yes, I'm sure. Look!"

Ernie dragged the digital capture from the Marriott's security camera next to the graphic he found on line. It looked more like a cake decoration than a Satanic Symbol.

"Good eye, Ernie. How did he put that thing on his jacket?"

"Looks like paint."

"Did he use his feet?"

"That's what happens when you cut a school's arts program."

It would have saved them a few minutes later in the evening had they taken a look at the origin of the symbol. As it was, they were both in linear mode and were only interested in getting the jacket ID'd.

"Okay. Print out both, and let's take a ride."

It was only 10 o'clock. The chances of finding at least one group of teens huddled under a street lamp were better than good. They drove past the church on Prospect Street. The parking lot was empty. Neither detective thought anything of it. They were bound for the Seven Eleven a couple of blocks away. Despite the "No Loitering" signs scattered about its parking lot, the "Sev" was always a good spot to rustle up some pimple-faced slackers. Sure enough...

"Whoah, whoah...where are you running off to there, buddy?"

"I've got to get home, sir. My mom is..."

"Hold on. Look. Badge...no uniform. You know what that means?"

"You're a NARC?"

"It means I'm a detective, which means that I spent more years than you've been alive working so that I wouldn't have to worry about busting kids for loitering."

The skateboard-carrying boy's eyes were not visible through his jet-black bangs, but Lynch could tell he still didn't get it. He pulled out his copy of the printout.

"What's your name?"

"Declan."

"I'm Sergeant Lynch. Ever seen this, Declan?"

"No."

"Give it some thought, and consider we got it from the back of a black trench coat."

"A what? Oh. Yeah. Gordy wears one of those."

"Who's Gordy?"

"A kid from school. He doesn't hang with us though. He doesn't skate. He rides his bike all over the place…dork."

"Does his jacket have this on the back of it?"

"No, he's got something else. I can't really describe it, but it's not that."

"You know where he lives?"

The boy whipped his hair to the side and stared sheepishly at his own Chuck Taylors.

"Okay, Declan. If I throw in a six of Red Bull, do you know where he lives?"

The boy re-whipped his hair and raised his head just enough to make eye contact. That was enough for Lynch. He turned to Gomez, who was questioning another fine young chap by the propane tanks.

"Ernie. Whaddayagot?"

"Word has it there's a fella named Gordy who might be able to help us out. My new amigo here is shaky as to a location though."

"Mine too."

Lynch turned and gave Declan a wink. There wasn't any real need for secrecy, but he knew the kid would get a kick out of it. They can cut their hair anyway they want, paint their nails any color they want. Boys are boys. They've all seen "Toy Story," and Declan had just been deputized.

21

4. St. Aloysius Rectory

The St. Aloysius rectory was conveniently on the same property as the church. Its small inhouse chapel was in the back of the building and flanked by trees. At night the lights could be on without attracting attention from the street. Father Leo was barely out of the hotel parking lot before he was on his cell phone to Pastor Karney. Forty-five minutes later, all three parish priests were in the chapel with the door closed. The prayers were short. Father Leo gave a detailed account of everything that happened, starting with Mass and ending with the security tapes. After that, it didn't take long for things to go from somber to borderline-hostile.

"Can we please forget about out our collars for one minute!? A man was killed tonight!"

"Lower your voice, Aiden. No one wants to be cold about this, but we all know what is going to happen tomorrow."

Father William Karney, the church's Pastor, fancied himself the most articulate of the three. When he spoke at Mass, he educated but rarely inspired. This had been his role so long that he found it difficult to switch it off. His pragmatism was irritatingly instinctual, especially in times of crisis. During the scandals, even with his title, no one let him near the press.

Conversely, the passion of Father Aiden O'Rourke lit up the sanctuary like a Christmas tree. Many of the confirmed would find out when he was leading Mass and work their weekend plans accordingly. They never knew what he was talking about, but it didn't matter. He was the only one of the three priests who'd grown up in Potterford. He was 26. Most of the neighbors still thought of him as a kid.

"What, Pastor? What's going to happen tomorrow!?"

"The same thing that always happens."

Pastor Karney was on his way home from St Joseph's University when he received Leo's call. Using the Bluetooth interface on his car, he was able to call the Archdiocese (hands-free) en route. The conversation lasted the full length of the drive.

"But surely *we're* not going to be seen as the bad guys this time."

"We shouldn't, Aiden, but…"

"But what!? I don't understand!"

Father O'Rourke had only been allowed 15 minutes to let the news sink in.

Father Leo spoke.

"What did the Archdiocese have to say?"

Pastor Karney took off his glasses and, as was his habit, let them dangle from his teeth as he talked.

"First I want to make sure I didn't lie to them. Leo, you're positive you've seen that jacket in the neighborhood?"

"I couldn't swear to seeing that *exact* jacket, but I've seen the gang. We all have. It's the same bunch that accosted Sister Edwina."

Father O'Rourke fidgeted uncomfortably.

Pastor Karney continued.

"Then, at least for starters, the diocese wants to keep the investigation local."

Both Leo and Aiden responded with expressions of skepticism.

"Involving the State or County Police or the FBI will intensify the media frenzy exponentially. Monsignor Edwards has already spoken with the Chief of the Potterford PD. The Chief wasn't exactly thrilled with the idea either, but he and the department will go along with the request, for now at least."

Aiden spoke.

"So where does that leave us?"

Pastor Karney put his glasses back on and directed his thought at Father Leo.

"Like I said, we have to talk about tomorrow."

Leo was familiar with the regular game plan…too familiar.

"What does the Archdiocese want to do about a public statement?"

Karney smiled at Leo sympathetically.

"Funny you should ask…"

There was a pounding on the rectory's front door. Whoever it was had to be using serious muscle in order for it to be heard from the chapel. Pastor Karney turned flush.

"Oh no. Not already."

Father O'Rourke stood, realizing the discussion had gone to a place that didn't include him.

"I'll get it."

The two priests continued to talk while Aiden jogged down the hall to the door. He did a quick inhale-exhale before he reached for the knob. He was bracing himself for a verbal head-butt from whomever was on the other side. He opened it, saw who was there, and instantly forgot himself. It wasn't a reporter.

"Jesus! What the hell are you doing here?"

The smell of mint tea just about knocked him off of his feet.

5. Declan's Driveway

"My mom is gonna freak! Can you walk me to the door in handcuffs?"

Lynch attempted to explain to the boy that cops don't take people *home* in handcuffs, but it didn't take. He walked Declan, his skateboard, and his six pack of Red Bull to his front door, met Declan's mother who was, as expected, in utter contrast with her son, explained to her what happened, and headed back to Gordon (Gordy) Weiss's house. He'd left Ernie to watch the house from across the street. Nothing had happened in the few minutes it took Lynch to drive Declan home.

An hour later, they were leaving the Weiss household with little more than they had at the Sev. Gordy was an angst-ridden youth who had attended a Forever Damned concert the previous year and wound up in general seating behind a group of guys wearing black trench coats with (what he interpreted to be) satanic symbols on the backs. He thought it looked cool, so he made one for himself. End of story.

"He's telling the truth, Detective. He's a good boy, but he doesn't keep a secret very well. We grounded him and made him get rid of the jacket. Besides, he's been home all evening."

"Apologies, Mrs. Weiss. He doesn't need an alibi. He's not a suspect. We didn't mean to give that impression."

Truly, he wasn't. Neither his jacket symbol nor his stature matched the gunman's. They decided to let him fester. Passive-aggression seemed to be the discipline of choice in the Weiss household. If the boy was hiding anything, guilt would get the best of him. The detectives took a courteous minute to calm the parents while Gordy went back to his room, then they left.

"Ay! Where to now, amigo?"

"Let's head to the coffee house. I think they do open mic on Saturdays. We're bound to encounter a decent amount of adolescent weltschmerz."

"What the fuck are you talking about?"

They got in the car, and almost immediately something caught the corner of Ernie's eye.

"Seriously, the kids in this town cannot all be this stupid!"

Gordy was flying up the street on his bike,…and he was wearing his trench coat. Lynch spoke.

"Wonder where he's headed."

"My guess is he's going to see the rest of…"

"I know. I was speaking rhetorically."

"Pendejo."

They followed at what seemed like a snail's pace for 6 miles to the overgrown grassy outskirts of Potterford. They turned on to a gravel road and shut off the car's lights. They were amazed that the boy didn't hear them. Little nitwit was riding with his buds in and his music cranked no doubt. They passed three farms and a weathered FOR SALE sign before…

"Now exactly what the hell is this?"

6. Near the Abandoned Meadowbrook Dairy Farm - In a Truck

About the time Declan was climbing into the back seat of Lynch's car, a black Ford F-150 was creeping down a gravel road 6 miles away. Two men sat in the back facing each other like paratroopers. Each, in his own cartoonish way, prepared himself for handing out an ass-whoopin'. The one behind the cab's passenger side repeatedly smacked the palm of his hand with the fat end of a baseball bat. The other nodded his head a lot and rubbed the back of his neck. The driver cranked the Skynyrd.

After passing 3 farms, their target appeared in the distance, looming under a single flood light. It was the old Meadowbrook Farm.

They stopped about 20 yards shy of the weathered FOR SALE sign that had been on the property for 9 years. The driver backed into the grass.

"Ready?"

"Hell yeah."

All three men deployed with the fervor of the Penn State Nittany Lions, got in single-file, and broke into a jog. They took a wide curve across the abandoned hayfield, failing to notice the trampled grass in their wake.

The floodlight acted as a beacon, throwing a vertical, cone-shaped beam onto the barn's broad side. Arcane symbols spray painted there boiled their insides as they approached. They halted just short of the light's perimeter. Music that sounded like someone being torn apart by jackals emanated from within.

They needed to get a look inside.

There was light coming through a small hole in the barn wall about chest-high. It was in an otherwise unlit area, so it would serve well. They took position. The man on point put his eye to the hole and beheld the cloister of the Unjudged.

The scene was as one would expect. 7 members were there that night. They were all in their late teens or early twenties. There was a fire pit in the middle of the room. Two of the boys were engaged in intense conversation by an antiquated CD player. The other three boys were taking turns throwing knives at a target that was nailed to one of the barn doors. One of the two girls was an obvious attention junkie, having stripped down to her bra and Hello Kitty underwear for no apparent reason. The other was sitting next to a pile of empty pizza boxes unlocking the mysteries of the universe by staring at the fire.

It took a mere 10 minutes for the paratroopers to discover the Achilles Heel in the gang's routine.

The room looked like a recycling center that specialized in Yuengling products. Obviously, the maid hadn't been in that month. Those in attendance, however, were hygienic enough not to piss in the barn. For that, and that alone, they removed themselves via a door opposite the peep hole and did their business by an ancient plow in the yard.

The peeper whispered to his team but had to stop abruptly because the barn went silent. One of the knife throwers was an arrogant looking twenty-something with platinum-bleached hair. He shouted with a rasp exerting his alpha maleness … or trying to.

"Hey! You homos deaf!!? The CD stopped!"

"We are talking here, Artie!"

"Just change it, asshole!"

The exhibitionist spoke up.

"Put on something I can dance to."

"Hear that, Rick? Hello Kitty wants to dance!"

The boy that Rick had engaged in intense conversation turned and walked away during the yelling.

"Where are you going, Jeremy? We're not done yet!"

"I'm takin' a pee. Calm down."

Jeremy heaved the door open with drunken momentum. The plow was visible in the moonlight. It acted as a good point of reference when the eyes weren't working so well. Singing the last few words of the song that just stopped, he stumbled forward and whipped down his fly. Inside, the music started up again. A moment later, 3 figures emerged from behind the plow.

And the boy was beaten within an inch of his life.

7. Near the Abandoned Meadowbrook Dairy Farm - On a Bike

Gordy's best kept secret was his encyclopedia-like knowledge of classic film and television. All the way through elementary school, he spent every afternoon with his Bubbe and Zaydee until his parents finished work. He was subjected daily to selections from his Zaydee's (grandfather's) vast library of DVD's. Comedies and War films were most common, but equal time was given to binge viewings of the Dick Van Dyke show.

For a single reason, his favorite film from the collection was a goofy comedy called *Guide for the Married Man,* starring Walter Matthau. There was a line in the film that Gordy came to regard as the "secret to an easy life." Matthau's co-star, whose name Gordy could never remember, was going through the steps one would take to successfully cheat on his wife. Among his pearls of wisdom was "the key to a good lie is making it as close to the truth as possible."

The key to a good lie is making it as close to the truth as possible.

The concept was simple, brilliant, and had served him well. It helped him deal with his nosy parents, his ass-hat teachers, and, most recently, a couple of fascist detectives.

He felt himself a genius.

With the accuracy, sincerity, and detail that could only result from the truth, Gordy had told Lynch and Gomez about the Forever Damned concert. He recalled, with all the trimmings, being in general seating behind a bunch of guys in trench coats. He listed what songs were played, gave them the exact time the show ended; he even produced the ticket stub. He, however, left out one pivotal detail. He had, in truth, gone to the concert *with* the guys in the coats. He spent the whole evening fetching beers, but he was with them, nonetheless.

He'd used his credo to get one over on the pigs, and now he was on his way to the barn, uninvited, to brag about it. He was not doing well on the gravel. He kept his head down, homing into the barn using moonlight and shadows. When the light behind the grass started to flicker blue and red, he brought his eyes forward discovering, to his horror, that the building was beset by the Potterford PD. Sloppily, he skidded around and tried to double back, only to find himself face to grill with a slow-moving car. The car's headlights instantly ignited, causing Gordy to fall sideways with a simian grunt.

The car came to a complete stop, and 2 men emerged. Gordy recognized their voices.

"You okay, Gordy?"

"Yes, Detective Gomez. I'm fine."

"Good. Get in the car."

This was their second crime scene in less than 5 hours. Sergeant Reilly, Sergeant Carrie Warner (Reilly's partner), and four uniforms were already there.

"Can you believe it? These little pricks did what they did, and now *I* have to work for *them*?"

"Take it down a notch, Reilly. What happened?"

"Seven of these Unjudged retards were partyin' in the barn. One leaves to take a piss and gets jumped."

"How bad?"

"He's still breathin', so not bad enough."

Lynch took a look around. Four of the gang members were spread around the scene, waiting for whatever was going to happen next. One of them, the arrogant one with platinum blonde hair, caught Lynch's eye and gave him a douchy thumbs-up with a douchier grin.

"Any chance the kid was jumped by his own gang?"

"Doubtful. We've questioned each one separately, and all the stories are consistent. Carrie's pretty good at trickin' 'em, and so far, everything stands up."

28

"Where are the rest?"

"Inside, except for the beat-up one. He left in the back of an ambulance maybe a half an hour ago."

Warner emerged from the barn.

"What are you guys doing here? We didn't call for back-up."

"Believe it or not, we're working our case. Whaddayagot?"

"Show me yours, and I'll show you mine."

The victim was named Jeremy Sokol. He was 20 years old, had a clean rap sheet, and according to the rest of the gang, was well liked.

The party started around 7:00 pm, as was normal for a Saturday. Everyone arrived in the same cruddy customized van nicknamed "Zed-Zed."

"Stupid thing to call a van."

"There are two Z's on the license plate."

"It's still stupid."

Those assembled represented a little under a half of the Unjudged or "UJ" membership. None of them left the building from the time the party started to when the police arrived: a rock-hard alibi for everyone if it held up.

"Okay, Kev. Ready?"

Reilly rubbed his hands together as if preparing for a meal.

"Born ready."

The uniforms gathered everyone and lined them up along the barn. Lynch did the talking.

"Thank you, ladies and gentlemen, for your patience. Now, if you would be so kind as to turn around and face the barn."

They complied, revealing the backs of their trench coats and a row of six white symbols. Lynch and Gomez held up their print-outs and walked along the line, starting at opposite ends and working their way to the center. Lynch walked especially slowly past the fellow with the platinum blonde hair.

"What's your name, son?"

"Arthur, sir. I have to tell you, I'm feeling a little like I'm in front of a firing squad. Should I ask for a blindfold?"

"Not yet."

Disappointingly, Arthur's jacket was not a match.

"If you just tell us what you're looking for, Sergeant, we can…"

Some loud words at Gomez's end of the line suddenly drew Lynch's attention. One of the other UJ's was not as lucky as Arthur. Hay dust billowed as the punk's face met the barn wall.

"Ow, man! What the hell!? The other cop said she didn't care about the grass!"

"Grass? What grass? I don't care about grass, acho. What I care about is your paint."

Lynch gave Arthur one last eyeball and walked towards the yelling.

"What's going on, Ernie?"

"Take a look."

As if playing "pin the tail on the pothead," Ernie slapped his print-out on the back of his new best friend. The symbols matched, but not exactly. The killer's was bigger and cleaner. That, however, didn't stop Lynch from getting into the guy's face.

"We have a little problem here."

"The niño's name is Steve."

"...Steve. The thing on the back of your gang uniform..."

"It's not a gang."

"Shut up. The thing on the back your jacket matches one that we picked up on a security camera couple of hours ago."

He thrust the picture under Steve's nose. The lad stopped wriggling around, stared at it for a few seconds, and reacted as though he'd seen a ghost.

"Holy...Samuel. That's Samuel."

The detectives would later learn that the jacket symbols were from the Theban alphabet and nothing more than the wearers' first initials. Steve and Samuel, therefore, had similar but not identical tags. Steve, able to explain the mistaken identity, became immediately more forthcoming, as did almost everyone else. Arthur was silent, but a widened shit-eaten grin revealed his feelings on the matter.

Disconnected, quick-fire information about Samuel went flying at the detectives from five sources. The comments ranged from high praise to throwing him head-first under the bus. Amidst the cacophony, Lynch picked out one snippet of interest. Samuel had a girlfriend. Her name was Kelly, and she was standing third from the left. It was the other girl, Traci the Hello Kitty exhibitionist, that outed her. Kelly was not pleased.

"Thanks, bitch."

Lynch stepped between them, much to Reilly's dismay. It was sounding like the whole mess could be resolved quickly if hands could be put on this Samuel guy.

"Let's take this into town. Come on, everyone. Saddle up."

In pairs, all six Unjudged delegates were split between the two patrol cars and Reilly's sedan.

Lynch and Gomez found Gordy smudging up his passenger window with handprints and juvenile finger drawings. Lynch spoke to him.

"Did you see anyone out there you recognized?"

"I told you. I saw them at the concert last year."

"And that's it? You can't tell us anything else about them? You don't know anything about a guy named Samuel?"

"Not a thing."

Lynch shrugged at Gomez and started the car.

"Let's get you home."

"I wouldn't want to be you right now, amigo. Sus padres va a estar muy pissed off at you."

"Yeah, right. You'll have to wake her up first."

The individual interviews were conducted two at a time, starting with Kelly the girlfriend and Steve the pothead. Since the two crimes had some overlap, all four detectives participated.

Lynch and Warner took Kelly.

"We were partying at the barn. We all passed out in the loft. The next morning, Samuel was gone. Poof, that's it. Hey, aren't you guys supposed to have pastry?"

"You don't seem that affected."

"It was March. I'm supposed to care about something that happened in March? We were going out for like three weeks. Whoop-dee-doo."

"Okay, well, if you're going to leave it up to us to find him, we're going to need his last name."

"I don't know it."

"What do you mean you don't know it?"

"None of us know each other's' last names…"

Lynch shot her a look as though he'd just heard the dumbest thing in the world. She continued before he had a chance to comment.

"…or age, or address, or occupation. We know cell numbers. That's it, and before you ask, I don't remember his, and I took it off my phone. You have it. Check it yourself."

"Thank you. We will. We'll need you to help us with a composite before you go."

"What? You mean like talk to a sketch artist?"

Overuse of the word "like," especially when used by someone out of high school, drove Lynch a bit mental.

"I mean *exactly* talk to a sketch artist. We're also going to need to talk to the rest of your gang…the members that weren't at the barn tonight."

"It's…"

"Not a gang. Yeah yeah. You guys hang out anywhere besides the barn?"

Silence.

"Please don't make me ask again."

She didn't make him ask again. The bar was called The Iron Wall, and, thanks to Pennsylvania liquor laws, had been closed for almost a half an hour. The information gleaned from the rest of the interviews was nearly identical.

Zed Zed had been driven by one of the uniforms to the station, searched in vain for the murder weapon, and parked in the lot. After fines were issued for the vandalism, the six members of the Unjudged were sent home.

Lynch was seeing double, but he and Gomez couldn't go home just yet. They had eight more black trench coats to track down. After watching Zed Zed's taillights disappear down Main Street, they caught up with Reilly, who was just ending his tour.

"Jesus, Jim. Get some sleep for chrissakes."

"Trust me, if we weren't talking flight risk here, I would."

"Is that the composite?"

Lynch had made a copy of the sketch. He'd forgotten it was still under his arm.

"What? Oh, yes. No match yet. You sure you've got nothing else from the barn?"

"You mean as in witnesses? None. Those shitheads have been hanging at the old Meadowbrook Farm for months. The neighbors complained a few times in the beginning, but…"

32

"Okay, okay. You answered my question."

"Crime Scene has given me all they can for now. I'll check back…" he looked at his watch. "…later this morning."

"Sounds good. Sleep well."

Reilly took hold of Lynch's shoulder.

"Remember…*in the loop*. Are you coming in tomorrow?"

"It depends on when the Fed's get here. I'll let you know when I do. Is that cool?"

Reilly made his eyes lazy and went slack-jawed.

"Absolutely."

"Kevin, stop it. The only person in the station that does a worse impression of Rocky Balboa is Ernie."

Gomez overheard and responded.

"Ay, Adriana!"

"Nice. Can we go, please?"

The other eight members of the UJ alibied out. Five of them were at the Iron Wall all night, according to the bartender. Two were at work, and the last was playing Black Ops with her cousins.

It all pointed toward Samuel being their man. They just had to find him. No one who looked at the sketch had seen him since he disappeared the previous March. The APB was put out, along with the sketch, but optimism waned as the wee hours of the morning ticked away. They didn't even have a last name for the guy.

It had been an extremely long night.

33

THE BASTARD WITH THE TAMBOURINE

Sunday

1. The Condo

Ugh…Sunday!

…was the second thing to go through Lynch's head as his eyes sprang open. The first was the earth-shattering sound of church bells. It was 10:00 in the morning, less than 5 hours after his face hit the pillow. As far as he knew, he didn't have to be anywhere for a few hours, but the odor of freshly brewed coffee and the pleasant shine of the sun through his bedroom window made him feel obligated to get up. He rolled over and stared at the ceiling for a minute as he worked his way into total consciousness. He became aware of a Fleetwood Mac song wafting softly elsewhere in his condo, mixed with the faint clickety-clack of a computer keyboard. Julie was working.

Maybe she got bagels.

…got him to sit up.

Maybe she's working naked again.

…got him on his feet.

Donned in his standard t-shirt and boxer-briefs, he walked to his living room. Julie was on the couch with her laptop set up on the coffee table. No nudity.

They'd been together for two and a half years. His place was her place now and had been since the previous summer. They'd discussed marriage a time or two, but, for many reasons, neither of them was ready, at least not yet. She was a food critic for Philly Neighbor Magazine and had a weekly spot on Fox 13.

"Good morning."

"Good morning, sunshine. Sorry I'm not naked. Did I wake you?"

"The Lutherans woke me."

He kissed her.

"I got bagels."

"I knew it! From Anna Maria's?"

"From Anna Maria's."

He kissed her again.

"You rock Ms. Calbraith."

"I know."

The day was kicking off nicely. Lynch went to the kitchen and got the fixins' out for his favorite Sunday breakfast. Julie talked and typed.

"I didn't hear you come in last night."

"This morning."

"Ouch. What happened?"

"Do you know who I mean if I say, 'Bishop Ryan'?"

"I do."

"Got killed last night."

"You're joking."

"Nope."

Julie reached for the newspaper. She had brought it in but hadn't taken it out of the plastic yet. She saw Ryan's photo on the front page before the paper was fully unfurled.

"There aren't any pictures of the crime scene."

"Yeah. We actually got in front of the media on this one. I'm sure the feeding frenzy has started by now."

Lynch didn't count the woman he loved among the Cyclopes who wrote for the local papers, and she knew it. She'd gotten used to sideways comments about her fellow journalists, and generally let them slide.

"When I got up, I saw you silenced the ringer on the land line. Now I get it."

Bagel toasting was underway. The kitchen was little more than a sectioned-off corner of the living room, so he didn't have to shout back.

"Clark will want me to make a public statement later today I'm guessing."

She put the paper down and resumed typing.

"You're the lead, then?"

"Oh, I'm sure the Staties or the Feds will take it."

She glanced back at the article.

35

"Your name isn't in here anywhere."

"It will be."

"I'm surprised Reilly didn't lunge for it."

Julie hadn't met anyone at the station apart from Ernie, but Lynch kept her up to speed. One of her favorite things about their relationship was the pulp-filled pillow talk.

"He wasn't around. Ernie and I didn't even know what we were getting into until we got to the Marriot."

"The Marriot...they've got good tilapia there."

"Really? Cool. Anyway, Reilly wound up with his hands full later on."

Lynch told Julie about what happened at the barn. By the time he was finished, his bagel was toasted, schmeared, plated, and on its way to the couch.

"The Unjudged? That sounds familiar to me."

"Familiar? How? Are they well-known in restaurant circles?"

She ignored him.

"Where the hell have I heard of them? Here...proofread this."

Julie turned her laptop to face Lynch. She got up and went for the stairs. Their place was a two-story condo. The second floor was more of a loft than a story, but it was big enough for a desk, a Bow-Flex, and small filing cabinet. The filing cabinet was Julie's and contained every issue of Philly Neighbor magazine since its inception in 2002. Lynch started to give Julie's article on restaurants with vegan options a read when the inevitable happened. Five hours ago, he'd draped his jacket across the nearby love seat. The inside breast pocket started to vibrate.

"Here we go."

He dumped out his phone and answered it.

"Hi Chief...Like a baby. What's up? Seriously? Why? I suppose it doesn't matter that I...Didn't think so...I'll be there in a half an hour."

He hung up and spun his phone like a Frisbee across the coffee table.

"Hey babe. I'm gonna shower. Gotta get to City Hall. The Staties and Feds are bailing. Looks like I'm the lead after all."

Julie was digging through the filing cabinet and replied without looking up. She was nothing, if not focused, when she was on task.

"Okay, hon'. Enjoy."

She was still digging when he left.

36

2. The Rectory

Leo Pascucci's meeting with the other parish priests had dispersed the previous evening, not long after the unexpected knock on the rectory's front door. With a head full of unprocessed thoughts, the good priest went to his room. His next cognitive sensation was sitting at his desk waiting for his laptop to come to life. Once it did, it was the only light in the room.

Hours passed.

The distant cry of a fox made him look at the time. He'd been staring at his monitor all night and had written but a single paragraph. It was probably enough.

On behalf of St. Aloysius Catholic Church, I thank you for attending this press conference today. Bishop Ryan was a beloved figure in the Catholic Community. He was, as you know, brought into our diocese under the worst of circumstances. As a diocese, we forgot that while we have devoted our lives to God, we have also devoted our lives to His children. And that helping to bring the community closer to God requires that we step back and look at ourselves regularly. I say that "we" as a diocese forgot all this, but Bishop Ryan did not. He was as devoted as any man who ever put on a collar was to assuring that we hold ourselves to the standards expected of us.

It was five o'clock in the morning. Across town, James Lynch had just gone to bed.

Leo rubbed his temples, then leaned forward and continued to type.

As we break ground on our new beautiful church next month, we will dedicate the project to his memory. No man will deserve it more.

He stared at what he had written for a bit. Then he typed the last two words.

God Bl

He stopped. Then, slowly, and after contemplation, hit his backspace key evenly 6 times. He looked down, looked up again, and pecked out the last two words one letter at a time.

Thank you.

He checked his voicemail. The press conference on the back steps of City Hall wasn't for several hours yet. This wasn't business as usual. He had to get going. He needed to do more than make himself presentable for the cameras. He was to be sharing the stage with someone very important.

3. Potterford Memorial Medical Center

Jeremy Sokol was still unconscious. His nose, jaw, and cheek bone had been broken along with his left knee and several ribs. He also had two black eyes, a punctured lung, a variety of ugly bruises, and a concussion. He was in the ICU and only allowed three visitors at a time. Kelly, along with Traci and Rick, clung white-knuckled to Jeremy's bed railing. Without prayer, there wasn't much to do other than stare at the broken ash tray that used to be Jeremy's face. Rick started errantly thumping the railing with the heel of his palm.

"Come on, man. Wake up. Wake up and tell us who did this. You can do it man. Wake up. Wake up and tell us who did this."

The feeble mantra persisted quietly. The rock in Kelly's throat started to expand. She became conscious of a faint tapping sound and then realized it was her tears falling on the edge of Jeremy's pillow. It was all Traci could take. The whole situation was eclipsing her senses. She closed her eyes and shook her head slowly.

Too much. Too much.

She wasn't built for this kind of reality. She had to do something to break it, *anything* to break it. She opened her eyes with a manic smile and did the first thing that came to mind.

"Hey, Jeremy! Look at this!"

The R.N. at the desk almost ruined an entire box of gauze with 22 ounces of spilled coffee. He'd not seen a patient get flashed before. Kelly, again, was not amused.

"What the hell is wrong with you Traci!?"

And Jeremy's eyes twitched. Rick was the only one who saw it.

"Really, man? Is that what it took to wake you up? Traci's knockers?"

The trio giggled with relief and exhaustion. Then Rick spoke.

"Can you hear me, man?"

Jeremy did what he could to nod.

"Do you remember getting beaten up?"

Again, a nod.

"Did you recognize who did it?"

Jeremy stared at Rick blankly for close to a minute. Then, with pain in his eyes, he rocked his head slowly from side to side...no.

Out in the waiting room, the wall-mounted lo-res TV was turned to the morning news. They had just finished stepping the greater Philadelphia area through a recipe for dill dip and were back to continuing coverage of Bishop Ryan's murder.

Arthur was watching.

There was to be a press conference at 11:30 am. Among those speaking would be representatives from St. Aloysius, and the Philadelphia Archdiocese.

"Alrighty then."

4. The Courtyard Outside Potterford City Hall

Philip looked down. He'd gotten something white and powdery on his shoe.

Where did that come from? Ain't no white powder around here. Topiaries, cobblestone, some trees, reporters, cops. Oh, that's right. My donut...I had a donut before...a good one. Anna Maria's kicks ass.

Going through City Hall security put a quiver in Leo's stomach. His last visit to a government building wasn't particularly pleasant. The quiver elevated to a swirl as he looked past the guard and got a glimpse of the man he was instructed to meet. It was Archbishop Fellini of the Philadelphia Archdiocese, the man brought in specifically to clean up the mess of the past two years. Leo had spoken to him only three times prior. The first was during Leo's official review of the diocese's restructuring. The second was right before his grand jury testimony. The third was four hours ago. The Archbishop's demeanor was notoriously, unnervingly pleasant. He made his reputation from an explosive temper that no one

39

ever saw. Leo gathered his personal effects from the blue security bin and approached with as much fortitude as he could muster.

"Your Grace. Hello."

"Yes, yes. yes. Hello, Father."

Fellini clasped both of Father Pascucci's hands in his own. They spoke in Italian.

"Did you make it in okay?"

"Yes. The Schuylkill Expressway was kind, surprisingly enough."

"Were you able to get something to eat?"

"Yes, yes. I'm good. Have you managed any food?"

"Food, yes; sleep, no."

"You'll do fine. We're all glad you're at the helm for this Leonardo. I was asked to pass that on."

"Thank you, Your Grace."

"I know it's been a few hours since we spoke. You haven't changed the speech at all, have you?"

"No, it's the same one I sent to you word for word."

"Good."

"I don't believe they're planning on this taking too…"

"Excuse me, gentlemen."

They were interrupted by Harry Clark, the Deputy Mayor. Next to him were the two detectives assigned to Bishop Ryan's murder. Everyone was being shuffled towards the building's rear entrance. The Archbishop maneuvered to the back of the pack. He wanted to be the last one out.

Philip dug out his cell phone.

What are the chances they're going to start this thing on time? It's 11:37…so…none.

He had no reason to be anxious; he had no idea what he was going to do. It seemed smart to check his exits.

Exits?

The poorly contained courtyard outside City Hall filled the block. A dozen uniforms, a single checkpoint, and some security tape were all that separated the public event from the riff-raff. There wasn't much tree cover. A speedy getaway would be tricky.

The area directly in front of the portable stage was sectioned off for the press. Philip and the rest of the onlookers bunched up behind. A hush fell on the crowd as the mayor and her entourage exited City Hall and descended the steps. Philip stood still with his hands in his coat pockets while everyone else fought for a better view. He double-checked the safety on his nine-millimeter. All good.

For Lynch, this was quite familiar territory. The back steps to City Hall emptied out onto a large courtyard that, with the help a few barricades and some yellow tape, was easily contained. Police were placed strategically about the perimeter and on the steps, as was the standard fare.

The speakers were the Mayor, who was introducing everyone else; Father Pascucci, who was issuing a brief statement from the church; and Lynch, who was fielding questions about the investigation. There was one other man from the Archdiocese that Lynch didn't know.

Clark gave the Mayor the high sign. She approached the microphone
.

Philip looked on.

Here we go...and the first one to the podium is (drum roll) of course, the mayor. She's more articulate than the last one. I'll give her that. Blah blah blah tragedy blah blah blah. Dear God, the guy next to me smells! Is he homeless? Maybe I should give him something. I only have two things of value with me. I need my nine, and I left my second donut in the car. There's no way he's getting that. He'd have to pry it from my cold, dead hand. Oy! What's she talking about now? Come on! Get in; get out! Go paint a bridge and let the people who actually know what's going on talk! Wow, I have to move. This guy reeks!

Leo glanced over at the Archbishop, who gave him a reassuring wink. Fellini's presence served a single purpose. Any Catholic watching the press conference would know that the Archdiocese was on the job. Anyone else would probably think he was just another priest from St. Al's, and that would be fine.

The Mayor finished. Father Pascucci was up.

41

Philip sashayed laterally to his left until he felt it was safe to breathe.

Whew, much better! What's going on here now? Ahhh, finally! She's done. Who's next? Oh, I remember him. He led the Mass...THE Mass...the greatest Mass ever...Bishop Dickhead's LAST Mass. Seems pleasant enough. What did they say his name was? Palucci? What is he? Italian? Greek? Russian? Now, HE'S got a nice speech...nonsense...but nice. Wow, they're breaking ground on the church next month. That didn't take long.

Lynch ran his eyes across the courtyard. Whether specifically assigned or not, everyone with a badge was on crowd control. He whispered to his partner.

"So far, so good."

"I'm bored."

"You want a disturbance?"

"I wouldn't *mind* a disturbance."

The front section was filled with reporters from Potterford to Camden, New Jersey and everywhere in between. Behind the press was a medium-sized crowd of regular folks.

"Nothing is going to happen. Put it out of your mind."

Father Pascucci finished, and the Mayor introduced Lynch. The opening act was over; it was time for the main event.

Aaaaand, here come the cops.

Philip and everyone else within a stone's throw of the stage had been scanned and frisked. It was a formality. With that kind of police presence, no one would be dumb enough to pack heat. That's why the evening before (DQ Peanut Buster Parfait in hand) Philip stashed his nine-millimeter in one of the courtyard topiaries. He knew there would be a press conference the day after the killing. He knew it would be open to the public. He knew where it would be held, and he was pretty sure who would be speaking.

These beat cop ding dongs weren't Homeland Security. They'd feel you up in a heartbeat, but they never swept for bombs.

The cop stepping up to the mic must be the lead detective. This interests me.

"Good afternoon. First of all, on behalf of the Potterford Police Department, I'd like to offer sincere condolences to Bishop Ryan's family, as well as those close to him. I've been asked to give the facts of the case up to this point as we know them."

I guess the sergeant likes prepositional phrases.

"The shooting took place between 7:00 and 7:15 pm in the parking lot of the Potterford Marriott. Some guests heard the gun shot and contacted the clerk at the hotel's front desk. Hotel security investigated, found Bishop Ryan's body, and dialed 911. It was a single, lethal shot with a small caliber bullet. We're still waiting for specifics from ballistics. We do have one strong lead. For various reasons, I'm not at liberty to discuss any specifics, other than to say that it is being aggressively followed, and we hope to have something positive within the next 24 hours. That's all we have at this time, but I'll be glad to take some questions."

The crowd erupted. Lynch pointed. He knew all the locals on a first name basis.

"Yes, Barbara."

"Detective Lynch, Barbara Edison Potterford Herald. Do you think this killing is at all related to the allegations against the church over the past 2 years?"

"No, we don't."

Idiot! When you start a question with "do you think", the guy can answer any way he wants. Ass-sucking Herald!

"Go ahead, Steve."

"Good morning, Detective Lynch, Steven Rameau also from the Herald. Do you think…"

Oh, for crying out loud! People waste so much time. What good…wait a minute…what's that sound?

43

Others heard it too. It sounded like a chant coming from PCHS stadium, but the Hawks didn't play on Sundays. Lynch looked up mid-sentence, and his facial expression went from "What can I answer for you?" to "You've got to be fucking kidding me." Everyone who had been giving full attention to Lynch turned around. The first thing they saw was a half-dozen uniformed police jogging towards the street side of the courtyard. Then they saw the first of the protest signs...then more...and more. The biggest read "THE CHILDREN KNOW THE TRUTH." Another was crafted as a train ticket to hell with the words "ONE WAY" stamped on it. Lynch thought that one was clever, but not clever enough to change his sudden shit mood. He turned to Gomez, who was smiling ear to ear.

"Got my back, Jaime?"

"Yeah, yeah, yeah."

To Philip, the protestors' chant sounded like "Sell the boot!" After listening to it for a minute, while local law enforcement formed themselves into a barrier, he could hear the actual words: "Tell the truth!"

Whatever.

Philip spun back around and clapped his eyes on his target. Could he chance it? Just like the conversation he overheard at St. Al's, the distraction caused by the protest seemed providential. He felt almost obligated to take the shot. He looked around. He could do it quickly. Gun out...pow!...gun in. Who would see him? No one! Why not? He flicked off the safety just in time to see the Deputy Mayor and two police officers corral everyone off stage and into City Hall.

Philip exhaled, scrunched his forehead, and laughed to himself.

What was I thinking? Yeah...like no one's gonna see me. Like no one's gonna hear me. Idiot. That's that. Time to go.

He flicked the safety back on and turned up his jacket collar.

Next time.

5. The Protest

The crowd of 200 or so was comprised primarily of married couples who had just finished either church, brunch, or both. Many of them enthusiastically shook sheets of poster board bearing references to bible chapters and verses. Others wielded pictures of their own children as they shouted barely intelligible slogans that took the moral high ground. Some sang. Some held up empty crosses, which made for some ominous shadows on the grass. Sprinkled among the couples were pockets of conscientious youths and a few lefties who looked for any reason to march on anything.

Lynch hated protests. Peaceful or not, the police always came away looking like fascists. His partner's opinion on the subject differed.

"Someone's going to do something, Jaime. I can smell it."

"A disturbance isn't enough? Now you want a riot?"

Music started. Beneath one of the larger placards, two guitarists and a cajon player laid down the chords and beat for a song called *Lord Knows*. Lynch, evidently in a minority, hadn't heard it before. The tune droned on with the monotony of most protest songs.

Lord knows that you can't hide,
Lord knows God won't abide,
Take a good long look; the mirror shows,
The truth will free you, Lord knows

...over and over again.

Gomez started humming along. Lynch gave him a backhand to the shoulder.

"Ouch! What!? It's catchy..."

And just when Lynch thought the morning couldn't get any worse, some bastard started banging on a tambourine.

"Ernie, get your cuffs out. I'm about to assault a musician."

With laser precision, the jingles shot through the discord and into Lynch's eardrums. The arty twat playing the thing had nestled himself between the two guitar players and was belting out the song along with everyone else.

"I'm telling you, amigo. We're gonna earn our overtime today. Just wait."

The passing of an hour proved Gomez to be wrong. All the protesters wanted were the sympathetic cameras off of the priests and on the placards, which they got. There was no need to get rowdy.

But the tambourine continued.

"Dude, I've got to say something to that bastard. Maybe I can appeal to his sense of humanity."

"I got your back."

"I don't need my back got."

"I'm coming with you anyway."

Two things drew Lynch's attention as he and his partner approached the crowd. The first was the banner being held defiantly above the protest's epicenter. Upon it was the high school yearbook picture of a good-looking young boy. Its caption was in large block lettering:

REMEMBER

The banner was weathered. It had been used before. The second thing that caught Lynch's eye was a quartet of young men clad in black trench coats. They'd staked a claim on the protest's periphery.

"Check it out, Ernie. You might get your wish."

Lynch only recognized two from the barn: Steve, the stoner, and Arthur, the cocky albino-haired son-of-a-bitch. The other two must have been with the crew at the Iron Wall. The bigger of them came in around 350 pounds. Gomez spoke.

"Did you see that?"

"The fat one reaching into his pocket? Yes, I did."

Arthur saw it too and reacted with a clutch of the wrist and a whisper.

"Not now, Bubbs."

The detectives stepped into view with their shields and side arms exposed.

"Welcome to the action, boys. You're late."

Arthur gave Bubbs a sharp, demoralizing glance before responding in an overly genteel manner.

"Well, good morning, detectives, or what's left of it."

Gomez was downright giddy.

46

"Whatcha got in your pocket there, hombre grande?"

Clarification from Arthur was required.

"He means you, Bubbs."

"Huh? Oh, you mean this?"

"Ah! Ah! Slowly. Nice and slow, junior."

Per Lynch's admonishing, Bubbs moved imperceptibly slowly and eventually produced an apple. He dangled it by the stem while Lynch and Gomez eased their stances.

"It's…uh…my lunch."

"Really? Your lunch? What do you think, Ernie? You think this gentleman maintains his girlish figure on an all-fruit diet?"

"No, Jaime, I would guess not. My guess is we're looking at a projectile there. You chicas looking to stir up some shit?"

Arthur appointed himself spokesman (long before they got there so it seemed).

"Stir shit? Detectives, will you please take a notice of our surroundings. Look at those nice folks peacefully exercising their right to assemble over there. Now look at us. Now look at your peer group over there in light riot gear. If someone throws an apple at a cop, who do you think is going to get tased first? I mean, let's face it. Running isn't exactly a strategic option for Bubbs here."

Lynch was borderline-impressed. Gomez was not.

"So, what are you doing here?"

"To tell you the truth, we came out here to see if we could peep Samuel for you."

"Really, did you now?"

Arthur was keeping the lie as close to the truth as possible. The little turd, Gordy, had rubbed off a bit.

"We figured the only way you're going to leave us alone is if you find the sorry-ass prick so…"

"Very well spoken. By the way, I talked to just about everyone in your 'not-gang' last night, and I never got a straight answer when I asked who your leader is. Has a good-night's sleep jogged your memory at all?"

"We ain't got a leader. Ain't no gang."

"Is that so, Bubbs? Who told you that?"

There was no response, but the reactive glances in Arthur's direction gave Lynch his answer. He spoke.

"Yeah...well, I got news for you, Bubbs. The guy that tells you there's no leader...he's the leader."

Bubbs processed Lynch's words for a pregnant moment before voicing his retort.

"Ain't no gang."

The City Hall Steps had long since cleared. Having made their point, the protesters started to disperse. Bubbs put the apple back in his pocket. He had been dangling it since he took it out. The tambourine stopped.

Lynch and Gomez were antsy to get started on the case. Arthur was antsy to get started on his Sunday buzz.

"Looks like things are breaking up, detective. May we go?"

"You're not gonna stay and help clean up?"

"Nah, I think we'll be taking off. There shouldn't be much to do anyway. The people in this town are pretty tidy as a rule...especially this crowd."

The four UJ's turned, revealing their Theban monograms. Lynch called after them as they walked away.

"You still have my card. Right?"

Arthur nodded his head and gave another sardonic thumbs-up without turning around. Gomez wanted to punch something.

"Little Aryan puta!"

"What're ya gonna do? Well...that was both time-consuming and bilaterally fruitless."

"You ain't kidding, partner whatever the fuck you said. I think the uniforms have this. Wanna get to work?"

Lynch checked the time. Julie had a review at 1:00. He was half hoping he could get home for a quickie before lunch, but his carnal window had closed.

"Let's eat first."

"Is Julie pissed that you have to work?"

"Not yet."

The small talk continued as they walked through the building to the municipal parking lot. Lynch took a quick look at his cell phone as he got into his car. There were three notifications: two texts and a voice-mail. The voice-mail was from a number he didn't recognize, so he gave it a listen.

Hi. Detective Lynch? This is Kelly Sanford. Um, you talked to me…well…interrogated…I mean interviewed me last night about Jeremy getting beat up.

A pause.

I need to talk, but we have to do it somewhere private. We can't do it at the barn or the police station.

The barn was still considered a crime scene and closed off anyway.

I'll be at the food court at the Galleria at four o'clock today. I'd really like to talk.

Another pause.

Okay, thanks. Bye.

He stared at his phone for a few moments, then took a look at the text messages. The first was from Detective Reilly:

THE JEREMY KID WOKE UP. HEADED TO THE HOSPITAL.

The second was from Julie:

FOUND IT.

6. St. Matthew's Catholic Church

Neither of them said it out loud, but both men were thinking the same thing.

Here we go again.

The event at City Hall probably could have gone worse, but in terms of what they were looking to accomplish, it was difficult to see how.

49

On the plus side, the protest distracted the press long enough for Father Pascucci and Archbishop Fellini to escape unaccosted. They needed to regroup, and St. Al's was not the place for it. Luckily, St. Matthew's, also a part of the Philly Diocese, was only a short drive away. They'd been given a small police escort, but both men agreed that the added protection wasn't worth the added attention. They sent all the officers away, save one. Once comfortably in the offices of St. Matt's, the Archbishop started calling every news contact he had in an attempt to head off the inevitable.

What a disaster.

Leo took a seat by a large window and stared out. He whispered to himself.

"Please God, I need a hand here."

It was the third time in twenty-four hours that his mind wandered to the Eric Bell trial. So far, he'd been too busy to let the memory take him. Now, with nothing to do but watch the traffic on Bridge Street, he needed to push it out of his head.

"Anything, Lord. Please."

Since childhood, Leo's life had been steered by pivotal moments in time that he called "water in the face." He was at a three-week sailing camp in New Hampshire the first time he put a name to it. Why his parents wanted him to learn how to sail was (and remained) a mystery to him, but there he was.

At the age of thirteen, his lack of enthusiasm for boats was only surpassed by his ignorance of women. Nonetheless, he'd spent the better part of the first week pining over a cute, early-developing cherry blonde from Norwalk Connecticut named Leslie. His two-part plan to become Leslie's summer boyfriend was the same that had failed over and over since the invention of puberty.

By his efforts, part one (enter the friend zone) worked. Part two (exit the friend zone) did not.

Her reaction was straight out of the teenage rejection handbook.

"You're a great guy, but I don't think of you that way. I just don't want to have a boyfriend right now."

The next day, he spotted her kissing his bunk mate. His heart sank into his boat shoes. There were ten days left in the session, and he was determined to mope through all of them. He walked the grounds slowly and ponderously like a beaten mule. When asked what was wrong, he blamed homesickness.

Sad stuff.

Then, one sunny afternoon during search and rescue training, his boat crossed another's wake. The craft jumped, and his face was hit with the spray.

The sensation flipped a switch.

Whoosh…

In that unexplainable instant, he realized that his summer, as well as his life, was moving forward with or without him, and he was ruining both with his own self-pity.

He returned to the dock a changed kid. For the remainder of the session, he was the happiest, friendliest, funniest, most active and adept sailor on the lake. He never did kiss Leslie from Norwalk, but it didn't matter. Life was good enough.

It was not the first time it happened. It would be far from the last.

It was salvation in times of need, but so much more. To Leo, it was proof of the existence of God. No argument put forth by any Atheist pseudo-intellectual could hold up against that second of pure clarity: that moment when Leo knew God was not only watching, but helping, guiding.

The biggie came while he was having a smoke behind his father's butchery. The shop was in South Philly's Italian Market. Leo was twenty-three years old. A scruffy old codger that he'd never seen before appeared out of nowhere and asked Leo for a match. They started talking about the Flyers and, by some serpentine route, wound up on the subject of happiness.

"You wanna be happy?" the codger soliloquized.

"Doesn't everyone?"

"In your short time on this earth, if you're lucky, you may find one thing that leaves you free of doubt. When you find that one thing, make it your life."

Then he tapped out his pipe and left, never to return. And that was that.

As Leo gazed out the office window, he mouthed the words of the old codger and managed a small grin. It wasn't "water in the face", but it did the trick.

51

He was summoned back to the present by the sound of the office phone being slapped back on to its cradle. He sat up straight and turned to face the desk. The venerated man sitting behind it offered no expression of assurance.

"Were you able to talk to anyone, Your Grace?"

"A few. We were lucky the protesters interrupted Sergeant Lynch and not you. Otherwise, the photos would have been…well…worse let's just say."

"But they'll still be on the front pages…the photos, I mean."

The Archbishop nodded and spoke.

"The same constitution that protects us also protects them."

He exhaled through his nose.

"Leonardo, do you think we're going about this incorrectly?"

The answer was "yes," but Leo chickened out.

"Well, Your Grace… I…"

"Yeah, me too. It's too familiar. It's too close to the way we did things last time."

Fellini tapped his fingers on the desk a few times and randomly browsed the room.

"Leo, what's the immediate problem? What are we trying to avoid?"

The Archbishop often held his conversations Socratically. Leo was relieved to have an answer ready.

"Anything that will hold up the construction of the new church."

"I agree, and I'm afraid you don't know the worst of it."

"Your Grace?"

"Father, this is not a done deal. Saint Aloysius has been filling two collection baskets for close to five years. One of those baskets has been going straight to the diocese. There's nothing keeping them…us…from building the new church a half an hour closer to Philly.

"Potterford is the place for it Leo. I've believed it in my heart from the get-go, but I have been in a minority. I'm the 'Head Ginney In Charge,' but I can be overturned. If this town becomes a hot bed of controversy, the project is sunk."

"So, we have to keep the site protected? We have to keep the press away?"

"I don't see vandals being a problem, not around here. The press *is* a problem, but only if there's a story to write. The real issue is the community. We have to get *Potterford* on our side. If we can get the town to say 'leave the Catholics alone,' then Potterford is off the news."

The room went quiet as the Archbishop withdrew into thought. Leo was anxious to offer suggestions for a starting point.

"I can get the deacons together. We can meet privately with some of the more visible members of our congregation. I couldn't see the protest from the stage, but I can find out who was there and meet with them as well."

Fellini shook his head.

"Forgive me Leo but appealing to either of those groups won't accomplish anything. Their minds are already made up. What we need to do is put a friendly hand out to the twenty thousand Potterford Protestants, Jews, Muslims, and Atheists that *weren't* at the protest. The message will eventually need to be more widespread, but we must start here!"

The Archbishop stood and walked to the window, seeking inspiration in the passing cars.

"Father, give me two names. Who is the most charismatic member of your church, and who has the strongest roots in the community?"

"Does it have to be two people?"

"Not necessarily. How many do you have in mind?"

There was no hesitation.

"One."

6. Uncle Walter's Woods

Son of a bitch!

The sound of metal against screaming metal echoed through the trees while Philip pulled down his shooting muffs and reached for another box of bullets. His uncle had owned and lived on the 75-acre patch of land for as long as Philip could remember. The two of them rode dirt bikes all over it when he was a kid. The trails were still there, but the bikes were on blocks. Lately, he just visited for the solitude.

Time to think...

One thing that irritated him about himself when he allowed it was the fact that, even though his adult life had been on a steady upswing, he still couldn't figure out relationships. When he was alone, he desired companionship; when he was with someone, he craved solitude. It was a crappy little fact about himself that was more than likely symptomatic of a bigger issue.

Whatever...(click)...

He'd set up an old-fashioned firing range complete with cans, bottles, and sawhorses. It was twenty yards into the woods with a couple of 4' by 6' pieces of plywood behind it. Philip had modified the cans slightly with some gold and silver paint. Otherwise, the range was free of ornamentation. He had been chomping at the bit to shoot something since he was denied use of his firearm at City Hall.

Okaaaaay, so it looks like the public shooting thing is only going to work once.

"Pow – ping!"

I've put the police on their guard, which makes life more difficult, but I knew that was going to happen.

"Pow – ping!"

What then?

He revisited the little speech he gave himself when he was thinking through the first shooting.

It's got to be quick. It's got to be painless. It's got to be free of fear.

"Pow – ping!"

Only now, it has to be with cops around. How the hell am I going to do that?

"Pow – smash!"

Well, obviously, I can't.

"Pow – smash!"

Soooo, what do I need? A silencer for starters.

"Pow – ping!"

And I need to find a time when there are no cops around. When are there no cops around?

"Pow – smash!"

He froze with his eyes fixed where the last bottle used to be. Then he moved his arm to hold the gun away from his body, scratched his neck, and spoke out loud.
"No way. It can't be that simple."
He put the gun down.
"What do I need? What do I need? What do I need?"
He started to pace.
"A map. I need a map. A map. A map. And a place to sit. Hunting gear. I need to find some hunting gear."
For what may have been hours for all Philip knew or cared, he paced the length of the range until, at last, he found himself next to his spot of origin.

Got it.

With an enigmatic smile, he scooped up his gun, and walked towards his uncle's work shed.

7. The Food Court at the Galleria

Julie wasn't about to make things easy on her cop boyfriend. She had been sending Lynch dirty text messages ever since he told her about his meeting at the Galleria. Each one shot home the benefits of sleeping with a writer.

The little bit of work that he and Gomez were able to do at the station yielded close to nothing. Samuel was a ghost. There wasn't a single namesake in the five surrounding counties that matched his description. Wherever he was living and/or working, it was under a different name. The only thing left was ballistics, which they didn't expect to see until the next day. He was, therefore, really hoping his conversation with Kelly would prove to be fruitful.

He and two tall lattes had been sitting at a café table in the Galleria food court for half an hour. Kelly was running predictably late. Lynch always kept a book of logic puzzles in his glove compartment for, among other things, killing time. He was filling in the last few boxes of a grid marked "challenging" and mumbling about how Sudoku is for pussies, when she suddenly appeared in the seat across the table. He understood why she chose the location. She said in her message that the police station and the barn were not options, which meant no local cops and no black trench coats. She wasn't likely to run into either at a crappy little mall two towns away from Potterford.

She wasn't in her UJ get-up, which made it easier for Lynch to be pleasant. Lynch preferred pleasant. He also preferred eye contact, which he wasn't getting.

"Hi, Kelly."

"I'm not late. I was over there."

"Where? In American Eagle?"

"I wanted to make sure you came alone."

"Very smart. Are you convinced?"

"What's in the book?"

"Oh…logic puzzles. My grandmother died of Alzheimer's, and I read somewhere that keeping your brain busy is good preventative measure. Who knows if it's true, but I get paranoid. It's a nasty way to die."

Kelly said nothing. Lynch wasn't even sure she heard him.

"I got coffee."

"Huh?"

"I wasn't sure what you liked. My girlfriend's niece is about your age, and she usually orders a caramel latte, so I got a caramel latte."

She broke from her erratic glancing about and focused in on the trendy cup in front of her. Lynch's words finally appeared to register.

"Thanks."

She picked up the latte and drew it to her face. Perhaps the conversation could start.

"Kelly? We good?"

She continued her gulp. She was obviously stalling. Progress was only going to be made if Lynch did the broaching.

"Kelly, did you want to tell me something abou..."

"Okay, look. I don't...I'm not...I don't know...dammit! A bunch of us went over to visit Jeremy this morning."

She told Lynch about what happened with Traci and the miracle cure.

"Really? Well, whatever works I guess."

"The thing is...the thing is, later on, a couple of guys came by. Cops. A guy and a girl, actually."

"Reilly and Warner."

"Yeah, that was their names."

"They're investigating Jeremy's beating."

"They are? I thought *you* were."

"No. The bishop's murder case is mine, but it's okay. Go on. What happened?"

Kelly suddenly got lost in thought, as though a bad situation just got worse.

"Kelly?"

She spoke slowly and angrily.

"The hospital only allows three visitors in the ICU at one time, so when the cops showed up waving their badges around, we had to leave. Rick and Traci headed for the exit, but I didn't leave so fast."

"What do you mean?"

"I don't know. I didn't want to leave. I kind of walked backwards slowly towards the door, so I saw what happened when...oh God."

"When what?"

"When the cops got close."

She stared at her cup.

"What happened when …?"

"Jeremy freaked the fuck out. That's what happened! They got up next to the bed, and all of Jeremy's vitals started to spike! He started to shake, stuff started falling off the bed table, and then he went back to being…being…"

She was welling up. Lynch was doing his best to hide his rage.

"Unresponsive."

"Yes, detective. Unresponsive, so you see why I couldn't come down to talk to you at the station."

Lynch let her calm down and allowed what he had just heard to sink in. Could Reilly have helped with the beating? He went through the previous evening's events in sequence. When did Reilly leave the squad room? He suddenly had a sharp recollection of the odor of mint tea. Indeed, Reilly stormed out right after he heard about Ryan.

Keep me in the loop! You hear me! In the loop!

Lynch didn't see him again until he got to the barn. Suddenly a chill darted up his back. There was something else. Reilly said something at the crime scene. It meant nothing at the time, but now…

"Did anyone else see this happen?"

"The intern…I mean the guy at the desk. I don't know what he's called. I'm pretty sure he saw."

"Okay, that means we won't need you as a witness if it comes to it. You hear me?"

He handed her his napkin so that she could wipe her eyes. She took it and nodded.

"Good. Now, I'm not going to jump to any conclusions with this. I'm just going to take what you told me and start asking some questions. I think that's all you want anyway. Right?"

"No. I want you to burn those sons of bitches!"

"If they had anything to do with Jeremy's beating, they'll burn. I promise."

He hesitated.

"What else can you tell me about Samuel?"

"Nothing. I told you everything last night."

He was dying to call bullshit.

58

"Anything would help. Just a way to get his last name would help. Did he work? Could I talk to his boss? How did he join the UJ?"

"I'm not sure. I think he and Arthur met at the Iron Wall. Work? I think he mentioned running errands for a photographer, but that was a couple years ago."

"You mean like a P.A.?"

"I don't know. I'm so fuckin' exhausted I can barely remember my own name."

They sat for a while. Then Kelly sniffled, offered her gratitude with a refreshingly firm handshake, and left. Lynch remained at the café table sitting in the middle of a cop's worst nightmare. He finished off his coffee and considered going over to the station. The drive would give him time to think. His phone buzzed. It was Julie's latest text message. It came with a picture.

Holy mother of...!

Reilly could wait.

8. Uncle Walter's Woods

Philip lay flat on his back, looking up at the tree where he was perched the minute before. A few feet from his head was the bottom part of his uncle's tree stand.

Yup, that was embarrassing. I'm reasonably intelligent. Why is this so damned difficult?

In the end, it didn't matter. He wasn't going to actually use the tree stand. He just needed to see the basic design. Though this fact didn't make his back hurt less.

"Pruners! I'll need pruners!"

9. En Route to St. Matthew's

Father Aiden O'Rourke had screwed up. He knew it, and he was pretty sure he was about to be told how badly. He was just helping out a family friend. At least that's what it felt like at the time. What else could he do? Reilly was shaking with rage over Bishop Ryan's murder. Aiden simply answered his question:

"What do you guys know about it?"

What could Aiden tell a cop that he didn't already know? That night…Saturday…standing in the rectory's front door, the young priest repeated what Leo said about the surveillance footage. He told Reilly about the black trench coat and how they all recognized it from the neighborhood. He told Reilly about the Unjudged, and divulged that he knew where the gang hung out on weekends. He had more to say, but he didn't get the chance. The instant Reilly heard about the barn, he slapped his phone to his ear and rushed off towards his car, whispering angrily all the way.

Uneasily, the young priest shut the chapel door and returned to the meeting with Fathers Karney and Pascucci, the rest of which was a blur.

Now he was headed to the Pastor's office at St. Matthew's. He'd been summoned by the Archbishop. This was not good. He knew nothing of the law. He didn't know what possible ramifications could exist for his actions. He maniacally flip-flopped between believing what he did was no big deal and envisioning himself being removed from the priesthood.

He parked and exited his car. There was someone practicing on the sanctuary organ. Aiden could hear it from the parking lot. He felt himself getting smaller with each step he took towards the church entrance. He wasn't sure where the office was. He piled disorientation onto his fragile mental state and started to sweat. The entrance was locked. He pressed the buzzer, and a familiar voice boomed out of the intercom.

"Father O'Rourke?"

"Yes, Your Grace. I'm a little early."

"Excellent. Come one in. The office is to the right after you walk in. Father Pascucci will flag you down."

The door clicked. Aiden entered. As he turned right, he silently observed how all the churches on Prospect Street smell the same. Indeed, Leo was down the hall motioning Aiden forward. He was smiling.

A minute later, Aiden was seated at the head of a hand-carved meeting table facing two men each of whom possessed the power to ruin him if he so chose. They had already exchanged pleasantries and had moved on to intimidating silence.

The Archbishop turned to Leo and nodded. Leo spoke.

"I'm not going to beat around the bush here, Aiden. You're about to be used, and you're not going to have much choice in the matter. Are you okay with that?"

The two seasoned men on either side of the table watched as the confused expression on the young priest's face morphed into a smile.

"Well, sure…as long as you put it that way."

The smile was mistaken for one of enthusiasm, rather than what it was: relief over not getting shit-canned.

10. Still Uncle Walter's Woods

Philip stood looking up at the pants that were once on his body. Now they were dangling from the stub of a broken branch ten feet above him. A mishap with his latest prototype left him hanging upside down. The only way Philip could free himself from the grasp of the tree was to undo his belt and fall.

Well crap.

He picked a bad day to go with the tighty-whities.

Well crappity crap.

The patent office was going to have to wait a little longer for a fully collapsible tree stand. He still had a few days to work on it.

His phone rang.

"Hey baby…No, I'm just fartin' around at my uncle's place. I'll be done in a few minutes… Half-n'-half…got it. See you in a bit. Love you!"

The sun was on its way to setting anyway. Soon it would be too dark to continue the experiments. He anticipated a horrible night's sleep.

11. The Condo at Night

"Doubles again you bastard!"

Lynch (James) and Julie had been nicotine-free for six months. Without smoking as an option, backgammon in bed was as good a post-coital activity as any. Julie was a better strategist, but James was luckier with the dice. One game usually took long enough for him to get recharged for round two.

"Doubles it is. Thank you very much."

Julie rolled over on her back, purposely averting her eyes from the board while James moved his pieces with little rhyme or reason. Ineptitude at any level put her out of the mood.

"So, what the hell was going on at the Galleria?"

"Don't want to talk about it. I can move this piece home, right?

She glanced at the board.

"Oh, dear God, yes! Didn't you teach me how to play this game?"

"I think so. 1 – 2 – 3 – 4 – 5...okay, done."

"Hand 'em over."

"Right. Here's the long and short of it. I met with my prime suspect's ex-girlfriend this afternoon, hoping to get some information on him, and as the result, tomorrow I've got to have a conversation I don't want to have with probably the worst person I could have it with."

"Let me guess. Reilly?"

"Yup."

Julie suddenly snapped her fingers and sprang to her feet.

"Shit! I almost forgot."

She threw on a robe without bothering to close it, kissed her lover on the forehead, and darted out of the bedroom. He heard her open and close the refrigerator and scamper up to the loft. She returned with a Mike's Hard Lemonade and a back issue of Philly Neighbor. She chucked the latter towards his groin. He caught it as a reflex.

"Here, check this out."

"What is it, and why did you throw it at my balls?"

"You got my text today, didn't you?"

"Ah! Your text. I guess it got lost among the others. This is what you found?"

She took a swig and pointed at the magazine.

"I knew I recognized the Unjudged from somewhere."

James turned to the page marked with a Post-it.

"How did a street gang end up in Philly Neighbor?"

"It didn't. That's why I had a hard time remembering the right issue. In the magazine, 'The Unjudged' wasn't a street gang. It was a painting."

James took a look at the article. He didn't read it right away. He just glanced at the title and scanned the pictures.

LOCAL ARTISTS PUSH THE ENVELOPE

Julie ditched her robe and resumed her supine position next to the backgammon board.

"That stupid article and that stupid painting almost shut us down."

The painting was shown right below the title of the article. There was a caption.

THE UNJUDGED BY WALLACE AVERY.

He couldn't tell whether it depicted a rite, or a rave, or some twisted combination of the two. At the center, being highlighted by some sort of mystical moonbeam, were three women in various stages of undress surrounded by an audience of twice as many men. In the background was a throng of young, good-looking people engaged in just about every known modern vice. There were pyramids of beer cans, tables piled with artery-clogging food, a multitude of drug paraphernalia, fist fights, acts of random destruction, and, if you looked closely enough, a smattering of public masturbators. Subscribers must have shit when they saw it.

"How old is this article?"

"Three years and a couple months. Do you see the robes?"

"I do, and the target."

Behind a pile of splintered furniture, hung a knife-riddled target, identical to the one at the barn. More obvious were the robes. Everyone in the painting wore a black robe, each bearing its own mystic symbol between the shoulder blades.

63

Now James started to read.

The article was about some sort of urban shock value modern surrealist doo-dah movement that was buzzing around the local art scene three years ago. Four paintings were featured. Avery's was first. The writer penned the article as though taking dictation.

"The idea for the painting coincided with the moment I felt I'd finally succeeded as an artist. I got a second to breathe and found myself reflecting upon everything I'd missed."

Avery self-indulgently continued with a story about coming home to the Philadelphia suburbs after struggling in a saturated New York market for six years. He eventually meandered back to the topic of his piece.

"I don't generally paint with insight. I report facts. I talk to people, a lot of people, and what I hear I put on canvas.

"Last year I went to Burning Man (a haven for gays), the Philadelphia Comic-con (a haven for nerds), and three raves (a haven for the young and privileged). I asked a dozen people at each event why they were there. There was one answer in common among them: 'No one judges me here.'

"I'm no psychoanalyst. I'll leave the whys and what-fors to them. I offer the stifling effects of judgment as a matter of testimony, not insight. The painting depicts a group, clan, tribe, that exists without it."

Then, contradicting himself, Avery went on to offer his thoughts on the oppressive power that conformity has over youth. He held that a person's potential for greatness peaks in his/her early twenties. The ignorance of our teens wanes, while mental and physical energies hold fast. The mind is fresh. The body is strong. The problem (according to Avery) is that this is also the time when a person becomes burdened with adulthood. Society no longer congratulates us on things like good grades and touchdowns. All of that gets replaced by how much money we earn and how often we demonstrate character traits like responsibility and temperance. We are forced to play this silly game, and we steer our lives based on what others think of us from our parents to our employers to strangers in line at the grocery store. And we, in turn, feel ourselves justified to judge others similarly. A vicious cycle is created, and the greatest years of our lives disappear before we know what's happened.

"The people in the painting don't compare themselves to the people around them, so there is no need for luxury. They have no religion, so they have no fear. If they're hungry, they eat anything they want. If something hurts, they ingest something to make the pain go away. If they want to fight, they fight; if they want to f***, they f***."

James murmured to himself.

"I bet Mrs. Schwartz looking for a good place to get her cat groomed loved that last one."

Avery never explained the knives, or the target, or the robes. In fact, James had to raise his eyebrows at the entire narrative. He had read more than his fair share of suspect interviews and criminal confessions. He could tell by word choice and the flow of the language whether or not a person meant what they were saying. Assuming the writer of the article wasn't taking creative license, Avery was spewing out some serious cow plop.

He took another look at the painting and thought about the gang at the barn.

"I guess the question is…what inspired what. Either way, I really want to talk to this guy."

"What's that, babe?"

"Just talking to myself. What do you think of this?"

"I like it."

"You like it?"

James was surprised. Julie knew her stuff when it came to art. Avery's sophomoric vision seemed below her.

"Yeah, I do. Look…"

She pressed up behind him and put her chin on his shoulder as she pointed out the elements of Avery's work.

"…some paintings look for two reactions; one at perception, and one at assimilation. At first glance, this bit in the middle comes off as misogynistic, but look at the postures. Look at the expressions on the women's faces. The men aren't being entertained; they're being held at bay. The background appears to advocate violence, but no one is getting hurt."

"What about the fist fights? These two guys are beating the snot out of each other."

"Yeah, but that's UFC/Fight Club stuff. They're having fun. There are also no weapons involved. The only weapons on the canvas are the knives, and they've been aimed at a thing, not a person. In fact, all of the violence has been aimed at *things*, and all of those things could be viewed as symbols of a judgmentally-driven, materialistic society. There's an HDTV, there's a Porsche, there's some high-end furniture. They haven't been destroyed purely for the sake of violence. They've been destroyed because they're not needed."

"What about the food and the drugs?'

"I don't see anyone obese or overdosed. People generally overindulge in their vices as a way to escape their reality. Maybe in *this* reality they do things in moderation because they're looking to enhance rather than escape. C'mon, open the unused part of your brain a little."

James gave it a shot, but all he could see was a bunch of eating, pill popping, and whacking off.

"Is all this off the top of your head, or have you been gazing at this thing all afternoon?"

"I had to do something while you were strip searching girlfriend at the Galleria."

"Shut up. That's not fair. Well...I don't get it, but if you think it's good, I'll give Avery his due props."

"I do think it's good ..."

James' body covered with goose bumps as a gentle hand grazed the length of his back and worked around to his front. Warm breath and a whisper filled his ear.

"...I also think you should put it down now."

James whole-heartedly agreed, and the magazine found its way violently to the floor followed closely by the backgammon board.

12. Sitting in Zed Zed

It had been two months since Gordy first worked up the courage to walk into a UJ party uninvited. Arthur had lost count of the number of times he wished he'd stuck one of his Doc Martins up that little puke's ass the instant his oxygen-stealing, pock-marked face came stumbling through the big barn door.

The specifics of that night were sketchy. Arthur must have been on at least four mind-bending substances most of the day. He remembered telling Gordy that he could hang out if he passed the initiation. There, of course, was none. Unjudged membership was by invitation only.

Arthur couldn't recall exactly what he told Gordy he had to do, but it must have involved Mayor Winkler's farm. Everyone was duly impressed and surprised when Gordy walked into the barn three hours later with one of Her Honor's cows in tow. Gordy was, as a result, allowed into the group at an entry level position. There, of course, was no such thing.

All three of them (counting Zed Zed) sat in silence across the street from a bar called Frankie and Jimmy's. The owners, Frank and Jim Cutillo, were third-generation Potterford natives. The friends they'd made through the years helped them dance around Pennsylvania's Puritanical liquor laws. Theirs was the only bar open on a Sunday night.

"You see, Artie! I told ya!"

"Don't call me Artie."

The little puke was right. Through Zed Zed's driver's side window, foggy from the mist of a zillion sneezes, Arthur saw Reilly.

What Kelly didn't know, and therefore didn't tell Lynch at the Galleria, was that the coffee-spilling R.N. at the I.C.U. had become rather smitten with Traci and her breasts. After he saw Jeremy's crazy reaction to Reilly and Warner, he chased Traci down in the hall and told her what happened. For his efforts, he got a peck on the cheek and a fake phone number. The information was quickly relayed to Arthur.

With great inner turmoil, Arthur broke down and called Gordy. The little puke was, shittily enough, his best resource in a situation like this. You couldn't trust him to wipe his own ass, but his talents were scary when it came to knowing the comings and goings of anyone around town. The kid did, however, need to be continually babysat, which was why Arthur came so close to slamming Gordy's head into the side of the van every time he opened his mouth.

"Every Sunday! Just like I said!"

Arthur didn't take his eyes off of Reilly as he walked into the bar with three other men.

"Just Sunday?"

"No. Most nights. It's his regular hang."

Arthur faced forward, took a joint off of the dashboard, and lit it up.

"Nice, Artie! I mean, Arthur! You gonna share that?"

"Fuck off."

"What are you gonna do about the cop?"

Arthur started the van. Zed Zed's engine spun up like a box of fighting alley cats.

"With you up my ass? Nothing."

HE JUST WANTED TO PAINT SOME BOOBIES

Monday

1. The Township Diner

"A koala bear sleeps twenty hours a day. Did you know that, Jaime?"

"What?"

Two or three times a week, Lynch and Gomez met for breakfast at The Township Diner. Potterford was only an hour from New Jersey and well within the boundaries of the state's diner culture. There were five within town limits, but only The Township made their bagel sandwiches with sausage from the Italian Market in Philly.

"Did you know a koala bear sleeps twenty hours a day?"

"I thought that was a sloth."

"A sloth's about the same, but you expect it from a sloth 'cause of the name."

"Fascinating, Ernie. Did you read the article on Avery yet?"

"I thought we didn't talk about work at breakfast."

"I'm not talking about work. I'm asking a question about a magazine."

"Yes. I read it."

"Then give it back. You're getting egg on it."

Gomez picked the magazine up by one corner and handed it across the booth as though it were a dirty diaper.

"Do we like this Avery guy for the murder?"

"Now *you're* talking about work. But, no, he had a well-attended event at his gallery Saturday night."

They went back to eating.

"Okay, listen Jaime. As humans, we're awake sixteen hours a day."

"Christ, are we still talking about this?"

"Yes, we are. Do you think koala bears lie on their death bed's wondering where the time went?"

"Is that a philosophical question, or are you trying out new stand-up material on me?"

"'Yes' or 'no' would have been fine."

"Okay, then no."

Gomez reached for his coffee.

"Whatever, puta."

Lynch glanced at his watch to change the subject.

"It's quarter of."

"When are we going over to Avery's studio?"

"Couple hours. It doesn't open until 10:00."

"Does he know we're coming?"

"No."

"What will we be interrupting?"

"A pottery class or something."

"No dick models?"

"No, no dick models."

"Good."

Between jabs, they managed to empty their plates and polish off their coffees. They had arrived separately, and it was Lynch's turn to pay, so Gomez waved a quick "see ya" and left. With the check in his hand and his book of logic puzzles under his arm, Lynch got up and walked toward the cash register. As he did, he spotted someone familiar eating at the counter.

"Hi there, Father."

Leo spun around in his stool with a mouthful of pancakes.

"Oh, hi!"

"Father Pascucci. Right?"

"Yes, Detective. Good to see you."

They shook hands.

"Please, it's Jim."

Lynch gave the priest a moment to wash down his food by acknowledging the diner with a general gesture in the air.

"You're a fan are you, Father?"

"Yes I am. I'm here a couple times a month. I wish it were more"

"How are you holding up?"

"Oh, you know. Everyone's doing their best, I suppose."

"Well, if you're here to clear your head, I'm with you. A diner is the perfect place for it, especially this one."

Leo's expression hardened a bit. Lynch feared he had crossed a line, although he wasn't sure which one.

"Sorry Father, I hope I'm not being…"

He was "being," or at least coming off as "being," but Leo, as was his nature, gave the benefit of the doubt.

"No worries. Truth be told, I didn't really know what to do with myself this morning. I usually use Mondays to start getting things organized for Mass, but Archbishop Fellini is doing all of them this weekend so I figure some good food is in order."

"You've tried the sausage here, I hope."

"Tried it? I made it."

"You made it?"

"My family did."

"That's about the coolest thing I've heard all week."

"No kidding."

"Hey, listen, are you going to be at the church today? I'd like to do a quick interview if that's okay."

"Sure, I'll be at Saint Matthew's trying to hide from the press."

"Mind if I stop by?"

"Come in the side entrance."

"I certainly will."

Then Lynch got the attention of the waitress behind the counter.

"Hey Rhonda, this guy's breakfast is covered okay?"

Rhonda nodded. Lynch paid his tab and left.

Leo did his best to enjoy the rest of his breakfast. He wasn't stupid. He knew the interview had already started.

2. The New Unjudged Cloister

It wasn't the barn, not even close. It was musty, dark, and creepy as shit. The location had been used by the UJ only once before. Now, at least for a while, they were going to have to call it home. This was the third time they'd gone through the drill. Bubbs and Rick were tagging the walls. Steven was working on firing up the generator and running extension cords. Arthur was off by himself sitting on a ratty old armchair with his feet up on an overturned waste basket. He was slumped down and staring at a pipe on the wall for no reason other than he needed a place to put his eyes. He'd been up all night; the other three hadn't.

If I can't sleep, nobody sleeps.

71

"You must be cooking up something good over there, Artie!"

Rick might as well have been talking to his spray can. Arthur's brain had been a freight train since he and Gordy pulled away from Frankie and Jimmy's. Every anger-fueled thought led back to a single sentence.

You really fucked up this time, Samuel.

He didn't know why Samuel wasted the Bishop, and he didn't really care. The last time the two of them spoke was the night the virtuous jackass disappeared. He left Arthur a bloody mess in the loft for no good reason.

If I could have gotten my hands on a knife, if we would have been scrapping near the target, the outcome would have been much different.

"Hey, Artie! At least we won't have to worry about crashing. There's like a hundred mattresses in here!"

There was no question. That piss-stain cop, Reilly, had to die. Is it what Jeremy would have wanted?

Who cares?

Arthur had no use for the silly Jew. He was one of Samuel's chosen. This had nothing to do with Jeremy.

In the UJ, they did *whatever* the fuck they wanted, *whenever* the fuck they wanted. Anyone who hindered that was one of "them," and the biggest "them" was the Potterford PD.

One of "them" had beaten up one of "us," and he had to pay.

Arthur could feel his heart start to pound again. His body was running on rage and adrenaline. In his mind, he was setting the whole town on fire. He saw himself driving Zed Zed down Main Street at 100 miles an hour, screaming with his head out the window and brandishing the biggest, baddest gun he could get off of one of the carcasses, all the time getting his dick sucked by the Police Chief's wife. It was beautiful. His senses writhed. Somewhere in the distance he heard Pink Floyd.

"Goddammit! How am I supposed to think with one of you prick-wipes blasting Floyd!?"

Rick answered.

"Relax, man. It's my ringtone. I'll take it in the other room."

"You and your fucking ring tones!"

"You want me to change it? I'll change it. Chill. Sit back down."

Artie did so. His mind had returned to him, but his body was still teeming with beating hot blood. Every one of his extremities felt engorged, especially his groin. He put his feet back on the basket and resumed staring at the pipe. His thoughts shot back to Reilly. He knew he wasn't going to be able to come up with a plan right there, so he settled for the thought of piss-stain cop's head on Zed Zed's hood. He felt a hand on his shoulder.

"Artie."

It was Rick. Arthur didn't budge.

"Traci just called from the hospital. Jeremy's dead."

Perfect.

3. The Station

It was an interview room. Lynch let the door swing open slowly. Reilly's big red freshly clipped head came into view. Lynch had rehearsed this moment twenty times to himself since he left the Galleria. The news he just received from the Chief, however, tossed the whole spiel out the window. This wasn't just about Reilly's badge any more. If he did what Lynch was about to accuse him of, he was now, at the very least, an accessory to murder.

He pulled his trench coat clear before closing the door. There was something about the way Lynch entered that particular room with that particular door that sometimes caused his coat to get caught in the latch. If he was distracted or in a hurry, he wouldn't even feel it, and, since the action left the door open a mere half-inch, wouldn't see it either. He'd only been caught twice, but the second time nearly got him suspended. He'd conditioned himself to check it, but one in ten times he'd forget. Luckily, this was not one of those times. The latch clicked. The room reeked of mint tea.

"Hey, Reilly."

"Hey."

73

Reilly was seated at the table, staring at six sheets of paper that he'd spread out in two rows of three. Lynch correctly assumed that they were the statements taken after the barn party. Reilly was looking for inconsistencies that might help him pin the beating on a few of the other UJ members. It was his latest theory, and he wasn't doing much to hide it.

"I heard your vic died at the hospital. Sorry."

Reilly did not look up.

"Thank you."

"Got any more leads without an eyewitness?"

"Workin' on it."

Lynch appreciated economic word use but also placed a great deal of value on common courtesy. Reilly's grunting was only making the confrontation easier.

"Can I ask you a question while you do whatever you're doing there?"

"Shoot."

"I told you how I wound up at the barn. Right?"

"Yup. Was that the question?"

Reilly had index fingers on two of the sheets of paper and was moving his eyes between them as though he was watching a tiny tennis match.

"You remember we followed a kid who lackeys for the Unjudged. Right?"

"Yup."

"And we found this kid by flashing around a picture of the symbol from Samuel's jacket."

"Yup."

"And we printed the picture from the internet…"

"Well, that I didn't know, but yup."

"…after you left."

"What do you mean?"

"You took lost time, walked out of the squad room, and then we found the picture. I don't think I ever showed you the original from the security camera either."

Reilly turned around and squared off.

"I don't think you did either. And?"

"Do you remember what you said to me when I arrived at your crime scene?"

"Refresh my memory, Lynch."

74

"I may be paraphrasing a bit, but you were taking exception to the fact that you had to 'work for these little pricks after what they did.' Ring a bell?"

"Sounds like something I'd say. Are you accusing me of something?"

"Call it what you want. I'm just curious how you knew about the connection between the UJ and Bishop Ryan's murder. I sure as shit didn't tell you."

Reilly rolled his eyes and sat back down.

"Oh God. Really? You thought I meant Ryan's murder when I said, 'what they did?' Jesus, Lynch! I was talking about the Satanist crap they spray painted all over the barn and the beer bottles and drugs and stuff. I wasn't talking about Ryan's murder!"

"Jeremy Sokol freaked when he saw you at the hospital, did he not?"

"He freaked *while* I was at the hospital. The fact that it happened while I was in the ICU was a coincidence. Look!"

Reilly swept his hand across the table, picked up whatever papers he could in the process, stood, and waved them in Lynch's face.

"Read these statements, Lynch! They all say that Jeremy went out to take a piss sometime after 10:00! Ask Warner where I was at 10:00! You think she'd let me beat up a kid half my size for no reason!?"

Lynch had no answer. Somehow the thought of first approaching Reilly's partner never occurred to him. Reilly saw the expression of defeat on Lynch's face and backed off.

"Okay, Lynch. You're just doing your job. I get that. I'd do the same, but you're barking up the wrong tree. You've got the real case here. Go find who did Ryan and let me find who killed the kid. Want some coffee?"

"No, I'm good."

Reilly started to leave.

"If for some reason you think any of these statements will help your case, help yourself. Make copies. Get the PDFs from my case directory. I couldn't care less."

The door slammed. Lynch got what he wanted. Reilly's answers were solid...locked and loaded before Lynch even entered the room.

4. On a Bench

So far, three people who knew Philip, or at least knew who he was, walked by him without saying anything. He was delighted to find that the art of camouflage had as much to do with setting as it did disguise. He didn't need a mask, or a fake mustache, or even a hat. All he needed was a park bench and a newspaper. Anyone who knew Philip, or had even encountered Philip, would never picture him on a bench at 9:30 in the morning reading a newspaper. The only person who approached him was a complete stranger.

"Excuse me, sir."

Philip looked up smiling and answered the woman.

"Yes, officer. What can I do for you?"

She smiled back and tapped her badge for clarification.

"School security."

"Ah, okay. Am I doing something wrong?"

"No. Just giving you some friendly advice."

Philip put the newspaper down and folded his arms comfortably.

"And what would that be?"

"Well, not to overstate the obvious, but you're in a school zone, and folks have a tendency to get antsy in school zones. You were sitting on that bench over there for about fifteen minutes, then you moved to that bench for ten more, and now you've been here for maybe a half an hour."

"Oh, I'm just reading my paper. The sun keeps getting in my eyes, so..."

"True or not, all it takes is one teacher looking out a window and getting the wrong idea."

"Wow! Thank you. That thought never crossed my mind, but it makes perfect sense."

"So, it's up to you, but I suggest you finish your paper on the other side of the park."

"I'm almost done. I have to get to work soon anyway."

"Have a nice day (pervert)."

Philip found it amusing that she noticed how many times he switched benches but failed to notice that he wasn't even looking at his newspaper. Had she seen him eyeballing the side of the building, he very well could have been explaining himself to someone else.

Regardless, it was a Monday morning. All he was doing was sitting on a bench, and he got noticed. The fine representative from Cardinal Romero Catholic High School Security was right. School zones are rank with paranoia. He could only imagine what it was going to be like on Sunday. He gathered himself and pretended to walk toward his car.

So, Sunday Mass is out of the question. Whatever, it was worth a look. On to plan C.

5. The Avery Art Gallery

Regarding the arts, what little Potterford had to offer was concentrated into the 200 block of Main Street. The Artisan Community Theater, The Thirsty Poet's Coffee Shop, and the Avery Art Gallery formed a pretentious triangle that stretched between traffic lights.

During Potterford's industrial hay day, the gallery was a four-story residential town house. Avery's renovations (which barely brought the building up to code) put the main show room on the ground floor. On Saturday evenings, it was awash with mood lighting, incense, piped jazz, and scores of tragic hipsters. During the week, it was an art supply store.

Lynch and Gomez entered.

Apart from the few spinning displays, serigraphs of the proprietor's creations, black curtains (for aesthetics), and a single inconveniently placed register counter, the place was empty.

"Wanna rob the place, acho?"

"Good God, no."

Lynch hollered "hello" a couple of times until the sound of a body hitting the floor came from behind one of the curtains. A dazed and unshaved fellow in his mid-twenties emerged nursing his left shoulder. He'd been napping precariously on a large roll of canvas. The dismount needed work.

"Good…"

He looked at his watch.

"…morning gentlemen. Welcome to the Avery Gallery. I'm Earl. What can I do for you?"

"Is Mr. Avery done with his class yet?"

"I…uh…he has a class?"

"It's supposed to be done at 11:30. Does he usually end on time?"

The line of questioning was too much for Earl. In place of a coherent answer, he pointed at a sign that read:

CLASSROOMS DOWNSTAIRS
WATCH YOUR STEP.

Lynch saw no value in breaking up the class and freaking out the students.

"That's okay, Earl, we'll wait. Mind if we look around?"

"Help yourself."

The clerk surreptitiously found his way back to his canvas while the detectives browsed. Lynch spoke.

"He smells lovely."

"Malaysian cologne and weed, if I'm not mistaken."

At 11:35, the class filed up from the basement. Bringing up the rear was Wallace Avery. He looked different from his Philly Neighbor photo. He'd grown out his hair and had different glasses, but it was easily the same guy.

He instantly pegged Lynch and Gomez as detectives. Only two types of people showed up at the gallery in pairs wearing neckties, and these two were too unkempt to be Jehovah's Witnesses. He smiled and waited for his class to exit before he approached.

"Are you here for Earl?"

Lynch chuckled and flashed his shield, as did his partner.

"No, Mr. Avery, but you might want to check on him."

"Earl! You okay back there!?"

The sound behind the curtain repeated, followed by a muffled "yup."

"Mr. Avery, you are not in any trouble. We think you might be able to answer some questions we have regarding a new case. That's all."

"Well, okay then. Earl! Out front! I'm going to be up in the studio for a while! ...Earl!"

They took the stairs up two stories to Avery's studio. The room showed him to dabble in several mediums. Only the tools of his trade were visible. Everything else was covered. Avery pulled out three chairs from the organized clutter and offered seats to his visitors.

"It's not the Ritz, but it's the only way I can be sure we won't be disturbed. And, please, it's Wallace."

Everyone sat and things began. The detectives minced no words explaining why they were there. Upon hearing, Avery leapt to his feet with an unbecoming yelp. Lynch put up a hand.

"Calm down, Wallace. Like I said…"

"Yeah, yeah, sorry, you just blew my mind a little bit. I mean, with what I do, I generally don't associate with the most strait-laced of characters, but Jesus! What do you think a bishop's murder has to do with me?"

Gomez produced a copy of the security camera capture. Lynch pointed out the trench coat and started to put forth the theory regarding its connection to Avery's painting. By his eyes, however, the artist had filled in the gaps himself.

"Follow me, detectives."

He led them down to the second floor, which was reserved for more exclusive showings and, Lynch supposed, the occasional orgy. As they stepped onto the carpet, Lynch couldn't help but wonder what sort of DNA it contained. He pictured Gomez hitting it with a black light and saying "Now that's what I call art." There was only one painting in the room. It was on a covered three-by-five landscape canvas and hanging on the wall to their right. Avery unceremoniously removed the sheet to reveal his most famous work.

"Here it is: The Unjudged."

Lynch and Gomez instinctively stepped forward in unison for a closer look. Avery, dust cover in hand, took position behind them.

"Want to hear a secret?"

"We'd love to hear a secret."

"I just wanted to paint some boobies."

Lynch waited for Avery to elaborate, but the artist (and his ego) would not continue unless asked.

"Boobies?"

"No, really. One afternoon, strictly for my own amusement, I got the urge to paint three perfect pairs of breasts. What do you think? I truly outdid myself, didn't I?"

He got no answer. He didn't really want one.

"Then I said to myself 'screw self-amusement. These must be seen.' The problem was my particular circle wouldn't accept boobies alone. I had to give them context."

"And this was the result?"

"The creative process is an organic one. The brush hits the canvas and starts moving from the center outwards. One thought begets another and another. Hopefully they line up into one stream of consciousness. By the will of the muses and a little luck, in the end, you find yourself looking at a whole. We create our own truths."

"So, all that stuff about the high point of our existence, and the burden of adulthood was all made-up?"

Lynch wanted to say "bullshit," but it would have been discourteous.

"You mean bullshit? Not entirely. But as far as the original inspiration for the work...boobies."

Avery was a talker. Lynch knew he was going to walk out of that gallery with twice as many answers as he had questions.

The artist introspectively worked his way through the painting's images. Julie was on point with all but the symbols on the robes.

"I had an intern with Theban tattoos. I can't remember her name. She didn't last long. Few do. Anyway, I needed an authentic yet unfamiliar unifying symbol, and it was the first thing that came to mind."

Avery strode between the detectives and re-covered his masterpiece. He turned and continued his train of thought with folded hands and a shrug.

"So, detectives, getting back to the gentleman in your photo, I've never seen him, and therefore have drawn no inspiration from him. If he drew any from me, it would have been due to a gross misinterpretation of my work."

The artist looked beyond the detectives, and inexplicably locked a stare on the far wall. When it came to arty-farties, Lynch could never tell how much of the persona was forced and how much was natural. Either way, he found their pensive little trances tiresome. The only thing worse was the weird half-schizo little tone they took when they snapped out of it. Avery did not fail to deliver.

"Which reminds me...where are my manners? I never offered you coffee. We're completely set up here. I can make lattes if you..."

Avery turned back towards the stairs. For the first time, Lynch viewed the area behind where they had entered. On the wall under the stairs were some pieces from a partially dismantled display. The pieces, however, were not paintings. They were photographs. His memory was stimulated. The situation may not have rung such a loud bell had Avery not mentioned lattes. He reached into his jacket pocket for the picture of Samuel. Thanks to Kelly, he already knew the answer to the question he was about to ask.

"I think he mentioned running errands for a photographer, but that was a couple years ago."

"Mr. Avery, have you ever seen this man?"

Avery barely gave the photo a glance.

"No. Don't think so."

"Can you take another look, please? It would have been maybe two years ago."

Lynch handed Avery the picture. The artist glanced again and handed it back dismissively. After all, his life was faces. He knew them well. If he didn't recognize the guy, he didn't recognize the guy. He could stare at it all day, and it wouldn't make a difference.

"I'm afraid not, detective."

This paint jockey schmuck wasn't going to make it easy.

"Okay. Thanks for looking."

"Wait a minute."

Avery pulled the photo back to his face. His expression changed.

"This is Matthew."

"Matthew?"

"I didn't recognize him at first. When he worked for me, he was heavier, and his hair was different."

"Last name?"

"Modine."

Lynch raised an eyebrow.

"Modine?"

"Yes. Matthew Modine."

"I see. You realize Matthew Modine is an actor, right? Full Metal Jacket? Private School? Ring a bell?

Avery tilted his head like a dog hearing a high pitch, wrinkled his forehead, and looked at the ceiling for a moment or two until the light dawned. If "ten" was how stupid he should have felt, he was around a "four."

"Oh yeah. Huh…probably wasn't real then."

"Probably not. What else can you tell me about him?"

Avery scrambled to redeem himself.

"This is starting to make sense now. You think he's the fellow in the trench coat. Don't you?"

"Why would it make sense?"

"There was an article in Philly Neighbor a couple years back. Do you know the magazine?"

"I do."

Gomez, chuckling, chimed in with "Intimately." Lynch flipped him off behind his back. Avery continued with a bunch of information that Lynch already knew regarding the article, and then came back to Samuel/Matthew.

"Not only did Matthew read it, he tore it out of the magazine and handed it to me like a resume."

"Sounds a bit zealous."

"Maybe. He certainly knew how to get a job at a gallery. That level of interest in a painting will get the attention of any artist. I don't care how bereft of ego we claim to be. Are you sure you don't want a latte?"

"No thanks."

"Anyway, I needed an intern."

"As in an *unpaid* intern?"

"Well, don't say it like that. I told you. He volunteered."

Lynch decided to ignore the name "Matthew." The suspect was introduced to him as Samuel, and that's what Lynch was going to call him until he saw a birth certificate that stated otherwise.

According to Avery, Samuel was a part-time intern but pulled a full day at the gallery every day. The boy was obviously in a position where he didn't need to earn a living. He always showed up to the gallery showered and shaved. His clothes were clean. He always went out for lunch and never asked to borrow money. None of his actions indicated that he was hurting for cash. He never complained about his parents, which meant he more than likely didn't live with them. He did his job well enough to be memorable.

The interview went back and forth, consisting of nothing but short questions and long answers. Then Lynch asked if Samuel ever caused any trouble.

"You know, I can't recall a single problem, and that's rare with the boneheads that…hold on, I lied. There was this one time."

"A problem, you mean?"

"Yes, but it wasn't him, actually. It was a guy he brought in to check out the painting. A spiky Billy Idol-looking panty waste. What was his name? Andrew? Alfred?"

"Arthur?"

"That's it, Arthur. I guess you've met him."

"We have. He's the leader of the gang."

"Don't think so."

"Really?"

"I don't know. I guess he could be. The first thing Arthur did when he walked in here was fill his pockets with the free scones we always have out. I didn't know the kid's situation. Maybe he was homeless or recently off his meds or something. I pulled Matthew off to the side and discretely told him what happened. The next thing I know, Matthew has that Arthur kid slammed up against the wall getting an earful. We got the scones back, but I had no idea what else was in his pockets, so I threw them out. Matthew tried to pay for them, but I didn't let him."

"So, you're thinking Matthew was the gang leader."

"I would say, at least that day, he was Arthur's leader."

"You said Sam-…Matthew brought Arthur in to see the painting?"

"I'm not sure what that was all about. After the scone thing got straightened out, they made their way up here. I don't know what they talked about, but Arthur left the place beaming. No… 'beaming' is the wrong word. He looked dastardly, like a maladjusted child who was just told that it's okay to play with matches."

"And that's the last time you saw Arthur?"

"That's the last time I saw either of them."

With the ballad of Matthew and Arthur complete, Lynch turned the questions toward Samuel's paperwork. As expected, Avery had none. He didn't keep paperwork on any of his interns. For a list of Bohemian reasons that gave Lynch a headache, Avery saw no need to keep paperwork on anyone. More accurately, Avery saw no need to pay anyone. This included any kind of bookkeeper. Like so many times before, Lynch handed over his card, and headed for the door feeling as though he had just run a marathon and tripped ten feet short of the tape. No one was that elusive by accident.

Who the hell was this guy?

Lynch had abandoned the notion that he was dealing with a professional hit two days previously, but why would Samuel use an alias to get a job at an art gallery? Or why would Matthew use an alias to join a gang? Either way, Lynch added "not sure of the suspect's first name" to his list of complications.

As he reached for the door handle, he turned, expecting Gomez to be right behind him. He, instead, discovered Ernie to be off in the distance nosing around Earl's counter.

"Hey!"

"What, jeffe?"

Lynch's cell phone buzzed. He unlocked it and put it to his ear as he replied to Gomez.

"You're looking for free scones, aren't you?"

"What if I am?"

Lynch switched conversations.

"This is Lynch."

The voice on the other end was excited, bordering frenzied.

"Jim, I think I just met our killer."

6. The Confessional at St. Al's

"Bless me, Father, for I have sinned. Was one week since my last confession. These are my sins."

A week's-worth of Constance Henderson's sins were usually atonable with half a "Hail Mary." Today was different...sort of. It had been explained to her time and time again that words alone don't mean much, and actions mean little more if done self-servingly. Still, she came every week and said what she thought would sitteth her as close to the right hand of God as possible.

"I've had evil thoughts regarding the person who killed Bishop Ryan."

84

Father Leo swallowed a sigh and spoke reassuringly.

"Go on."

"I picture myself in Heaven looking down upon him and smiling as his soul burns eternally in Hell."

"You want him to go to Hell then?"

"Oh yes, Father! With every fiber of my being I do. I've also had the desire to hurt him myself."

"How so?"

"I want to kick him. I want to tie him down and hit him with something hard like a stick."

"Do you want to kill him?"

There was silence. He could tell she was searching for the most righteous answer.

"No. Of course not. I just want to help deliver justice in some…" more searching "…way. A humble way."

Father Leo continued hoping the fiftieth time would be the charm.

"You know that's not how it works. Only God can pass judgment like that. No matter the circumstances, He doesn't want us to wish harm on each other. It's our job to live our lives as Jesus did. Jesus wasn't just the Son of God; he was an example. God could never show himself to us in his true form, so he sent down a piece of himself to set an example. Do you think Jesus is happy when another one of his Father's children goes to Hell?"

"No. I suppose not. Thank you, Father. I understand now."

She didn't.

"Also, just for the record, picturing yourself in Heaven is almost as bad as picturing someone else in Hell."

"I understand."

Nope.

"Is there anything else you wish to confess?"

"I made three pies for the capital campaign last Friday. I said I would make four, but I decided to keep one for myself."

And everything was back to normal. Constance began the wrap-up. Dr. Phil was on in twenty minutes.

"Sorry for all these sins and the sins I cannot remember."

"I don't think you need to worry about the pies, but for the act of hubris, say five 'Our Fathers' and try to remember that he who exalts himself shall be humbled and vice-versa."

"Thank you again, Father. Sorry for my sins with all my heart. In choosing to do evil, and do not do well, I have sinned against you whom I should love above all things. I firmly intend, with your help, to do penance, to sin no more, and to avoid anything that leads me to sin. Amen."

"Your sins are truly forgiven. Go in peace."

"Thank God. Oh, and Father, I got a good picture of the Bishop after Mass last Saturday. Let me know if you'd like me to send it to you."

Mrs. Henderson was a piece of work, but not, by any means, unique. For some folks, especially those generationally set in their ways, the broad picture was just too broad.

She's a good soul. The salvation is in the attempt, not the...

"Bless me, Father, for I have sinned."

Leo didn't even hear him enter the confessional. He didn't recognize the voice.

"It has been a long time since my last confession. I don't remember exactly how long."

"That's okay. What are your sins?"

There was a disturbingly long pause.

"I've done...horrible things, Father."

"Involving what?"

The entire box creaked as it did when a person shifted their weight on the bench.

"My sister."

Leo's face tightened.

"What happened?"

"I'm not a freak!"

Father Leo's voice had a magical calm to it.

"It's okay. Ba assured. You've come here. That's a very good start. God forgives the penitent, but you have to confess your sins out loud."

The box creaked again as the man moved his face to the latticed opening.

86

"You know, you spend your life with a person, and then one day you're in the pool, and you're swimming, and she's sunbathing, and the sunlight catches her just right, and suddenly you realize you have an erection."

Leo heard a soft, slow thumping as though the man was beating his head against the wall behind him. The anonymity could only be broken as a last resort, and Leo didn't feel it had gotten there yet.

"I'm not going to insult your intelligence by telling you that what you described isn't a sin, but there's a big difference between having an impulse and acting upon it."

"But I did act upon it, Father."

Leo could feel his eyebrows meet. There was no creaking. The only sound in the confessional was the man's labored breathing.

"Did you…have sexual relations with her?"

The man let out some kind of hiss. Leo sensed that he touched a nerve and braced himself for the answer.

"No, I didn't. I wanted to, but I didn't."

"Then you did the right thing coming here. Have you sought thera…"

"But I did masturbate right in the pool."

"Oh, I see."

"Then I hid a webcam in her room and masturbated more."

"You did?"

"I mean a lot…and everywhere. I spanked it in my room. I waxed it at school. I cranked out a few out in my car. I even shot one in the parking lot of a hotel."

"Okay, okay. God knows the details. Have you sought therapy?"

No answer.

"Look, if you are truly sorry and are willing to repent, God will forgive you, but you should also talk to someone."

Leo waited close to a minute. The confessional creaked again…then, again.

"Bless me, Father, for I have sinned."

A woman's voice.

What the…?

Leo pulled the curtain back and looked out into the sanctuary. It was empty.

Hold on…shot one in the parking lot of a hotel?

He sat back with a jolt.

"Carol…I mean…my child, did you see the man who was in here before you?"

Leo suddenly felt as if a helicopter was about to take off in his chest.

"Uh, not really. He was tall, but everyone looks tall to me. He had on a wool hat, so I couldn't see his hair. He walked out facing the wall, so I couldn't see his f…"

"Did you see where he went?"

"No. He was walking towards the back of the church, but I don't know if he was walking to the offices or the side exit. Was two weeks since my last…"

A Bishop gets killed two days earlier, a man runs out of confessional in a wool hat being very careful not to let his face be seen, and this woman didn't think anything of it?

"Thank you. Hold that thought. I'll be right back."

Leo threw the curtain open and ran to the side exit. He slammed his hands against the switch bar, and the door to the courtyard flew open. There were two gardeners.

"Did someone just run through here!?"

The gardener that was pulling weeds looked up at his co-worker who was pruning the rose bushes. The pruner shook his head. The weed puller looked at Leo and did the same. Without response, Leo slammed the door shut and stood alone in the sanctuary. The whole room seemed to expand and contract as he did his best to pull himself together. The killer must have run to the offices.

Lynch. He had to call Lynch.

Even under normal conditions, getting to his pants pockets while wearing his vestments wasn't easy. The sound of the zipper echoed through the empty room as he wriggled his shoulders out of his robe, revealing his clerical garb underneath. With a pile of black cloth around his ankles, Leo pulled out his cell phone and his wallet, but he couldn't get his fingers to work, and his wallet flew out of his hands as soon as it cleared his pocket. The muffled sound of leather against carpet caused Leo to look down just in time to see it bounce under one of the pews. He dove for it, slamming down the kneeler and almost crushing his right thumb in the process. Near injury was quickly joined by insult as he snatched up his wallet, tried to stand, and realized his feet were still tangled up in his robe.

His last sliver of calm left him.

He started kicking furiously. The robe flailed up and down like a hooked marlin, until Leo, at last, felt full range of motion in his legs. His phone and his wallet never left his hands. He pulled himself onto the pew and sat up in an attempt to regain his sanity. It wasn't working. He looked up and widened his eyes upon the crucifix to try to gain some focus but found it to be spinning with the rest of the room, so he shook his head with a hard blink and looked back down. The finger situation was not improving. Fed up with himself, he flipped open his wallet with one hand, dug out Lynch's card, abandoned his wallet, held up the number, braced both hands on the pew in front of him, and dialed.

"Jim, I think I just met our killer."

He thought he heard detective Lynch say something about scones.

"Father Leo?"

"Si...I mean, yes."

"Where are you?"

"I'm at the church. St. Al's, I mean."

Leo briefly went through what happened.

"Is he still in the building?"

"I don't know. He could be."

"Okay. Get out to the street. If there's anyone else in the church that you can take with you safely, do it. We'll be there in five minutes."

Leo instantly felt the blood return to his head.

"Okay. Sure. No problem."

He hung up and reached for his robe. The woman inside the confessional had overheard the conversation and was halfway out of the church.

The room was still spinning but not as quickly. Fear gave way to relief.

"They'll be here in five minutes...(sigh) five minutes..."

He eyeballed the door to the offices and had a thought that he and his pastor would later describe as uncharacteristically stupid.

"If he's still here, that's where he is...maybe I can get a look at him."

He stood and, without any real sense of self, started walking. There was a two-by-four against the wall, used for propping open the door to the courtyard. Barely breaking stride, he picked it up.

"Just a look: enough to help with a sketch or a line-up."

Maybe the killer was sneaking around the offices looking for a safe way out or crouched behind the water cooler...unlikely, but the priest was jacked. On top of everything else, the little prick had pissed on the sacrament of confession.

The hallway behind the sanctuary was L-shaped and lined with six doors. Leo edged his way along the wall, holding the two-by-four like a tennis racket. He stopped two inches short of the Church Secretary's office and peered around the jamb to find her obliviously typing with earbuds in.

No killer there.

"Hesper! (son of a...) Hesper!"

"Hi, Father. What's with the wood?"

"Rat...a big one. Take the rest of the day off."

"But I told Edith..."

"I'll let her know. Scoot. Go do something fun."

Next was a closet that, to his knowledge, hadn't been opened for three months. He tried the handle. It didn't budge, as if welded shut.

Next was his office. The door was closed just as he left it.

A glimpse, that's all.

He crept forward and turned the knob slowly. St. Al's was built when Eisenhower was in office. All the doors were original. Even with slow, careful motion, the latch popped like an old-fashioned pinball machine rendering any further attempts at silence moot. Leo pressed his ear to the door.

Nothing.

If the killer was in there, the racket didn't spook him. The good priest considered the absurdity of what he was about to do for a fleeting moment before being taken over by the false notion that it was too late to turn back.

He tapped himself on the forehead with the wood to psyche himself up, held his breath, ducked down, re-popped the knob, and slid into the room.

Barren and almost unchanged...almost.

"Phew! Yuck!"

Leo's office had its own bathroom, complete with a sink, toilet, and sixty years of embedded odors. It helped to keep the door closed. When left ajar, even slightly (as it was), urine, mold, and disinfectant went straight up the nostrils.

The priest was getting used to his situation. He spoke to be heard. "Someone left the bathroom open, and it sure as shit wasn't me."

Done fuckin' around.

Three angry strides took him to the stinky door. He gave it a yank. Empty.

The hand soap wasn't where it usually was, but that was easy to explain. It was always falling on the floor, and Archbishop Fellini had used the bathroom the day before.

Leo checked the window. As expected, it was swollen and could only open downward a few inches. No one could fit through it. He looked out. Through the leaves of the courtyard's large maple tree, he saw a gardener pulling weeds but nothing else. No killer in sight.

He checked the remaining two rooms, including the pastor's office. The only door left was the fire exit at the end of the hall.

"Yeah, that's how he got out...shit."

The guy was just a little too fast for the Dirty Harry wannabe from South Philly.

In the distance, he heard the main entrance to the sanctuary open and close... Lynch and Gomez no doubt. They were probably going to tear him a new asshole for not going to the street as instructed.

7. Sitting in Zed Zed

Silently, Arthur acknowledged that the Unjudged was Samuel's idea, but that didn't change the fact that, despite his strength of vision, Samuel was no war-time president. Arthur had finally come into his own. Everyone rallied behind him as he waved an invisible banner bearing the sigil of Jeremy. There was no confusion on the matter. They were at war.

Sitting in Zed Zed, once again across the street from Frankie and Jimmy's, Arthur wished his wimp of a former advocate could see...

You'd have just let this bastard slide. I know it! Take a look! This is what you do when someone throws down the gauntlet! This is how you repay someone who is trying to take it all away from you!

91

The van was almost full. Traci was in the passenger's seat. Bubbs, Rick, and Steven were in the back. Traci tapped Arthur on the shoulder and pointed down the street.

"How about that alley?"

"Too close to the bar."

"We can't run him all over town."

"I said it's too close."

Rick spoke up.

"I don't see what the problem is. The industrial complex is right across the bridge."

"Too far."

"Artie, it's not too far. It's just across the bridge."

Artie turned ready to jump over the seat and pummel Rick for his impudence, but Traci got herself between them.

"Artie come on. He's just throwing out ideas like the rest of us."

"Fucking stupid ideas!"

Rick refused to let up.

"The industrial complex will work."

"It fucking will not! How are we going to outrun an entire bar from here to the industrial complex, jackass?"

"You just got done saying the alley is too close!"

"Fuck you!!"

Steven and Bubbs thrust their arms in front of Rick, partially to shield him and partially to shut him up. Arthur took a sloppy swing around the back of his captain's chair and caught Bubbs on the forearm. It was like punching a bowling ball. He let out an intimidating scream to hide the pain, but no one was fooled. He faced forward to wiggle his fingers in private.

Rick swatted away his protectors and pressed his lips together to show he'd surrendered to the futility of arguing.

At the risk of making things worse, Traci made herself heard again.

"We don't have to run."

Arthur didn't have friends. His ambition, self-absorption, and general assholiness left no room. He allowed no one into his life that didn't have something he could exploit. Bubbs had moron strength; Steven could get drugs; Rick hated cops; Traci had a devious mind and a sweet ass…and whenever she made one or the other available, Arthur paid attention.

92

"Explain."

"We'll need a patsy."

She paused to make sure she had Arthur's interest and approval. She had both, so she continued. She also knew she needed to clarify things for Bubbs.

"Someone will need to risk getting caught. I was thinking maybe someone…with a bicycle."

The corners of Arthur's mouth turned up slowly. He didn't much relish the idea of dealing with the little puke again, but he had an inkling of where Traci was going, and he liked it.

Without taking his eyes off of her, he turned on the radio and slid his hand up her shirt. The three in the back collectively rolled their eyes, broke out the cards, and played Skat for cigarettes while Traci hopped onto Arthur's lap and rode him like a ranked bull.

Ah! The spoils of war!

8. Father Leo's Office

Leo sat behind his desk still recovering. Lynch sat across.

"I thought you said you were going to be at St. Matthew's today."

"Yes. I meant to be. Pastor Karney got called to the Diocese and asked me to hear confessions."

Lynch had been writing in his notepad since he sat down. Leo might have felt more intimidated were he not preoccupied with adrenaline and feeling stupid.

"Do you know why?"

"Why what?"

Lynch didn't look up.

"Why he got called to the Diocese?"

"He didn't say specifically… (topic shift) …Jim, I hope you don't think I was trying to throw you off my trail this morning when…"

"No, no, no. Not at all. I get it."

He tapped his pencil on his pad and locked eyes without lifting his head.

"What I *don't* get is why you were in the church when I arrived and not out on the street like I told you."

"Oh yeah. About that… I'm a moron."

Lynch laughed.

"Fair enough. May I guess that you wanted a look at the guy in case he got away?"

"You may, and you'd be correct."

"I'm not gonna lie to you. It was pretty dumb, but no blood no foul. You got a Mulligan so…"

"So, in the unlikely event that I ever find myself in a similar situation again, my ass is in the parking lot."

Lynch smiled inquisitively. He'd never heard a priest swear before. Leo read the look correctly and responded to it.

"The word 'ass' is in the bible you know."

"Yes, but in the bible, it means 'donkey,' doesn't it?"

"Fine, then I'll bring my donkey to the parking lot."

"Well played. So, what happened today?"

Leo recounted the events from the moment Constance finished her confession to the moment Lynch arrived as they were forever burned into his brain.

"Well Father, the guy has…"

Balls? Stones? Cajones?

"…nerve. I'll give him that."

He flipped over another page and clicked his mechanical pencil.

"Mind if we talk about Saturday, Leo?"

Do I have a choice?

Lynch started off with all the standard questions: "Can you think of anyone who would want to hurt Bishop Ryan?" and so forth. Leo wasn't much help. As he'd said, he didn't know the Bishop very well. Then the questions turned to the hotel arrangements.

"Who knew where the Bishop was staying?"

"There was a big foul up when he arrived. I was told he wanted to get together after Mass to talk about the groundbreaking ceremony."

"At the steak house. Right?"

"Yes. I, however, was *not* told that he never drove on the highway after dark. Apparently, the church always put him up somewhere in town if he chose to stay late."

"Who made the arrangements, then?"

"I did, about ten minutes before Mass started."

"Cutting it close."

"Tell me about it. That's usually when I write the Homily."

The joke was completely lost on Lynch.

"So, who knew?"

"Just Bishop Ryan, Pastor Karney, and me, as far as I know."

Leo realized how that sounded but figured it would be best to let Lynch ask for an alibi. He didn't. By the surveillance footage, the police knew when the murder took place. From the server logs, they knew that the church voicemail was checked from Father Pascucci's office phone twelve minutes later. Even with no traffic and all green lights, (which never happened in Potterford) it would have taken just about that much time to get from the Marriott to St. Aloysius. When they tacked on a few minutes for things like getting from the crime scene to the car, parking at the church, and actually getting to the office phone, Father Pascucci was all but taken off the suspect list. Lynch still asked about Pastor Karney.

"Like today, he was at the Diocese. Someone there can vouch for..."

Suddenly ...

BRRING BRRING BRRING BRRING BRRING

...the room was overtaken by a deafening alarm. Lynch looked wide-eyed at Leo and hollered.

"Exactly what is that!!? The fire alarm!!?"

"I don't know!! I never heard it before!!"

They both rose to investigate. The din stopped as Lynch broke the plane of the doorway. The silence revealed screaming...in Spanish.

"I wonder who that could be."

With hands in pockets, he took a few casual steps to his right, looked to his left, and discovered Gomez having a fist fight with the fire exit.

"The puta went off when I opened the door!!"

Leo returned to his office to call off the fire department. Lynch filled a cup at the water cooler and handed it to his partner.

"Here."

"Thanks, and by the way, it took me a few minutes, but I realized why you had me interview the landscapers, and I don't fuckin' appreciate it."

"I have no idea what you're talking about."

"You figured they were Latino."

"They weren't?"

"Eastern bloc asshole!"

Leo reappeared. Lynch spoke.

"Father, do you have a key to the rest of these doors?"

"There's one in the secretary's office. Why?"

The priest answered his own question. The killer couldn't have gone out through the fire exit. He would have tripped the alarm. If he entered the hallway, there was only one possibility: He locked himself in one of the other rooms, and if that was the case, he was still there. Leo's chest revved up again. Lynch spoke slowly and calmly, confident everyone was on the same page.

"Father, Detective Gomez and I have this. Where is the key, exactly?"

"Top desk drawer on the right."

"Do you remember what you said earlier about finding yourself in this situation again?"

Leo nodded and made his way to the street.

Gomez drew his sidearm and planted himself in the corner of the hallway, while Lynch retrieved the key. The half-century old hard-wood floors and wainscoting amplified Gomez's voice.

"Okay, jagoff! Here's the deal! We know you're in one of these rooms! We are assuming you are armed! Under that assumption, we are going to open all four of these doors, one at a time! If anything moves on the other side of any one of them, we are going to start squeezing triggers! That means that things will go a whole lot smoother for everyone involved if you come out on your own!"

Nothing happened. Lynch walked from the secretary's office and jingled the key.

"You hear that, jagoff? That's my partner with the key! Let's get this party started!"

They opened all the doors. They found nothing. Lynch spoke.

"Let's get this party started?"

"What should I have said?"

"Not that."

"Whatever. You wanna hear this?"

Gomez did his interviews with a digital recorder. Lynch normally cursed the device, saying it slowed things down and made two steps out of a one-step process, but he gave in. It was the voice of one of the gardeners, and he might as well have been speaking Spanish.

Dee man come to da door. Den vee vork. Den man ask if vee see a man running. Vee tell him no.

For better or worse, it confirmed Leo's story.

"How in the sweet name of Elvis did he get out of here, then?"

Crime Scene had arrived, so Gomez went to see if they had any success getting prints from the confessional. Lynch met Father Leo in the parking lot. The priest had kept his word.

"What happened?"

Lynch told him what little there was to tell. Leo replied with five words that he found, considering the day's events, difficult to say.

"Jim, I have an idea."

9. A Random Intersection

The elderly couple at the stop light felt compelled to say something. They had their windows up, the radio on, and they still heard the screams coming from the car next to them. At first, they thought something was terribly wrong. The man in the car appeared to be having some sort of mental or nervous breakdown. Muffled waves of guttural agony spilled from within, accompanied sparsely by the thump of his fist against the roof of his car and the staccato honks of his horn as he beat his head against his steering wheel. They feared for the man's safety and were about to call the police when they curiously realized that he wasn't screaming; he was laughing. He was hysterically laughing. They went from being scared to being puzzled. They still suspected some sort of psychotic episode and were only put at ease when the hysterical laughter was halted by a victorious cheer. The man wasn't out of his mind; he appeared to be, to their best estimation, celebrating something. Relieved, the elderly woman rolled down her window, managed to catch the eye of the elated man, and signaled for him to roll his down as well.

She hollered across the white line with a thumbs-up.

"Congratulations on whatever it was!"

Philip answered.

"Oh! Thank you very much, ma'am! It has been a good day at that!"

There was another longer honk from behind them. The light had turned green. The woman waved goodbye as she and her husband drove past and into the intersection. Barely able to see through his tears, Philip spit out another guffaw and turned right.

Gotta love Bill Clinton. No one used the term "sexual relations" before him. When Philip told the priest he was lusting after his fictitious sister, he was hoping for "fornication" or "carnal knowledge of," but the priest exceeded all expectations by replying with "sexual relations". Philip suspected the priest heard him say "yessss" under his breath when it happened. He almost flat-out lost it after confessing about the (also fictitious) boner in the pool but managed to get himself back in check by beating his head against the wall. He was sure the priest heard that, but it didn't seem to matter. Neither misstep invoked a comment, so Philip figured he was clear to launch into the masturbation portion of his story. Once he felt he had the priest off balance, he threw him the bone about the hotel parking lot and left. It was brilliant. The only thing more brilliant was his escape.

He didn't quite execute *Plan C*, but he now knew it was possible. He checked his watch. As usual, he was running late.

10. Lunch

Gomez drove. Lynch chewed over his notes. Leo's idea was scribbled in at the end:

Father L. will email blitz his congregation for pics taken at Sat's Mass – mentioned someone named Constance???

Why not? Couldn't hurt.

They'd heard from ballistics. No match was found locally, but they were still waiting to hear from a few nearby jurisdictions. In the meantime,

Lynch decided to roll the dice and check the system for Matthew Modine. Also, no match…big surprise.

It was a bit after three o'clock. As long as they were in a holding pattern, the detectives decided to get lunch.

"Now, in contrast to koala bears, pigeons…"

"Oh, sweet Jesus, Ernie."

"And I'm not sure I completely understand this."

"Then don't talk about it."

"There's something about a pigeon's eyes. The frame rate or whatever it's called. It's like ten or twenty times faster than in humans, so they see shit in slow motion. That's why pigeons wait until the last second to jump out of the way when they see a car coming."

Silence followed. Gomez had, once again, stopped a few yards short of his point. Lynch let all the air out of his lungs with a sigh.

"And?"

"That's the shit man. That's how you live."

Lynch had no idea where to even start with a response, so he returned to the task at hand.

"Julie told me Steaks n' Stuff has a new sandwich."

"What's it called?"

"The Barn Yard."

"What's it got on it?"

"A bunch of crap and a fried egg."

Done.

All twelve seats in the Steaks n' Stuff deli were occupied, so they got their sandwiches to go. The bag weighed close to three pounds and gave off an aroma that was as glorious as it was disgusting.

For Lynch and Gomez, eating lunch in a parked car traditionally led to playing a game they called "What If?" It was, more or less, an exercise in creativity, which was much needed when a case hit a dead end. In the absence of a dead end, they used it just to pass the time. It also put the brain to work, which appealed to Lynch and his irrational fear of Alzheimer's.

The premise was semi-simple. Step out of the realm of possibility as to not be confined by it. In other words, they would look for motive, means, and opportunity among those who *couldn't* have committed the crime.

The first round always started the same. Lynch went first.

"What if you did it?"

Gomez had to play along, or the game wouldn't work.

"What's my motive?"

Lynch went for the first commonality between Gomez and Bishop Ryan that came to mind.

"You're Catholic. Right?"

"Yes, I'm Catholic, dumb-ass."

"Maybe you blame Ryan for the diddling."

"I don't blame Ryan for the diddling. He wasn't one of the diddlers."

"But he's part of the diocese."

"A diocese that he helped to clean up."

"Doesn't matter. You're still angry, and he's the only member close enough for you to get your hands on."

"I can buy that, but you know I have an alibi."

Again, the rules were contrived but needed to be followed.

"Okay, I guess you're off the hook."

"What if you did it?"

"What's my motive?"

"Maybe you hate Catholics."

"Why would I hate Catholics?"

"Any number of reasons."

"Too broad. Narrow it."

"Fine. Maybe you just hate the Diocese. Maybe you think they got off easy, and it's Ryan's fault."

Lynch thought for a moment.

"I can see that. How did I get Samuel's Jacket, then?"

"Samuel gave it to you."

"There's no evidence that I knew him."

"You found it, then."

"Where?"

"In the trash."

"Why would he throw it away?"

"He got fed up with the gang and bolted."

"So why was I digging around in the trash?"

"You're homeless."

"Homeless with a 9-millimeter?"

"You're a garbage man."

"A garbage man with a 9-millimeter that has it for the diocese?"

"Sure."

"Except you know I'm a cop."

"Right. Not you then."

It was Lynch's turn again. The game had only one rule: They had to stay within the confines of the case. In other words, they couldn't try to pin anything on Mickey Mouse.

"What if Father Pascucci did it?"

"What's his motive?"

"Same as ours; he's got it in for the Philly Diocese for some reason, and Ryan was handy."

"Gonna need a reason."

"How about an intense feeling of betrayal?"

"Okay, but we've got the same problem with the trench coat though. Gift? Trash? Neither is likely."

Lynch put his sandwich down.

"Why did we settle in on the trash? He could have found it somewhere else."

"Okay, where?"

"No idea."

Gomez put his sun visor down and cocked his head to one side.

"So Pascucci has it in for the Diocese, decides to kill Ryan and pin it on Samuel because Samuel's a Godless twat. Samuel's coat somehow falls out of the friggin' sky and into the good Father's hands, so he puts it on, speeds to the hotel after dinner, waits for Ryan to arrive, shoots him, gets back in his car, goes to the church doing about seventy miles per hour in zero traffic…mind you, this is 7:30 on a Saturday evening in a town notorious for speed traps…hitting all green lights. And he does all this to give himself an alibi by checking for a voice-mail message form a hotel security guard that he doesn't even know he's getting?"

Lynch picked up his sandwich before speaking.

"You're not following the rules, Ernie."

"Sorry. What if Pastor Karney did it?"

"I don't know enough about him to play him."

"Fellini?"

"Even less."

Gomez grinned.

"What about Avery?"

"Good one. Motive?"

"Diocese and diddling acho. Same as the others. The jacket's not a problem either, since he knew Samuel."

"I'd buy it except that makes the killing an act of taking the moral high ground. That made sense with the other suspects, but Avery? Moral high ground?"

"Okay fair enough. What if Gordy did it?"

"Really?"

"Right. What if one of the UJ's did it?"

"We can't do them. They're not eliminated yet."

"Oh, come on acho. It'll be fun."

As they were merely killing time, Lynch partially complied.

"Just Arthur."

"Okay, just Arthur. Fish in a barrel. The motive is easy. He hates the Diocese and all Catholics because their ideology clashes with his, plus he believes he's entitled to do whatever he wants."

"The jacket's a problem though."

"How is it a problem?"

"All of the UJ's fingered the guy in the surveillance photo as Samuel. That means they had no reason to believe anyone else had his coat."

"So, they lied."

"All of them? Even Kelly? I don't see it."

"Some of them could have lied. It's obvious that Arthur has his own little Gestapo within the ranks."

Lynch pulled off a dangling piece of bacon and pointed it at Gomez thoughtfully.

"That I can see. Samuel sees the writing on the wall and decides to leave before he's overthrown."

"Assuming he was the leader, we could run with that."

"But then why would he give Arthur his coat?"

"Passing the torch?"

"What torch? It's a coat with a Theban 'S' on the back. What's Arthur gonna do with it?"

"So, the jacket is still a problem."

Lynch chucked the bacon into his mouth.

"It is."

Gomez took a massive bite and chewed for a while. They were both losing steam on the sandwich front.

Gomez spoke. "Here's a thought. What if this was a set-up from the get-go, and the jacket wasn't Samuel's?"

"I'm listening."

"It wouldn't take much to make one just like it."

Lynch shook his head. Gomez wasn't ready to give up.

"Come on. It takes the jacket problem out of the mix."

"All the UJ's positively identified it."

"Oh yeah. That's right. Still a problem then."

"Still a problem."

They stewed for a few minutes before wrapping up the better portions of their Barn Yards and dropping them back into the bag. Simultaneously, they tried to remember what they were thinking when they ordered them, but the majority of their blood had moved from their heads to their stomachs. Gomez started the car.

"So, if it winds up Samuel didn't do it, what are we thinking? A garbageman?"

"Sure. Why not?"

It was almost 3:30. Their shift was over in a couple of hours, so they decided to go back to the station and do some more research on Ryan.

"But Samuel did do it."

"Of course he did."

11. The Cardio Room at the "Y"

You could say what you wanted about the Potterford YMCA. It was still the best deal in town. It was built when "Happy Together" topped the Billboard Charts. A couple of the wings resembled (both in look and smell) those of a minimum-security prison, but it had a pool, an indoor running track, free weights, Nautilus machines, three cardio rooms, and aerobic dance classes up the wazoo all for around fifty bucks a month.

It was also the one place in town where Aiden O'rourke could take off his collar without being looked at sideways.

Even before Aiden left the meeting at St. Matthew's, he knew who he was going to contact first. Pastor Carl Seymour of The Potterford First Baptist Church had the ear of the town's young black community. More importantly, Aiden and he had two crucial things in common. They both graduated from Potterford High School in the same year, and they both preferred the elliptical machine to the treadmill.

Seymour thought nothing of it when he looked to his left and discovered the energetic priest on the machine next to his.

"Hi, Carl."

"Aiden, how've you been man?"

Aiden chose his words carefully. Regardless of the moral fiber of his intentions, he was acutely aware of how he would come off if his wording was disjointed, or his tone was insincere. Carl had a very keen sense for when he was being hustled. At least the young priest didn't have to worry about his old classmate seeing him sweat.

"Been better, Carl."

"Oh, of course, what was I thinking? Thoughts and prayers to all of you, brother."

A good guy.

"That means a lot, Pastor. Thanks."

Aiden wasn't lying.

They continued their cardio workouts in silence. Aiden's assigned task was proving to be significantly more difficult than he had anticipated. At regular intervals, he lifted his head towards the pastor and inhaled as if preparing to speak, but nothing came out. Somehow the words weren't traveling from his brain to his mouth with any kind of syntax. Aiden looked down at the timer on his machine. Three minutes had passed. He could have sworn it had been at least ten. The situation had officially turned awkward, and it was about to get worse. Pastor Seymour had been on the machine longer than Aiden realized.

"See you around, Father. Give my regards to Pastor Karney and Father Leo. Okay?"

By the time Aiden realized what was going on, the pastor had dismounted and was half way across the room. Winded and at a loss, Aiden called after him.

"I certainly will Carl. Thanks again."

Great! Now what?

He couldn't jump off and follow the man. He just got on. This was supposed to be a covert operation. Fake a pulled muscle? Feign exhaustion? For crying out loud! No! Two faces flashed before his eyes as he watched Seymour exit the room. The first was Archbishop Fellini's. His Grace had put a great deal of faith in Aiden's people skills…skills that, as it would seem, were rendered useless in the presence of self-consciousness. The second was that of Jesus. At age 33, the man cleansed the world of sin by escaping death. At age 26, Aiden couldn't even escape from a piece of damned exercise equipment. This was horrible. He looked down at his sweaty white knuckles and whispered to himself.

"Okay, O'rourke, what's your next move?"

Next move? All he wanted to do was have a conversation with the guy, not sell him vinyl flooring. Still he found himself helplessly strategizing. Did Carl just finish his warm-up or his cool-down? If it was his warm-up, he'd be starting on his lower body. If it was his cool-down, he'd be headed to the showers. Aiden checked the timer…six minutes. He whispered again.

"Screw it. Maybe he won't notice."

He went into the hallway, feeling like a completely ineffectual idiot. He knew that Catholics were often erroneously looked upon as self-loathers. He never bought into it, but he was feeling the part as he walked toward the men's locker room shaking his head in disgust.

He slapped the door open and made a bee-line for his locker, all the while looking for Carl out of the corners of both eyes. He opened his locker, pulled out his cell phone, and pretended to check his text messages. Pastor Seymour was nowhere to be seen, so Aiden replaced his phone, used two fingers to push his locker shut, and retraced his bee-line back to the hallway.

He was reaching for the door when it opened by itself. A familiar face appeared.

"Hey Aiden. Forget something?"

Dang!

"Carl! Hi! Uh, no…I'm expecting a text from Pastor Karney. I forgot to check it before I started my cardio so…"

105

He had over-explained himself just like a fifth grader who hadn't finished his homework.

"Okay, well...enjoy."

And Aiden found himself in the hallway once again. On the opposite side of the door was Pastor Seymour. The situation had turned from awkward to comical. Exasperated, he threw his towel over his head, sat on the floor with his back against the wall, and started to laugh uncontrollably. The towel came off once he composed himself.

"This is stupid."

He stood defiantly and re-entered the locker room. Pastor Seymour was sitting in front of his locker undoing his sneakers. He saw Aiden right away.

"Wow! That was quick."

"I'm cutting it short today, Pastor. My head's not really in the game."

Again, not a lie.

"Listen, Carl..."

"Is it okay if I go first?"

Aiden had no idea what the pastor was talking about but nodded and smiled anyway. Addressing one or a thousand, Carl Seymour was an excellent speaker, and he meant everything he said from the depths of his soul.

"On behalf of maybe a dozen members of my congregation, I'd like to apologize for yesterday."

Aiden correctly guessed he was talking about the protest.

"Oh. I didn't realize your congregation..."

"They didn't organize it, but they were there. It's not our way. Once the law has its shot, it's up to God to do the rest. Alleluia."

"Amen."

It just slipped out.

"Anyway, for what it's worth, I spoke to them and the rest of the folks at First Baptist. Nothing like that will happen again, at least not by our doing. I was trying to work up the courage to talk to you about it out there, but...I don't know...it's supposed to be easier to approach a friend with this sort of thing, but somehow it just isn't. You know?"

All that stress for nothing. Aiden apologized to God for his lack of faith. Now it was time to come clean.

"Actually, yes, I do know."

He explained everything.

"It's probably small consolation, Carl, but I came to you first."

Pastor Seymour belly-laughed. He hadn't stopped smiling since Aiden started talking. The only thing he enjoyed more than Sunday worship was an opportunity for forgiveness.

"That depends on who you were planning on going to second."

"Would you laugh harder if I said Rabbi Sager?"

"Good choice…"

Pastor Seymour did laugh harder, and then suddenly turned serious.

"…but you won't get him today if that was the plan."

"Oh no. I don't like the sound of that."

"It's a sad one, Father. One of the boys from his synagogue was killed. He died in the hospital this morning, and the family's level of orthodoxy requires a burial before sundown. It's understandably quite a scramble."

"You said he was killed. You mean murdered?"

The pastor stood and unzipped his sweat jacket.

"More or less. He was at a party on Saturday night and got jumped. The poor kid was beaten almost beyond recognition. The doctors were surprised he lasted as long as he did. The family wasn't even given word as to what had happened until it was too late. Real shame."

"Where did it happen?"

It was a question that begged a benign answer.

"The Old Meadowbrook Farm."

Pastor Seymour turned around to find Father O'Rourke bracing himself against the wall of lockers and breathing heavily as though he was about to pass out.

"Are you okay, Aiden?"

Aiden looked up. His face was a shade whiter than normal. Carl was surprised that was even possible.

"Been better."

12. Back at the Station

Lynch rolled back from his desk and looked at the ceiling to give his eyes a rest. He felt like he hadn't blinked for three hours. Gomez was in the bathroom recovering from lunch. He'd exited the squad room with his regular eloquence, stating that his Barn Yard needed to take a swim.

As they'd discussed after the feeding frenzy, attention turned from the assailant to the victim.

They were approaching the end of the all-important first forty-eight hours. Standard operating procedures had yielded nothing. No irregular or telling cell phone activity. No sketchy relatives. No personal threats. Nothing. Ernie's earlier speculations were dead-on. All the local Catholics saw Ryan as a savior and adored him. Everyone else saw him as Internal Affairs for the Philly Archdiocese and admired him. Archbishop Fellini had chosen his man well.

Regardless, neither Lynch nor Gomez was ready to explore the possibility that the act was random. The shooter was caught on tape, tagged with a pagan symbol. That was enough to keep them from going down that hellish path. They were, however, more than ready to explore the possibility…the strong possibility…that Bishop Ryan, while the victim, was not the actual target.

Over the previous two days, dozens of boxes filled with Philly Archdiocese hate-mail had been brought into the station and stored in one of the smaller interview rooms. Two of the boxes were now stacked next to Ernie's desk. He'd piled the first dozen letters from the top box in front of his monitor, save one that he took with him to the toilet.

Potterford did not have a full-time Computer Crimes Division, so Lynch called in a favor and sent the hate-emails to one of his counterparts in Morrisville.

For his part, he decided it was about time he learned more about Archdiocese's recent legal problems. The information was not difficult to hunt down.

He used newspaper articles as a quick way to establish the sequence of events, then he dug up the police reports associated with each article. He divided all the digital documents into three folders, which he named T_JARVIS, E_BELL, and C_INGRAM. Then he threw out a bigger net to gather documents for a fourth folder that he eventually labeled PORTLAND. He worked through the cases backward from least to most recent. Once he got organized, he was able to see the whole terrible story from start to finish.

PORTLAND

The problems for the diocese actually began in the Pacific Northwest. Eighteen months before everything started locally, a priest from Portland, Oregon was accused, tried, and found guilty of child molestation. There was more than one count. There was more than one boy. There was substantial compensation for the families involved. The families went through great pains to make sure no one outside the closed courtroom knew the exact figure, but the church, in an act of insanity, stupidity, negligence, or sheer genius, allowed the information to leak. On one hand, it utterly sold out the convicted priest who maintained his innocence throughout the proceedings. On the other, it set up reasonable doubt should similar accusations fly later on. There was, of course, no way to confirm how the leak occurred. It very well could have been an accident. To make matters worse, there were several people on both sides of the aisle who believed that the prosecution failed to make their case.

T_JARVIS

The three accusations within the Philadelphia Archdiocese couldn't have happened in a worse sequence. The first was quickly discovered to be a sham put forth by a pair of unfit and mentally unstable parents. The church was exonerated, but only after an intense series of hearings that wound up putting a nine-year-old boy named Timothy Jarvis into therapy.

Then came the second.

E_BELL

A teacher in one of the Main Line Parochial Schools was accused of attempted sexual assault on a sixteen-year-old boy named Eric Bell. The act was said to have taken place in the locker room showers after a swim meet. The only evidence was Eric's word along with some bruises on his back and arms. There was no DNA, since the assault was only attempted. Months of investigation and hearings resulted in both sides getting creamed financially as well as tortured with the same questions over and over again. When the case finally went before the Grand Jury, the church went into survival mode and pulled out the money card that they pocketed during the Portland case. This was, obviously, dangerous since the Portland priest was found guilty, but it paid off. All they had to do was

109

attach it strategically to the Timothy Jarvis case to spark reasonable doubt. The final nail in the coffin was a convincing character witness testimony from none other than...

I'll be damned.

Then the third.

C_INGRAM

An eleven-year-old boy named Charles Ingram returned from a nature retreat..."changed"... as the parents described it. Something had happened. Father Braniff, the priest supervising the retreat, claimed he had noticed the boy's sudden reclusiveness, but didn't think much of it. His exact statement was:

Many boys his age discover things about themselves and the world around them when convening with God's green earth the way we do on these trips.

The statement was boorish with lascivious subtext and under any other circumstances would have set off a battering-ram-style inquiry. In the light of the previous two accusations and their outcomes, however, the parents were viewed by the public and the courts as bandwagoners. Relatively little effort was put into the initial investigation. Ultimately, nothing came of it legally, but that didn't stop the press form going for the throat. The Philadelphia Archdiocese learned many new meanings for the term "damage control." After several months, thanks to the efforts of the Archdiocese, things had almost gotten back to normal.

Then Ryan was killed.

Lynch let his eyes blur on the florescent light above him. The sound of water rushing through pipes in the wall caught his attention. Gomez must have flushed. He pulled himself back to his desk and re-opened the E_BELL folder. Ernie entered the room to find his partner lost in thought.

"What's going on, Jaime?"

"Skeletons Ernie...lots and lots of skeletons. How about you? Any revelations on the crapper?"

110

Gomez tossed the letter onto his desk and sat down.

"None."

Lynch neither budged nor responded.

"What's up, Jaime? Did life just get complicated?"

Lynch exhaled and replied.

"Difficult to say."

13. 3rd Street

Traci closed her eyes and shivered as the cool air from the river blew across her shoulders. Other than the occasional burst of laughter coming from the direction of Frankie and Jimmy's, the block was dead. She glanced to her right as she walked. Her reflection in the Tru-Value's darkened window confirmed what she already knew. She looked perfect.

She was naturally pretty. She neither denied it nor apologized for it. She could have disguised herself in utter contrast, making herself "plain", but she knew better. Guys could see through plain. A guy couldn't be manipulated with plain.

She had a better way to go. Firmly, she held a theory that pretty had five basic subcategories represented succinctly by the Spice Girls. Jumping between these subcategories, without fail, left guys blind and clueless (even more than usual).

She strutted towards Reilly's nightly haunt, looking as though she just stepped out of a limousine. She'd dyed her hair golden blonde with subtle streaks of red. Her dress was classic black, knee-length, and tastefully backless. Her shoes were strappy, three-inch heels over nude stockings. Her jewelry was all gold, and thin, and her make-up was straight off of the cover of Vogue magazine. Indeed, she'd successfully jumped subcategories of pretty: wild to sophisticated (Scary to Posh). She reached for the big oaken door to Frankie and Jimmy's and smiled as she thought about how Reilly wouldn't be able to take his eyes off of her. Less than forty-eight hours ago, he was grilling her for information about some dead minister or something. Tonight, he'd have no idea who she was...fuck head.

***

Gordy's instructions were simple: Hit the shamrock with the brick and ride like hell for the bridge. He wasn't told what to do if he got caught. For that, he had a plan of his own.

This was the night...what he'd been waiting for ever since he dragged that stupid cow from the Mayor's farm to the UJ Cloister. It was a two-mile walk, and the thing shit about every ten feet. After tonight, he'd have his real jacket. After tonight, he wouldn't have to fetch beers or endure a regular helping of boots to the balls. Arthur told him so.

The Reillys moved to Potterford when the steel plant opened in 1898. Sean Reilly worked the furnace and, as the story went, was so callused he could light a match on the tip of his index finger. His son Liam worked the line. He was short and wiry but could still drag a girder the length of a football field if needed. Liam's son, Martin, was on the loading dock and died saving the lives of seven men when a suspicious fire almost took half of the factory in 1984. Martin and his wife June were blessed with four children. Beth, their only daughter and second oldest child, sold insurance. Petey, their youngest boy, drove a semi. Ian, their middle (and largest) boy owned a local trophy shop. Kevin, their oldest, became a detective for the Potterford P.D.

Despite his upbringing, Kevin Reilly had all the characteristics of a second or third generation cop. He wore his love for the job prominently on his sleeve and went after bad guys with a zeal that bordered frightening, depending on the case. Potterford was his town. His family had been walking its streets and praying in its churches for four generations. He took every crime as a personal insult, and that drive kept his arrest record unsurpassed. Not that things like arrest records and commendations meant anything to him. They didn't. What mattered to him was hearing the town say "thank you" every time he closed a set of handcuffs. No one killed a man of God in his town and just walked away.

Still, the Jeremy kid wasn't supposed to die. Until two days ago, Reilly's passion for the job had granted him self-justification for his pliable interpretation of the law. He'd looked the other way here and there when it served the greater good. He'd taken down a pimp or two and sampled the wares afterwards. He had a couple of paid informants that weren't on the books, but what happened Saturday night was different...big-league different. Reilly had ordered a hit. He could talk to himself all he wanted to try to convince himself otherwise, but it was what it was. Nothing was going to change the fact or bring that Jeremy kid back from the grave.

He'd been putting up a front all day. Now he was exhausted and paralyzed. Staring deeply into a pint of Guinness was the only activity he could manage. His brother, Ian, was sitting across from him. Their server's name was Angie. It was the Reillys' table, literally. A bronze plaque bearing their father's name said so. Anyone that wanted to sit at it was told that they had to give it up if any Reilly walked in. Ian was not helping matters in the least, but his heart was in the right place. A heart he had when it came to his family. A brain? It depended on the day.

"Kev man, you gotta snap out of it. I'm gonna say it again. You went to the source, you got your info, and you did what your heart and your gut told you to do. That's what a man does, right? Pop said that over and over again right before beating the shit out of us, right? That kid was in a gang. If he didn't shoot Bishop Ryan, then one of those other limp dicks in the gang did. And now they're going to think twice before doing it again. And let me tell you something else. That kid didn't die because he took a beating. We all take a beating. He died because he was too stoned to defend himself. When you go at a guy with a bat, you expect him to cover up or put his arms over his head. You don't expect him to give you a clean shot. Man, I gotta tell you…"

"Ian, will you shut the fuck up?!"

Right now, all Reilly could think about was how to make it all go away. Carrie Warner, his partner, wouldn't be a problem. The two of them had been through a lot. She had no idea what he'd done and would have his back as long as he didn't give her a reason to suspect him. They were in the station together when the beating took place. That would be enough for her. If he could just find enough red herrings and follow them to enough dead-ends, he might just be able to put this one in the loss column, try to make amends in some anonymous way, and move on. But why did that Jeremy kid freak out in the hospital?

His thoughts were interrupted by a gorgeous blonde entering the bar. Was she lost? No one went walking into F and J's on a Monday night looking like that. He took a pull off of his Guinness and watched her make her way to the bar. She sat and looked around as though she was supposed to be meeting someone. Jimmy was tending that night. Ian started yammering on again, but Kevin didn't hear a word. The woman absently tried to order a drink, but there was some problem with her ID. Jimmy was a stickler for such things. He'd had to make a ton of concessions in order to keep his place open every night of the week, and one of them was agreeing to check every single ID at the bar…no exceptions. The woman appeared to take it in stride. Jimmy offered her a free Coke or something, but she opted to slide her ID back into her little wallet thing-a-ma-bob and exit the bar, but not without giving Reilly a little wink. He appreciated being given reprieve from his problems, if even for one fleeting moment. He wiped the brown, foamy mustache off his lip with his sleeve.

The Potterford Industrial Complex was eight blocks of connected buildings and numbered lots. A railroad track divided the property into two regions, referred to as the river side and the street side. A second railroad track skirted its southern edge. The most visible part of the complex from the road was the scrap yard. That was partly due to its size and partly due to its majesty. A ten-foot corrugated metal fence separated the yard from the road and railroad track with a dozen or so piles of indistinguishable metal scraps looming as high as twenty feet above. Those who didn't know any better considered the yard an eyesore, but hard-core Potterford residents knew it was beautiful. Not only was it the geographic center of town, but it represented Potterford at its finest: a reminder of what it used to be and, deep down, still was.

Arthur's eyes passed across the yard. He was starting to understand how it was organized, although he didn't really care. He, Bubbs, Rick, and Steven (The Gestapo, as referred to by Ernie) were each crouched behind their own pile of castaways. They appeared to be in the area reserved for iron, as indicated by the heavy mechanism towering above them. It was one of those flat, round, ultra-powerful swinging magnet things that always foiled robots in 1970's cartoons.

Arthur was expecting the fun to start at any moment. He was looking eastward. The small section of chain-link fence that broke up the corrugated metal and formed a lockable entryway was forty or fifty yards in the distance and lit by two street lights. Soon, that little puke, Gordy, would scurry over the fence, closely followed by anyone who chose to follow him from the bar. Reilly would be one of them, and the UJ would be ready.

Then…a voice.

"Well, well well! And just what do we have here!?"

Traci dug through her purse. The quiet of the night amplified the sound of her three-inch heels as she left the bar and took a sharp right on to the pavement. Another of Jimmy's many concessions to the Town of Potterford was opaque windows. If there was to be debauchery on a Sunday, it was to stay in the bar where the good folks of Potterford couldn't see it. It would have been cheaper to simply paint the front windows over, but Frankie and Jimmy opted for dark stained glass. This caused a problem. The UJ had a package for Detective Kevin Reilly, and the little puke courier needed to know exactly where the man was sitting. Luckily, the little puke courier went to high school with Braden Reilly, Ian's son.

Braden was very proud of his father and talked about everything he did, including going to F and J's every night with his uncle, "Kev." The boy knew about the Reilly Table, but, thanks to the bar's strict "No Kids; No Exceptions" policy, had never actually seen it. All he knew was it was one of the tables against the front window. He didn't know exactly which. Consequently, neither did Gordy, and, until three minutes ago, neither did Traci.

Now it was up to her to make Gordy's part of the plan as dirt-simple as possible. He couldn't be trusted to remember instructions for the fifteen seconds it would take him to pedal his bike from the hiding place to the window. He needed a target…a clear, easily seen and easily understood target.

The tiny black purse she bought to go with her disguise was essentially a wallet with a shoulder strap. Her regular Hello Kitty purse was a shopping bag by comparison. Inside it were her phone, lipstick, debit card, keys, and a pad of shamrock-shaped sticky notes which she deftly extracted.

She peeled off a single shamrock, stuck it on the pane next to Reilly's table, crossed the street, walked two short blocks, backed herself up against a parked car, and waited for the little puke to emerge from his hiding place.

She hadn't anticipated the problem with her ID, but it solidified her theory regarding the subcategories of pretty. To Jimmy Cuttillo's eyes, it didn't look a thing like her.

Gordy looked on. Traci had done it. The target was in place. He readied the brick and balanced himself. Arthur wanted him to use a whole brick, but Gordy could neither get his hand around it nor carry it on the bike without toppling over, so they had to break it in half.

It would do the trick.

The handlebars wobbled as he struggled to work up his momentum. Like a steam train pulling out of a station, he felt himself working towards break-neck speed. All he had to do was hit the shamrock with the brick. He couldn't see it yet, but he knew it was there. There wouldn't be much time to think, and there was no second chance. Missing was not an option. The wind caused by his forward motion made his eyes tear. Through the fluid, the window came into view. The little green target was beautiful and, thankfully, obvious. He slowed down just enough to focus and, with all the nerd-strength he could muster, backhanded the brick into the glass. It was a direct hit. He saw it. He heard it. He felt it. His eyes continued to well up, only now with pride. He skidded to a stop and turned to see Traci's reaction. It was not congratulatory as he'd hoped. She was irritated and mouthing something.

"Will you fuck a goat?!"

After a few confused seconds he realized that what she actually said was "Will you fucking go?!"

And he went. He went just quickly enough that Reilly would see him head for the bridge and the surprise waiting for him in the scrap yard.

Everyone else in the bar heard two sounds: the crash of the window, and the brick landing on the table. Kevin Reilly heard nothing. He only saw the writing on the brick. Had he not lifted his arm to down the last of his pint, the thing would have shattered his wrist. It was perfectly placed. One moment he was lost in thought about a horrible mistake he'd made; the next he was looking down at a broken brownstone brick with three words etched into its surface: EAT SHIT REILLY. He didn't connect it with any particular person or action. He'd made plenty of enemies around town in his chosen profession. He stood immediately as did his large brother. Next, he heard Jimmy Cutillo.

"Those sons of bitches!"

Everyone in the bar headed for the door. Jimmy, with baseball bat in hand, got there first. The man weighed 300 pounds if he weighed an ounce

116

and could still move like lightning if he had to break up a fight or chase after vandals. In true managerial form, he put on a loud but friendly voice and insisted everyone stay in the bar and continue enjoying themselves.

"The Reilly boys and I will take care of this. Next round is on the house! Angie! Tend bar! Don't let anyone drink without ID!"

Everyone complied. No one messed with Jimmy…ever.

Reilly found himself outside. He could hear his brother breathing heavily, the way he always did when he was pumped to rip someone's lungs out. All three of them tried to get a bead on their surroundings. He reached for his cell phone and discovered that he'd left it on the table inside.

A woman's voice cut through the frenzy.

"He went that way!"

The fantasy woman with the hinky ID was on her cell phone across the street and two short blocks towards the bridge. Could she have done it? No. Third Street was four lanes wide. She wouldn't have been able to cover that distance so quickly--not in that skirt and those heels. No way. Kevin Reilly shouted to her.

"Are you calling the police?"

"Yes, sir. I am!"

All four of them looked down the street just in time to see a kid on a bike take a left and head for the Industrial Avenue Bridge. Jimmy's '65 Fleetwood was parked in its regular VIP spot. The three men bolted for it, and Kevin shouted to the woman again.

"Tell them to send cars to the Industrial Complex. Tell them it's me! Detective Kevin Goddam Reilly! Word it like that!"

She nodded and called Arthur. She had every intention of calling the cops…in about fifteen minutes. They would be too late…just like they were for Jeremy. Oddly, Arthur didn't answer.

The Fleetwood squealed out of its spot and front-heavily fishtailed all the way down Third Street. The front of the car made the left towards the complex, but the back almost didn't. Kevin and Jimmy were pissed. Ian was psyched. He all but hollered, "Yee haw," as they caught air, speeding over the bridge. They screeched to a stop under the spot-lit shadows of the scrap yard. The kid was nowhere to be seen. Kevin thought quickly. A left would have taken him to Franklin Village. No kid would ride his bike through the Village at that time of night.

"Take a right, Jimmy!"

Another squeal and a fishtail pointed them towards the gated entrance. They slowed to take the curve. That's when they saw the bike. It was abandoned on the ground. No doubt the kid heard the squeals and shit himself. Kevin signaled for Jimmy to stop the car.

"He jumped the fence! I'm gonna follow him. Go around to the north side in case he makes it through. You coming, Ian?"

"You bet your pasty Irish ass I'm coming!"

Traci's plan, for the moment, was working.

Kevin and Ian had been jumping fences since they were in diapers. The action appeared almost choreographed, from the leap at the fence to the dramatic billowing as their feet simultaneously hit the dirt road on the other side. Then it was a sprint. The kid couldn't have been that far ahead. They had to either catch him or flush him out. Either option required speed and a load of shouting.

Then…noise.

There was activity a short distance ahead of them. They saw it at the same time and stopped in their tracks. The head of one of the people involved drew attention. The hair was almost metallic white and unmistakable. Kevin had been poring over crime scene statements all day. He knew exactly who it was. Arthur. The kid's name was Arthur. Ian recognized him from the barn.

"Hey, Kev…that's…"

"Yeah."

Arthur was fighting. They all were. It was a rumble with another gang. One by one, he picked out the other members of the Unjudged and started to put two and two together. The brick. The bike. He and his brother had played right into their hands, but something went wrong. The UJ got jumped. Why the hell did they get jumped? And, more importantly, what was he supposed to do now? The police were on their way (as far as he knew). If any of these guys got taken in, yet another investigation would start. God forbid Lynch would get assigned, and in a few days, it would be "game over" for him and everyone involved. He couldn't leave his mother with all her boys in jail. He had to make them scatter somehow. He didn't have his badge. He didn't have his gun. All he had was the darkness, his voice, and his shithead brother.

"What do you want to do, Kev?"

Kevin Reilly did his best to explain the reality of the situation before sounding the charge.

"Now follow my lead. Don't let yourself be seen."

Then Kevin cupped his hands around his mouth and inhaled deeply.

"Break it up! This is the po…"

And Detective Kevin Reilly's lights went out. His last sensations before hitting the ground were a shadow, a brief smell of iron, and the stars above him changing colors.

FIVE MINUTES EARLIER…

The voice came from behind.

"Well, well, well! And just what do we have here!?"

There were five of them. How that many large black men managed to be that stealthy in a yard filled with scrap metal, Arthur could only imagine. The smallest of them was easily over six feet tall, and their average BMI had to come in under nine percent. They also appeared to be inked up, although it was impossible to tell to what extent because, curiously enough, they were dressed in suits and ties. The one who had spoken approached with a smile. Arthur responded in kind.

"Nice suits. Don't mind us. We're just waiting on a friend."

"Ha ha! Like my man, Mick Jaggar! Right?"

Arthur didn't get the reference.

"Guess you're not a Stones fan. That's okay. I don't much care for Jay-Z to tell you the truth. But thanks for the compliment. A brother likes to look good, you know."

The speaker had worked his way into an exaggerated street accent, which he snapped out of in order to continue.

"Seriously, you boys hiding out here looking to score some blow? Some hookers maybe?"

Arthur barely let him finish the sentence.

"I'm not sure how that's any of your business."

Bubbs chuckled, as did all the suits. Steven and Rick shot terrified glances at Arthur. They were both thinking the same thing.

Shut up! Dear God, Artie! Just shut up!

119

Nineteen-year-old Tony Evans, the spokesman for the suits, took another step forward, locked eyes with Arthur, and, still chuckling, pointed toward a barely visible skyline of townhouses on the other side of the yard's western fence.

"You see that window over there?"

Arthur feigned politeness with a quick glance. Tony held his pose in intimidating silence for a few seconds before folding his arms and proceeding with his story. His speech was slow and mellifluous, just like his pastor's.

"I've lived in Franklin Village my whole life. I hear it was a nice place back in the day. Loaded with nothin' but hard-working white folks. You look like a pretty young bunch of fellas…older than me but still probably too young to remember the Village when it was cool. See what it is now? That's what happens when people like your grandparents get greedy. Factories close down. Hard working white folks move on to greener pastures. The whole area falls into disrepair. The land values go down the crapper. Slum lords buy the empty homes and fill them up with desperate black folks looking for cheap rent."

Tony moved closer. His smile disappeared, as did Arthur's.

"And, let me tell you brother, they are welcomed with open arms."

The rest of the suits joined in like a congregation with a chorus of subdued "Amens."

"Open…mother…lovin'…arms…but, guess what? It doesn't last long. Not at all. Once they hand over their security deposits, the black folks are on their own. Ain't no Tenants' Association. Ain't no landlord to call when something breaks. Over time, they realize that nothing's any better than it was before. They start thinking to themselves, 'Nobody else gives a shit. Why should I?' so they stop caring about their community and themselves. That's when the drug dealers move in. Now take another look."

This time Athur's eyes didn't move. Tony didn't care but had to put on a good show. So far, the lines weren't coming out in the order he had rehearsed, but he was getting the point across.

"Me and the rest of the brothers here could have wound up just as messed up as that building. I'm talking that building right there, you belligerent mother fucker! The building where I grew up! That window right there is my bedroom window, asshole! You know what kept that from happening!?"

Tony didn't wait for a response. He quietly answered his own question. "God."

Both smiles returned. Neither was sincere.

"And that's why we're here, my white brothers, to spread the word of God. Brother Michael?"

"Yes, Brother Anthony!"

"What do you think would be an appropriate verse for my new white brothers, my NWB's?"

"How about Corinthians 15:33?"

"Perfect, Brother Michael. Thank you! Hear the word of the Lord my NWB's! Corinthians 15:33 says 'Do not be deceived: Bad company ruins good morals.'"

The suits emphasized the words with fist bumps and more "Amens." Tony turned to receive a few high fives and, with running back speed, pivoted back to relock eyes with Arthur.

"So, you've heard the word of the Lord…now get out of here."

Arthur looked down and thoughtfully wrinkled his brow, as if considering Tony's demand. Bubbs stood fast with his regular lazy grin. Steven and Rick swallowed hard and continued to think in unison.

Come on. Let's cut our losses and go. There will be another night for Reilly. It isn't worth this!

Arthur spoke.

"That's the word of Paul."

Tony raised his eyebrows.

"Excuse me?"

"You just quoted a letter from Paul to the Corinthians. That's the word of Paul, not the word of the Lord."

"I said get the fuck out of here."

Arthur's phone buzzed. It had to be Traci. What little time he had for these sharply-dressed bozos had run out. He squinted and licked his lips. Steven and Rick knew the look: that look of Arthur's that said "I'm just going to say what it takes to start a fight." They feared the worst.

"I'm afraid we can't do that …"

121

For chrissake, Artie, don't say it.

"…Nigger."

Arthur's hand flew from behind his back, along with an iron bar he'd been slowly and quietly freeing from the debris since the start of Tony's story. Had Tony not been literally dodging bullets for fifteen years, Arthur might have had a chance of finding his mark. As it was, all Arthur found was air and a fist slamming into his kidneys. His mouth wrenched open in agony, but nothing came out. His vision blurred. He didn't even realize he had doubled over, until Tony's elbow went into the back of his head with the force of a sledge hammer. Like a sack of potatoes, Arthur went to the ground. A well-polished shoe thumped into his ribs. He opened his eyes as the air came out of him. In silhouette, he saw Rick and Steven. He wouldn't have recruited them if they didn't know how to fight. Both of them seemed to be holding their own. At least they were still on their feet. Struggling for breath, he went fetal. He had no idea where Tony was or where he was aiming the next assault. His face bled. Either by falling or writhing, he'd cut his cheek.

This was all Traci's fault; it was her plan.

No, it was Rick's fault; it was his idea to do this in the yard.

Screw that; it was Samuel's fault; he did the priest. Everything that came after that was on him.

The next blow went into the small of his back. He arched, leaving himself exposed. His assailant was giving him a clean fight…not a favor Arthur intended to return. He reached behind his back for something to swing…anything. The action was too obvious. Tony leapt into view and thrust his knee into Arthur's already tender ribs, simultaneously grabbing his wrist and twisting it into the air. More kidney punches followed. Tony, apparently, still had a free hand. Mercifully, so did Arthur. He pawed around, hoping Tony would be too preoccupied to notice. He could feel his shoulder on the verge of dislocation and let out an agonizing scream. The sound energized Tony, who hollered triumphantly as he took a break from kidney punches to go to work on Arthur's fingers. The movement brought a split second of relief to Arthur's shoulder, and in that moment, his free hand rested on something flat. He had no idea what it was, but it was just light enough to lift and heavy enough to do some damage. With a savage wail, Arthur brought the object up with enough

122

speed to knock Tony off of him. Arthur felt the weight leave his body. He scrambled to his feet to see Tony shaking off the blow. He looked around for another weapon. He saw a second pipe, smaller than the first, sticking out of the ground. He tried to wield it, but it was wedged fast. Tony was coming back at him. It was okay. Now it was a fist fight. Arthur had a chance against a dazed Tony toe-to-toe, or so he deluded himself to believe.

He looked over his opponent's shoulder and saw that Bubbs was getting double-teamed. Arthur would have been surprised to know that only ninety seconds had passed since he antagonized the suits with the mother of all racial slurs. The suits outnumbered the UJs by only one, so they decided to use the extra man against the biggest target. Unlike Jimmy Cutillo, Bubbs was not fast for a big man, nor was he burdened with an overabundance of intelligence. Within seconds, he managed to get himself cornered. Arthur offered the only help he could.

"Bubbs! Look down!"

Fatefully, Bubbs had stumbled backward onto a pile of rusty brake drums. He played to his only strength, which was brute force and pulled one out of the pile. He had no idea what to do with it. Noticing the action had caused his two opponents to take pause, and he started swinging it like a battle axe. His lazy grin returned, and he walked forward. The suits kept a close but safe distance. At first, they were taken aback by the ease at which the white gorilla was able to one-handedly scoop up twenty-five pounds of iron. When he started to swing it around, they realized the moron was going to wear himself out. When he lumbered into the open, they decided to speed up the process by getting on either side of him. Only by a rare and fleeting moment of cognition was Bubbs able to see what was going on. With his shallow idea pool empty, he grabbed on to the brake drum with both hands and started to spin. All the suits could do was step back and watch as Bubbs whirled around and around like a maniacal discus thrower. He tried to use what little sobriety he had to keep himself oriented, but none of his reference points seemed to stay in one place. There was nothing for it. He knew he wasn't going to be able to keep it up for much longer, so he did the only thing he could think of. He let go.

One of the suits hollered.

"Heads up!"

Reactively, everybody stopped and ducked. It was in that silence that they heard a voice in the distance.

"Break it up! This is the po..."

Bloody and exhausted, they all looked at each other. Had they heard what they though they heard? Then a second voice rang out, a frantic voice, a desperate voice.

"You bastards just killed a cop!"

Like cattle, the two groups gathered and ran in opposite directions.

14. The Condo

James and Julie were too tired for sex. She'd had a late dinner in Wilmington, Delaware. He and Gomez had pulled an extra half shift to get through the rest of the letters in the first box of diocese hate-mail. All the letters were variations on the same theme. The majority suggested castration for the accused priests and Archdiocese leaders, but not death. Those that did mention death put it in the context of eternal hell fire. The lefty letters with P.C. slants attempted to appeal to reason. The militant ones contained a bunch of name-calling and not much else. Nothing popped.

She patted him on the chest.

"I can tell you're still awake, baby."

He pulled her close.

"Yeah, I'm still awake."

"Anything you want to talk about?"

He thought she'd never ask.

"Did you keep up with any of the Philly Archdiocese molestation stuff?"

"Here and there. Do you think the killing had anything to do with them?"

"Maybe. Do you remember the one from the school? One of the teachers..."

"The shower thing. Yes, I remember sort of."

He adjusted his pillow as he tried to form a complicated thought into coherent sentences.

"I'm not sure what to... it probably doesn't have anything to do with anything, but you know Saint Al's is building a new church. Right?"

124

"Yes, I do. The magazine already has copies of the blue prints."

"Then you've seen the press. The Diocese is hailing the project as a symbol of Catholic strength. Saint Al's has been the fastest expanding parish in the territory for the past five years, and the Diocese didn't seem to care until the trials started."

He paused and rubbed his temples.

"I'm sorry. I digress. What I'm getting at is the church is important. Getting a position there would be a big deal."

"Sounds like it."

"The priest that's been in the middle of this case…Father Leo…he seems like a good guy. The thing is he's only been at Saint Al's for three months, and I think his appointment was a 'thank you' for services rendered during the Bell trial."

He told Julie about Leonardo Pasucci being a character witness for the defense and how the accused priest probably owes him his freedom.

"Do you think he perjured himself?"

"No. And look, I work for the city. I know everything is political. If he's getting his back scratched for scratching someone else's, more power to him. But facts are facts. He's one of three people who knew where Ryan was staying the night he was murdered. We've got a guy who, according to Leo, confessed to the killing in a confessional and then disappeared into thin air. If the killer was going to try something else, the press conference would have been the perfect place."

"And Leo was on the stage."

"Leo was on the stage. Yes. Then again, he all but alibied out the night of the killing. So far, I haven't allowed this garbage to pollute my thinking because I thought Leo was a good guy, but now that I see him connected with the trials and sitting pretty at Saint Al's…I don't know. None of this is changing the investigation. Samuel is still our Prime Suspect, even though we have no idea where he is."

He wasn't making sense and he knew it. What could any of this have to do with Ryan's death? What was he trying to reconcile?

Julie propped herself up on one elbow. She knew he wasn't going to get any sleep unless he could settle his mind. Practicality was usually good medicine, so she asked him a practical question that required a practical answer.

"Are you going to talk to him?"

He looked up at her. Even in the dark she was beautiful.

"Definitely."

"Why?"

"To get the full story."

"Can't you just get the transcripts from the trial?"

"I want to hear it from him first. I want to hear his version of the truth before I get the facts. I also want Ernie to read him."

She collapsed her arm and snuggled next to him again.

"Okay. Doesn't seem like there's much else you can do until then."

Lynch instantly felt his eyes start to close.

"I love you, Ms. Galbraith."

She didn't answer. She didn't have to.

They were both just about to nod off when Lynch's cell phone buzzed. He lazily scooped it up from the corner of the bedside table and looked at the screen with one half-opened eye.

It was Sergeant Warner, Reilly's partner. As Lynch was pulling the phone to his face, he noticed that he'd missed a text message. He decided to grab a quick look at it before talking to Warner. It was from Kelly.

I DIDN'T HAVE ANYTHING 2 DO WITH IT.

"What the hell, Kelly? I know you didn't have anything to do with it."

He answered. Julie put her chin on his chest and listened. She was praying that he didn't have to go to the station.

"Hey, Carrie. What's up? Oh no! You're kidding! Where? I...Do you want me to come? Okay, tell me if that changes. Who's got it? You? Good. Are you going home tonight? When are you getting there? Okay, I'll see you then. Hang in there, okay? Bye."

Julie sat up while James returned his phone to the table.

"Everything okay?"

"No, actually. Reilly is in the hospital."

"Dear God. What happened?"

"He was at Frankie and Jimmy's with his brother, and they chased some vandals into the scrap yard. I guess one of them threw a brake drum at them and nailed him on the forehead."

"Is he okay?"

"He's got a depressed skull fracture. Luckily, they got him in the OR quick enough. He's alive, but the jury's still out on the effects of the damage. I didn't follow everything she said."

A part of Lynch couldn't help but feel it to be poetic justice for Jeremy.

"I'll go with you to the hospital if…"

"No. It's okay. I'm going in the morning. Warner says there's not anything to do. She's taking lead on the investigation, and she's got it under control."

He was starting to babble and slur his speech. Julie decided that if he wasn't going to worry, neither was she.

Lynch's last thought before he fell asleep was of Kelly's text message.

I DIDN'T HAVE ANYTHING 2 DO WITH IT.

He wouldn't understand what she meant until the following evening.

BATTLE OF THE BANDS

Tuesday

1. The ICU

"We'll get him for you, bro."

Ian Reilly was in the ICU with his wife, Molly, and son, Braden. His daughter, Sian, was a freshman at Northwestern University and wouldn't get the news of her uncle for another hour.

Sons of bitches

Ian lied to his brother's partner. Kevin was clear in his instructions before hollering at the punks in the scrap yard. No matter what happened, the cops could *not* be put onto the Unjudged.

"Don't worry, Kev. I got this."

Ian would find who sent that brake drum flying, and he'd make them pay. The cops and the criminal-protecting justice system they represented could suck it.

Braden had just turned fifteen, and like many of his generation, didn't deal well with things that required a response beyond a text message. He loved his Uncle Kevin. The thought of losing him sent the boy to a horrible place. All he wanted was to recede into his secret pastime: the only activity in his life that gave him pleasure. He kept it all in a trunk under his bed. His mom would shit if she found it. His dad? Hard to say.

Please open your eyes, Uncle Kev.

A familiar, heavy hand fell onto his shoulder.

"After we leave, son, I'm going to tell you what caused this, so you understand sacrifice…so you understand what it means to be a man."

Braden had heard the phrase "what it means to be a man" at least twice a day since his first Communion. It no longer had any meaning or effect.

Please.

128

The operating surgeon said the injury could permanently affect Kevin's eye movement and ability to speak. The chances of him returning to the Detective Squad were slim at best. The most he could hope for was a crappy desk job and early retirement.

Molly knew that Kevin would rather hear the news from a family member than a doctor. Neither of his brothers would be able to get the words out. It would have to be one of the women. It would have to be her…that is, if he ever woke up.

She put her head on her husband's shoulder and spoke.

"Kevin is tough, and this is a good hospital. He's going to be fine, boo."

Ian didn't hear a word.

"We'll get him, bro."

The Reillys had been weakened. The other cheek would not be turned.

2. The ICU - a bit later

Lynch stepped out of the hospital elevator a little after seven am. The automatic doors swung open as he approached the entrance to the sixth floor's south wing. The ICU entrance was in view, so too the edge of the waiting area. There were a few chairs lining the hallway. Carrie Warner was sitting in one of them. Lynch could see the Reilly family gathered in a circle. His instinct was to go toward them, but Warner waved him off. He wanted to offer his sympathies and ask permission to see Kevin, but Warner was right; both of those things could wait. With a gentle smile and open arms, he walked to her. She stood, and they shared an embrace.

"Carrie, I am so sorry."

"I know, Jim. Thanks."

He pulled a chair next to her.

"Any news?"

"No. They just need to keep an eye on him until he comes out of it."

There was a folder and a note pad on the floor next to her. She'd already started interviews. The name "Ian Reilly" was at the top of the first page with noticeably little writing below. He nodded towards it.

"What have you got so far?"

Warner picked up the pad and handed it to him, leaving the folder on the floor.

129

"A little bit more than I told you over the phone. Three witnesses: Ian Reilly, Jimmy Cutillo, and the kid they chased."

Lynch read Ian's short and semi-accurate account of the evening.

"So…am I reading this correctly? They just happened to stumble upon a rumble?"

"That's what he said."

"And neither Reilly recognized anyone in either gang?"

"Nope."

Lynch flipped the page to find the notes taken from Jimmy Cutillo's interview. By his own account, he drove his Fleetwood around to the north gate, per Kevin's instructions, and spotted the kid sneaking between telephone poles. Lynch was not surprised to discover that the kid's name was Gordon Weiss (Gordy familiarly). He lifted his head to say something, but Carrie beat him to the punch.

"Jim, we're not New York City, right?"

She wasn't making eye contact. Something was up.

"What do you mean?"

"We do our best. We've all been trained as well as any other cops, but Potterford's a small town. We don't get a crazy amount of murders. We don't get the practice or have the gear that the big cities do. We miss stuff, don't we?"

Lynch turned his chair to face her.

"Carrie, I'm not following you."

She reluctantly picked up the folder from the floor and held it out to him. He took it and opened it, recognizing the contents immediately.

"I've read these already, Carrie. They're the UJ statements taken from Saturday."

She nodded.

"They were taken at the barn, not the station."

"I know."

"And Kevin took all of them while I was dickin' around with Crime Scene."

"I know. I still don't follow."

Carrie rubbed her eyes.

"Read them again. Read them as though Reilly isn't the lead investigator, and you are."

"What am I looking for?"

130

"I'm not going to tell you. I just want to see if you notice the same thing I did. And if you do, I want to hear your explanation…because there has to be one. Reilly wouldn't…I mean he's a small-town cop like the rest of us. He could have just made a mistake. He could have accidentally forgotten…just read it."

Lynch took the folder and read the statements for the third time, only now in the manner that Carrie suggested. The words hadn't changed. Every UJ member set the time line the same way. They showed up at the barn at seven pm. Around ten pm, there was a break in the action while Rick changed CD's in the player. Jeremy went out to take a piss. Twenty minutes later, Traci was wondering where Jeremy had gotten to, so she went outside to look for him and found his body. The first squad car was there by ten thirty. Then …

Wait a minute.

Lynch hurriedly flipped through the statements, shooting his eyes to the end of each one.

Who called it in?

The sound of rustling papers filled the hallway.

None of them mention calling the police. Who called the police?

After his second scan, he looked up at Warner. She spoke. "Yeah…that's what I thought."

3. The Cloister

Arthur didn't startle easily, but he wasn't expecting Rick to be right in front of him when he woke.

"Dammit, Rick! What!?"

Rick had been sitting a few feet from Arthur's cot for the better part of an hour. He hadn't slept a wink. Traci had nursed them all back to health as best she could. Rick was not surprised to find her in bed with Arthur, but he *was* surprised that she'd fallen asleep in her party dress. Maybe she

131

wanted to get her money's worth out of it since she'd never be able to wear it again. Rick had been stewing silently since the mad dash from the scrap yard. Of all the things that happened after Gordy threw the brick, the getaway was the only thing that went according to plan.

They were supposed to be wearing masks when Reilly jumped the fence. If there were others with him, and they were few enough to handle, Bubbs, Steven, and he were supposed to ambush from the side, leaving them unconscious while Arthur had his fun with Reilly. No guns were to be involved; guns were traceable. Reilly was to be hog tied and gagged, while Arthur explained to him why he was about to die. Then Arthur would stomp on his head with his steel-tipped Doc Martins until the job was done. If there was any variation…if the cops spotted them in the yard before Reilly arrived, or too many people came over the fence…the UJ would disperse and save vengeance for another day.

None of that happened.

As far as Rick could tell, they had three hopes. The first was that the black guys in the suits were just as eager to put the evening behind them as the UJ. The second was that whoever shouted the thing about bastards killing cops was too far away to positively ID anyone. The third was that Gordy's silly little scheme for dealing with the police actually worked. Neither Rick nor anyone else in the UJ had considered the possibility that Reilly might still be alive.

"So, I suppose we're calling this a victory, eh Artie?"

Arthur winced and sat up.

"Richard, I would kick your ass sideways right now if I didn't have three bruised ribs. What's on your mind?"

Rick instantly felt like the straight man in a comedy act.

"Dude…what was that shit with the n-word? We're militant racists now?"

Arthur's favorite douchy grin appeared.

"Oh, come on now, Richard. You know me better than that. I see no reason to cast hatred upon an entire race of people when there are plenty of good reasons to hate people individually. I just wanted to throw the guy off balance."

Rick drew an invisible line connecting Arthurs many injuries.

"And how'd that work out for you?"

"I'm telling you. You're asking for it."

"We were supposed to run if anything unexpected happened."

"Yes, Richard. And?"

Rick sat in gaped silence for a moment before responding.

"And I'd say five huge Reservoir-Dogs-lookin' black guys appearing out of nowhere qualifies."

Arthur chuckled.

"What can I say? I thought we could take 'em."

Rick was crippled for a retort. A dozen thoughts bundled into a single knot in his brain.

Steven chimed in from across the room.

"What about Gordy?"

Arthur rubbed his eyes and answered.

"What about him?"

"The kid is a moron, but he gets smarter every time you kick him in the balls. We hung him out to dry. If he realizes that, he's gonna rat."

"Exactly, Steven! The kid! The KID! He's a minor! His parents were called the second he set foot in the station! We said we'd bail him out, but we can't help it if mommy and daddy got there first! You get it? The turd brain had no idea we had no intention of bailing him out! All he knows or cares about is that thinks he's full UJ now! He's not gonna rat!"

"Is he?"

"Is he what, Steven?"

"Full UJ."

Arthur looked over at Rick who, by his expression, had the same question. Arthur had an answer.

"Fuck no. He's not full UJ. We'll let him wear the colors. That's it. He can fetch beers and get kicked in the nuts wearing the colors."

Traci rolled over in her sleep, losing her blanket in the process. She was on her stomach, breathing softly while Arthur ogled her lower half. She awoke when he started to hike up her skirt for a better look.

"Come on, Artie. Not now. I'm tired."

With a frustrated growl, Arthur sprang up as quickly as he could with three bruised ribs, grabbed his shirt from a nearby chair, and stormed toward the adjoining room.

"Has everyone lost their goddam minds around here!? Has everyone forgotten what the UJ is supposed to be about!?"

133

Rick and Steven looked at each other and shrugged as Arthur stomped over the threshold. Traci raised her head an inch or two in response to the yelling, then put it right back down. There were a few seconds of silence before Arthur returned with his shirt half buttoned and a cigarette dangling from his scabbed-over lip.

"Anyone know where Bubbs and Kelly got to?"

4. On the Way to School

Gordy was grounded.

What a joke...friggin' grounded.

He walked to school, reflecting fondly upon the events of the previous evening.

He understood what happened. Arthur would have bailed him out of jail if he could. Everything happened so quickly. How was the UJ supposed to know the massive bartender would drive his massive car right to where Gordy was hiding? The schmuck almost tore Gordy's arm off dragging him to the yard.

That sucked. But...man! Everything up to that point was incredible!

They all scoffed when he suggested the role play. He couldn't wait to tell them how well it paid off.

Twenty minutes before Traci sauntered into F and J's in her black dress and high heels, several Potterford residents saw Gordy on his bike, bound for Third Street. It wasn't unusual; Gordy rode his bike everywhere. Five minutes later he was approaching the bar. There was a man flagging him down in front of the Tru-Value. Gordy stopped, and the dialogue began.

"Hey kid, you want some easy cash?"

"It depends on what I have to do to get it. I'm not getting down on my knees or anything."

"No kid. Nothing like that. I'm going to give you fifty bucks and a brick. After I hand you the brick and the cash, take your bike and hide in that alley. Wait fifteen minutes."

"Why do I have to wait fifteen minutes?"

"Do you want the money or not?"

"Yes. I'm sorry. What do I do after fifteen minutes?"

"Ride your bike in front of Frankie and Jimmy's and throw the brick through the window."

"That's it?"

"Yup. That's it. Hide where you want afterwards. I suggest the industrial complex, but that's up to you."

Gordy thought for a moment before he answered.

"Okay. You've got a deal."

The man handed the brick and fifty dollars to Gordy. There was one last instruction.

"Kid, I'm going to be watching you to make sure you don't screw me over. I don't want you to see where I'm hiding, so turn around and count to 100."

"Got it"

The man sighed.

"Is that good enough, Gordy? I feel like an idiot."

Gordy didn't care what Steven felt like. This wasn't about dignity. It was about having a story that would hold up under scrutiny. The only thing left for Gordy to concoct was a bogus description of the man, and he had that covered.

He wished that Arthur could have been there to hear the pat and natural answers he had for every question the cops threw at him. He was most proud of the moment he shut down the line of questioning about the money by reaching into his pocket and producing a brand new folded fifty-dollar bill. It was folded because Steven had folded it. Steven folded it because that's how a person palms money to a stranger in the street. That's how you make a lie as close to the truth as possible.

He knew he'd have to do some community service and probably bus tables or something to pay off the fine, but it would be worth it.

He smiled as he recalled saying "Yes, that's the guy," when the sketch artist showed him the completed drawing.

Had his parents not whisked him out the station, he would have heard a brief and amusing exchange between the sketch artist and the Chief of Police.

"Hey, Chief, take a look at this."

"Yeah, it's a sketch. What's wrong with it?"

"Nothing's wrong with it. Who does it remind you of?"

"I don't know. Looks a little like Walter Matthau."

"Who?"

5. On the Gravel Road

The sun was still low in the sky when Lynch and Warner turned on to the gravel road that led to the old Meadowbrook Farm. According to 911 Dispatch, the phantom emergency call was made anonymously from a pre-paid cell phone. The caller was male and disguised his voice with a horrible Southern (or British?) accent. The phone hadn't been used since.

Of the three possibilities, least likely was the caller being one of the Unjudged. None of their cell numbers matched the 911 record, and none of their voices, no matter how disguised, were anything like the British cowboy's. Still, the implications sent Lynch's head reeling.

Suppose the caller *was* one of the gang. That meant a missing burner phone. Why would someone ditch a phone, if not to hide a picture, text, or call record? And whose picture, call, or text would a UJ feel the need to hide? Lynch had a wishful guess.

If the phone was still at the barn somewhere, and they found it, and anything on it led to Samuel, he was planning on kissing Warner full on the lips.

Warner was differently preoccupied. She loathed discrepancy. Seven years as her partner had earned Reilly the benefit of the doubt. Intimidate witnesses? Yes. Dance around procedure? Yes. Sleep with prostitutes? Yes. Manipulate an investigation? No fucking way.

Yet the crummy feeling she'd had in her gut since Saturday night remained. True, she was with Reilly when the beating took place, but she didn't have eyes on him the entire evening. A guy *that* angry and *that* well connected could do a lot of damage with a cell phone and a few moments alone.

And...

Shit.

...there was a discrepancy.

Lynch wanted to go back to the barn to look for the missing cell phone. Perhaps, in the process, the discrepancy could be explained. Even if not, the situation deserved a second set of eyes.

They decided to step through the events of the evening, starting with the arrival of the attackers. Carrie was resistant to the idea that one of *them* dialed 911, but that was the more favorable of remaining two possibilities (strangely enough).

They left Carrie's car at the barn and walked to the truck-shaped patch of flattened grass where the assailants had parked. Several trampled paths led to and away from the area. Each one had been labeled by Crime Scene as either "Coming" or "Going."

Lynch snatched up one of the "Goings" and held it out straight.

"Does this mean 'Going' *to* the barn or 'Going' *away from* the crime scene?"

"To the barn, if I remember correctly."

"Good. That's the one we want. A little less polysemy would have been nice. It's too early for that shit."

"No, it's too early for the word 'polysemy.'"

They walked in the assailants' footsteps through the field all the way to the peep hole.

Lynch crouched and took a look inside. It was his first glimpse of the UJ cloister since visiting the Avery gallery. The effort put into recreating the artist's vision was recognizable but hardly valiant. The target once used for bouts of knife throwing hung in the distance, nearly hacked to bits. The remnants of the fire were still on the ground, surrounded by piles of empty pizza boxes and, no doubt, a mound of maggots. There were enough beer bottles scattered about to make a stained-glass window for Saint Patrick's Cathedral. If these were the symbols of freedom, Lynch would take his oppressive condo and brainwashed bourgeois girlfriend thank you very much.

Carrie spoke.

"Ready to see where Jeremy was found?"

Both knees cracked as he stood.

"Lead on."

They walked to the far side of the barn and stopped at the old plow. Lynch took a whiff.

"Piss?"

137

"Yup."

Ten feet away lay a dried pool of blood and the remnants of two passes by Crime Scene.

He'd read the statements, and Carrie had gotten him up to speed on the suppositions. There was no reason to suspect that Jeremy Sokol was targeted specifically. The outnumbered assailants hid behind the plow, so they could take out the UJ one at a time. Jeremy was simply the unfortunate soul that had to pee first. Traci was the next one out. She screamed when she saw the body, but the music was too loud for the rest of the gang to hear her, so she ran inside for help.

"So, you and Reilly think the thugs ran when Traci screamed?"

"Or when she went back in, yeah."

She pointed towards the blood.

"Now, look at the dirt. I want to show you why I don't think the truck guys made the call. See the footprints? The assholes went in hard and close. None of them ever so much as took a step back. There's nothing in the patterns here to indicate any kind of remorse, and a call to 911 shows remorse."

"Devil's advocate?"

"Go ahead."

"What if murder wasn't the plan? They think they've worked him over enough, so they go back behind the plow to wait for their next victim. They realize Jeremy's a sack of meat, and they get scared. Maybe it wasn't remorse so much as fear."

"Fear? These guys? Scared? Does that seem right?"

"No, I guess not...all the more reason not to abandon the idea that there might be a cell phone around here somewhere."

Lynch held his breath, got on all fours, and scoured the plow for the burner. No dice.

His lungs gave way.

"Dammit!...ack!"

He gagged, coughed, and stumbled to the edge of the tall grass. Once the fit passed, he threw back his shoulders and happily breathed in the piss-free air.

The field met the horizon just past the long shadow cast by the barn...real John Steinbeck stuff. Warner came up beside him with her note pad tucked under her arm.

138

"So, where do you want to look next?"

"I don't know."

He shifted his gaze from the grass to the barn and back again, hoping for a crumb of inspiration. He was woefully in need of a starting point, and nothing was jumping.

"I couldn't find an elephant in this shit, much less a goddam call phone."

They were officially stymied. Warner tried to get things moving again.

"They left tracks in the field and a body in the open. One thing's for sure. These boys are *not* brain surgeons."

A breeze blew across the property, causing a wave through the grass. The mad flap of tiny wings caused both detectives to look up. Two barn swallows flew in tandem over their heads and disappeared into one of the barn's upper windows.

Something unlocked. All the information Lynch had absorbed throughout the morning got into line.

"That's right … the barn has a loft."

"What?"

"Wait here."

He didn't need a starting point; he needed a vantage point.

"No problem, bossy-pants."

Whoever nailed up the only access ladder must have had shoulders that were half as wide as Lynch's and legs that were twice as long. Still, he managed to reach the loft alive, which, judging by the odor, was more than he could say for some other poor creature.

He dusted himself off and took a look around. The UJ's had set themselves up surprisingly well. There weren't any bed frames or box-springs, but there were five queen sized mattresses, three hammocks, and a cedar cabinet filled with blankets and pillows. Everything had been mothballed.

Really? Fry your brain, hump everything in sight, and then put out mothballs?

On the far end of the loft, there was a window overlooking the old plow.

"That works."

After a tiptoe through the mattress maze, he looked out. Three farm houses separated by acreage equal to Meadowbrook's were visible in the distance.

Carrie called up from the ground. "What are you looking for?"

"I'm not looking; I'm waiting."

"You really are a dick. What are you waiting for then?"

"Another breeze."

The breeze blew. From north to south, across the expanse of Meadowbrook Farms, the breeze blew. As Lynch had hoped, a trampled path he hadn't seen before became exposed, only this one neither snaked back to the truck nor emptied onto the dirt. It started ten feet away from (or stopped ten feet short of) the crime scene and appeared to lead all the way to the next property. The grass in that part of the field was some of the tallest. Someone of average height could stand in it up to their chest. Someone of less-than-average height, especially at night, could likely go unseen.

Tah - dahhh!

"Guess what, Carrie."

"What?"

"Option number three."

Her teeth glistened in the low morning sun.

"A witness we missed?"

"Boo ya!"

6. Up a Tree

Philip awoke the same way he had the day before: In pain. He was encouraged by the fact that his current pain was only in his balls. That meant he was making ergonomic progress with the seat. It was impossible to have a completely accurate test environment. Nature wasn't a fan of repetition as was demonstrated in things like snowflakes, fingerprints, and, yes, trees.

This was the second day in a row he'd gotten up at the crack of dawn and driven to his uncle's place for the sole purpose of climbing a tree and

140

falling asleep. By his stopwatch, he made it to forty-five minutes, a vast improvement over the day before.

He braced his feet on opposing branches and leaned back with a yawn and a stretch. He grabbed a look at his watch as it cleared the cuff. It was getting close to eight o'clock. He'd have to climb down soon and spend some time on the bike.

Dammit.

It was an obstacle of his own making. He got pissed at himself every time he thought about it. He needed an excuse for his sudden change of morning routine. He couldn't lie about his whereabouts. There were too many ways to find him.

The bike story was perfect.

For years Philip had talked about rebuilding it. Everyone close to him knew the fond nostalgia with which looked back upon his teen years and the afternoons he spent racing with his uncle around the woods. When he announced that he was finally going to dig out his tools, no one so much as raised an eyebrow. The problem, as he came to realize, was that at some point he was going to have to show the fruits of his labor, which meant taking time each day to actually work on the fucking thing.

His stomach growled. He reached into the breast pocket of his jacket for a protein bar and laid his fingers on something he didn't recognize by touch. He pulled the thing out to take a look and broke into a hearty guffaw. It was the disgusting set of yellowed false teeth he'd shoved in there the day before. He held it to the heavens and sang half of a chorus to "You Are My Sunshine" before winding up and chucking it far into the woods.

In the distance he saw his makeshift shooting gallery. He considered not wasting the bullet, but the moment of caution abandoned him as he whipped the nine-millimeter out of its holster and took a million-to-one pot shot at one of the painted cans.

"Pow – ping!"

Yes. That morning, in that tree, even with aching balls, it was good to be alive.

7. Father Leo's Office

"Leo, I'm so sorry."

After six hours of penance and a sleepless night, Aiden finally found the courage to approach Father Leo.

The young priest was a mess.

"Please Aiden, calm down."

It would have been unfair of Leo to be angry. He couldn't ask the man to use his neighborhood connections to help the church, and then condemn him when those same connections *may* have landed the church a couple of degrees separated from a major felony.

"Father, I should have known. I should have known what he was going to do."

Leo took Aiden's hands in his.

"You don't even know that he did anything."

"I know him. I know Kevin…"

He came dangerously close to saying, "I take his confessions."

"…this is something he would do or get someone else to do. He'd mean well. He'd be doing it for the church and for the town. He sees things in absolutes."

Aiden was getting irrational in his speech. Leo needed to awaken the South Philly son of a butcher inside him.

"Will you fucking get a hold of yourself!"

The young priest looked up in shock.

Leo continued.

"Don't look at me like that. The f-bomb isn't listed among the deadly sins. *We* decided it's vulgar, not God. What do you think Jesus hollered when they drove in the first nail?"

Aiden couldn't help but burst out in exhausted hysterics through his blood-shot eyes.

"Look, Aiden, all we have to do is go to the police. I have a new friend there. Just tell him what you told me. This is evidence in a murder case, that's all."

Aiden wiped his eyes and nodded. Leo stood and walked to his half-opened window so that Aiden could have a moment alone to collect himself. They'd leave for the police station as soon as the young priest was ready. Leo breathed in some fresh air and looked out at the courtyard.

Pastor Karney was there. He was pruning the rose bushes. Leo found that odd for some reason.

8. The Strausser Farm

Lynch and Warner decided to grab some breakfast and come back. Eight-fifteen was too early to go banging on someone's front door, even a farmhouse door.

It was on the road side of a sizeable piece of land that was divided into sections by electrified fence. Various breeds of livestock inhabited each paddock. What little Lynch knew about animal husbandry made him believe that the majority of the animals were for showing rather than butchering.

They were a few steps away from the front porch when Lynch stopped and subtly pointed toward one of the distant fences. There was a boy there, perhaps sixteen or seventeen years old.

"Carrie, check it out."

"Yup. I'd say that's about right."

Before he and Warner left for breakfast, they gave the once-over to the area where their witness had stood. What they found gave them an idea, at least generically, whom they were looking for.

From the farmhouse, it was difficult to tell what the boy was doing. It looked like he was scratching a cow's back with a fire poker. Lynch spoke up.

"Hey buddy!"

The boy spun around nervously.

"Yes, sir?"

"What's your name?"

After regaining control of his bladder, the boy answered.

"Elliot...Strausser...Elliot Strausser."

"How old are ya, Elliot?"

"Sixteen, sir."

Warner swore to herself as Lynch hollered back. They would have to talk to his parents first. Neither of them bothered to ask the boy what he was doing at home at nine-thirty in the morning. No doubt, the boy was home-schooled.

A woman's voice came from the porch.

"You folks lost?"

A conservatively dressed woman in her late thirties stood at the house's entryway with her right hand out of view. Considering the high probability that it was wrapped around a shotgun, the two detectives wasted no time showing ID. Carrie spoke. It was her case.

"Good morning, ma'am. Detectives Warner and Lynch. We were hoping we could speak with Elliot. Are you his mother by chance?"

The woman made her shooting hand visible and put it in the pocket of her apron.

"I am. Is this about the hoo-hah Saturday night?"

"It is. We have reason to believe your son witnessed the crime and called 911."

The woman amusedly wrinkled her brow.

"You are more than welcome to talk to him, but, like I told the two fellows in uniform on Saturday, none of us left the house that night."

Lynch spoke up.

"You were in your son's presence all evening?"

"No, but I know he didn't make any calls from the house, and he doesn't have a cell phone. He also knows what happens if he lies."

Warner's blood pressure jumped. She'd spent time in Social Services and could never let a comment like that slide.

"Is that so? What happens when he lies?"

The woman's expression instantly went from pleasant to placid, as though the Prozac had just kicked in.

"He goes to hell, of course."

Lynch looked over his shoulder toward Elliot, whose eyes were riveted to the conversation, even though he couldn't hear a word of it. He turned back to the boy's mother.

"It was nice meeting you, ma'am. We won't be long."

The woman had every right to be part of the interview, but Lynch thought it best not to offer. She went back into the house. The two detectives shared a chuckle and walked at a friendly pace towards Elliot. Lynch spoke.

"Whatcha doin' there, buddy?"

Elliot's voice shook. What words he was able muster came out in a scared whisper.

"Getting Daphne ready for show."

"Oh! The cow's name is Daphne?"

Elliot nodded. Lynch continued.

"What's the poker for?"

The boy looked at the hooked rod in his own hand as though he'd forgotten he was holding it. His voice became steadier and his posture more at ease as he backed into his comfort zone.

"It's a show stick. It's for positioning her legs. See?"

He used the hook to move Daphne's ankles a bit. Danged if the slight change didn't somehow make the animal look more regal. Elliot spoke again.

"You have to position them for judging just like a dog at a dog show."

The boy had an endearing quality, despite what Lynch and Warner had found in the field. The next question was Carrie's.

"We saw you scratching Daphne's back with that thing. What does that do?"

Elliot was smiling now.

"It's called loining. It makes the cow pose with a straighter back. Watch."

He demonstrated. Lynch continued.

"What did you see on Saturday, Elliot?"

Daphne twitched as animals do what they sense apprehension. The shake returned to Elliot's voice.

"Nothing. What do you mean?"

Lynch put his hand on the boy's shoulder. Warner stepped away. This was definitely a conversation that needed to be had between two fellas.

"Elliot, if it makes you feel better, you're not in any legal trouble. But I'd be remiss in my duties as a cop and a man if I didn't...uh..."

Ernie should be doing this.

"...That stuff isn't cool. It's intrusive and causes problems later in life. It dehumanizes people, especially women, and can lead to erectile dysfunction."

Dear God, Ernie should be doing this.

145

Elliot put down the show stick in defeat and took a seat on a nearby hay bale. Lynch went to lean on the fence, but Elliot quickly reacted.

"Don't do that."

Lynch jumped, realizing that he had just been saved from electrocution.

I hope Carrie didn't see that.

She did.

With effort, he used his foot to nudge a second bale beside Elliot's and plopped down upon it. It was the boy's turn to speak.

"How did you know?"

Lynch chose his words carefully.

"Honestly? We found your spot in the field, and the trail to it, and the binoculars...and the towel."

Elliot pinched his eyes shut in embarrassment. Unfortunately, it was Carrie who found the towel and unscientifically surmised what was one it. Lynch spared the poor kid the details.

"We also know you called the police on a phone that your mother doesn't know about."

Elliot pulled his beet-red face away from his hands and cleared his throat.

"The girl with the colored hair likes to get naked sometimes. Not every time but...look, my mom..."

"Don't worry. I'm not going to tell your mom. I've said my piece on the matter, but you can help me out if you can tell me exactly what you saw on Saturday."

Elliot didn't hesitate. He recounted what he could remember in explicit detail, confirming just about everything Warner and Crime Scene had guessed. The gold that Lynch thought he struck, however, lost its luster as the boy started to describe the attackers.

"...orange...two of them had ol' wooden things, but the third used an aluminum softball bat, and it was orange. I couldn't see their faces, though. They had camouflage masks."

WTF?

Lynch's heart sank into his stomach and then worked into his lower intestines as Elliot answered question after question with crappy answer after crappy answer:

Yes, the assailants kept their masks on the whole time.

No, they never spoke.

Yes, every member of the UJ arrived when and how they said they did.

No, no one came or left otherwise.

"…until the girl in her underwear started screaming. I don't know what happened after that. I ran."

Lynch clenched his teeth and stabbed a period onto his last note before pocketing his notepad.

"Thanks buddy. The girl with the colored hair owes you a great deal. That'll give you a little redemption."

Elliot shifted on his hay bale as if his overalls were suddenly uncomfortable.

"Really? Cool!"

Lynch mussed the boy's hair and gave him a little punch. He hoped he wasn't pouring it on too thick.

An orange bat…well, it's something, considering everything else has gone to shit.

Elliot Strausser was tapped. It was time to go. Lynch shook hands with him and walked over to Warner. She could tell the interview had yielded nothing, but she asked anyway.

"So, a step forward or a step backward?"

"About three steps backward. Every member of the UJ now has an alibi for the shooting…"

Warner interrupted.

"You pretty much knew that though."

"Yeah, but my quality of life would have improved greatly if one of those ecstasy-popping losers would have gotten their hands on Samuel's jacket and…"

He was half talking to himself. Warner interrupted again.

"The beating, Lynch! Come on!"

Lynch begrudgingly repeated what the boy told him.

147

"So, the good news is there's no way Jeremy Sokol could have identified Reilly; the bad news is there's no way Jeremy Sokol could have identified *anybody*. Why the hell, then, did the kid flip out in the ICU?"

Like Lynch, Warner had mixed emotions, but there was no denying the meteor-sized weight that left her shoulders.

"I don't know…"

She panned one last time across the tall grass, dirt, and cow manure.

"…we should probably say good bye to Elliot's mom. What's her name again?"

"She didn't say. I'm guessing something biblical"

Lynch's cell phone rang. He answered it. The few words he spoke put a noticeable pep in his step. He switched it off, playfully tossed into the air, caught it, and slid it into his shirt pocket.

"Well, Carrie, the Lord taketh away, and the Lord giveth."

"How so?"

"That was Gomez. Chester County Ballistics got a match on the bullet they pulled out of Bishop Ryan."

They said a quick good bye to Mary Strausser and headed for the car. Warner checked her e-mail en route. She was expecting a scan of Gordy's sketch. She was pleased to find that she'd received it…that was until she opened the file."

"Oh, for fuck's sake!"

She speed-dialed the station before Lynch had the chance to ask what was going on. The sketch artist's name was Danny.

"Hi Boris. Get me Danny. Danny, how old are you? Thirty-five and you've never seen The Bad News Bears? I'll tell you what I'm talking about. That Gordy kid is screwing with you. The sketch isn't real. Just tell Gomez to call the parents and get the little asshole back in there. I don't have the number on me."

Lynch couldn't leave it alone.

"What was that all about?"

"I swear to Christ, Jim. I sometimes wonder how we stay in charge of this town! I really do!"

9. PMMC

Ian Reilly kissed his mother on the forehead, zipped up his wind breaker, and looked toward the elevators. His eyes stung from hours of welled-up tears. He clutched his stomach as it hurt physically to leave his family in the hospital, but he had no choice. It was getting close to ten o'clock. His trophy shop needed to be opened, and the only set of keys was on a hook in his garage. He wouldn't be gone long. He just needed to unlock the doors and disable the alarm. Quentin, the assistant manager, could handle himself for the day.

He called the elevator by pressing the down-button an unneeded number of times. His vision blurred, and his eyelids twitched as he waited for the doors to open. His toes started to tap inside his sneakers. He felt his fingernails dig into his palms. A doctor was paged, but Ian barely heard it over his own grinding teeth and impatient humming. It was obvious that he wasn't going to be able to stand still for six floors, so when the chime that announced the elevator's arrival finally sounded, he gave it the finger and headed for the stairs.

He entered the lobby without any recollection of the descent. The room was air-conditioned unlike the stairwell, and it made him realize how much he was sweating. A man his size didn't take stairs in any direction without doubling his heart rate. Thoughts of keys and revenge were overtaken by the need for fluids.

His eyes fell on the vending area. A machine bearing the blue Deer Park logo beckoned. He started walking. As he got closer, his periphery widened. To the right of the Deer Park machine stood the obligatory rotating sandwich dispenser. There were tables nearby. Sitting at one of them was a man, a man Ian might have passed without notice were it not for three things. He was black; he was nursing a head wound, and he was wearing a suit.

Ian made his purchase and tried to catch the man's eye. The man, Tony Evans, just stared at his own bruised and folded hands.

"Hi."

Tony looked up from his trance and responded quietly without emotion.

"Hey, what's up, man?"

Ian uncapped his water and took a swig.

"Everything okay?"

149

The answer didn't come right away.

"Yeah. Just thinking."

Salesman Reilly gave a charismatic smile, nodded, and sat. Then he spoke.

"I saw you last night."

Tony got up to leave, but Ian grabbed him non-confrontationally by the forearm. Tony balled up his fist.

"Get your hands off me!"

"Hey, hey, hey. Calm down. Better yet, sit down. That wasn't a threat. Come on. Sit."

He did.

"Sounded like a threat to me."

"My fault. The guy that got hit with the iron is my brother."

Tony's face relaxed. He was relieved to hear the pasty, sweaty, Irish butter ball say "*is* my brother," rather than "*was* my brother."

"How is he?"

"How is he? He'll live, but we're not sure of much else. Look, I know you didn't throw the brake drum. I know this because I know the piss-holes you scrapped with last night. They call themselves the Unjudged. Can you believe the arrogance?"

Tony laughed.

"Pretty bold. You got that right."

"I mean, I don't care who you are. No one goes through life without judgment. I bet you believe in God. Don't you?"

Tony nodded with resolve.

"Yes, I do."

All the torturous thoughts and memories that had robbed the young man of his sleep spilled out uncontrollably. He told fragmented anecdotes of his childhood in Franklin Village. He spoke of the scrap yard, his bedroom window, drug pushers, gun dealers, and pimps. With a lump in his throat, he spoke of his father who died of a heart attack when Tony was still in his mother's womb, his sister who got clean and now worked as a pet groomer, his mother: his rock, his reason, his world. He spoke of his church and his pastor. It all wove together and formed into the story of a community's triumph. The struggle was far from over, but where there once lay piles of garbage, now stood planters. Every street lamp now had a working bulb. The drugs were still around but no longer blatantly pushed in the open like ice cream.

"...and the scrap yard is clean. Pastor Seymour did that, Mr. Reilly. There's still a great deal of work to do, but he'll be the shepherd. He'll be the vessel of the almighty. You'll see. The drugs and guns are out of the yard, and they aren't coming back!"

Tony was first in line when the good Pastor announced formation of the Village Crime Watch. Seymour pitched the idea to the Borough with little resistance, but there had to be rules, strict ones. And these rules had to be explained clearly and specifically to the angry youth who wanted so desperately to be the good Pastor's right hand.

"Anthony, look right into my eyes. I want you to gather four of your biggest friends. All of you put on suits and walk the east side of the Village three nights a week. You are to be Boy Scouts: helpful, courteous, the whole deal. If you see anything happen, you make your presence known and that's it. If that doesn't work, you call the police right away. If they aren't there in ten minutes, you call me. Otherwise, you do nothing."

Tony remembered being held firmly by the shoulders as his mentor drilled in the most important of the Borough's stipulations.

"You do *not* patrol *anywhere* outside the Village. Not the park, not the boulevard, and especially not the scrap yard. It's dangerous, it's trespassing, and Potterford will shut the program down over it. Understand? If I find you in the yard, you're out of the Watch. I'll find someone else. I'm serious about this, Anthony."

Ian nodded with false sympathy.

"So, what were you and your friends doing in the yard last night?"

In truth, Tony and his friends went there every night, whether on patrol or not.

The drugs are out of the yard, and they aren't coming back!

"They swung first. That's all I've got to say."

Ian got up and bought a second bottle of Deer Park. He handed it to Tony who distractedly accepted it. Ian sat.

"I know they did. That's what they do. They're jumpy little Godless freaks that think they answer to no one. You did the right thing. I admire

151

you. If your pastor finds out about last night, it won't be from me. I promise."

"I don't even know why I came here. All I needed was a Band-aid."

"I know why. You wanted to find out for yourself what happened to my brother. See? Now, that's being a good person."

Tony sniffled.

"I just hope God forgives me. That's all."

"Forgives you? For what? Look at me."

Tony did. Ian Reilly couldn't have given two shits about the snazzy underprivileged youth. He needed information, that was all. Even as he offered reassurance, he considered ratting the kid out to his pastor just for being a whiney little bitch.

"Son, those boys were going to kill my brother, and they would have succeeded if you hadn't shown up, and I'll swear to that on a stack of bibles."

For reasons Ian couldn't begin to understand, Tony folded his arms on the table, put his head down, and wept uncontrollably. Ian allowed himself a triumphant grin before putting his arm across Tony's shoulder.

He leaned in and whispered. "Tell me son ... who threw the brake drum?"

10. The Shed

Philip had abandoned working on the bike and was sitting in the corner of the shed. The past hour was a harsh reminder that he'd forgotten more about motorcycle repair than he'd ever learned. He was staring at the gas tank, which was propped up against his standing tool box. He decided it looked like a face and would make a good sounding board.

"When it comes down to it, I don't really need to fix it; I just need to make it look like I tried, right?"

He was kidding himself, and he knew it. His mind was on it now. His obsessive personality wasn't going to let it go, even if it was both a mistake and an inconvenience. One way or another, that bike would run.

"Take the good with the bad when you've got a brain like mine, I guess."

He stood with a grunt and walked over to the work bench where he'd left his cell phone. Someone had tried to call him.

"Oh bollocks!"

He displayed the call and touched "Reply".

"Hey baby…no, I didn't forget. I just lost track of time. Tell him I'm leaving right now. Yeah, I'm an idiot. I know. I love you, too. Bye."

He hung up and turned back to the gas tank.

"One of these days, my friend, I have to learn how to prioritize."

Again, he was kidding himself.

11. The Station

Gomez met Lynch outside the squad room. It was Tuesday, which meant there was a cart of free coffee and donuts from Anna Maria's in the hallway. There was a single apple fritter set aside with a note that Lynch read with mixed emotions.

FOR SGT. REILLY WHEN HE GETS BACK. DON'T F&@!ING TOUCH IT.

Gomez stood with a full, un-lidded insulated paper coffee cup and no apparent sense of urgency.

"What the hell, Ernie? I thought we were checking out that hit from ballistics. You ready to go?"

Gomez turned towards the squad room and pointed at Lynch's desk.

"I don't know, acho. You tell me."

Not one, but two priests were waiting to see Lynch. One was Father Leo. The other…the one that looked like he was about to throw up…Lynch hadn't yet met.

Leo had been eyeing the hallway in anticipation of Lynch's arrival and smiled when the detective came into view. Both priests stood courteously as Lynch approached with an outstretched hand and a half-bewildered expression.

"Good to see you again, Leo. Free coffee and donuts from Mama M's, did you see?"

"Yes. Thank you. Neither of us is all that hu..."

"Jeremy Sokol's death is my fault."

153

The words shot from Aiden's mouth like a champagne cork. Leo grabbed the young priest's shoulder harder than intended and spoke with nervous laughter.

"No, it isn't, Father. We talked about this. Jim, is there somewhere the three of us can go?"

Lynch recalibrated. The day started with learning how to loin a cow, and it was just getting weirder.

"Yeah, sure. The interview rooms are down the hall. I'll have to get Sergeant Warner."

Leo released his grip, leaving Father O'Rourke wincing and rubbing his own shoulder.

"Is that necessary, Jim?"

"Yes, it is. It's her case."

"It's just that...Father O'Rourke...I just think it's best if we make him as comfortable as possible, and I don't think talking to a stranger would..."

"What do you mean? He doesn't know me."

"No, but I do, and I kind of vouched for you."

"Well, that's very nice of you, but this is a police station, not the Elks Club. There are protocols."

Lynch started around the side of his desk bound for the donut cart. Earlier, Warner said she needed to put some things in her car, but she was most likely pouring herself a dark roast by now. Leo squeezed around Aiden and stood in Lynch's way. The detective spoke calmly.

"Leo, I'm sorry. Like I said, it's her case."

He shuffled to his left. Leo shuffled right with him.

"Look, Jim, what if he made an unofficial statement to you first? Let him wade in and get the words out. Then he can talk officially to whomever you want."

"What are you worried about?"

Leo practically mouthed his response.

"Good lord, Jim. Look at him. The guy is thirty seconds away from confessing to the beating himself. How does that help your investigation?"

"I don't know. Did he do it?"

Leo didn't bat an eyelash.

"No, he did not."

154

In the anxious pause that followed, Lynch heard a woman having harsh words with the desk sergeant. The voice was familiar, but he couldn't place it entirely.

"Fine."

He motioned the two men toward the back hallway and got in Leo's ear as he walked past.

"This will not be friendly if it comes out that anyone at St. Al's suppressed evidence."

"I'm not sure what that entails."

"Then I guess we'll find out together."

Lynch opened the door to the interview room and quickly made sure that Reilly had gotten all of his crap off of the table before letting Leo and Aiden enter. The faint odor of mint tea remained.

He was distracted. He was in a hurry. And, unfortunately, this was the one time in ten he failed to notice that the latch didn't click when he closed the door. Had he not gone straight from his car to the donut cart to his desk, he might have removed his trench coat. But he did, so he didn't.

They took their places at the table.

Leo was apprehensive. Aiden was nauseous. Lynch was downright confused.

Father O'Rourke spoke.

"I grew up here, Sergeant. Did I tell you that?"

Lynch glanced over at Father Leo, who non-verbally pled for some leeway. Of course, Aiden hadn't told Lynch anything of the sort. The young priest was on the verge of losing it. It was obvious that the guilt had taken him, and Lynch had to figure out a way to let the air out slowly if he was to make any sense of the man's story.

"You didn't tell me that, but that's okay, Father. Start from the beginning."

Leo spoke up.

"No. *I'll* start from the beginning."

Without pulling any punches, Leo told Lynch about the meeting that took place in St. Al's chapel the night of the murder. He ran through everything that was talked about, including the security disc footage.

Lynch added it to the list of things to discuss with the good father…loudly…once he got him alone. Now was not the time. He turned to Aiden.

"So how does this make you responsible for the beating? It sounds like Father Leo here…

Fucked up

…made the mistake."

Aiden processed for a moment and answered.

"Well, like I said. I grew up here."

The statement had even less relevance than before. Lynch took a not-so-subtle look at his watch and braced his feet on the floor to stand and leave. Leo reached out to stop him, but Aiden continued before either man left his seat.

"The Reillys grew up here, too. Their family moved here at the turn of the last century. They've got a lot of roots in this town…a lot of clout. Especially Kevin, you know, being a cop and all. Not that that's the reason I told him. The Reillys are family friends. They're all our parishioners."

Now Lynch was listening.

"Told him what?"

"Everything that Father Leo told us at the meeting…"

The young priest's shoulders broadened, and his spine straightened as the torturous guilt left his body.

"…plus, I told him where he could find the Unjudged."

He spared wide-eyed Sergeant Lynch the trouble of asking the obvious question by telling the story of sister Edwina and the Clean Streets Project.

Sister Edwina, as Aiden put it, *stood out*. She had an infectious smile, a flawless complexion, and a pair of big blue eyes that sparkled nonstop, especially when she was doing the Lord's work. She loved the Clean Streets Project. It never ceased to amaze her how the waters would part when a parade of nuns marched down a street. It didn't matter how sordid the neighborhood. When she and the other habit-clad women came into view, people often stared, sometimes giggled, but always got the hell out of the way. Picking up trash and painting over graffiti along the way made the experience all the more satisfying.

Aiden's anecdote started with Edwina entering the church after an afternoon of planting flowers. That day's task took the sisters one block away from the Iron Wall Tavern.

"She was flustered, and she doesn't fluster easily. She'd been accosted, you see, by a boy from the Unjudged named Gub or Dubby or something."

"Bubbs perhaps?"

"Sure...sounds right. He really got under her skin. He started off acting about as you'd expect...juvenile comments, lewd gestures, and so forth. *That* garbage she could deal with, but then he invited her to a party that night, and it got real."

"He told her where the party was?"

"At the Meadowbrook Farm. He was wasting his breath; she didn't even know where the Meadowbrook Farm was. She still doesn't..."

The young priest adjusted his collar.

"...but I do."

There were a few moments of silence broken by Father Leo.

"Tell him what you did."

"About the stupidest thing I could have done. I went to the party. And I went alone. And I didn't tell anyone."

Lynch could have responded a dozen different ways, most of them inappropriate.

"Exactly what the hell did you do that for?"

Leo mercifully answered for the young priest.

"Father O'Rourke is ambitious and gets restless. He often feels as though he's not answering his calling because our parish, to put it simply, doesn't have many problems to fix. He has trouble understanding that the mere fact that St. Al's is free of drama demonstrates that we're doing the job. He saw an opportunity to save some souls, and he took it."

"Did it work?"

Aiden wiped his brow and snickered.

"No."

"He almost got his ass kicked."

"The big guy...Bubbs, I guess...and the hot head with the spiky yellow hair gave me a couple of shoves, but the leader broke it up."

Lynch dug Samuel's sketch out of his shirt pocket and slid it across the table.

"Was it this guy? Did this guy break it up?"

Aiden took a look.

"Yes. That's him. Why do you have this?"

Lynch didn't want to get off-topic.

"Another case, …"

He tried to ask another question, but Leo interrupted.

"Tell him why you think Kevin took part in the beating."

Aiden repeated what he told Leo earlier, including his conversation with Reilly as close to verbatim as he could remember.

"What happened afterward?"

"He left."

"That's it?"

"He made a call."

Lynch did a little victorious fist pump under the table. After hitting brick walls for three days, he was amped to feel as though he was making progress on a case, even if it wasn't his.

"Any idea to whom?"

"His partner, I assumed."

"Not an option."

Aiden cluelessly fished about the walls as though the answer would be written somewhere. The break in the action allowed the enormity of the situation to creep back into his psyche. He clasped his hands, and the panic returned to his face.

"Then I don't know. If he did this thing…what am I saying? Of course, he did this thing. He did this thing, and I helped! Dear God, I helped!"

Leo turned his chair to face Aiden's, reached over, and spun the young priest to face him, chair and all.

"Knock it off, Aiden! God does not condemn what you've done!"

Lynch spoke.

"Neither does the law."

"You can help! Do you have a guess who Sergeant Reilly may have called when he left St. Al's?"

Aiden sniffled. The young priest was bouncing up and down like a basketball. Things had gotten loud. No one in the room wanted that. Lynch offered to get him some water, but he meekly refused it. After a few deep breaths, he was ready to continue. He turned back to the table as he answered Leo's question.

"Someone who owes him a favor, I guess. That could be anybody. I don't travel in those circles."

He picked up his head to match eyes with Lynch.

"There's more, Sergeant…"

Leo curiously raised one eyebrow and folded his arms. Apparently, whatever Aiden was about to say was news to *him* as well.

The young priest pointed at the unfolded sketch on the table.

"He came to see me the next day."

By Father Leo's expression, one would have thought that Aiden had just confessed to being a woman. Lynch slid to the edge of his seat.

"Father, I don't know how to ask this politely: Didn't you see the sketch on the news?"

Aiden hadn't read a newspaper or watched a lick of television since Fellini sent him on his quest, the details of which he was too drained to reveal.

"No, I've been … busy. I was at the water cooler, and he just walked up next to me as if he wanted to compare fantasy football scores."

"Well, dang, what did he say?"

"I'm paraphrasing here…he said that he'd hit a crossroads in his life where he had to choose between a group of people he'd grown to be very fond of, and what he felt was right. Then he whispered something to himself about a misguided a-hole and things not being the way they were supposed to be. I tried to give him some advice, but he said there was no need. Then he thanked me and left."

"When did this happen?"

"Last March. That's when the Clean Street Project did the flower beds."

And when Samuel disappeared.

The revelation caused a dull ache behind Lynch's eyes. Samuel's last act before leaving town was confiding in a priest. Why, then, would he come back months later and murder a bishop?

He was getting handed tiny pieces to two puzzles in no particular order.

So…Jeremy Sokol couldn't have identified Reilly as one of his assailants.

So…Reilly used Father O'Rourke to get to the UJ.

So…Samuel left the UJ and skipped town because it was *the right thing to do* (whatever that meant).

And?

Aiden allowed his body a moment to send the blood back to his extremities. Leo gave him a comforting pat on the back. The young priest had been absolved of his naivety and ignorance in lieu of sin. Lynch leaned back and rubbed his forehead in an attempt to corral his thoughts.

Was his biggest fear in all this coming to fruition? Was the big white Theban "S" that had been staring at him from the top of his suspect list starting to fade? Even worse, could he now extrapolate that Samuel simply abandoned his trench coat, along with everything else in his life? Was the coat dumpster food? If it was, anyone could have picked it up.

That fucking trench coat.

He just thanked God that Chester County came through on Ryan's bullet.

He turned his attention back to Aiden, who didn't have much more to add. It was just as well. The young priest was soon going to have to retell it all to Sergeant Warner. Lynch would follow up with her as well. The honor of tracking down the recipient of Reilly's phone call would be hers. While the two cases were starting to bleed together around the edges, Lynch was too far up to his balls in his own lack of evidence to clog his brain further.

The three men exchanged courtesies, and Lynch excused himself. He made one more offer to fetch coffee or water before leaving, which was kindly declined. He reached for the door.

Uh-oh!

A sliver of fluorescent light from the hallway shone on the floor of the interview room. The door hadn't latched. In a single panicked motion, Lynch whipped it open and popped his head into the hall. It was empty. The old break room was directly across from where he stood. There was someone in it who sounded like the Chief, but the door was closed so he couldn't tell for sure. Whoever it was, they couldn't have heard anything that went on between Lynch and the two priests. The latch faux pas must have gone without notice.

Lucky.

Gomez was still at the pastry cart. Lynch could only imagine how many French crullers he'd fired down since he left him there.

"You ready, Jaime?"

"Put a lid on your coffee, would you? I'll tell you about my boned-up morning on the way to Ellisport."

12. The Old Break Room

Thirty seconds...Gordy was left alone in the old break room with the door open for thirty seconds. The idiot cop in the room across the hall failed to close his door completely. When the sketch artist he'd played for a fool returned, he brought the Chief of Police with him. They barely had the door closed before the bucket of intimidating B.S. began. Ten ridiculous minutes later, Gordy turned on the waterworks. Walter Matthau and Dick Van Dyke would have been proud.

Between spasms and snorts, he squeaked out an apology and swore that the man outside F & J's threatened to hurt his mother if he went to the cops.

The pinheads fell for it.

What did Gordy care? He'd just give another description, this time of the bass player for Forever Damned. No one ever noticed the bass player in a band. He probably should have done that the first time around anyway. Maybe they'd believe him; maybe they wouldn't. Maybe they could eat shit.

As he tried to fake-stop his fake-crying, he did his best to catch a couple more words from across the hall, but it was no good with the door closed.

Gordy hadn't been able to see what was going on in there, but he'd heard everything...for thirty seconds. It was enough.

13. Southbound on Route 202

Gomez drove.

Lynch had copies of the ballistics and related incident report and was smiling wider and wider as he flipped through the pages. The bullet had been dug out of a wooden barrier fence that bordered the property of...

"A church. Do we find that interesting? Do we call that a connection?"

"I dunno. It's something'"

161

"Yeah, it's something."

The Fellowship Church of Ellisport was located right along the Schuylkill River about an hour from Potterford. It was known locally as the "Church of Rock," due to the Battle of the Bands benefit concert they held every summer.

The last one was held, July seventeenth, the date of the report.

"It says a junkie named Eddie Williams pulled a gun on some musicians behind the church. According to *them*, he squeezed the trigger by accident, scared the piss out of himself, and ran. Nobody was hurt. They chased after him, but he ditched the gun before they caught up. When they did catch up, they *kept him*…whatever the hell that means…until the uniforms arrived."

Lynch's smile faded when he read that the gun was never found, and Williams was discovered dead some weeks later from an overdose.

Well, that sucks.

Ellisport was a great hang. The restaurants were fantastic, the streets were clean, the people were friendly, and all the retail businesses were family-owned. There was also very little crime, which made Lynch optimistic that people would remember the incident behind the church.

"It should be at the end of this street."

Both detectives felt as if they'd entered some alternate universe where everything went smoothly. They'd called the Ellisport P.D. en route. Since Potterford ballistics had requested PDFs of the paperwork, the call was expected and Lynch was (shockingly) put on the phone with the arresting officer. His name was Blakely and was possibly the most agreeable flatfoot that Lynch had ever met. Blakely enthusiastically agreed to meet Lynch and Gomez at the church, and said he'd also try to contact one of the witnesses.

"There's only one explanation, partner."

"What's that, Jaime?"

"Robots…Ellisport is populated by robots."

The well-kept brownstone church was almost as old as the town itself. Like all the other buildings on its street, it sat atop a fifteen-foot riverbank and was separated from the water by a sturdy elevated wooden walkway edged by a thick barrier fence.

The minister was Danielle "Dani" Adams, a petite woman in her early fifties with red graying hair and permanent dimples. She, along with Officer Blakely and a man who obviously had fond nostalgia for the eighties, were waiting next to Lynch's reserved parking space when the detectives arrived.

"I'm tellin' ya, man...robots."

Blakely filled in a few gaps as the five of them walked back to the wall. The eighties throwback guy introduced himself, with a complex handshake, as Chaz. He was the drummer for the band that encountered the meth-head.

"We're called *Generation Us*. We do 70s and 80s covers, but it's like we choose songs where the lyrics can be like reinterpreted to mean faith and stuff."

He was forty if a day.

The wooden walkway behind the church connected all the neighboring structures. It functioned as a mini-boardwalk, although it appeared to have restricted access. The cedar pole fence designed to keep people out of the river came up to Lynch's chest. Blakely (probably for the first time ever) pulled out his expandable riot stick and used it to point out the bullet hole. Lynch gave it a quick look and turned to the drummer.

"Okay, Chaz. Give it to me"

Chaz recreated the event with stunning accuracy.

"So, like the van was pulled up to the door, and we were rolling the amps out over here. Then some guy in a tank top and a poser flak jacket appears out of nowhere waving a gun around."

Gomez almost took a pinky in the eye as Chaz demonstrated.

"Easy, hombre!"

"Bro! We had no idea what to do. I think he wanted the gear. He was, like, looking around at all of it like he was trying to figure out how to get it home. Anyway, the door to the church opened, and the gun went off. He scared the be-jeepers out of himself and ran so ..."

He started to jog along the fence.

"... we chased after him. Dangerous I know...*pant pant*...but we were...*wheeze*...pumped I guess."

When he got to the far side of the neighboring property, he trotted to a stop and pointed at the fence. He was doubled over with his free hand on

163

one knee as he struggled to both catch his breath and speak loudly enough to be heard from a distance.

"He chucked the gun...*wheeze*...into the river! We caught him...*gulp*...and pinned him..."

He stumbled over to the center of the walkway and collapsed in a seated position.

"... here. It took all four of us! Dude was jacked!"

Lynch hollered through cupped hands, while the others applauded the performance.

"How long after you caught him did you call the police?"

Chaz struggled to his feet and shuffled back towards the church.

"No call needed, bro. Geoff...I mean Officer Blakely was pulling security duty at the Battle of the Bands, same as all the other Ellisport cops."

Lynch and Gomez took a look over the fence. The river was twenty feet below them. Anything that went over the fence would have landed in the water. Gomez felt a presence next to him. He turned his head to find Officer Blakely also looking into the river as if that's what every cop on the walkway was supposed to be doing.

Gomez spoke.

"Did you scour the bank?"

"Yes, sir."

"Did the river get dredged?"

"There was no need. The case never went to court. The kid OD'd before the date. Besides, the bank is sheer, and the river moves pretty fast in the summer, especially last summer with all the rain. What goes in doesn't come out."

But it *did* come out. It came out, found its way into the hands of a killer, and expelled a bullet into the head of a bishop. Lynch's brain revved up. A myriad of schemes resurrecting the murder weapon from the depths of the Schuylkill went past his eyes. All were ridiculous.

Another item for the complication list.

He was brought out of his trance by Chaz hooting "whew!" as he backed against the fence with a thump.

164

Gomez wanted to take him back to Potterford as the police station mascot.

"So, Chaz mi amigo. Did you win?"

The drummer looked up, finally able to speak normally.

"Win what?"

"The Battle of the Bands, hombre. How'd you do?"

"We came in third. *We're All Lazarus* brought their A-game."

"Sorry to hear that, bro. Are they local?"

The drummer wiped some sweat off of his upper lip with the cuff of his Members Only jacket.

"Maplewood Evangelical…it's in Potterford."

14. The Burger King Parking Lot

Bubbs was the perfect grunt. He had no delusion or pretense regarding his limited intellect. He knew he was at his best when working under orders. He knew that the world was a better place when he wasn't thinking for himself. On occasion, however, he *would* act under orders that he considered implied, and that never yielded positive results.

This was one of those times. No one told him to track down, follow, and mess with Reilly's bitch partner. No one had to.

Bubbs knew Sergeant Warner. He'd seen her and Reilly at the Iron Wall. The place was a hotbed for dealers, and Bubbs was the bouncer for the club's rear entrance. He had neither the inclination nor the mental capacity to remember everyone that went into the club, but he did take notice when someone went out in cuffs. He'd witnessed Warner in action. She was fast and had an impressive amount of upper-body strength, but not enough to give the big-boned moron cause for concern.

Bubbs wasn't much for concern in general. His needs were Cro-Magnon-level simple: eating, sleeping, screwing, partying, being bigger that everyone else, and riding his bike.

Bubbs had a Harley Davidson Softail. Bubbs liked his Harley Davidson Softail…a lot.

So, upon his hog, the grunt sat and waited with no specific idea what he was going to do. He was in the Burger King parking lot across the street from the Potterford Police Station. He was good at sitting and waiting…or anything that resembled sitting and waiting.

Half way through his second Double-Whopper, he spotted Warner exiting the lot in a black Ford Fusion with municipal plates. She was alone.

With an enviable belch, he fired up his bike and eased out on to Main Street. As he struggled to stay unseen, a plan-slash-fantasy started to form beneath his thick skull. He'd definitely knock her out and cut her. He wouldn't sever anything major. He just wanted to leave a visible scar. The bridge of the nose would be good, or her ear. If he had time, maybe he'd strip her, or just yank down her grannies and write "PIG" on her ass. Then he could take a picture for Arthur and the rest of the crew. That would be cool.

He nearly missed her taking a right onto Prince Boulevard. The only thing of interest on South Prince was a ramp to the highway. His afternoon was about to get complicated.

They were both soon racing east on Route 422. When they passed the second exit, Bubbs thought about bailing. Three more, and she'd hit either Route 76 bound for Philly, Route 202 bound for Delaware, or the Pennsylvania Turnpike bound for just about anywhere. When her blinker went on at the sign for Morrisville, he breathed a sigh of relief inside his helmet and almost blinded himself.

The traffic thinned out at the exit, so he backed off several hundred feet. Less than a mile after taking the ramp, she turned left. She was just going home for lunch.

Gotcha!

Her house was set back in the woods far enough so that it couldn't be seen from the road. Bubbs' brain seized as he passed the driveway. He was going to have to find a place to park and think.

He didn't know the area. The green sign at the ramp said MEMORIAL PARK DRIVE. That could only have meant a couple of things.

Some brown signs appeared. There was a one-lane bridge coming up that crossed over Pickering Creek, then some historical thingies and a picnic area.

Bubbs managed to suss out that he was in a park…a *memorial* one in fact.

The Softail rumbled over the bridge and into the picnic area's lot. The grunt, flustered but not beaten, shut off his bike, put down the kickstand, and leaned on the handlebars as something akin to a linear thought started to percolate.

He kept his eyes open for other vehicles. A few passed. None took notice of him, save one black pickup truck. It slowed down, but it didn't stop. Bubbs figured he'd scared the driver off.

"That's it pencil-neck. Keep driving."

There were maybe fifty tree-covered yards between the lot and Warner's house. It wouldn't take him long to sneak through and catch her as she left the house. Easy in; easy out.

He thought about fingerprints. That was an easy fix. He'd leave on his riding gloves. He thought about being recognized. Even easier, he'd leave on his helmet. What else was there?

Nothing. Time to teach a bitch cop a lesson.

He did one last check to see if anyone was around and made his way into the woods. The helmet made negotiation difficult as he'd been denied the ability to look down comfortably. Every third step he went into a hole or catapulted a stick into his crotch. Crouching made things easier, but he still looked like a drunkard trying to find a contact lens. It never occurred to him to take the thing off. Such was what happened when Bubbs thought for himself.

Eventually, the trees thinned, and the ground hardened. He'd found the edge of the driveway. Now he could sit and wait. He was good at sitting and waiting. He could see Warner walking around inside the house.

Heh heh.

His little field trip had turned out well. He didn't mind giving himself a pat on the back and indulging in a devious chuckle...which came out his nose and stimulated a cluster of nerve endings.

Not in the helmet. Not in the helmet.

"Achoo!!"

Ughh!

Once the fog cleared, he looked through his own saliva spatter to see no change inside the house. He hadn't been heard.

For the amount of grief the helmet was giving him, Bubbs had yet to realize the tragic irony in his choice to leave it on.

He'd had the thing *customized*. The airbrushed head of a honey badger (meanest animal alive according to Google) covered it front to back. By design, the helmet was one of a kind, just like a finger print or hair follicle, and the dumb-ass had left it on so he couldn't be identified.

Oblivious to this colossal blunder, he still couldn't wait to take it off. The thing was hot, smelled like onions, messed up his hair, narrowed his vision, and, as he realized when the orange aluminum bat crashed into his spine, muffled his hearing.

A sharp rock dug into his abdomen when his body flattened. He felt his honey badger helmet get yanked over his ears and a second blow to the back of his head. It was a blackjack. He knew what a blackjack felt like. It was definitely a blackjack. He would have no other sensation for the better part of an hour.

The Reillys were hunters. They knew how to sneak up on their prey. When you weigh north of 325, dress like an Aryan Race reject, and set up a stakeout across the street from your latest victim's place of work, you make yourself easy to find.

They'd followed him all the way from Potterford.

Fat idiot.

15. The Maplewood District

Potterford's Maplewood District started at the Creekside Golf Course and worked its way, block by pristine block, to the edge of East Main. The town's aristocracy called it home and had done so since the Second Industrial Revolution. Its spotless streets were lined with Victorian and Georgian manor homes separated by perfectly coiffed shrubbery and cobblestone sidewalks. The beauty of the architecture and landscaping was topped only by the palpable aura of Doctorate Degrees and old money.

In 1998, a God-fearing landowner's dying wish cleared the path for the only modern structure in the District, Maplewood Evangelical Church.

Lynch and Gomez left Ellisport armed only with two facts: Their murder weapon was otherwise used at the Fellowship Battle of the Bands. And, one...*one* of the participating acts *happened* to belong to a church in the town where the murder took place.

"Ernie, did you know the phrase 'grasping at straws' refers to a drowning man trying to hold onto anything to stay afloat?"

"Sounds right. How do you want to play this?"

"There were six other bands at the show..."

"Right."

"...and an audience of about 1200..."

"Right."

"...and who knows how many of them were members at Maplewood."

"Right."

"So, I say let's just do a general stir of the pot and see what bubbles up."

"Right with you, partner."

"Don't put your fist up."

"I wasn't gonna!"

"You want to take lead? These are musicians. That's your lane, not mine."

"I would love to."

Lynch had called Maplewood Evangelical from Ellisport and spoke to Mick, the church's sound tech. The band had regular rehearsals on Tuesdays and Thursdays, starting around 4:30. Mick instructed them to use the side entrance, cut through Community Hall...

"...and then follow the music, man."

He failed to mention the clothing drive.

The large, general-purpose room, known as Community Hall, teemed with protestant housewives who were taking time from their busy schedules of society teas and yoga classes to volunteer for charity. The donated clothes were in several piles about the perimeter. On the wall above each pile was a tacked-up piece of printer paper with a two-letter code. One said "SM." One could only assume that meant "small." There was another marked "XL." That made sense too. So did "ME." Others, however were more random. One was "SA;" another was "F." Perhaps those piles were being graded: "satisfactory" and "fail?" The "fail" pile was pretty big.

Neither detective had much time to think about it as the muffled sounds of Christian Contemporary kicked off somewhere beyond the far wall.

"Follow the music. That's what Mick said."

So, follow they did, through the vestibule, under an ostentatious blue and gold sign that read "WELCOME ALL", and into the worship hall. The space rivaled most venues on the Vegas Strip. Its amphitheater footprint and angled pews were covered in purple velvet and custom-embroidered cushions. The rest of the room was finished wood, acoustic panels, and brilliantly shaped stained glass.

There was no pulpit. The minister walked the room during his sermons, wearing a wireless headset so both hands were kept free to manipulate his Good News Bible. This left the bulk of the sanctuary empty for the church's award-winning praise team, also known as We're All Lazarus.

It was a five-piece group: guitar, bass, drums, keyboard, and singer, or more accurately: a teacher, a general contractor, an electrician, a network administrator, and a hospice caregiver. They were all trained musicians, each of whom had taken a shot at the music business in some way. Different sets of circumstances individually took them off stage, but their love of the Lord collectively put them back on.

Lynch and Gomez entered the room during the bridge of a song called "No Cross, No Crown." It was right in the meat of the singer's range, and she belted it out to the angels' applause.

169

Mick was behind the sound board directly to the detectives' right. He looked up from his sliders and dials when he saw the light from the opened door.

Lynch recognized him instantly as the bastard with the tambourine.

This is the bunch that set up at the protest.

He beckoned the detectives closer and hollered to Gomez over the song. "The tune is almost done. Is it okay if they finish!?"

"By all means! Hey man, she's good!"

Mick smiled ear to ear.

"That's why I married her!"

The song ended on a stinger that held in the air until the acoustics allowed it to die. Mick spoke into a gooseneck mounted microphone.

"Sweetheart, the police are here."

Gomez and Lynch made their presence known with a silly little wave, as the musicians de-instrumented themselves. Everyone gravitated to the front pews, except Mick who stayed behind the board to mark levels.

It was Bill the guitar player who spoke first.

"If this is about Sunday at City Hall…"

Gomez replied.

"No. Not at all. Man! You were shredding up there! Nice! What's that you were playing on, a PRS?"

"Wow, yes, it is. I hope it sounds good. It cost enough."

"That's Carlos Santana's axe. Isn't it?"

"Wow again…yes."

It was Gomez's way. He fancied himself the Puerto Rican Columbo. If he had a zinger in his pocket, he'd save it for his way out the door.

"We're following up on the shooting at the Ellisport Battle of the Bands. Did you see any of it?"

They all stared back with vacant expressions. They were clearly puzzled by the question. PJ, the bass player, cleared his throat.

"We were on stage when it happened. We didn't even know anything went down until after the set."

They all started to speak at the same time, but Gomez prevailed.

"Hold on everyone. The upshot is you guys saw nothing."

They all nodded and shrugged. Gomez took a thoughtful pause as he stared down each musician individually.

"Fair enough, amigos. Sorry to interrupt…"

Both detectives turned to leave. Lynch counted down to himself in anticipation of his partner's next move.

With a thoughtful hand in the air, Gomez did an about face and delivered his exit statement.

"...because the kid's gun was used to kill Bishop Ryan, and we're shaky on how it made its way from the bottom of the Schuylkill River to the Potterford Marriott."

All five musicians responded with looks of confusion and alarm, although in the silence, Lynch was sure he heard one of them whisper "good" under his or her breath. Patty, the singer, spoke.

"I'm not sure what to tell you."

Gomez scrutinized the room one last time, stroked an invisible beard, tipped an invisible hat, and pivoted towards the back of the room. Lynch followed.

"Good one, Ernie."

"We'll talk."

"About what?"

"I don't think they're lying. If they are, it wasn't agreed upon. When I asked them about the shooting, they looked at me, not each other. There's also no ringleader."

Lynch reached for the door but was halted by the voice of Sound Man Mick.

"You'll want to talk to Brother Devlin."

Irritated that his exit had been ruined, Gomez replied.

"Who's Brother Devlin?"

"You don't know? He's the big guy, the minister here."

"Why do we want to talk to him?"

Mick's expression ebbed, as if he was disclosing something that wasn't his business.

"He knew Eddie Williams"

This was interesting. Eddie Williams was the boy who shot the Ellisport fence.

"Knew him, how?"

"They developed a relationship after the incident."

The detectives' nonverbal, yet telling, reactions caused Mick to backpedal quickly.

"No, no, no, goodness, no. Not like that. He took Eddie under his wing, tried to help him. Brother Devlin can give you the whole story. I don't know it."

"Fair enough. Do you know why he took such an interest?"

Mick went back to his notes. He was obviously trying to dive out of the conversation.

171

"I think he felt responsible."

"For the shooting?"

"Yes, and for Eddie's death."

"Did he sell the kid the meth? Did he give the kid the gun?"

"Of course not, but you know the kid pulled the trigger when the back door to Fellowship opened suddenly, right? Well …"

"Brother Devlin was the one who opened the door?"

Mick nodded.

"His office is upstairs. You can't miss it."

16. Near Pickering Creek

Bubbs owed his rescue to his cheap-ass phone. The slam of Carrie Warner's car door woke him up. He could only open one eye. He spit out a mouthful of blood and grunted one word.

"Pussies."

This was nothing…an average Friday when he was in high school. In his delirious state, it was difficult to tell where the pain was coming from. Having been on the giving side of several such ass-kickings, Bubbs figured they'd gone at his midsection the hardest. No problem. That part of his body was like a cast-iron pot, but standing up wouldn't be possible for a while. He wiggled his toes and squeezed his fingers to make sure he still had use of his limbs. That was when he discovered they'd put his cell phone in his right hand. He managed to move his head enough to look at the screen. A better phone would have been in sleep mode. His piece-of-shit pre-pay displayed his contact list with all the entries, of course, being members of the UJ. He aimed for Arthur with his thumb, but his eyes blurred. By the sound of the ring, he could tell that his new special friends had left the phone on "speaker." Whoever jumped him wanted him to be together enough to make the call.

Someone answered.

"Whatchaneed, Bubbs? I'm at the garage."

It was Rick.

Fuck!

He then noticed that the left hip pocket of his jeans was turned out. That was where he kept the keys to his Harley.

Now he was angry.

17. Devlin's Pad

Pastor Richard Devlin's persona did not match his appearance. To look at him, you'd think everything about him was contrived, from his untucked, black, band-collared shirt with the rolled-up sleeves to his Caesar haircut to his John Lennon glasses to his soul patch. His speech, however, was smooth and honest; his posture, modest.

He welcomed the two detectives to his little pow-wow room that he called an office and told the heart-breaking story of Eddie Williams.

"Do you have his mug shot with you?"

It was with the incident report. Gomez pulled it out and placed it respectfully in front of their host. The good pastor looked upon it with affected familiarity.

"That's not Eddie; that's the drugs…"

He reached for one of the pictures on his desk and spun it around for the detectives to see.

"*This* is Eddie."

Like just about everyone else he'd met since he walked into Maplewood Evangelical, Lynch recognized Eddie (and consequently, Devlin) from the protest. The yearbook photo under the good pastor's index finger was the same that was on his banner two days earlier. The banner that read "REMEMBER"

Devlin continued the story, scowling with distain every time he said the word "Catholic."

"Both his parents were killed in a meth lab explosion when he was five. Foster care did him no favors. Everyone was well meaning, but that counts for very little when a kid ends up with a (finger quotes) *good Catholic family* who believes the only way to set him straight is to make him Catholic too. Baptism, CCD, confirmation, he got the full treatment, including the required serial fondling by a crusty old priest.

"And Eddie was so brainwashed by his Catholic foster family that he didn't say anything until he was sixteen friggin' years old. You know what happened as a result? As usual, nothing. The family retreated into denial, and his church tried to convince Eddie he imagined the whole thing. Eventually, the boy snapped and ran. He found his only comfort in the streets and wound up a meth head like his parents. Do you know how I know all this, Sergeant Gomez?"

"Mick told us you got to know the boy after his arrest."

"Yes, and then it was *my* turn to fail him. I visited him in jail, stood up for him at his hearing, posted his bail, agreed to take him into my care until the trial…the whole boat. It all sounds very noble, but in *jail* he would have been protected from himself. In *jail*, he wouldn't have been able to

173

steal a hundred and fifty dollars, sneak off to his dealer, and put enough chemicals in his body to kill a buffalo."

Devlin slid the mug shot back to Gomez.

"Like I said, that's not Eddie. Please don't remember him that way."

Ernie took advantage of the emotional lull to broach the subject of the murder weapon.

"Did Eddie tell you what happened to the gun?"

"He wouldn't talk about it. His lawyer told him to keep any information about the gun to himself…some garbage about 'no gun; no crime. Anyway, you can see why I have a vested interest in anything involving the Philly Diocese. I'll take full responsibility for Sunday's protest. If it caused the Potterford P.D. any grief, all I can do is apologize and say I'd do it again in a heartbeat."

Lynch held the yearbook picture next to Eddie's mug shot. It was a horrible night and day. He spoke.

"Would it be alright if we kept this photo? We'll make sure you get it back."

Devlin smiled and nodded. Lynch took the photo out of its frame and tucked it into his shirt pocket. Ernie asked the good pastor to give his version of what happened behind Fellowship. His account of the shooting, though less flamboyant, matched Chaz's to the letter.

The return walk through Community Hall and across the Maplewood parking lot was a low-spirited one.

They had no murder weapon.

They had no trench coat.

Their number one (only) suspect was weakening by the hour.

The two detectives sat for ten minutes in defeated silence in Lynch's car before Gomez worked up the nerve to voice what they were both thinking.

"Is it time to cry, uncle?"

Lynch didn't answer. Instead, he leaned his head back with his eyes closed and punched the passenger window with the side of his hand.

He turned to his partner.

"What if you did it?"

Gomez started the car.

18. Father Leo's Office

They spoke in Italian.

The Archbishop sensed something wasn't quite right before he picked up the phone, so he answered with four words that would have been two in English.

"Cosa c'è di sbagliato? (What's wrong?)"

Father Leo suppressed a sigh and answered.

"I don't know that Father O'Rourke can continue with his assignment."

He explained everything that happened at the police station.

Then...relief.

"Would it help if I talked to him?"

Leo slumped in his chair. The world had been lifted from his shoulders.

"I would be most grateful, Your Grace."

"I can be there tomorrow by 9:00 am. Would that be too early?"

"Not at all. Thank you."

Leo had left Aiden to his prayers. Now he had to explain to him what was going on and that the Archbishop's visit was not a punishment. It would be a tough sell.

19. The Cloister

Arthur had put the word out for the entire UJ membership to get to the cloister ASAP. This was rare for a Tuesday; unheard of for six o'clock in the evening. Not all of them would be able to make it on time. Two were out of town; Traci had to work late.

The general rule was you arrived either in Zed Zed or on foot. Steven parked his car at a poorly advertised shop that sold Celtic paraphernalia. No one would look twice. Most of the other members did the same at various unmonitored businesses within walking distance of the cloister.

Steven ascended the stairs, figuring Artie's call to arms had to do with the upcoming painting party. What he saw when he entered the main gathering room made his jaw drop a foot. Sitting in the center of the room, as if on two thrones, were Arthur and the little puke Gordy, drunk as a couple of monkeys. Arthur hollered sloppily as he clapped eyes on Steven.

"Okay! That's just about everyone! Listen up, brothers and sisters! I need to introduce you to the UJ's latest member!"

Everyone commented in unison with some variation of *"the fuck he is!"*

"Pipe down!"

Arthur put his hand on Gordy's shoulder and continued.

"Our boy here has been doing some recon, which is more than I can say for the rest of you pubes! He spent the afternoon in the company of our friends at the Potterford P.D.! It seems that we have the nice folks at Saint Aloysius Church to thank for the death of our comrade! I'm too drunk to give you the details in a way that makes sense, but suffice it to say, they've got some payback coming! Tonight, we drink and chew over ideas! Tomorrow we act!"

175

Everyone in the room looked around as though Arthur had announced an attack on the Pentagon. Steven was about to voice an opinion that was sure to get him jumped when the roar of duel exhaust game from outside the building. Arthur jumped up. Gordy also stood but stumbled back to his seat realizing that it wasn't matter of *whether* he was going to throw up, but *where*.

They all scrambled to various windows. The gathering room was one floor above the street. No one had seen Rick's car before. Steven stated the obvious.

"It's not a cop."

His words were enough to prompt a swarm down the nearest stairwell. When they got to the tire-marked plot of grass outside the building's entrance, they saw Rick open the passenger door of his Mustang and lean in with both arms. He spoke loudly enough for everyone to hear.

"Gonna need a hand Artie!"

A bloodied Bubbs sat in the reclined passenger seat. He had the word POCKET written on his forehead in red magic marker. Arthur spoke.

"What the fuck is this?"

Rick explained how he'd gotten a call from Bubbs. All he heard was: "*Come get me ... Morrisville ... Park ... picnic tables.*"

Bubbs's crappy phone died after that.

"It took me an hour and a half to find the tool bag. He's lucky the cops didn't find him first!"

Arthur looked at Bubbs.

"What's the shit on his forehead?"

Rick produced a piece of paper.

"This was in his pocket. They wanted him to be found."

Arthur read the note through booze-soaked eyes.

No police from now on. Just you and us you prick. The gloves are off. Next time consider who you're fucking with.

Much love.

The Reillys

Arthur looked up, handed the note back to Rick, and spoke in a manner of an Olympic gold medal winner.

"This could very well be the best day of my life! Come on, Unjudged! Back upstairs before someone sees us! Eric, Frankie, help Bubbs! Rick, get this noisy piece of shit off my lawn."

Steven had worked his way next to Rick. He read the note and did his best to be heard over the revelry.

"What does this mean?"

Rick answered dismissively.

"I'll tell you what it means…it means we're a gang."

20. Taking a Moment

Philip sat cross-legged at the edge of a parking lot, smoking one of his dozen daily cigarettes. What happened earlier was unexpected but not necessarily bad. He just needed to figure a way to push things up a couple of days.

"I just wish I knew what was going on there this week."

He took a deep drag and watched the smoke dissipate into a breeze as he blew out. He used a Pepsi bottle for an ash tray. He had too much respect for the property to tap onto the grounds.

Ten variations played in his head from start to finish before he concluded that he was simply going to have to take his best guess and let the plan fly.

Tomorrow…I'll go tomorrow.

He dropped his butt into the bottle with a hiss, stood, and walked back to the building whistling a reggae version "Ave Maria."

21. The Condo

Lynch had to step away from the case for a bit. At the end of his shift, he called his awesome girlfriend. The stars had aligned, and they both had the evening off. Julie didn't become a restaurant critic by happenstance. She was an astonishing cook, and when she found out that her cop boyfriend was going to be home for dinner, she headed to the market and crafted a meal fit for foreplay.

They prepared it together. Lynch had learned his way around a kitchen over the previous two years. He was assigned to prep work while Julie masterfully worked the appliances. They set up Julie's iPhone and wireless JBL speakers, punched up the soundtrack to Purple Rain, and danced as the meal was created, taking make-out breaks when necessary. They ate by candlelight in their underwear.

Lynch talked about his day. The nearly naked woman across the table from him got turned on by cop talk, otherwise he would have just as soon pretended none of it ever happened. Chaz was the highlight of the story.

"We're watching this high-haired drummer who is hopelessly lost in the eighties run the length of the property, giving himself a coronary in the process."

"Any moonwalking?"

"If only. If I weren't on duty, I'd have recorded it. It was truly viral."

Neither of them had to make lewd gestures or eat seductively. Just them being them was enough.

He stood behind her as they washed the dishes together. The album looped back to the beginning, and they went to the bedroom as "Let's Go Crazy" played for the third time.

Are we gonna let the elevator bring us down? Oh no, let's go!

Afterwards, Lynch got up to fetch the backgammon board, but Julie pulled him back.

"Screw board games. I don't need a round two."

"Good. Me either."

She snagged her iPhone and switched off the music. They watched the ceiling fan for a while, holding hands, before Julie decided she wanted to hear more cop talk.

"So, you're sure Samuel didn't do it?"

"I'm not *sure* of anything, but it's unlikely at this point."

She turned on her side and stroked his chest.

"I lost track of the Unjudged in all this."

He took her hand and kissed it. He knew she was hoping that at least one of the UJ had something to do with Ryan's murder, since she was the one who made the connection to the painting.

"They all have alibis."

"Does anyone like them for Reilly's injury?"

"You'd have to ask Warner. I'm going to keep my nose out of it, unless she asks for help."

"What about the girlfriend?"

"What girlfriend? You mean Kelly?"

"The pedo-bait you met at the mall."

"You're funny."

"Did she reach out to you again?"

Lynch grabbed his cell phone from the bed table and brought up his texts.

"She sent me a text last night."

I HAD NOTHING 2 DO WITH IT.

178

Julie squinted at the screen and spoke.

"Nothing to do with what? Ryan or Reilly?"

"Ryan...well, now that you mention it, I'm not sure." He sat up and tapped out a reply.

DO YOU MEAN RYAN OR REILLY?

He reached to put the phone back, but it buzzed in his hand before it made it to the table.

SAME PLACE 2MORROW 10:30?

Julie sat up and read the text. Lynch could see her eyes twinkling with excitement in the screen's glow.

SURE

Kelly replied seconds later.

THX

Julie waited for her cop boyfriend to put the phone down before hopping up and straddling him. Needed or not, there was going to be a round two.

22. The Cloister

The gathering was winding down. Bodies covered the room. Traci finally arrived shortly after eight o'clock and patched up Bubbs as best as she could. Other than his pride, all of his wounds were superficial. She, once again, had found her way out of her outer vestments and into Arthur's cot...face down and passed out.

Arthur was slumped on one of the couches next to a lesser-active UJ member named Eric. They lit up and passed a bong back and forth simply for something to do.

"Eric, my man, when was the last time you saw Kelly?"

After an absurdly long toke, Eric exhaled and replied.

"I don't know. Couple o' weeks maybe."

The thing Arthur liked the most about him was the fact that his physical features were relatively nondescript. It made him perfect for situations that required being forgettable. He also had a knack for getting things...specific and unusual things.

179

"I think she's going astray. Find out, would you?"

Eric answered with bloodshot eyes and a huge craving for pistachio nuts.

"No problem."

THE PAINTING PARTY

Wednesday

1. The Shed

Philip looked at himself in the cracked, full-length mirror next to his uncle's work bench. The bare-chested man in a diaper staring back didn't exactly give off the musk of the hero he felt himself to be. He had to make a joke of it, or he'd never leave the shed. He puffed out a faux-Asian grunt, took the stance of a sumo wrestler, and stamped his feet on the weathered hardwood floor one at a time. He tried a second, beefier grunt, but all that came out was a snort and a laugh.

The day was going to be either a major triumph or a colossal waste of time. With music that reminded him of a happier time blaring from a dusty, paint-spattered boom box, he got dressed and checked his gear.

He'd dug up an old backpack that no one knew he owned and filled it with his weapon, ammo, the latest incarnation of his collapsible tree stand, three bottles of water, a handful of protein bars, a tan wool hat, and a camouflage bandana that was pre-tied to fit over his face.

He dressed in earth tones that wouldn't draw attention when he walked from his parking space to the church. He knew the resulting investigation would be intense, and the police would probably find fibers and DNA all over his perch. It wouldn't matter. He wasn't in the system. He hadn't received so much as a parking ticket since he was in high school. True, after today, he (or at least his remnants) *would* be in the system, but that wouldn't be an issue until they caught up with him. By then, it would all be a moot point.

He would get caught in the end. He knew this. It was not only anticipated, but necessary.

The half-fixed motorcycle sat before him as he pulled on his green windbreaker. Slinging the backpack over his shoulder, he felt two different kinds of pride.

The smell of wood and motor oil permeated his senses. He took a quick look out of one of the windows. Through the smoke-stained glass, he saw the sunrise.

"Okay, Lord. Let's rock."

2. Out for a Run

Kelly had her morning routine. The veterinarian she assisted normally didn't expect her in until 10:00, which gave her time to run three miles, shower, and eat her cream-cheese-slathered whole wheat bagel without having to wake up before the birds. Today, she would have to call in sick so she could meet with Lynch. Her boss would be cool with it. She never called in sick.

She also never burdened herself with keys or a cell phone when she ran. She could trust an unlocked apartment for an hour. It was that kind of neighborhood.

She glanced at her wall calendar on her way out the door. There was a UJ painting party that night. She, to put it lightly, didn't want to go. She enjoyed illegal drugs and acts of depravity just as much as the next person, but things had changed since Jeremy's beating. The "fallen comrade" noise that Arthur spewed forth was all wrong. The UJ paradigm was supposed to have been built off of enlightenment, not muscle. That prick, Reilly, should have been exposed for the fascist bully he was. Instead, he was put in a hospital…the ultimate cliché. She didn't join the UJ to be counted among the like-minded; she didn't join to kick anyone's ass. She joined for the freedom. She joined simply for what the group's moniker implied. Where was all that now? What does a group stand for if problems are solved with force? That's what the cops do. The ideals of the UJ had been swallowed up by the will of the few. The general membership had allowed themselves to become what they themselves despised.

All this occupied her mind as she ran. Manatawney Creek flowed across the street from her path, but she couldn't see it through the row homes and shrubbery. She did a mile and a half out, and then the same route in reverse. A few horny, but harmless old farts always made it a point to be out on their porches or granite slabs when she passed. She would wave just to be friendly when the mood hit her. If only they knew what she got up to at the cloister when the mood hit her.

The cloister. She didn't even know where it was. The turnover rate of burner phones left the UJ's communication system, at best, convoluted. An unreliable texting pyramid, along with word-of-mouth, did the trick for simple, cryptic messages such as "gathering tonight 7:00." More specific, important, and/or secret information simply wasn't sent. Learning, for example, the latest cloister location was the responsibly of the individual members.

Kelly hadn't done her due diligence, and she didn't intend to.

She wiped the sweat off of her face with her t-shirt sleeve as she slowed to a walk outside her building. She did a quick cool-down stretch on the sidewalk and took a swig from the bottle of water she'd left right outside the entrance to the stairwell. She poured the rest over her head before the last part of her workout, which was an easy jog up two flights of stairs to her apartment. She, as a matter of routine, pushed open the unlocked door.

She was half way into her living room before she saw the note that had been taped to the window directly across from her.

DON'T TURN AROUND

There wasn't time to react. A gloved hand clapped over her mouth, and she was pulled against the body behind her. The intruder's free hand appeared in front of her face holding her cell phone. The screen showed her last text to Detective Lynch. The intruder threw the phone at her couch and started digging in his pocket. The next thing he showed her was a piece of paper he'd stolen from her memo pad. It read "What did you tell him?"

He loosened his grip around her mouth just enough so she could answer, but kept her against him with his forearm and elbow. Her whole body moved forward and back with his deep and erratic breathing.

"Nothing."

It was an answer he was expecting. A second piece of memo paper reading "I don't believe you" was held in front of her nose. He crumpled it and tossed it across the room before forcefully pointing at the note taped to the window.

DON'T TURN AROUND.

He stepped back and ran his hands down her sides as if he was checking her for a wire. It made no sense. She just got back from running. Why and how the hell would she be wearing a wire? Her panicked thought process went to figuring out who this dickbag could be. He was too thin to be Bubbs…too strong to be Arthur…too tall to be Steven. She held back a scream as she felt him grab the hem of her shirt. He jerked it up over her breasts, exposing her sports bra and ankh belly ring.

She spoke in a forced whisper.

"Lynch wanted to know what happened to Reilly. I have no idea what happened to Reilly. I don't even know where the cloister is! Traci sent me two text messages. One said 'Irish Pig Roast tonight.' The second said 'It's over. Sorry you couldn't make it.' That's it! That's all I know!"

He slipped his thumbs under the elastic of her shorts. She hedged her bets on a name.

"Goddammit, Rick! I didn't say anything, you cock!"

The intruder's hands stopped. He stood motionless except for his breathing, which was becoming more controlled.

183

"I'm not begging you, Rick! Kill me or get the fuck out of here, but whatever *else* you're expecting to happen…"

She felt him back off. As she looked down at her own bare midriff, it occurred to her that her intruder never produced a weapon. She also realized that there were only a few people who knew her morning routine, none of whom were in the UJ, not any more. Then she heard a familiar voice.

"It's not Rick."

She spun around. When she saw who it was, every emotion she experienced during the previous five minutes went into her fist, causing it to ball up and thrust into his gut. He fell to the floor with a grunt. She stood over him, dripping with sweat and spring water.

"Bastard!"

What little air he was able to take in was coming out as a laugh.

"That's right, asshole. Laugh it up…and if you think you're getting laid this morning…"

The intruder closed his eyes to cough twice. When he opened them, Kelly was almost at her bedroom door, and her t-shirt was slung over a lamp shade.

"…you're absolutely right. Now, quit coughing like a little bitch and get naked."

3. Father Leo's Office

A good night's sleep had done Aiden well; not so for Leo. The time spent at the police station the day before, along with Aiden's guilt-induced breakdown, had drummed up memories of the Eric Bell trial. Leo knew he would have to retell his part of it sometime before the investigation was over. Lynch would explore all possibilities before giving into the notion that Bishop Ryan's murder was a random act. The detective had put the revenge killing scenario on the back burner for the time being, but it was only a matter of time before he and Gomez would return to it out of necessity. That would mean going back to all of the diocese trials, opening up transcripts, and re-interviewing every witness, character witnesses included.

One thought led to another, and he found himself looking around his office. He'd only been in it a few months, but he'd miss it. He liked to think it was similar to the old church offices in Vatican City, more so than the one he'd be moving into at least.

Despite the events of the previous five days, he was happy; happier than he felt he deserved. After all, what had he done to earn his position at St.

Al's? He sat in a witness box and answered a few questions before a grand jury. It wasn't even a real trial.

Maybe that's the point.

He couldn't even completely remember what he said. He could, however, remember what he left out.

Dammit.

How many times had he promised himself that he wouldn't let his thoughts wander back to that dreary place? He didn't lie on the stand. He was instructed to answer the prosecution's questions truthfully and directly without embellishment. To his own satisfaction, Leo did that.

The D.A. asked him a total of ten questions. Three were about his years in seminary. Of the three, only one really mattered.

"Based on your years at school with the defendant, do you think he could have done what he is being accused of?"

Leo answered with an unhesitant "no."

It wasn't a lie.

Rationally, after sharing four years of seminary with the accused priest, Leo's honest general impression was that the man wouldn't hurt a fly.

But the D.A. didn't ask the question correctly. If the question had been worded something like "Did anything specific happen while you attended school with the defendant to make you think for even a second that he would be capable of that which he is being accused?" Leo's answer would have been different. It may have changed the outcome…or not. He'd drive himself crazy if he thought about it too much.

Son of a bitch! Stop it, Leo. Stop it!

Too late.

He'd worked himself into the middle of the argument that he'd had with himself countless times since he was asked to testify. Once, a few weeks before the trial, he raised the subject during his weekly confession but found that his confessor, Bishop Haas, had little to offer in the way of objective advice. It was a fair assumption that it would be the same story all over the diocese, so he chose, with God's help, to deal with it on his own.

He prayed and prayed, to no avail, for some water in the face.

185

A test...it was a test...I was being tested...God was testing me.

The day of his testimony, Archbishop Fellini met Leo in the courthouse to offer some last-minute support. It was the last thing he needed. Regardless, the single sentence of advice offered by the Archbishop became forever embedded in his memory.

"Just do what you think is right, Father."

The phone on Leo's desk rang. The Archbishop's ears must have been burning.

"Hi, Leo. How goes it with Father O'Rourke?"

"Better, but I still think you..."

"I'm happy to do it. I'm just calling to let you know I'm running late."

"Anything wrong, Your Grace?"

"No, just had an early meeting run over. Pastor Karney asked me to pass on his regards. Oh, and they're making me bring a security detail. It's just two guys. Where should I tell them to stand?"

Leo answered quickly. The church's vulnerability had entered his thoughts many times since Saturday.

"The front door and the entrance to the courtyard."

"Excellent. See you soon."

Comforted, Leo went into his bathroom to wash the sweat off his hands and face. The old porcelain tap squeaked as water dribbled out painfully. The sound startled a squirrel in the tree outside the window. It was still stuck open an about six inches, due to the swollen pane.

"The water doesn't work. The window won't close. The bathroom door doesn't lock..."

He spun the little handle and the dribble stopped.

"...I'm still going to miss this place."

Leo shook his hands dry and looked out the window. He remembered seeing Pastor Karney pruning the rose bushes and tried again to recall why he found that so strange.

4. The Galleria

Kelly was late *again*. Two lattes sat on the café table just as they had Sunday afternoon. Lynch rubbed his eyes. His book of logic puzzles, like most others, increased in difficulty as it progressed, and he was closing in on the back cover. The first half of the puzzle he'd reached went quickly. The second half was pissing him off.

If Mrs. Elverson bought her poodle on Tuesday, and Mr. Gadd (whose first name wasn't Edward) didn't buy his schnauzer on Friday, then...

186

"Hello, detective."

His tablemate had snuck up on him again. Only this time, the voice was not one he expected...male. Lynch gave the corner of his eye to the seat across from him. A reactive surge of vital fluids caused him to sit up straight and all but become aroused.

"Hello, Samuel."

The tablemate gave a small but genuine smile and nodded toward the severely dog-eared puzzle book in Lynch's lap.

"Kelly tells me you're into logic puzzles."

The detective went cold.

"Where is she, (*you bastard*)?"

"At work, as far as I know. She was as surprised to see me as you are...happy though."

It wasn't enough for Lynch. He referred back to the book.

"Did she tell you why I do these things?"

"She did. Alzheimer's is a bitch. I've seen it up close."

Okay, so Kelly probably *wasn't* laid in a ditch somewhere. Lynch exhaled and allowed himself to catch up to the weight of the moment. He had no idea where to start.

The two men stared at each other. Both of them knew the next move belonged to Lynch. Samuel reached for Kelly's latte and took a healthy pull. Lynch folded his puzzle book and stuffed it in his trench coat pocket without breaking eye contact. Five days' worth of investigation data ricocheted through his head as he attempted to find the one perfect, succinct, powerful set of words that would kick things off.

Fuck it.

"Who are you?"

Samuel leaned back and widened his smile, as if he'd waited his whole life to be asked that very question.

"Detective Lynch...I'm the guy everybody hates. I am, to put it plainly, heir to a sizable business empire. I prefer not give you my last name, but I will if you ask me to. Suffice it to say, you'll recognize it."

"I can't say that I particularly care what you prefer."

Samuel gave his last name. Lynch recognized it. It made no difference.

Samuel slid the latte aside and folded his hands on the table, palms down. Lynch could tell that he was being very careful not to appear as though he was reaching for his pockets...smart lad.

"But, detective, the reason I'm here instead of Kelly is to save you some time. I realize that I am in no position to negotiate, but I would humbly ask for ten minutes of your time in return so that I might explain myself."

"I get the feeling you don't do *anything* humbly."

"I can help you. We can help each other. Kelly tells me you're very good at your job…"

He pulled his hands back to his chest, snarkily leaving a small folded piece of paper on the table.

"…so, I'm hoping that makes sense."

Lynch could clearly see what it was.

"Cute, you can put 'slight-of-hand' on your resume right below 'heir to a sizable business empire.' What does a receipt from Dave & Buster's have to do with anything?"

"It's proof that I wasn't in Potterford Saturday night."

"This? This is proof?"

"Not by itself of course. Damn, Sergeant, I'm sure Dave & Buster's is loaded with CCTV's, and there's at least one witness…"

"Alright, shut up. We'll see."

Lynch pocketed the receipt, thus closing the book on his prime suspect.

There it is. "Yay!" and "Shit!" at the same time.

"You've got your ten minutes. Explain how you can help me."

Samuel gleefully picked up where he left off.

"You see…my dad is in pretty good shape for his age and isn't in any hurry to retire, so, since I'm not taking over the empire any time soon, I generally spend my life traveling the world in search of things to keep me from getting bored."

"And you wound up in Potterford?"

Samuel grinned and nodded.

"By way of Downey's about three years ago. Do you know Downey's?"

"In Philly?"

"Yes, one of three Irish pubs in the city that actually knows how to pour a Guinness."

"Marvelous, what happened at Downey's?"

"Whoever had the table before me left a copy of "Philly Neighbor" on the seat. Do you know…?"

"Yes, I know "Philly Neighbor," and I know the article you're about to ask me to read. Is there any special reason you told Avery your name is Matthew?"

Samuel was clearly impressed.

"No, no reason. I'm rich. I get bored. I find biblical aliases amusing."

"Who doesn't? Back to Downey's."

"I usually can't stand rags like Philly Neighbor, but what else are you going to do while you're waiting for the bartender to complete a three-stage pour?"

"Holy crap, you fully intend to take the *entire* ten minutes, don't you?" Yes, he did.

"I tell you, I don't know if it was because I was twenty-two years old. I don't know if it was because my great-aunt had just died, and it was the first time in my life that I was forced to face my own mortality. I don't know if it was the residual effects of what I put in my body the night before. Somehow what Avery said in that article got to me.

"I mean, you've met him...the dude's a charlatan. I spent a year working for the guy, trying to tap into his genius. The man has talent, but insight? No way. He *is* right about one thing though. We do make our own truths. I don't care what he meant by the painting; I know what it meant *to me*. The mistake I made was assuming anyone else in my shoes would be affected the same way."

"You mean Arthur."

"Yes, I mean Arthur. Did Kelly tell you why I left the Unjudged?"

"She said she didn't know."

"That was smart. She's the reason I stuck around, you know."

"You've been in town this whole time?"

"Atlantic City, but I've been reading the Potterford Herald every day on line."

Lynch chuckled as was his instinct every time that snot rag of a paper was mentioned.

"What the hell for?"

Samuel shrugged.

"I was keeping an eye on Kelly. When I left the UJ, I realized it meant leaving her, but I figured it was worth the trade-off. I mean, I'd left stuff before. Well, detective, I was wrong, and it took me way too long to be honest with myself about it. So, I started reading the Herald. I figured as long as I didn't see anything in the police briefs about the UJ, everything was okay. There was a part of me, though, that hoped I'd read something that would give me an excuse to swoop in and snatch her out of harm's way...yuck, right?"

The word "right" upwardly inflected at the end of a sentence bugged the shit out of Lynch, almost as much as overuse of the word "like."

"So, you saw the Meadowbrook arrests in Sunday morning's police briefs, along with Jeremy's beating."

"Yes, and the front-page write-up on Reilly's assault two days later."

"Why did it take you until this morning to show yourself?"

189

"Pathetically enough, I was working up courage…then there's this."

Samuel stood slightly and produced a copy of that day's Herald, upon which he had been sitting. Had he done it a few minutes earlier, he would have been staring down the barrel of a police issue Glock .38.

He handed the paper to Lynch. It was open to an article about a motorcycle that was pulled out of Pickering Creek. A fly-fisherman stumbled across it around sundown the night before. The tag had been removed.

"Did you read this, Detective?"

"I glanced over it. They pulled it out in Morrisville…not my beat."

"The bike belongs to Bubbs. I assume you've had the pleasure."

"I have, but that's a stock Softail. It could be anybody's."

"The *bike could*…"

Samuel pointed at the Herald's photo, specifically at a uniformed police officer in the background bagging evidence.

"…but not the helmet. That's a custom-painted honey badger. Don't ask."

Lynch struggled to put the pieces together as he read. Samuel was kind enough to get him started, using insight that was off of Lynch's radar.

"Something's going down between the UJ and someone close to Reilly. The Bishop is killed; Jeremy is attacked; Reilly is injured while trying to (finger quotes) 'break up a gang fight;' Bubbs's bike ends up at the bottom of the Pickering. It's back and forth. The next hit is on Reilly's crew, and I'm getting Kelly out of here before she finds herself dead or in jail."

Lynch finished the article. For a fleeting moment, it occurred to him that Carrie Warner lived in Morrisville. The relevance escaped him. He gave a terse, but sincere, reply.

"This is helpful."

Lynch stared at the floor while he processed everything. The mall was almost empty. Samuel let a half-chorus of *"I Say a Little Prayer for You"* go by over the piped music, before offering his next nugget of chesty advice.

"It's your investigation, but if I were you, I'd question…"

"Ian Reilly."

"The article on Reilly said that he and his brother chased after a kid named Gordon Weiss."

"That's right. He goes by Gordy."

"Kelly told me about him. He's a lackey for the UJ. I don't know the kid. He joined after I left. Has he been questioned?"

Lynch's expression revealed exactly what he was thinking.

I can't answer that, and even if I could, you're not my boss so go piss up a rope.

Gordy *had* been interrogated about the vandalism, but his lips were vacuum-sealed regarding the UJ. All they had on him was the fact that he wore a similar jacket (which he could explain), and that he appeared to be riding out to the barn the night of the murder. He fell off of his bike before he got there, so no one saw him interact with any member of the UJ. It all added up to a big stinking pile of circumstance. Gordy, at least for now, was useless, unless Kelly was willing to go on the record…unlikely.

Samuel took the hint and backed off the question.

"Detective, I'm just saying that Reilly didn't follow anybody anywhere; he was led. He didn't stumble upon a gang fight in the Yard; the UJ was waiting for him there. Beyond that, I don't know what happened. The only person conscious and not in hiding who *does* know what happened is Ian Reilly."

Samuel took a breather. The man had obviously indulged in a few courtroom dramas too many. It didn't mean he was wrong. As a cop, Lynch wasn't able to comment on any of it, but he silently stayed on board. Still, it was all conjecture. No arrests would be made on the merit of Samuel's theories.

"You said we could help each other. How does this help you?"

Samuel looked around.

"I want you to fuck up Artie for me, or at least fuck him over."

The statement was absurd.

"Samuel, you don't appeal to me as an idiot…"

"Are you hungry, detective?"

"No. Not really."

"Good. Me neither. In the course of your little dance with the UJ, have you ever heard the term 'painting party?'"

Lynch shook his head.

"I have not."

"That's surprising. Well, I'm going to have to familiarize you with the term before I can explain myself."

"If you must (*jackass*)."

Samuel stretched but showed no signs that he was tired of talking.

"Basically, it's a unifier for the UJ. The one downside of being part of a group without rules is that after a while, it ceases to feel like a group. So, once a month, the UJ gather in the cloister for a painting party. We *recreate Wallace Avery's painting*. It's pretty impressive. We…I'm sorry…*they* break out the hookahs; they bring on the junk food; they haul in all sorts of furniture to destroy; they fire up the knife-throwing target and bring handfuls of ecstasy tablets for…I'll get to that in a minute. Anyway, the most important part of it, as you can imagine, is…"

"The boobies?"

Samuel laughed and hooted out loud.

"Fuckin' Avery. The UJ call it The Rite."

"I'm assuming that's a euphemism for sexual free-for-all."

To Samuel, The Rite was so much more, but how could he expect anyone outside the cloister to understand. He'd had enough trouble getting those *inside* the cloister to understand. He decided the best route was to just describe it rather than try to explain it.

"They position the hookahs and the food and the furniture roughly as it appears in Avery's painting. Then each person in the cloister picks a figure to be."

"A figure?"

"A person in the painting. They pick a person in the painting to act as…to stand in for. They're recreating the painting so everyone needs to become a part of the painting. You follow?"

"I think so."

"They have a copy of the thing handy for reference. They also have a digital alarm set to make the sound of twelve bells at midnight. When the time is getting close, everyone starts hovering around the area of the room that represents their area of the painting. Still with me?"

"Keep going."

"On the first bell, everyone strikes their figure's pose and holds it until the eleventh. On the twelfth, the room goes bat-shit nuts. Seriously, it's beyond description, but, amidst the chaos, the painting's prominent elements are upheld. Everyone tosses their handfuls of ecstasy tablets in the air. The music wails, knives go flying at the target, pizza gets woofed down as if it was the last food on earth, furniture gets destroyed, drugs are all over the place, and…yes…people have sex. Sometimes it's depraved; sometimes it's flat-out messed-up, but it is always consensual."

"And something happened at one of these things last March to make you leave?"

Samuel took a moment.

"Yes, something did. You see, painting parties are also used to bring in possible new members."

"That's kind of a baptism by fire, isn't it?"

"They have to know what they're in for. No better time than day one. Look, maybe I wasn't clear about this. No one is forced to do any of this stuff. If you want to come to a painting party, hang out on the sideline and watch, or put in your earbuds and fall asleep then go for it."

"Well, that's good. You're getting off subject here."

"I am not. The UJ is about freedom. Arthur never got that. To him it was always about the sex. He fed me a good line when we first met at the Iron Wall. I don't know. Maybe he started the whole thing with the correct mindset, but his true colors came out soon after we set up the first cloister. I thought I could turn him around, but I was wrong. Eventually the best I could do was keep him in check. I wasn't about to kick the spiteful little prick out of the group. He would have made it his life mission to destroy everything. As it winds up, he did that anyway!"

All linear aspects of the conversation were starting to disappear. Samuel had worked himself into a rant. Lynch had to repeat himself in order to reel him back in.

"What happened in March?"

"Arthur brought a girl to the party. I have no idea how old she was. The general rule…we do have a few…was recruits should be out of high school, but I don't know. I don't remember her name. I barely remember what she looked like. Arthur talked her into being one of the three."

"The boobies."

"The center piece, yes. The implication is that if you are one of the three, you are having sex in some fashion with at least one other person, but, again, nothing is required, and no one is supposed to get shitty if they're refused."

"Did she go through with it?"

"Yes, but she bailed almost immediately. It was no big deal. She got dressed and hung out by the food tables. She appeared to be really enjoying herself. I thought she might be a good match for the UJ, even if Arthur only brought her to mount her."

"I'm guessing the mounting didn't happen."

Samuel's expression turned grim.

"He was chucking knives. He does the same thing every time. He waits until he wins a match before he joins the orgy. He needs to feel like a conqueror, as if he's collecting a reward or some shit. So, I don't know how long it took him, but he eventually strutted over to the center of the cloister, expecting to get laid and discovered that his conquest had left him high and dry."

"Poor fella. What happened?"

"I quite honestly don't remember. Kelly and I decided to have an evening of intimacy rather than public fornication, so after getting high and stuffing our faces, we headed up to the loft. We fell asleep early. That's partly why I woke up in the middle of the night."

The word "partly" seemed to jump. Lynch braced himself. He sensed that the crappy part of the story was but to be told.

"Go on."

"It was dark. Any other night of the month, and I probably wouldn't have been able to see what was going on. It was Arthur and the girl. The bastard propped her up face down with her knees tucked up under her chest. She was moaning in protest, but I don't think she had any idea what was happening. Either he doped her up, or she doped herself up. I don't know. She had a skirt on, which he'd hiked up over her hips. Her underwear was half way down her thighs. I know this because I was the one who pulled them up."

Lynch's jaw locked.

"Please tell me you stopped him before…"

"Just barely. The girl was lucky in one crucial regard. Arthur was having trouble…you know…no boner. He had backed off and was (pantomime masturbation) working on it when I finally got to my feet. I asked him what the fuck he thought he was doing, and he laughed. The evil little ass-hat had the nerve to ask me if I wanted a turn while he got his problem sorted. I said two words… 'zip up.' He looked at me as though I'd just sent him to his room. He then called me a faggot and stomped off in a huff. I assumed he was either having a smoke or taking a piss. I got the girl situated and went to look for him. He had a serious verbal beat-down coming. I didn't even make it to the ladder. I don't know where he was hiding. All I know is I was slammed into a dresser, and I didn't much like it."

"I'm surprised he had the balls to fight you on his own."

Samuel allowed himself a smirk.

"To be honest…it wasn't much of a fight. Arthur's good with the hardware, but he can't throw fists. I messed him up pretty good. When I figured he'd had enough, I just let him fall to the floor in a heap. I admit, I took sadistic pleasure in crouching down next to him and watching him struggle for air. I looked around. Everyone had slept through the whole thing, even Kelly. I couldn't believe it. I must have muttered something to myself because Arthur spoke up…as best as he could anyway."

Samuel proceeded with an unflattering impression of Arthur.

"Yeah Samuel, they're still asleep. Do you have any idea what would have happened to you if they weren't? If Bubbs was awake? If Steven was awake? Or Rick? I've pulled a Stalin on your ass. It's just a matter of time before you pay for this, faggot! First you, then your little whore! I'm paraphrasing, of course. And it wasn't his lame threat that made me leave. They wouldn't have done anything to Kelly, or me for that matter."

"Then what made you?"

The answer did not come easily.

"Because the little platinum jerk-off was right. He'd taken the whole thing for himself. We still had the gatherings and the rituals, but the UJ

194

had become a pathetic shadow of itself. It was…done with me. It just took the rambling of an impotent, bloodied waste-of-space to make me face it. And it's gotten worse since I left. Kelly got me caught up this morning between orgasms…"

"Come on. Really?"

"Sorry. That was uncalled for. The point is, even the painting parties are all but unrecognizable. We had *forty members* at our peak. What do they have now, fifteen, sixteen? They're lucky if eight members show up to a regular Saturday gathering. There's no anonymity; there's no center. The only thing they've managed to rally around is Jeremy's death, and that's just a pointless revenge thing. The land and the king are one. Just like Arthur, it's all about kicking ass and getting laid. It's a goddam joke!"

Samuel slumped back. Lynch could feel his own feet beating inside his shoes, so he could only imagine what was going on inside his tablemate.

"…so, detective, if you would be so kind, I'd like you to fuck up Arthur for me."

It was the request of an entitled little prick with no grip on reality. Lynch spoke.

"I'm going to do two things: I am going to assume 'fuck up' means 'arrest,'"

"It doesn't…"

"…shut up. And I'm going to try to bring you back to Earth by stating the obvious. The only way any of this means anything is if it's true."

Samuel gave an understanding nod and randomly crumpled up his napkin.

"Sitting at this table, all I have today is my word. If there's anything else I can give you, tell me what it is."

"This whole thing locks in, and your boy goes to jail if I can get in touch with the girl who was assaulted."

"Oh…is that all? I told you, man. I don't know who she is. Kelly says the girl left the painting party and disappeared. I've seen nothing in the local news about missing persons or suicides. I don't think she's from Potterford. Even if you found her, she wouldn't remember a thing. How's she going to come forward?"

"Kelly…"

"Ain't happening."

"You…"

"Completely ain't happening."

"Then think hard, and give me something else."

For the first time since he sat down, Samuel found himself wrestling with is words. Lynch recognized the look as that of a man protecting a loved one, and he had a pretty good guess as to who it was.

195

"Samuel, whatever you tell me, Arthur's the target. Unless he knows the location of Hoffa's body, he isn't plea-bargaining. We're not going to allow him to cop a lower charge to turn in the rest of the UJ."

"Wow. You are way off."

"Okay. What then?"

"Look, if you want Arthur, go get him at work. He's a sales rep for..."

"That's no good. No one's accused him of anything. If you won't come forward, and Kelly won't come forward, and we don't know where the girl is..."

"You've got Ian Reilly."

"Not yet, I don't. Without a witness or an accuser, I need to actually catch Arthur doing something, or nothing will stick long-term. Do you understand?"

Samuel rubbed his eyes with the heels of both hands and stared at the ceiling.

"How about this? I was thinking about this the other day. And I'm admittedly just spit-balling here, but The Herald said that Reilly was hit with a brake drum, right? There's no way Arthur could have thrown one of those things hard enough to hit anyone in the head. My guess is that it was Bubbs, but on a good day it could have been either Rick or Steven. If you can convince Arthur that a witness came forward, and the witness is claiming that he...I mean Arthur...hit Reilly, the prick won't hesitate to rat out the guy that actually did it. Believe me man, all four of them will instantly turn on each other. You will get more ammunition than you can handle. With a little creativity, you might even be able to get Arthur to cop to the assault on the girl if he thinks it will clear him of any participation in..."

"I still need to get my hands on him, and I need a real reason to bring him in."

Samuel hung his head in thought. He spoke without looking up.

"Would drug possession be enough?"

"More than enough."

Samuel scratched his chin, swung his head back up, and regained eye contact with Lynch.

"There's a painting party tonight."

Lynch nodded with satisfaction.

"Talk to me."

"It's the second reason I chose today to return to Potterford. I wanted to make sure Kelly wasn't going to the fuckin' thing. There will be plenty of drugs...maybe even a few concealed weapons."

"Then we've got him."

196

"Not quite. I don't know where it's being held, and neither does Kelly."

He explained the UJ's ineffectual communication procedure and Kelly's failure to check in.

"Well, can't Kelly just send the text and ask?"

Samuel leaned forward and jabbed his index finger in the air toward Lynch's nose. This was obviously the suggestion that he'd feared all along.

"If she does that, then you can't whiff it. If the cops don't show, or even worse, if they *do* show up, and the bastards get off…"

"We won't whiff it."

"You've got to promise me, man."

"I promise"

Samuel reluctantly pulled out his cell phone, punched in a quick text, and placed the phone on the table.

"I don't know how long this will take. She's at work like I…"

The phone buzzed. Samuel picked it up with a chuckle and read Kelly's reply. He turned the phone around so that Lynch could read it too.

"I guess she beat us to the task…it's at the old flag factory in West Springfield."

"Springfield? Kind of far, isn't it?"

"It's far, but it works. The cloister location only requires two features, but they're features that aren't easy to come by. One, it needs to be a place that no one pays attention to and, two, it needs to have some kind of skylight with access to moonlight."

"Come again?"

"The painting…the boobies…the center of the room needs to be lit. That's why this month's painting party is tonight."

Samuel took another drink while Lynch asked his next question.

"What's tonight?"

Samuel gulped and let out a satisfied sigh before answering.

"Full moon. You're right though. Not only is it far, it's probably the worst backup location the UJ has. It was our first one, the 'Beta-test Cloister' if you will. They must have been all kinds of hard-up if they had to relocate there."

Lynch pictured the factory and thought ahead to the take-down. It would be easy. Three cars, tops. He couldn't wait to tell his partner. Ernie was nothing if not entertaining when there was blood in the water.

Samuel stood. Lynch reacted.

"Whoah! Where do you think you're going?"

"Dude, I'm done. I gave you my whole story, along with everything I know that could possibly help. Get busy on that receipt."

197

"With all due respect, Samuel…no, of course no. Your ass is mine until your alibi checks out."

"Really? You're going to arrest me? Put me in jail for Bishop Ryan's murder? You know I didn't do it. That receipt can't be the only thing you've got."

Every fiber of Lynch's being wanted to drag Samuel into custody, but, unfortunately, the wordy blueblood was right.

"Give me your number and stay available until this painting party tip pans out."

Samuel did so, bowed respectfully, and turned to leave. As he walked away and adjusted his coat, something in Lynch woke up. Like a shot, an intense feeling of stupidity surged from his neck to his fingertips. His tablemate had faded him out of position. Lynch had become so engrossed in Samuel's story that he forgot to ask him question number one.

His voice echoed through the empty food court.

"Samuel!"

The former president of the UJ took an irritated pause in his stride and slowly pivoted back around with his hands in his pockets.

"Yes, detective?"

"What did you do with your trench coat?"

"The day after I left the barn, I went…"

"…to St. Al's and talked with Father O'Rourke. I know."

Samuel was again impressed.

"I left it on a pew in the church."

5. By the Schuylkill River

Indistinguishable Eric made his promise to Arthur when he was stoned out of his mind. He had *no idea* where to find Kelly, but he couldn't renege. Losing face with Arthur just wasn't done. After a morning of driving around aimlessly, he found himself parked by the river staring at the sky.

He reached for his glove box.

When the going gets tough…smoke a bowl.

As the THC started to do its job, he remembered Arthur's words: "I believe she has gone astray." He turned down his radio so he could talk to himself.

"Astray…where would she go if she's gone astray? To the enemy? Who's the enemy? The cops? The cop that beat up Jeremy? Would she visit him, maybe?"

He took a massive hit.

"What the fuck; it's all I got."

He made his way to the hospital after a stop at Taco Bell.

As far as he could tell, the detective's condition hadn't changed. The family remained in the ICU's waiting area crying, praying, and squeezing rosaries.

Kelly was not there.

A woman arrived. She was welcomed like a family member, but she wasn't a family member. She didn't act like a family member. She wasn't dressed like a family member. She was more like…

"A cop. Shit, that's Reilly's partner, isn't it?"

He wouldn't be able to stay much longer.

It was noon. His buzz was wearing off. He was irritated, slightly nauseous, and stuck with two options: take another lap around town or give up and face the wrath of the UJ.

… or …

As Carrie Warner circulated, embracing and consoling each Reilly individually, Eric got an idea. If he couldn't deliver Kelly, maybe he could deliver something better. He pulled out his burner phone.

"Hey, Artie, it's me."

"Eric, my man! Find her yet?"

"No, but…"

"Don't sweat it. She sent me a text. It's all taken care of."

They both could have left it there. They didn't.

Eric spoke.

"So, I was thinking…do we need a third chick for the party tonight?"

"Until a couple minutes ago, we needed a second *and* a third, but yeah, we could use one. Why? What are you thinking?"

The nondescript little ass-kisser gave his own shoulder a little brush and tried to think where he could get his hands on some chloroform.

Meanwhile, Samuel and Kelly had just past mile marker 184 on the Pennsylvania turnpike. They were westbound in Samuel's red Alfa Romeo…never to return to Potterford.

6. Driving Up Prospect St.

Lynch checked in with Gomez on his way to St. Aloysius. Ernie had been on a video conference call with Pastor Karney and a few members of the Philly Archdiocese most of the late morning. Collectively, they'd reviewed the short stack of filtered hate mail that the two detectives put together. Through the course of the call, eight letters and three emails were deemed worth pursuing.

"You sure you don't want me to come with you, acho?"

"Trust me. You are much better utilized doing what you're doing. Good job with the diocese, partner."

"No problem. Son mis hombres hombre. Ay, my desk phone's ringing. Later, bro. You know what to do if things get dicey. I can be there in three minutes."

"I truly doubt it will be necessary."

Father Leo met Lynch outside the Pastor's Office with a smile and a friendly hand. The hand was acknowledged; the smile was not.

Leo spoke.

"We'll talk in here, if that's okay. My office in use."

Lynch said nothing, breezed past the priest, and disappeared into the room. A confused Father Leo followed and closed the door behind them.

"Won't you take a seat?"

The detective answered with a confrontational tone.

"I'm alright."

Leo, as was his nature, gave Lynch the benefit of the doubt and would remain pleasant until given a reason not to be.

"Jim, what's going on?"

It took a lot for Lynch to censor his language.

"A freaking murder investigation, in case you haven't been paying attention."

"I'm sorry Jim. I don't..."

"I am going to start with some basic facts...no inference...no detective work...just freaking facts! Day one of the investigation, I gave you one simple instruction. Don't discuss the case with anyone."

"I know... and I did. I'm sorry."

"Sorry!? Freaking sorry!? Do you know now why I gave you that *simple* instruction?"

Leo opened his mouth but was denied the chance to speak.

"Because word travels like wildfire in a crap little burb like Potterford...quite often to the wrong ears! Ever heard the legal term *proximate cause*?"

Over the past two years, he'd become extremely familiar with the term, but saying so would have been pointless.

"The long and short of it is that *you*...not Father O'Rourke...are second on the list of people responsible for Jeremy Sokol's death after the guy that actually slammed the bat into his head! YOU, FATHER!"

It wasn't entirely true. The tactic may have worked on someone else, but after twenty years of sitting in a confessional, Father Leo knew smoke and mirrors when he heard it. He kept his mouth shut and continued waiting for a question that wasn't rhetorical.

"Why did you do it?"

The answer came with neither stutter nor apology.

"Because we needed to get ahead of the press."

The floor creaked as the detective shifted his weight.

"You know, Leo, I just noticed something. This office has no private bathroom. Yours does. This wasn't the Pastor's office, originally. Was it? Yours was. In fact, I'm betting the diocese made the Pastor move in here when you came on board."

"That is true. I would have fought it had I known. It was all set up before I got here."

He was telling the truth.

"Well, father, there would have been no point. The diocese insisted. Fellini insisted. You did them a solid during the Bell trial. It was only fair. I get why you never brought it up. It had no real relevance to the case. It would have been nice to know for some back drop though…for the big picture."

He was playing to the good priest's sense of guilt. It wasn't working.

"Believe me, Jim. If I thought the Bell trial had any…"

"I'm just saying that I'd understand if there was anything else you failed to tell me at the insisting of your superiors."

Leo was taken aback by the implication.

"My superiors had nothing to do with any of my actions."

"Or lack thereof? The thing is…now I find out that Samuel's trench coat…the only solid piece of evidence we have…was left on a pew in your church. If you were me, what would you conclude?"

Leo was sick of being interrupted. He answered without fully realizing what he was saying.

"That someone here picked it up, obviously."

"Obviously."

The look on Lynch's face brought forth a rumble of South Philly in the priest's gut.

"Wait a minute, Jim. You don't think I had anything to do with Bishop Ryan's death, do you?"

"In my experience, when someone holds back information, it's because they're either guilty or covering for someone."

"Yes or no, do you think I had anything to do with it?"

"Bring it down, father. I'm the one…"

There was a knock on the office door.

"Come in!"

It was Father O'Rourke. He realized he was interrupting something and stood poised to either enter or exit the room. He spoke quickly.

"Father Leo. We're done. You can have your office back."

"How are you feeling?"

"The man's good at his job. There's a reason he is who he is. I'm ready to pick up where I left off. I figured I'd try to set something up with Reverend Beech over at Xavier Lutheran. Does that sound okay?"

"Sounds perfect. Nice to have you back, Aiden."

Aiden started to exit.

Lynch had a thought. He was probably way off base, but he didn't care. This was about posture, not accuracy. He pointed at the young priest and spoke to Leo.

"Is that it?"

"Is what it?"

"Are you covering for Father O'Rourke?"

Aiden's face turned white. Leo's turned red. The time for manners had passed.

"Have you completely lost your mind, Jim?"

"You have an alibi...sort of...for the night of the murder. Does he?"

"I'm not even entertaining this."

"He's the only person that we know was in the room with the jacket after Samuel left. He dimed the UJ to Reilly. Maybe that was to throw him off the scent. Makes sense."

"No, it does not. If you spent any time with this young man, you'd know that what you're saying is absurd!"

Lynch turned to O'Rourke.

"What do you have to say for yourself, Father?"

"Don't say anything, Aiden!"

Lynch was ready to put the last nail in the coffin. He pulled his jacket back, and reached for his handcuffs.

"Still obstructing, Leo? Fine. Turn around."

"You have got to me shitting me."

"Wow...mouthy. And here I was trying to censor myself. If I'm wrong, I'll fucking apologize. Turn around."

Lynch approached. Leo instinctively put up his fists.

"It's like that, is it, Leo?"

"Aiden, go get the Archbishop."

"Aiden, don't move."

The young priest turned to stone in the doorway. Follow his mentor? Follow the law? He whispered a prayer for guidance, but there wasn't time to wait for God to respond.

"I'm sorry, detective."

He was out of sight before Lynch had a chance to react.

"Father, wait!!"

Aiden found the door to Leo's office open. The room was empty.

"Your Grace? Your Grace!"

The muffled answer came from father Leo's bathroom.

"I'm in here, Father. It's okay. Come on in."

The urgency of the moment disallowed Aiden to notice the voice's unfamiliar timbre and missing accent. He barreled forward and gripped the door handle for dear life.

He wrenched his wrist to the right.

The latch popped.

The door opened…pushed ajar by the body resting on the other side.

Aiden stepped back and froze in horror. What lay before him made no rational sense. There was blood. There was a man in a black shirt lying face down with his body twisted in the doorway. There was a crossbow bolt in the back of the man's head.

When the surreality of the scene subsided, and Aiden fully realized what he was looking at, he sunk down to the floor burying his face in his hands.

He started to scream.

"Father!! Detective Lynch!! Holy mother, full of grace!!"

Archbishop Fellini had been assassinated…a single shot to the base of the skull…painless, but tragically undignified.

7. Just Driving Around

Eric was good at getting stuff. He made another call to Arthur.

"We're set on this end."

"Eric, you're the man."

"A few more things have to fall into place, but it should be a very interesting evening."

"It's going to fucking rock."

"Out of curiosity, Artie, we've got Traci; we've got my girl. Who's the third?"

"Brother, you wouldn't believe me if I told you."

Eric was *not* set on his end. The idea was crazy. The plan was ridiculous. It *should* have failed miserably.

8. Outside St. Aloysius RCC

Gomez met Lynch in the church courtyard. Crime scene had not yet arrived. Lynch was standing under a tree located near a partially opened window. He was looking up in disbelief at an ambiguous apparatus stuck into the trunk about ten off of the ground. Sirens filled the air. All available uniformed members of the Potterford P.D. locked down the church and closed off Prospect Street.

Ernie spoke.

"They're on their way."

"I know."

There was a bullet placed in plain sight by the roots. It had been through a gun.

"That's weird."

"Yup, and I'll bet you dollars to donuts ballistics matches it to our bullet."

"Holy shit, the guy wants us to know he did both shootings."

"So it would seem."

Twenty minutes later, the FBI arrived.

9. Under a Tree

Thank you.

Philip sat in his uncle's woods gazing upward.

So much, thank you.

The recon that he'd done leading up to his perfect moment was nothing short of pure artistry. The floor plans of Cardinal Romero High School and St. Aloysius Church were easily found on the internet. He trashed the former. The latter saved him a great deal of time when he did his walk-thru and wound up in Father Pascucci's confessional.

Thank you.

He allowed himself full credit for the preparation but not the killing itself.

Dear Father, thank you.

It was no secret that Archbishop Fellini was leading all St. Al Masses over the upcoming weekend. Philip figured that His Eminence would be hanging out at the church at some point during the week. He also figured that the man would eventually have to defecate, and while the toilet in the (former) Pastor's Office wasn't the *only* place to poop, it was certainly the most private. Philip's investigation of the tiny bathroom yielded two astonishing bits of luck.

First, there was the tree.

The tree itself was not a surprise. He'd seen it when he compared the church floor plan to the satellite rendering he'd printed from eMaps. Still, the wide and towering maple couldn't have served more perfectly. The middle branches were long and strong. The leaves were big and provided ample coverage from trunk to top.

Then, there was the swollen window. Its position was satisfactory for a headshot, but its frosted glass made it impossible to tell who was on the other side. He dreaded the thought of jamming the thing open, until he discovered that the century-old building and years of moisture had done half the job for him. A little hand soap between the pane and the frame guaranteed that the window wouldn't budge.

The unknown quantity was the timing.

Man...the first day! He was at the church the first day! I was in the tree; he was right there...on the crapper! There wasn't a thing to stop me! Not a thing! The path of frikkin' Moses wasn't clearer!

Some would have called it fate; others would have called it a progression of logical circumstance; still others...like Philip...divine intervention.

From the bottom of my heart and soul, thank you.

The plan's *only* glitch was fixed *by a priest*.

Philip guessed that the Archbishop would be guarded. He dismissed it as a non-issue, believing that everyone would scramble to the body once the deed was done, thus leaving his exit clear. The problem was the body had to be *discovered* in order for this to happen.

No one knew the killing had taken place.

When he asked his uncle for a silencer that would fit his nine, the old man laughed in his face.

"You've been Hollywooded boy! Silencers don't work like that. You're going from freight train to jackhammer. You want silent? *This* is silent."

His words were true. The crossbow pistol did the trick. The tradeoff was a dead Archbishop that no one knew about, and a goon blocking the way out.

Until the young priest showed up.

Philip let out a snicker and recreated his estimation of the Archbishop's voice.

"I'm in here. It's okay. Come on in."

The rest played out according to design.

No pain; no fear.

Philip tilted his head back as far as he could. His face showed no expression. It was the first time in his life that he'd experienced absolute euphoria. No facial expression or kinetic activity could do the feeling justice. So, he sat...and listened to the birds.

10. Father Karney's Office

Leo had been offered medication by one of the EMTs. He refused it. It was a time for faith, not drugs. With closed eyes, he searched the Gospel, the Psalms, and all of Paul's letters, finding little comfort. The image of Christ on the cross served as a reminder to all humanity that there is no life without death. There is no heavenly reward without sacrifice. What higher purpose could have been served by the pointless slaughter of Archbishop Fellini?

He didn't know how long the FBI had been there. They'd requested anything that the church could provide pertaining to Ryan's last Mass, including the yellow confirmation inserts that were distributed before the service and collected afterwards. The building was overrun. All Leo could do was sit in Pastor Karney's office away from the crime scene and await his interview.

The Special Agent's name was Marjorie Beck from the FBI's Critical Incident Response Group. The line between compassion and condescension was a thin one, and Special Agent Beck walked it well. She entered the office with sympathetic eyes and an apologetic handshake.

The delicate silver chain around her neck adorned with a small crucifix did not escape Leo's notice.

She asked him for his version of the past 4 days. He spoke without self-awareness, as if listening to a recording of his own voice. He recalled the fouled up hotel arrangements, the dinner at Sullivan's, the voicemail message from the hotel security guard, the viewing of the security video, the meeting in the chapel, the press conference, the protest, the plan to send Father O'Rourke unto Potterford's non-Catholic communities, the masturbator's confession, the chase afterwards, Father O'Rourke's near breakdown, the visit to the police station, Archbishop's Fellini's offer to help, the confrontation with Lynch, and the rest.

They took a short break. Then she asked him to go through it all again, focusing on details and anything that struck him as odd.

Leo's eyes turned vacant. The vapor that was serving as his consciousness held nearly every recent memory at bay...*nearly* every memory.

"Pruning the roses."

"What's that?"

He wasn't sure what to call her.

"Ma'am, is Pastor Karney here yet?"

"He's en route."

Leo gave his jowls a vigorous shake and slapped himself on both cheeks.

"May I call him?"

"It's better if I do."

Between the three of them, and Ernie's digital recorder, they'd figure out how Leo's sister-lusting confessor got away, but that would be all. They were about to be interrupted with another crisis.

11. The Sanctuary at St. Aloysius

Carrie Warner's words rang in Lynch's ears. She was absolutely right. They *weren't* NYPD. He woke up that morning (feeling, at least, like) an above-average detective. Now he was just an ineffectual little turd acting as a facilitator for the investigators who actually knew what they were doing.

Everyone was brought back for second interviews, starting with the two women who entered the confessional before and after the incestuous jerkoff. Lynch observed but, by request of the questioning agent, did not participate. He was to listen for inconsistencies, nothing else. He heard none, although the timbre of every word made him want to ram a spike in his own eye. The abrasively pious woman remembered nothing. The non-sequiturial one didn't see the man's face but described him as medium-built with dark clothing, and shoulder-length blond hair under a black wool cap.

"Thank you, ma'am. We may be in touch."

The acting church secretary was next. Lynch didn't conduct her initial interview, so he was off the hook until his assistance was specifically requested.

They should have brought in the feds right away.

He took a seat in a pew and, head in hands, recalled Sunday morning's one-sided phone conversation with his boss.

"Listen, Lynch, as silly as it sounds, the Philly diocese wants to keep the investigation local."

"Seriously? Why?"

"The *excuse* is that the evidence points towards a local pagan whacko and therefore best followed up by cops who know the area. The *reason* is they don't want the FBI and the Sherriff's Department putting more eyes on this thing than necessary. They think it'll stir up the shit from the past two years."

Yeah yeah yeah, blah blah blah. Great call. What did it get them?

"Thanks to me, a dead Archbishop, that's what."

He wanted to nail a picture of himself to a wall, piss on it, and spend the rest of his life flipping it off.

Special Agent Beck appeared in the distance. She was walking toward him with purpose.

"This can't be good"

Earlier, he told her about Samuel and how he went from prime suspect to being eliminated from the inquiries. Apart from a thoughtful chew of her pen cap, she barely reacted. Either she was satisfied with Lynch's work or saving the ass-handing for later.

And it was later.

He clenched his buttocks as she took a seat next to him. With a facial expression that was impossible to read, she dug into her jacket pocket and produced Ernie's hand-held digital recorder. Lynch sensed that his injury was about to get a helping of insult.

"We just got off the phone with the landscaping company that services the church. There were only three workers here Monday, and *none* of them were allowed near the rose bushes. Only Pastor Karney does the rose bushes. That's a rule, and the landscapers know it. That makes one man too many in the courtyard. Now, check this out."

She pressed the recorder's PLAY button. Lynch heard the same portion of the same interview that Gomez played for him on Monday.

Dee man come to da door. Den vee vork. Den man ask if vee see a man running. Vee tell him no.

As if Lynch didn't feel like enough of an idiot...

"You see, detective? He's talking about two different men. One of them *come to da door*; the other *ask if vee see a man running*. Gomez assumed it was the same guy, so he didn't pay it any mind."

"So did I for that matter."

"Of course, you did. I would have too. That's not the point. Father Pascucci can't remember a thing about the perp, but the other guy...the guy legitimately from the landscapers...he got a short but close look at him. We've got a shot at a sketch here."

Lynch forced an enthusiastic smile as the dial that adjusted his feelings of inadequacy clicked up a notch. She'd been on the case four hours, and she already caught a break, a *real* break.

She thumbed through her notes.

A discussion needed to take place. Now was as good a time as any

"Agent Beck, how much do you need Gomez's and my help with this?"

She responded pleasantly.

"Why? What's wrong?"

"There's another case. I was helping out with it because..."

The situation seemed simple until he tried to explain it.

"...I thought it skated the edges of mine, but I was wrong. One of our guys is in a coma, and his partner is working two cases. One of them is his assault. She's by herself on the other."

"Then help her."

He couldn't tell whether she was being glib or kind. Either way, he knew she'd be happy to get him off her coattails.

"Thank you. I appreciate it. So will Detective Warner."

"Give me your time for the rest of today and tomorrow. After that, just make sure you and Sergeant Gomez have your cell phones on you with the ringers audible. Okay?"

"I need to be somewhere at midnight tonight, if that's alright."

"Midnight? Really? Sounds fun. Let me know if..."

A voice boomed from the church lobby. "Agent Beck!"

She stood to face the source. A broad-shouldered agent was in a dead sprint, clutching a folded piece of yellow paper.

"Agent Beck! We've got a bomb!"

12. Riley's Trophy Shop

"Goddam kid."

Ian Reilly was crouched down in the front display window of his trophy shop. He had to rotate the ribbons, or they'd fade in the sun.

He was alone, and he was stewing.

None of the Reilly men were particularly good at letting anger subside, but Ian, as a rule, didn't even try. His mother gave him flack at the hospital for wanting to leave.

"Pimple-faced jackass."

Quentin, Ian's assistant manager, had been in the shop by himself for a day and a half. The guy needed a break, that's all.

Ian would never abandon his brother. That's the word his mother used, "abandon."

"The balls. The absolute balls."

He wasn't surprised that he'd gotten a fight. With June Reilly, family came first no matter what. And she was used to getting her way. Ian expected that kind of crap from his mom, *but not his son*.

"Twerp's still having wet dreams, and he's trying to tell *me* where I can and can't go."

He never should have told the boy what was going on with the UJ. Emotions were running rampant Tuesday morning in the hospital. For reasons he couldn't remember, he felt the need to use his brother's injury to teach his son about the price of being a man. It was a mistake. It was a *big* mistake. It was a mistake big enough to leave Ian in a display window talking to himself.

"I just want to get through the afternoon, close the shop, and go to F and J's. I missed last night. I want to go tonight. I need a goddam drink."

He used the hem of his golf shirt to wipe the sweat from his forehead, exposing his hairy gut to Cherry Street. He was going to have to get out of the window soon; otherwise, he'd start dripping all over the display's tissue-papered matting. Every joint cracked as he eased all 250 pounds of himself onto the empty shop floor. Once fully upright, he took a proud moment to look around the store (as he often did). The bulk of the landscape was taken up with cups and statues customized with bogus names.

"So that's that."

It was his shop...*his* empty shop. Quentin had gotten caught up with the engraving the day before. All of the orders were met. Ian's customers would understand if he locked the door and went back to the hospital.

"No way. I am getting drunk tonight. If I don't... those Unjudged fuckers win."

13. The ICU Waiting Area

Braden Reilly knew what was up. He was a smart kid, especially when it came to his father. He didn't mean to start a shoving match in front of the hospital elevator, but he knew his dad was only going to the trophy shop so he could go to Frankie and Jimmy's afterwards. Braden had been hearing about the UJ for two days. He knew it was their turn to strike. He also knew what would happen if his father went to the bar. He would plop his fat ass down at the Reilly family table and drink himself silly until the place closed.

The tussle was broken up by a couple of orderlies. Ian was still hollering from the elevator as Braden turned the corner towards the ICU.

"That's right, Braden! Run back to mommy! It's a weeknight for chrissakes! I'm not even gonna drink that much, so everyone just leave me the hell alone!"

Wasn't going to drink that much? Bullshit.

He'd already self-justified his bender. He'd be drinking alone, and Jimmy wouldn't cut him off. He'd be off his tits by dusk.

Braden's insides churned as he took a seat next to his mother. She didn't know about the UJ. He was sure of it. He could tell her. He could squeal, but God help him, his father had bashed the disgrace of being a snitch so deeply into his head and heart that the words wouldn't form.

The same question scrolled before his mind's eye over and over...

What do I do? What do I do? What do I do?

...until he came to realize that he didn't have to squeal. He didn't really have to do anything. His mom would know where her husband was and would fetch him herself if he wasn't home by 10:00.

No worries.

211

Whether by a hangover, getting his ass kicked by the UJ, or receiving a massive earful from his wife, Braden's dad would regret going out.

He checked the time. It was getting close to 5:30. The hospital would be clearing out the visitor centers in three and a half hours.

"He'll be sorry."

"What's that, sweetie?"

"(Huh?) Oh, nothing, mom. I just got in another fight with dad. That's all."

"He's hurting, Braden. Try to go easy on him."

So am I, damn it.

"I'll try."

Most of his predictions would fail.

There would be no hangover, the UJ would not kick anyone's ass, and his mother would never make it to Frankie and Jimmy's.

But Ian Reilly *would* regret going out...oh so much.

14. The Sanctuary

One would have thought the single piece of yellow paper to be a holy relic. Lynch was able to snag a brief look at it before it disappeared into one of the FBI vans for at least three kinds of digital scrubbing. Someone doodled a pipe bomb on one of the Confirmation prayer supplements. Anyone looking over the shoulder of the artist wouldn't have been able to tell what it was. It was a bare, narrow rectangle surrounded by arrows, measurements, and chemical symbols.

The analysis would reveal nothing useful. The paper had been sitting in a box with several hundred others like it. The agents may as well have found the thing on the floor of a men's restroom for the worthless hodgepodge of DNA it yielded. There were fingerprints from five to seven different sources, but no matches in the system.

The entire congregation would need to be fingerprinted and swabbed, but that decision wouldn't be made for several more hours. In the meantime, both the church and Cardinal Romero High School needed to be swept for explosives.

Lynch and Gomez helped unload and unpack an array of high-tech gadgets. Leo and Aiden allowed themselves to be peacefully escorted to the street as instructed. Pastor Karney, in contrast, circled his wagons around the ciborium. If that area of the church was going to be swept for a bomb, the feds would be handheld through the entire process. He'd see himself face-down in handcuffs before allowing the Body and Blood of Christ to be desecrated.

Finding choice moments amidst the chaos, Lynch, bit by bit, told Gomez about his meeting with Samuel. The conversation wound up next to the confessional.

"What did Beck say about the painting party?"

"I haven't told her yet."

"Man. You're a glutton for punishment."

"The jacket's not connected with the UJ anymore. I'm not sending the fibbies out to Springfield on a flimsy …"

Special Agent Beck appeared, shaking her cell as a visual aid.

"I just got done with a very frustrating conversation with the archdiocese. Saint Aloysius is proceeding with all Masses as usual this weekend. They're even making arrangements for Cardinal Romero to lead them. The guy is in Batswana! They're bringing him back to lead Mass in Potterford!? For real!?"

Neither detective knew what to say.

Agent Beck took some deep breaths and continued with a tone that showed she was at least *trying* to understand the words coming out of her own mouth.

"They think canceling services will make the church look weak. They feel like they'd be giving into a terrorist…as if the shooter did all this to stop the Masses from taking place! You and I know damned well this maniac didn't commit murder to stop a Mass! He doesn't want the clergy to hide. He wants them out in the open! I have to sit down."

Beck gathered herself on a nearby bench. Finding the moment humorous was vastly inappropriate, but neither Lynch nor Gomez could help it. They were desperate for some levity, and watching a superior blow a gasket was always entertaining.

Gomez spoke, interrupting the agent's mumblings about "what the diocese wants the diocese gets."

"Can I get you a paper bag?"

She looked up to see if he was serious. He wasn't. She turned her head and coughed out a laugh before responding.

"No thank you, detective. I'm fine."

Lynch spoke next.

"For what it's worth, we've never had any trouble getting extra help from the surrounding counties. I can ask the chief to make some calls."

She smiled appreciatively.

"I may take you up on that. In the meantime, we do have a game plan. It's not terribly creative, but it'll keep Cardinal Romero from being served up on a platter. Tomorrow the diocese is going to make a general announcement to St. Al's parishioners that services will not be held at either the church or the school. They'll wait until Friday afternoon to select a location, and they'll keep it a secret as long as they can. When they make a decision, they'll let us know first, and we'll lock it down until show time. Assuming a pipe bomb hasn't been put in every building in Potterford, we should be okay."

She wasn't looking for a response but got one anyway in the form of some quickfire repartee.

Lynch went first.

"Doubtful."

"You might find a fridge full of sauerkraut in every building."

"Or a NASCAR T-shirt."

"Or a stack of lottery tickets."

"Or an indoor thermometer."

"A neglected fish tank maybe, but not a bomb."

Beck had worked cases all over southeastern Pennsylvania. Her experience with local law enforcement was wide and varied. She liked these guys.

She stood.

"Okay fellas. Here's the deal. We've got a rough … and I mean rough … sketch of a pipe bomb on a piece of yellow paper. It could mean nothing, or it could mean we're dealing with a separatist freak with a warhead in his basement. It doesn't matter. That piece of yellow paper changes everything. We've gotta ramp up. We've gotta revisit every dead end. Everything we were planning on taking a week now has to take a couple of hours."

She eyeballed Lynch. The look said "we don't have time for another screw-up."

"We're the FB-friggin-I. Not much scares us; *Bombs* scare us. Now, what can you tell me about these Unjudged assholes?"

Lynch thought about all the possible answers he could give and followed them through to conclusion. It took him about six seconds.

"I think I know where most of them will be at midnight, and arrests won't be a problem"

15. Philip's Home Office

Philip would have sat placidly under his uncle's tree all afternoon were it not for the inconvenience of having to earn a living. He worked from home, and made his own hours. As long as he hit his deadlines, his employer usually let him be.

This left him with time on his hands…too much as it turned out.

With an arched palm, Philip double-clicked his trackball mouse, revealing a list of similarly named spec docs.

IYP_dbase_spc_900
IYP_dbase_spc_901
IYP_dbase_spc_902
(etc.)

He was about to open the one most recently downloaded, when his eyes fell on the only file in the directory that wasn't supplied by the company. The naming convention made it stand out.

StAloysius_floorplan.pdf

He sat back in his ergonomic chair, shoved his hands into his armpits, and stared at the tiny icon for a good long time. Then he reached for his mouse.

"Oh, why not?"

The map of the church popped open. He had a dual-monitor setup, so he could keep the image opened to full-screen without covering his workspace. He spoke the immortal words of Warren Zevon as he faced forward and commenced pecking away at his keyboard.

"Enjoy every sandwich."

This was *his* day. If he had to spend three hours of it masturbating digital information like the code-monkey he was, he would do so with a symbol of his triumph a mere head-turn away.

So, he worked glancing to his right on a regular basis and dreaming about his next perfect moment. The material was prepared, and he knew exactly where it was going. He just had to figure out how to get it there.

Not going to worry about it right now.

A solution would present itself as all others had. He had help. BIG help. He was sure of it.

He was watching the blue progress bar as his final updates were being complied when he heard footsteps behind him accompanied by a familiar voice.

"Hey, goofball."

The woman he loved put her cheek against his and kissed him on the neck. She thought nothing of the church floor plan. He always had weird stuff on his desk top.

"Hey pretty lady."

"Almost done?"

"Completely done."

"Good. I'm hungry."

"Me too. Five minutes, I promise."

"I'll be in the car"

He closed all his sessions and shut down his computer. His phone buzzed. It was a text. Seeing the sender, he deleted it without reading.

You know better than that.

16. The Cloister

It wouldn't be midnight for another two and half hours. Arthur didn't care.

Less than half of the UJ's members were present. Arthur didn't care.

He had his three women for the rite. That was all he cared about.

He popped an ecstasy tablet, washed it down with a swig of Bacardi, and surveyed his bevy.

A full set.

The first woman was a willing participant. The second was a trophy. The third…just a novelty really.

Arthur understood what it meant to be a man. He understood it in the truest sense. He knew, as a gender, men weren't smarter than women. Men weren't more emotionally stable than women. Men weren't better equipped to handle high pressure situations than women. Men weren't better leaders than women. Men were superior in only one, single-purpose characteristic: physical dominance. They were put on this earth to serve humanity's primal instinct to perpetuate itself. Eating and screwing were a man's only two obligations.

But, somewhere along the line, men messed up. They talked themselves into believing they were hunters, protectors, providers, and even warriors. Perhaps they were those things when the fight was easy to

216

win. When it wasn't, they were hiding in the trees along with everyone else.

No.

Men were physically dominant for one reason and one reason only: to force women into submission. Humans were the only species that had forgotten this basic evolutionary fact. Every other species could mate whenever and wherever they wanted, regardless of the female's willingness. Nature called this arrangement neither cruel nor misogynistic. Nature wasn't sexist. In the insect world, the whole thing was flipped. Ask a male praying mantis who was in charge; he'd tell you. But human males, men, were forced by the society they created to suppress their urges. Every ugly stain on human history existed due to this basic truth. Arthur didn't know how the first war was *fought*, but he was willing to bet that it was *started* by something with a vagina walking up to something with a penis and saying "go get me that thing, and you can have me."

Arthur knew he wasn't alone in his beliefs. It did seem, however, that he was alone in his willingness to verbalize them. It wasn't long after his second written warning at work that he met Samuel at the Iron Wall. He thought he'd finally found a kindred spirit. After they went to Avery's gallery together, he was sure of it.

How could he have been so wrong? Samuel was a douche. The guy had a brilliant philosophy coupled with a silver tongue, and he wasted it on idiotic high principles like freedom and love.

We're men. We ejaculate. That's what we do. Why does it have to be more complicated than that?

In the end, it didn't matter. Arthur won. The douche was long gone…merely a necessary stone in the stairway to greatness. Arthur had no problems admitting it: from Nero to Stalin, men like him needed men like Samuel.

The painting party (a lame-ass stupid thing to call it) was ready to start.

Eric had just laid his unconscious and, so far, unspoiled victim on one of the mattresses near Arthur's feet. His facial expression and demeanor were those of a little boy brandishing a good report card.

The drug he used wasn't chloroform. His buddy on the phone advised him against it. Chloroform wasn't the efficient knock-out fluid that James

Bond fans were led to believe. At best, it was high maintenance; at worst, lethal. Eric didn't want to fuck with lethal. When he asked for an alternative, his buddy told him not to worry about it and hung up. As far as anyone else in the cloister knew, the stuff in the bottle was chloroform. Eric didn't actually know what it was. He guessed it was some sort of homemade something-or-other. It was given to him with one simple instruction written on its otherwise blank label:

ONLY WHEN NEEDED

Fair enough.

Whatever it was, it did the trick. The results pleased Arthur, and that was all that mattered to Eric.

Music was playing at a deafening volume. Arthur approached Eric, slapping his arm over both shoulders. He got close enough to speak without breaking Eric's eardrum.

"Hold out your hand."

Eric did so, and he was rewarded with a half-dozen pills. He clenched them in his fist, and the two of them shared a comrade's embrace.

The drug-addled moment was broken by an angry holler from the other side of the room. Arthur looked towards it. It was Rick. He'd just arrived, and he was angry about something.

Arthur spoke. No one heard him.

"If this cocksucker ruins my buzz…"

17. Difficult to Tell

Mothballs…

When they finally stopped jostling her around, the first thing she sensed was the unmistakable odor of mothballs.

There was music. It was loud and violent. She heard voices every once in a while, but nothing distinguishable. At one point, a screaming argument erupted behind her. She could hear morsels of it over the buzz-saw guitars and cannon-fire drums. None of it made sense.

"…what is this!? What does any of this have to do with the bullshit you fed me when you brought me in!!?"

"…you wanna go to the cops? Go ahead! You were in that junkyard with the rest of us!"

"…She's got nothing to do with this!"

"…you're outnumbered, faggot! Get the fuck out of here!"

Considering the stupor she'd just left, she was surprisingly lucid. Her abductors hadn't used any of the standard knock-out drugs. She had no personal experience with any of them, but she knew the recovery symptoms. She was on her side lying upon a soft surface that she (by the mothballs) guessed to be an old mattress. Her hands were tied behind her back, and she was blindfolded, but she wasn't gagged.

Good. She could scream.

By the sensations against her skin as she inhaled, she could tell they hadn't removed her top or undone her belt. She wiggled her toes. Her shoes were still on.

Good. She could run.

Her heart thumped inside her chest as she fought to keep her breathing under control. She didn't want to give the dickless cowards an excuse to dose her again. Her instincts conquered her fear: fight or flight…a no-brainer. None of this ended happily without a clear escape route. She had to get a glimpse of her surroundings. She slowly and repeatedly squinted, manipulating her blindfold upward until a sliver of viewable space appeared under her left eye.

She was facing a couch. She could see the knees and feet of the couple sitting on it. The woman had on strappy shoes and was getting cozy with a guy who had on …

What is that? A black skirt? A long black coat?

The guy didn't seem to be terribly into it.

It wasn't enough. She couldn't get the blindfold up any higher while her head was resting on the mattress. A tiny lift was all she needed. She tried to constrict her neck on one side, and a glaze fell over what little vision she had. She rested her head back down, but it didn't help. The room started to spin. Stars darted around the insides of her eyelids. There were heavy footsteps near the couch. Her struggle with equilibrium and her instinct not to be stepped on made her roll onto her back.

She screamed, realizing what she'd done.

219

She expected a rag over her mouth, but instead felt a gentle hand against her face, accompanied by a cloud of cheap perfume. The touch turned into a caress fueling her rage. She spit and gnashed at the hand. She heard laughter. Something small and plastic landed on the floor next to her head and dribbled away...a bottle cap. She felt a drip on her arm. They were loading the rag again. She tried to kick with both legs, but they had the drug over her face before she could find her purchase.

The second dose sent her further into oblivion than the first. Once, maybe twice, she faded into dim consciousness over the next two hours until she woke up in the driver's seat of her car. She was in her own driveway. She felt her face peel off the window as she sat up. She was dazed, and it was dark, but the light of the full moon allowed her to stay oriented. She slid to the left slightly as she fumbled for the driver's door handle. There was pain...a distinct pain.

18. The Old Flag Factory, West Springfield

Like a mule train, Beck, Lynch, Gomez, and assorted utility FBI agents pulled into West Springfield with a paddy wagon at the rear. It was close to midnight when the abandoned flag factory came into view. It took them twenty-five minutes to get there from Potterford. It took them almost the same amount of time to find the only open area with access to moonlight. Samuel was right. If the UJ ever set up camp there, it would have been as a last resort. The building was on the edge of a scarcely populated industrial complex similar both in appearance and consequence to Potterford's. Its six stories of brick, mortar, and mold threw an uninspiring silhouette against the night sky. The stench of a nearby landfill was in full force as it was most nights. The only way to the top floor was via an unlit concrete stairwell with no railing. Schlepping up as much as a case of beer would have been a chore.

Shafts of light from five government-issue flashlights skidded across the floor, walls, ceiling and dilapidated amenities. Apart from the swirling dust, the room was without activity, as was the rest of the building. There was no point in looking for a fuse box. The company's electric bill hadn't been paid since the reign of the Broad Street Bullies. There were mattresses, beer bottles, hundreds of cigarette butts...everything that would

220

indicate that at least *someone* used the room for a party at some point. It was Gomez that found the kicker.

"Hey, Jaime. C'meer."

There it was, lit in all its glory by Gomez's torch. It looked barely used.

Lynch spoke. "The knife target…sweet. The tip was only ninety percent bad then."

En route, they'd received a sketch based on the description given by the St. Al's Slovakian landscaper. The poor fellow was short on observational skills. The perp had a black wool cap, shoulder-length cherry blonde hair, and bad teeth. He couldn't even give a detailed description of the teeth. He only remembered that they were comically horrible.

Gomez could tell his partner was seething.

"What are you thinkin', Jaime?"

"Either I got sent here by Kelly, or Kelly got sent here by Arthur. If I'm the stooge, I get it. If it was supposed to be Kelly…see what I'm saying?"

Gomez nodded. Arthur wouldn't have sent Kelly to a false location just to waste her time. He was an arrogant prick, but he wasn't a petty arrogant prick. His plan would have been to see if she'd dime the UJ to the cops. If that was the case, then someone was watching the building. Or, more than likely, someone *had been* watching the building and bolted when they saw the flashlights and suits.

Beck approached from behind. She was angry, but it was difficult to tell at whom.

She spoke.

"If I understand your informant, Jim, the painting party is going on somewhere tonight. Not *here*, but somewhere."

"That is correct."

"You said you have physical addresses for all these UJ ding-dongs."

Gomez answered.

"Some of them"

The beam from her torch whizzed around the room as she turned toward the exit.

"Okay gentlemen, reroute. It looks like we're doing this the hard way."

19. On a Bus

The bus.

Gordy's first painting party, and he spent it in West fucking Springfield. His superiors had dropped him off a stone's throw from the flag factory and told him to take the bus home. The stop for the only bus that ran all night was a half mile from the factory, and the stop in Potterford was close to three miles from his house.

Pain in the ass.

He'd tried calling Arthur when the fibbies showed up, but there was no answer.

The party must have been rockin' beyond belief. Arthur must have been kicking so much ass and getting so much tail that he forgot about the stake out. It was Gordy's special assignment, the one that would *finally* make him full UJ.

Gordy could see his reflection in the bus window from the shoulders up. He turned as far as he could to see the back of his UJ uniform. They'd allowed him to paint a slash through his generic symbol and put a Theban "G" underneath. It looked like a flaccid penis, but he'd take it. It was the greatest moment of his life.

His intel from the police station put St. Aloysius RCC in the crosshairs of the UJ. Why this pleased Arthur so much, Gordy could only guess, but what did he care? He was full UJ now. There would be other painting parties. There would be drugs. There would be women. There would be all the things he'd dreamed about since the first night he followed Zed Zed out to the old barn.

He found himself staring into his own eyes.

Ha! Grounded!

A Mack Truck could barrel through his parents' bedroom, and they wouldn't wake up. Thank G-d for Ambien.

He would have trouble keeping his mouth shut at school the next day, especially around Braden Reilly.

"Schmuck."

What Gordy would have given to tell the dicky red-headed tool bag mama's boy *exactly* what happened to his uncle. Then he'd see how trivial his good looks, his batting average…

…the science fair award he got in the ^h sixth grade that should have been mine…

…and his underserved boost on the PCHS freshman food chain were compared to the power of numbers. Compared to the UJ. Compared to the flaccid penis being reflected on that bus window. It killed Gordy knowing that he had to keep his triumph to himself.

He sat back in his sticky seat.

Maybe I'll try Artie again.

Gordy would, indeed, get his chance to tell everything to Braden Reilly, but the circumstances wouldn't be at all what he dreamed.

20. The Condo

Julie was understandably in bed when Lynch got home. The door clicked behind him as he trudged up the fourteen carpeted steps to his living room. On the end of the dividing wall that faced him when he reached the top, there hung a wood etching of the Irish Blessing:

May the road rise to meet you
May the wind be always at your back
May the sun shine upon your face
May God hold you in the palm of his hand

It had become a part of his environment, like any piece of home décor. He rarely paid it any mind, but a memory was tapped as he absently tossed his coat on the couch and went for his bottle of Chivas.

He gave the etching a hard look as he recalled the day he received it. It was given as a congratulatory gift for passing his Sergeant's Exam…a gift from Kevin Reilly.

He ran his index finger across the piece's surface. It was made from a beautiful piece of cocobolo. The lines in the recessed lettering were smooth and precise. The stain and the finish brought out the contrasts in the grain.

"I wonder…"

He lifted the piece off its nail and flipped it over to see if the maker left a signature or a stamp. What he discovered was a brass plate.

Reilly's Trophy Shop
305 Cherry Street
Potterford, PA

"There's a coincidence, considering tomorrow."

The giving of such a gift must have been a Reilly tradition. Lynch remembered Gomez saying that he'd also received one, except his was etched in Spanish.

The moment was easy to recall:

"The Irish Blessing in Spanish? Isn't that like going to Taco Bell and ordering in Old English?"

"Right, hombre. Me thinks I shall have a Chalupa."

He tried to replace the etching but wound up missing the hole and pushing the nail all the way into the drywall. He was in no mood to screw with it, so he tossed Reilly's gift onto the nearby dining room table. When he did, something on the table caught his attention. It was a promotional poster for the last battle of the bands in Ellisport.

?????

Julie had printed it from Fellowship's website. Publicity photos for all the participating bands were placed willy-nilly around the event info by someone with a rudimentary knowledge of Photoshop. The photo for Generation Us lay in the upper right corner in all its 80's-camp glory. And there was Chaz. He was making a peace sign with one hand and twirling a drumstick with the other. Of the five band members, he was the most svelte. Perhaps girth was their gimmick. Next to the poster was a note written by Julie.

I HAD TO GET A LOOK AT CHAZ.

Lynch smirked and walked around the island to his kitchen. Irish Blessings and promotional posters weren't going to keep him from his scotch any longer.

Per Special Agent Beck's orders, the fibbies would stake out the addresses they had, wait for the respective UJ members to get home, let them sleep off their binge effects just enough to be sober yet vulnerably groggy, and then drag them to the station.

Lynch was off the hook. Beck gave a respectful, no-frills explanation.

"Don't misunderstand me when I say this, Jim. You already brought these guys in once, and you got nothing. If you're in the interview room, they're going to look at you as a guy they beat. It wouldn't matter, except we don't have anything *now* either. We need to approach it from a position of strength, and you, frankly, could hurt us in that regard. Understand?"

"I do, and I'm cool with it."

Cool with it...*relieved* was more like it. He'd get back with Carrie and continue the work on Kevin Reilly's assault. Gomez would be available too. All three of them would go to Ian Reilly's house. It was the big guy's turn to do some tap dancing.

Chivas

Scotch glass.

One ice cube.

Pour until the cube floats.

Done.

He took a sip and closed his eyes as the warmth and tingle went from his lips to his extremities.

I'm telling you, Samuel, if you've jerked me around in any way, I'll find you and kill you myself.

THE BIG RED ONE

Thursday

1. The Condo

Lynch awoke to the sound of his cell phone and the sight of his girlfriend rummaging through his wallet.

"What the hell are you doing?"

"I need cash for tolls. I'm going to Jersey today."

Lynch fumbled for his phone and dropped it on the shag carpet, causing it to bounce under the bed.

"And you expect to find cash in *there*? I thought you had EZPass."

She waved the wallet around demonstratively, while her boyfriend lumbered out of bed and disappeared from sight.

"Why do I need EZPass when I've got you? Who's this?"

Lynch put his hand on his phone, resisting the temptation to fall back to sleep while he was on the floor. He tilted it to see who was calling. The one caveat for being released from FBI gofer duty was he had to keep himself available by phone…always. The caller, however, wasn't Agent Beck. With effort, he stood, although not quite erect.

"I've got to take this, baby. What did you ask me?"

"Who's this?"

She was holding Pastor Devlin's picture of poor Eddie Williams. Lynch had taken it out of his shirt pocket and laid it on their dresser.

"He's my lover…Hello?"

She gave him a severe "idiot" stare and leaned against the dresser without putting the photo away. He mouthed "I'll tell you in a minute," sat on the edge of the bed, and held his conversation with Father Leo.

"You still talking to me, Jim?"

"Of course, Leo. I have a ton of things going on today, but I haven't forgotten that you have a major apology coming your way."

"No apology needed, but I would like a favor if possible."

"Tell me what it is."

"Whatever you're doing this morning, postpone it an hour."

"I can do that. Want me swing by the church?"

"No, not the church."

Julie had gone to the kitchen to make breakfast, but left Eddie's picture prominently displayed on the dresser next to her boyfriend's empty wallet. She was putting her dish and tea cup in the dishwasher when Lynch emerged from the bedroom, fully dressed and gravely concerned about something. She could only assume it had to do with the phone call.

On the way to his coat, he slapped Eddie's photo on the dining room table.

"That's Eddie Williams, the guy Chaz tackled. I've got to go."

He grabbed his coat and went to give his girlfriend a kiss goodbye. Before he was able to pucker up, she burst into laughter.

"I don't have time for this, babe. What's funny?"

"Well, c'mon. Are you kidding me?"

She strode over to the dining room table, picked up Eddie's picture along with the promotional poster for the Christian rock concert, and held them side-by-side. She referred to the photo of Generation Us first.

"You mean to tell me *these* guys…caught up with and tackled…*this* guy? You buy that? He looks like a track star; they look like five marshmallows."

Lynch shook his head, looked at his watch, and backed toward the stairs.

"That's Eddie's 'before' picture. He was wigged out on meth that night. I'll show you the mug shot some other time."

He blew a kiss from the top step and trotted down. She flipped both pictures around to take a second look. She looked at one, then the other, and back again. When she heard the deadbolt turn, and the door open, she shouted.

"Okay, but still!"

2. PCHS

The teachers' lounge at Potterford Central High School was comfy (as teachers' lounges go). It was thirty minutes before homeroom, and the "A" seats by the water cooler were occupied by two well-liked ninth grade math teachers.

One of them got up to get coffee.

"Can you check my attendance while you're over there?"

"How long have you been waiting for me to stand up, asshole?"

227

The attendance office posted absences on the school's internal network, and there was only one computer in the lounge.

"Looks like you've got three out today: Jenny Weaver, Frank Barbera, and…that's weird…Braden Reilly."

"Why weird? He's been out most of the week."

"I thought I saw him this morning as I was driving in."

"Really? Where?"

"Walking across the baseball field. I must have been mistaken. Whoops…hello."

A "ding" came through the computer's external speakers. An urgent instant message was being sent to all the terminals by the administration.

"What's going on?"

"Damn! Gordon Weiss is being picked up by his parents. If I'm reading this right…"

"Reading this *correctly*…"

"(middle finger) …if I'm reading this *correctly*, Gordy got the shit kicked out of him, but he won't say who did it. I guess we're supposed to ask around."

"Ouch. Who would have it in for Gordy?"

"No idea."

3. St. Helena's

It was Lynch's first time in a convent. The little of it he noticed as he powerwalked through the entryway was a stone's throw from medieval. There was a single phone for common use that may as well have had a crank. He got a brief accidental look inside the only first floor bathroom and saw a pull-chain on the toilet.

And no one ever complains, I'll bet.

The doctor from Mercy Fitzgerald was waiting for him in the parlor.

"Did Father Pascucci fill you in, detective?"

"Briefly."

"She's sitting quietly in the Convent Chapel now. Physically, she's fine. She has some bruises and scrapes, but she wasn't violated…sexually anyway."

Lynch was becoming accustomed to the mix of relief and frustration that accompanied his dealings with Father Leo.

"That would have been nice to know up front. All he told me was she'd been kidnapped and assaulted."

"I think he called you before I was done."

"He could have called back."

All three St. Aloysius priests and the Mother Superior were outside the chapel. Pastor Karney took a step forward, but Lynch put up a hand to stop him. He didn't want to hear anyone's version of anything before he talked to the victim herself.

Leo spoke.

"She's expecting you."

The chapel door creaked open, revealing an elegant tabernacle and ten rows of pews. Sitting in the front pew was Sister Edwina. She was just as Father O'Rourke had described.

Her chance encounter with Bubbs outside the Iron Wall, and Lynch's open-door mistake at the police station, made her a target. Arthur exploited what Bubbs told him about "the hot nun" and what Gordy overheard at the PPD in order to indulge a sick fantasy, a fantasy that went mercifully unfulfilled.

Gregorian Chant on vinyl droned quietly in the background as Lynch made his way down the aisle and slid onto the pew.

He'd prepared only one sentence.

"Take your time, Sister. We've got as long as you need."

She spoke with precision, leaving space at every cadence.

"He called the convent a little after 9:00. He asked for me specifically. He spoke in a whisper; he said he had a cold…stupid. Then he said someone had donated some mums, and he needed help getting them out of his car…ludicrous. We never keep the flowers here. It's easy to see that now, but at the time, I was taken by the idea that a respected member of the Catholic community wanted *my* help…so stupid. I didn't even notice it wasn't his car."

She ridiculed herself with a laugh.

"So, I walked through the *unsecured* parking lot *alone*, and I saw who I assumed to be Father O'Rourke digging something out of his back seat. He was bent over, so I only saw his backside. He had on the vestments, although, in hindsight I suppose it could have been a long black coat."

Lynch felt a guttural wail halt in his chest.

"When I got close, two gorilla arms wrapped around my neck and choked me out."

She pulled the neck of her habit aside. Lynch winced at the bruising.

You may get your wish Samuel.

229

"When I came around, I was in the back seat of the car, and it was moving. I had a cloth around my eyes, tape over my mouth, and I think some sound-cancelling head gear.

"I was between two of them getting groped. My hands were tied in front of me, so I fought back as much as I could…pointless. I'd like to tell you how long we rode around, but I don't know. When we finally stopped, I was pulled out of the car and led through some grass…then some gravel…then two flights of stairs. Then they dragged me across a floor and threw me onto a couch. There was someone sitting next to me. I think it was a woman. Her touch was soft, and she had on some wretched perfume. I got the feeling that whatever was going to happen…she was going to get the first crack."

"How did you get away?"

She crossed herself.

"An angel rescued me."

Lynch wasn't sure how to react.

"Forgive me, Sister. You understand I can't put that in a report."

"I do…"

She touched his leg as if to pity him for not believing that God took part in her escape.

"…a strong pair of hands suddenly pulled me from the couch and led me back down the stairs. He took the gear off my head and prompted me into the back seat of his car. Again, I don't know how long we rode."

Her eyes started to tear.

"The next thing I knew, I was being put on solid ground. He took off the blindfold and whispered, 'keep your eyes closed and walk forward,' so I did. When I heard the car peel away, I looked up and saw I was home. That's it."

Lynch fought back his own tears and put his hand on top of hers.

"You kicked ass, Edwina."

She sniffled. Then her face changed.

"He spoke to me."

"Yes, you said, when he dropped you off at the convent."

"No, he *whispered* to me at the convent. He *spoke* to me in the car. The motor was loud. I couldn't distinguish anything in his voice, but I could tell what he said. I was confused by it. He said 'You missed me bitch.'"

The phrase echoed in Lynch's distant memory somewhere.

"Was that all?"

"That's all he *said*, but when he took off my blindfold, I felt something heavy, like a bracelet, fall here."

She pointed to her left shoulder.

And he was behind her. Left wrist. Got it.

"Detective, promise me one thing. If this goes to trial...I mean, if the whole gang is arrested, please find out who this man was. Then put me on the witness stand. I want to speak on his behalf."

The UJ would pay for this. "You hit me, so I hit you," is one thing, but this was a pure innocent who, months ago, happened to plant some flowers near one of their hang-outs. The bastards were being corralled at that very moment, courtesy of Special Agent Beck.

Edwina's choker was undoubtedly Bubbs, O'Rourke's imposter was probably Arthur. Traci was the woman on the couch.

He started to put together what he knew about UJ painting parties and had a thought.

"Sister, this is extremely important. If you were where I think you were, there would have been a third woman: you, the woman on the couch, and a third. Did you get the sense at any point that there was someone else there against her will?"

Edwina dug as deeply as she could. She'd spent the last eight hours looking forward to putting the event out of her head, but now there was the possibility of a second victim, a victim probably less lucky than she.

"I don't know, maybe. While I was sitting on the couch, I felt something fall directly in front of me. I suppose it could have been a body. And when I was pulled off the couch, I may have I heard a woman scream. It was hard to tell. The music...the things on my ears. I can't be sure..."

He wanted to give her a hug. He wanted to take her out for coffee.

"Please, detective, just promise me I can speak on the man's behalf."

It was a promise he couldn't make. Whoever saved her left another woman on the floor screaming. Still...

"I'll try."

The peal of church bells reminded him that he had to meet Warner and Gomez at the station for a very important ride across town.

"I'm going to call a uniform and have them take your official statement. You won't need to tell the story again; just write it down."

He pictured Karney, Leo, O'Rourke, and the Mother Superior with their ears pressed against the chapel door. He leaned forward and spoke in a whisper.

"One more thing...do everything you can to stay away from those clowns outside."

And Detective Lynch got his hug.

"You missed me, bitch!" Exactly what the hell could that possibly mean?

231

4. The Station

Rick had an intense hatred for cops. His teenage experiences with police brutality left him a perfect candidate for Arthur's elite. He'd been convinced by Arthur that there was safety in numbers, and nothing shuts down a cop faster than a corroborated alibi. Arthur offered him an entire crew willing to fall on a sword if it meant doing the Potterford PD up the ass.

Rick was fine with the plan to waste Reilly. He was fine with anything Arthur had in store for any member of the Reilly family. If you shared blood with a cop, if you shared a bed with a cop, then you were a cop. That's how deeply his hatred ran. The only thing worse than a cop was a Fed.

"Hello, Rick. I'm Special Agent Beck. I'm with the FBI."

Two hours had passed since the jag-offs pounded on his door and hauled him into town. Déjà-fuckin'-vu. He was in that very room sitting at that very table Saturday night and walked away without giving the police shit. He intended to do the very same before his twenty-four hours of non-charged custody were up. He would admit to nothing. He would roll over on no one, not even Arthur, who was all but dead to him.

They were using every lame trick in the book to break him. He was to be questioned about crimes relating to the death of Bishop Ryan. That is all he was told, yet he'd been sitting in an empty room for almost two hours and hadn't been asked a single question. Every time he dozed off, a pinhead in a blue suit stormed in with a cup of coffee. It was a different pinhead each time to give the impression that the station kept forgetting he was in there. Each pinhead said the same thing.

"Just finishing up in another room. Shouldn't be long. What's your name again?"

He was being watched, and they had no interest in keeping him awake. The coffee was disgusting but not so much that Rick was fooled. He knew decaf when he tasted it. They wanted him groggy and needing a piss.

Now Special Agent Beck was sitting across from him with a legal pad and a bottle of water. Rick figured it was just a matter of time before the air conditioning inexplicably konked out.

"Rick, I won't keep you longer than necessary. The locals are at sort of a standstill with this Ryan thing, especially now that Archbishop Fellini has probably been killed by the same person. They've called us in to help, so we're just following up on a few things. You know…these guys miss things from time to time."

"Yes, Special Agent Beck. I'm sure they drive you nuts. You and I are on the same side. Go team."

She was genuinely amused.

"What do you do for a living, Rick?"

"If you found where I live, then you know where I work."

That was all Agent Beck needed for now. This boy needed to be taught the penalty for being glib with the FBI. She took a sip of water, which was the signal for her to be interrupted. In seconds, a man with rolled up sleeves and a loosened tie popped his head in the room.

"Special Agent Beck, we've got something in the next room."

"Thank you, Henry. Hold tight Rick. I'll be right back."

As she walked out, pinhead number seven walked in with another cup of coffee.

"Oh, for the love of…"

All this pretense and game playing over a murder that had nothing to do with him? They must have been setting him up for something else. Reilly's injury, the painting party, there were so many loose ends all around.

He went through his list again. He wouldn't have to worry about any serious charges regarding the kidnappings. He took part in neither (quite the opposite). Fingerprints and DNA at the junkyard weren't a concern. They were all very careful to wear gloves. There could have been some hair flying, some blood maybe, but finding it uncontaminated amidst all that garbage…unlikely. None of it would hold up anywhere. The whole thing relied on eye witnesses. Ian Reilly wasn't coming forward. He was in just as deep as the UJ at this point. The sanctimonious black guys from the rumble? If any of them had spoken up, Rick's apartment door would have been broken down with a battering ram.

Maybe he slipped up with the nun.

No, I was careful.

Heroism was uncharted territory for him, but those bastards forcibly brought a nun to a painting party… a NUN! It seemed like a strange place

233

to draw the line, considering he was perfectly willing to take part in the brutal murder of a policeman, but he had his reasons.

All members of the UJ were guarded when it came to their personal lives. Rick had plenty of secrets, not at the bottom of the list was his favorite aunt…Sister Catherine of the Holy Trinity in Dover Delaware. He hadn't spoken to her for a while.

I should call her.

He considered his surroundings.

Maybe tomorrow.

5. The Emergency Room at PMMC

"Mom, I'm fine. I had a fight. Kids get into fights. It happens every day. Stop touching me mom!"

The Weiss's were in the hospital emergency ward six floors down from Kevin Reilly. The doctor had just finished up with Gordy and was one-handedly typing something into a tablet. Mrs. Weiss had requested a pediatrician but had to settle for one of Southeastern Pennsylvania's finest emergency room specialists.

"I'm going to have your son sent for x-rays just as a precaution, but I doubt they'll find anything. Whoever did this knew how to administer pain without causing any permanent damage."

Mrs. Weiss wasn't buying it.

"That's ridiculous! Something's broken. I know it!"

"Mom!"

"No really, Mrs. Weiss. Trust me. I've seen this before. Now, the nurse will be in soon to take him to radiology. In the meantime, here's a prescription for painkillers and the name of a top-notch counselor who specializes in teen trauma if Gordy needs…"

"I don't"

Gordy didn't care about his superficial injuries, or trauma therapy, or even lovely, lovely painkillers. Braden Reilly had broken him. He recalled what the punk Irish mama's boy screamed at him while he was delivering the beating.

"Where are they!!? Where's the UJ Gordy!!? Who are you more afraid of right now!!? What could they do to you that's more painful than this!!? You Freak!!"

What worse could the UJ do? Physically, nothing, and that's all that mattered to Gordy as Braden's knee grinded into his spine, while both arms were being pulled back to the point where it felt like his shoulders were about to separate. He could have lied. He could have given Braden any location in Montgomery County, but his lie construction process was too complicated, and his brain froze, causing him to blurt out the truth.

What worse could the UJ do? They could kick him out. His life would mean nothing. He'd spend his days riding around town on his lame-ass bike avoiding anyone in a black trench coat, only to return to his shitty life with his shitty parents. Braden had probably already gone to his dad. His dad would go to the cops. The cops would go to the cloister, and it would all come back to Gordy. He couldn't lie to Braden, but he would have to lie to Arthur. It would need to be one of his genius lies, which meant his starting point would be the truth.

And the truth was he was a pussy.

5. The Woods

"Pow – ping!"

Philip needed to think.
"How the hell am I going to pull this off?
He'd gotten away with superficial disguises up to this point, but those days were over. In order for the next great act to work, he'd have to impersonate a priest.
"It won't be enough to look like one. I'll need to actually *be* one. We're talking identity theft here. Now, who do I know that dabbles in identity theft?"

"Pow – ping!"

This one was risky. Executed perfectly, his new target would share the fate of the previous two. Executed less than perfectly, perhaps a dozen innocent bystanders would be killed as well. There was also no option to

235

pull out. "Maybe next time" wasn't going to fly. Once in motion, the plan would go to the end.

"I'll need the key. How do I get the key? I doubt Karney keeps it on a hook in his mud room."

"Pow – ping!"

He had two days.

6. Outside the Reillys' House

Ian and Molly Reilly's house was a red brick Cape Cod nestled in a neighborhood less than a mile from Braden's school. Lynch pulled up to the curb right behind Warner and Gomez. All three of them dismounted, closing their doors with a cluster of slams.

"Been waiting long?"

"Five minutes tops, acho. You ready?"

"Beyond words."

The driveway wound around the house to the back yard and the garage. The detectives were relieved to see the front bumper of Ian's truck peeking around the side. They were hoping he was home. They didn't want to have to deal with his rotundity at the hospital if things got ugly.

They ascended the porch stairs and slapped on some smiles as Gomez rang the bell. The door was answered by someone they did not expect. Carrie, the only one who recognized the woman, spoke.

"June! I didn't expect you to be here. We didn't get an update on Kevin today. I hope nothing took a turn…"

The elderly Irish mother of four looked as if she'd been without sleep for weeks.

"Oh no, Carrie, no. Bless your heart. Please, all of you, come in."

Mint tea.

The house was wall-to-wall, floor-to-ceiling, rank with mint tea. Lynch and Gomez suppressed their gag reflexes while Mrs. Reilly shuffled to the source.

"I'm not going to visit Kevin 'til later. Molly is sick, and Ian wants to take Braden to the baseball field for some hitting practice. It'll be good for them. The two of them went at it pretty loudly yesterday at the hospital.

As long as I was here, I figured I'd whip up a batch of the ol' Fowler Brew. All my kids drink it like water."

Lynch exhaled forcefully. He tried to pass it off as a cough, but there was no disguising the sound of a man reaching his breath-holding threshold. June Reilly snickered.

"That's alright, detective. The recipe has been in my family as long as anyone can remember, and it's been an acquired taste for just as long."

He collected himself.

"We were hoping to speak to Ian. Is he here?"

"*Three* of you want to talk to my son? Must be serious."

"Not really. It's just some time has passed since Kevin got hurt, and we were hoping…"

"If that's all you wanted to talk to him about, there would be no need for three of you. My other son's a copper, Detective Lynch. I know a few things."

I bet you do.

Gomez came to the rescue.

"Ma'am, the Feds have taken over Bishop Ryan's murder, which means Jim and I are free to help Carrie close your son's case. We, quite literally…and I mean this in the best way possible…have nothing better to do."

Mrs. Reilly leaned against her daughter-in-law's kitchen counter, shifting her gaze between her two male visitors. Her facial expression was one only a mother could summon. She sucked her teeth twice with a thoughtful little kissing sound before settling her eyes on Gomez. She uncurled a pale freckled index finger and pointed at him as if a decision of epic proportion had been made.

"You're my favorite."

That done, the kind matriarch stoically returned her attention to the Fowler Brew, poured herself a cup, and spoke with her back turned.

"He's out back."

The three detectives thanked her and headed for the door that led to the patio. On the way, Carrie pulled Ernie aside and mouthed two instructions.

"Stay with her. Don't let her look out the window."

He silently agreed and strode to a hutch in the living room.

"You know, Mrs. Reilly, you're my favorite too."

Lynch walked out and held the door for Carrie. Ernie's voice faded as the door was brought to a slow close by its hydraulic arm.

"You're right, abuela. All three of us don't need to be out there. Now tell me about the kids in these pictures over here..."

Ian was standing in the bed of his black pick-up, messing with a canvas bag that closed with a pullcord. He looked up and exasperatedly shook his head.

"Well...top o' the mornin' to you, detectives. Come to offer your best wishes for my brother's speedy recovery, have you?"

Something was off. His eyes were crazed. His breathing was irregular. His voice was jumping octaves uncontrollably. Carrie did the talking. This was her case.

"Your mother caught us up."

"Yeah, so...you know then...nothing new. Good, depending on how you...look at it, I guess."

"How 'bout you come down here and talk to us for a minute."

"Why would I do that? ...I mean...Why would you...I'm taking my boy out to the field. Things have been rough. We've got to blow off some steam, or at least get our mind...uh...minds off of...things."

"We'd still feel better if you came down here."

"I'll stay up here, thanks. What do you want?"

A 250-pound angry Reilly with the high ground...not a good thing.

"We feel like we're closing in on what happened to your brother, and we want to go over your story with you one more time."

"Why do you want to do that? It's all in the...whatchacallit...the report you took."

He gestured toward Carrie with an unsteady arm.

"You questioned me already. Nothing's changed. Would you get out of here? I mean...I'm sorry. Please leave. My wife is sick, and my boy needs batting practice."

"I'm afraid we can't do that. We have some new..."

"I'm trying to be nice. Just go. I'm not talking to you right now, and you can't make me."

Oh yes, they could. Lynch stepped up next to the truck. Between inappropriately grilling men of the cloth, running errands for the FBI, and being a day late and a dollar short in the assassination of an Archbishop,

238

he'd been mulling over his conversation with Samuel. He'd been sold on the theory that the UJ was at war with someone. Who that was depended on the answer to one question: Whom did Kevin Reilly call after he talked to Father O'Rourke? Not surprisingly, his regular phone records yielded nothing. By his brother's or his own doing, the burner he used for his extracurricular activities had undoubtedly been deep in a landfill since Monday.

Ian was holding back to protect his brother, himself, or both. There wasn't a doubt in Lynch's mind. Carrie agreed. They'd be damned if they were going to leave the Reilly residence without getting at least a half an inch closer to the truth.

Lynch stood flat-footed on the recently sealed asphalt, looking up at Ian. Carrie didn't need his help otherwise.

"Where is your son?"

"He's in his room. He has been all morning."

"Does he know he's going to the field? Have you talked to him about this? Shouldn't he be helping you load?"

"He knows. He knows. He overslept like he always does. Kid would sleep all day if I let him."

Lynch would stay silent unless, in the course of their visit, he spotted treasure. If he, somehow, deduced some slam-dunk bit of evidence that would break Ian Reilly, then he would speak…only then.

To that end, he listened intently to Carrie's interrogation pitting Ian's answers against the facts, the conjecture, and the unknown of the case.

The facts:
Bishop Ryan is killed.
Leo is shown a surveillance video of the murderer.
Leo recognizes the symbol on the back of the jacket.
Leo tells the other priests at St. Al's.
Reilly finds out about the murder.
Reilly tracks down Father O'Rourke.
O'Rourke tells Reilly about the UJ and where to find them.
Reilly makes a call.
Jeremy gets attacked by three men.
The men are masked; one has an orange bat.
Kevin Reilly has an alibi for the beating.

In the hospital, Jeremy freaks out when he sees Reilly.

Jeremy dies from his injuries.

The Reilly brothers chase Gordy into the junkyard of the Potterford Industrial Complex, stumble upon a gang fight.

Kevin Reilly is badly injured.

Bubbs' motorcycle gets dumped in Pickering creek.

The conjecture:

Reilly's phone call triggered a war between the UJ and someone else.

The UJ was one of the gangs in the junkyard.

The UJ's enemy dumped the Harley.

The unknown:

Who is the UJ at war *with*?

Who was the other gang in the junkyard?

Why did Jeremy freak out when he couldn't have identified Reilly?

Who...in the hell...did Reilly call?

"Ma'am and sir, I really don't have time..."

"We know your brother made a call the night Jeremy Sokol was attacked. Was it to you?"

"No!"

Sooo many lowlifes, some of them violent, owed favors to Kevin Reilly. If it was one of them, it might explain who jumped the UJ in the scrap yard.

Then again, it could just as easily have been someone he trusted, rather than someone he owned. That would mean family. That would mean Ian.

"We know the attackers drove to the barn in a truck like yours."

"Look down this street! Every third person in Potterford owns a truck like mine!"

If Ian had any other last name, they could pummel with accusations just to see what stuck, but he was a Reilly. The cops loved the Reillys. The local judges loved the Reillys. The Potterford Herald loved the Reillys. If they were going to pummel, they'd need a solid starting point. They'd need treasure. They'd need that all-important slam-dunk that Lynch was waiting for.

"Take it easy. Just wanted to make sure it was in your driveway that entire evening."

"It was."

"Didn't loan it to anyone?"

"No."

Plus, there was the ICU conundrum. No matter *who* did it, Jeremy couldn't have identified them, so why did the sight of Kevin Reilly make his vitals go haywire?

"Again, as I understand things, a low-ranking member of the Unjudged gets you to chase him to the Industrial Complex. You see his bicycle on the ground outside the junkyard. You figure he went in there, so you follow him and witness a gang fight?"

"For the third time, yes."

Carrie's interrogation strategy was a standard one: a commonly used lawyer trick. She'd ask him a bunch of questions. She'd work in a bunch of giftwrapped "outs." Then she'd go back to the top and ask them all again with different wording, hoping to catch him in a lie.

"And you didn't recognize anyone in either gang?"

"For the third time, no."

"Man, that's weird. Busy night for gangs."

It wasn't working. As strange as Ian was acting, he wasn't struggling with his answers. Either he was telling the truth, or he'd rehearsed his story so many times that, to him, the lies *seemed* like the truth.

"We heard you and your boy had a little fracas yesterday. I'm sorry to hear that. It's probably the last thing you needed."

"Yeah, well, we're Irish. Emotions run high."

Who did Reilly call? Why did Jeremy Freak?

The facts:

Bishop Ryan is killed.

Leo is shown a surveillance video of the murderer.

Leo recognizes the symbol on the back of the jacket.

Leo tells the other...

Whew!

On top of everything else, Lynch couldn't get the smell of Fowler Brew out of his nostrils.

Then he realized…

Oh my God.

…it wasn't in his nostrils.

Treasure…Slam dunk.

Warner had started repeating her questions.

"I just think it's a freaky coincidence that you and your brother just happened upon the UJ in the junk yard. Don't you?"

"I never said it was the UJ. I don't know…"

"Detective Warner, may I interject something?"

Carrie's eyes brightened as she looked upon the face of her companion to discover a Cheshire Cat grin. *Fuckin' A* he could interject. She motioned for him to proceed, then stood back to watch and enjoy.

Lynch spoke.

"Your brother told you what happened when he visited Jeremy Sokol in the ICU, right?"

"He mentioned…"

"But you blew it off because you knew he couldn't have identified any of you."

"What do you mean 'any of *us*?'"

"Yeah, it was a real puzzler. I was ready to blow it off myself as a coincidence. But I just realized something."

"Oh, did you, now?"

"The masks don't figure into it. Jeremy didn't think he *saw* one of his attackers in the ICU. Jeremy … thought he *smelled* him."

Ian threw back his head and cackled.

"You've lost your mind, copper."

"By your mother's own words, all of you drink the Fowler Brew like water. You all smell like it too, especially when you sweat. Right, Sergeant Warner?"

"Dear God, yes."

"He smelled it on your brother at the hospital; he smelled it on you at the barn."

Ian used his t-shirt collar to wipe his upper lip, while he tried to remember the term "admissible evidence."

"You call that monkey shit admissible evidence?"

"No, but I'm going to make a guess...several guesses actually, and you don't need to confirm any of them, so please just listen. I'm not even going to tell you where the guesses came from. We've got witnesses and revelation. That's all you need to know.

"I'm guessing, Mr. Reilly, that in that canvas bag that you are *not* packing for your son's batting practice, there is an orange softball bat. I'm also guessing that, while your brother would have been smart enough to scrub that bat down after using it to beat a man to death, you were not. I'm also guessing that sending said bat to the lab would reveal all sorts of blood evidence and DNA from Jeremy Sokol.

"Right now, you are packing up for another bludgeoning. I don't know if you're going by yourself, but that's where you're going. That means the UJ got back at you for dumping Bubb's bike into Pickering Creek. What'd they do Ian?"

The oaf fumed. His words left his mouth like dragon's breath.

"You know goddam as well as me that you aren't getting your hands on this bag or anything inside it, without a warrant. And there ain't a single judge in town that will issue a warrant against a Reilly on what you got."

"We can if it's evidence."

"What the shite are you talking about?"

"Well...let's say you suddenly pulled the bat out of the bag, took a swing at me, and then used it to go after Detective Warner. Then we could do whatever we wanted with it."

Ian laughed.

"Yes, you could, but I'm not going to do that."

As much as I'd like to.

Lynch gave an ironically cheerful reply.

"Sure, you are."

The veins in Ian's forearms protruded as he realized what was going on.

"Like hell you bastards!"

Warner chimed in.

"According to you, your son's asleep, and I can personally guarantee that about now your mother wishes she could adopt Detective Gomez. There's no one looking. If you shout, we can have you in cuffs before anyone takes interest. Basically, your best course of action right now is to come quietly and spill your guts at the station."

Ian stared back at her with murder in his eyes.

"Oh Ian, knock it off. Don't look at me like that. We're working straight out of your brother's playbook and you know it."

Later, at the station when Ian was questioned as to what happened next, his reply was "They were going to accuse me of it anyway, so I figured what the hell?"

With surprisingly fast reflexes for a man his size, Ian kicked up the canvas bag and grabbed the end of the first bat that poked out of the end. As fate's colossal joke, it was the orange one. Lynch immediately put a bead on him with his .38. Carrie did the same.

"Hey, hey, hey, Ian! Calm down!"

June Reilly's middle son was a fast thinker, but not a terribly efficient one. In his mind, the best he could do was get between the two detectives. They wouldn't risk friendly fire. One or both of them would drop their guns in the confusion, and maybe he could club one and take the other hostage long enough for him to get out of town, hold up somewhere, and think. He was a Reilly. Someone would bail him out.

The problem, simply put, was in order for his brilliant plan to work, his 250-pound ass had to run and jump. He took a running step toward the truck's gate, putting pressure on his heavy-duty shock absorbers, essentially turning the vehicle into diving board with wheels.

On his second step, the open gate bounced up catching him off balance just long enough for Lynch to reach around the corner of the truck and grab an ankle.

Ian took a header into his new drive way. The bat went flying into the grass as his hands hit the surface, softening the crash. He lay on his belly, stunned. The two detectives shared a satisfied nod and re-holstered their pistols.

Just then, the back door to the house opened.

"Ian, my boy! What did they do to you!?"

Both detectives took their eyes off of their perp just long enough to regard the furious woman at the top of the granite steps.

Thanks, mom.

The interruption was just what Ian needed to get to his feet and lunge for Carrie. Lynch reached for his gun, but there was no need. Carrie knew whcrc that spot was on the jaw that turned out a guy's lights. As fast as Ian Reilly was up, he was down.

Lynch took out his cuffs and went for the butt-crack showing mass before him, while Carrie tried to console his mother.

"I'm sorry, June. We had no choice. He came at us with a bat."

The matriarch was about to start screaming and wagging her freckly finger, when a deep Puerto Rican voice sounded behind her.

"Think about it. Think about what you know about your son. Think about what you know about Carrie. You can do what you want, but I know who *I* believe."

7. A Chat Room

Philip, (Screen name: MonkeyOnABike) and BOYBANDH8R had not met in person, otherwise the anonymous, private chat room conversation would never have taken place.

MonkeyOnABike: Sup?

BOYBANDH8R: Sup?

MonkeyOnABike: You never got back to me last week. How'd the upgrade go?

BOYBANDH8R: Pain in the ass just like you said, but the specs you gave me def helped. Thx.

MonkeyOnABike: Nice!

BOYBANDH8R: Yep.

A noticeable lull.

BOYBANDH8R: Still There?

MonkeyOnABike: I am. Remember the night you were waiting for CAD Drawings from Vegas. and I was waiting for an email from my idiot boss? We bullshat until four in the morning to keep each other awake.

BOYBANDH8R: Sure.

MonkeyOnABike: Remember that thing we talked about?

BOYBANDH8R: We talked about a lot of things. Which thing do you mean?

MonkeyOnABike: The thing you said was expensive.

BOYBANDH8R: ?

MonkeyOnABike: The guy you said you knew.

BOYBANDH8R: ???

MonkeyOnABike: I think you said his day job was sculpting.

Another lull.

BOYBANDH8R: Oh! Him! Not sculpting, engraving. He's a digital engraver.

MonkeyOnABike: Were you serious about the other thing you said he did, or were you just trying to keep the convo interesting?

BOYBANDH8R: I was serious.

MonkeyOnABike: Then I have a question.

BOYBANDH8R: Shoot.

MonkeyOnABike: How expensive?

8. Outside the Reillys' House

Gomez gave a little wave as he watched the squad car disappear around the bend. Ian Reilly was in the back seat. His bulbous head and red buzz cut were visible from two blocks away. Victory removed, the five minutes it took for the uniforms to arrive were not pleasant. Lynch and Warner cuffed Ian's hands and feet and kept him in the garage in case Braden looked out his bedroom window. The boy was about to go through enough without seeing his father in chains. They sat in silence. Gomez had taken June Reilly aside and asked her to let Molly and Braden know what was going on. No one had emerged from the house since. When the black and white arrived, Ian stood with all the dignity he could manage and shuffled toward it with humiliating assistance from his captors. All he said was "keep your hands off my head."

Once their perp was safely seated with all four limbs cuffed to the floor, Lynch and Carrie headed for the station. Carrie drove. Gomez stayed behind with Lynch's keys.

"Make sure the family is okay. Alright. Ernie?"

"Don't worry partner. I got this."

Gomez knocked on the front door, but there was no answer. He poked his head in.

"Abuela?"

Still no answer. He entered.

Finding no master bedroom on the first floor, he walked up the stairs and, as he hoped, heard June's voice coming from beyond a set of closed double doors at the end of the hall. He approached, knocked gently, and spoke.

"Molly? I'd like to talk to your son. I'm not questioning him. I just want to see how he's doing. But I need your permission."

After some unintelligible whispers, it was June that replied.

"Go ahead, Ernie. It's the one on the end."

The walk took him past Sian's room. The door was open, revealing a collection of Maroon 5 posters and Northwestern University swag.

247

She's going to find out about this over the phone…damn.

Braden's door was closed.

Is that kid still asleep?

"Hey, Buddy. It's Detective Gomez. I work with your uncle. Can I come in?"

No answer.

"I'm going to open the door, okay? If you want me to go away, just say so. You hear me, amigo?"

The door slowly creaked open. Braden was not in his room.

"I'm not liking this."

The boy had left in a hurry, too much of a hurry to turn off his computer, and too much of a hurry to close a foot locker he normally kept under his bed. It had been concealed by a ten-wide stack of (probably his parents') DVD's that now lay scattered.

"Not one bit."

Jewel cases cracked as Gomez crept towards the trunk. sensing that he would discover nothing good inside.

His blood turned to ice as his line of sight cleared the rim.

"Madre Dulce de Dios."

Powders. Wires. Casings. He was no expert, but he knew the ingredients of a bomb when he saw them.

He pulled out his cell phone and jogged down the hall, nearly side-arming Sian's graduation picture off the wall in the process. He skidded to a stop at the double doors, eased the left one open six inched, and spoke as calmly and controlled as he could.

"Ma'am…"

In the space, he made eye contact with Molly Reilly. She was on her bed. She'd been crying. She would have known about her husband's arrest for only fifteen or twenty minutes. She'd been crying much longer than that. She was in the fetal position with her comforter clutched against her chin so tightly that her feet poked out at the bottom. They were crossed…clenched tightly, and she still had her shoes on. She looked at him pleadingly as if she wanted to tell him something that she couldn't bear to tell her mother-in-law. The detective's heart sank. He knew the body language. He knew the face. He'd seen it so many times before, on the job, and in his old neighborhood.

Molly Reilly wasn't sick.

Molly Reilly had been, at best, attacked; at worst, raped.

9. A Police Cruiser

Ian stared beyond the backs of his chaperones' heads to the asphalt rushing beneath the car. The car smelled new.

"Truesdell, right? Officer Truesdell?"

"Yes sir."

"And you...Brian something. I forget your last name."

"Simon, Mr. Reilly. My last name is Simon."

A short burst of puerile laughter shot from Ian's diaphragm.

"Tell me, Kelly, or Brian. I don't really care. Is this car new?"

Kelly answered.

"It is, sir. Few months old."

"Ah...so this is where my taxes are going. My brother, who is *supposed* to be your brother too, is in a coma. The people who put him there are running around scot free. Meanwhile, I'm arrested and being driven to jail by a woman and a Jew in a car that I paid for. Love it."

Brian answered.

"Not jail, Mr. Reilly, just the police station."

"Are you even supposed to be working? Isn't this the Sabbath or Sabbat or whatever the fuck? Shouldn't you have your nose buried in a book you can't even read with a beanie on your head?"

"Not quite. A couple of hours yet. But somehow..."

He turned to face his sardonically grinning passenger with a grin of his own.

"...this doesn't feel like work."

Kelly happily contributed to the discourse with a snicker made inaudible by the gratifying sound of chains jerking against their restraints. Temper, temper.

Then, the radio.

"P12, this is Detective Lynch. Kelly, you there?"

Brian answered.

249

"We got you, Jim, What's up?"

"Pull over."

"Come again, detective?"

"Wherever you are, pull over. We'll be there in thirty seconds. When you see us park, unlock your back doors, both of them."

Brian looked over at Kelly, who could offer nothing but a shrug as she put on the flashing lights and turned the wheel to the right.

The car shifted and bounced as the back doors were yanked open and detectives Lynch and Warner leapt in, landing on either side of Ian Reilly. Warner asked the question.

"Does your son know what happened to his mother!?"

Ian turned beet red but said nothing.

"Quit fuckin' around, Ian! Did you tell your son what happened to his mother!?"

"Why don't you ask…"

Lynch's fist met Ian Reilly's ribs. The big guy wheezed and hollered to the uniforms.

"Are you guys watching this?"

"I'm just a stupid girl."

"Sorry…Sabbath…Baruch atah Adonai…"

Warner put an open hand to Ian's face to regain his attention. Knowing what they knew, she and Lynch probably owed their perp a little sympathy, but there was a bomb in Potterford. Going in soft would have been a slow strategy. At the moment, slow was not a part of their universe.

"Now listen, Reilly. It appears that your well-adjusted teenaged son made a bomb. We don't know what kind, or what he intends to do with it. There's a good chance he's going to try to hit the UJ *if* he knows what happened to his mother. If we confirm that, we can put all our resources on one path. If we don't, we'll have to split things up, and there's a better chance he'll be successful. If that bomb goes off, it will be considered an act of terrorism, and I don't have to tell you what happens next. He's only fourteen. It won't be Guantanamo Bay, but it will be pretty damned close!"

Warner couldn't be sure, but in recollection, she swore she saw a smirk on Ian Reilly's face as if to say "atta boy." He wasn't budging.

Lynch tried to think like Gomez. What was the one thing that would hit home with this sled head? Putting his mind on his partner took him back to the arrest. The Reilly house. June Reilly, the matriarch.

She'll have one son in the hospital. She'll have another son and her only grandson in jail. They're dropping off like…

He was driven where he needed to go. He spoke as if musing.
"The line ends with him, doesn't it…?"
Ian's breathing stopped.
"…probably anyway. Your sister has two daughters. Your younger brother is on the road 300 days a year. He's not starting a family. Who knows what kind of permanent damage Kevin has suffered, and your wife may never have sex with you again after last night."
The detective leaned in and lowered his voice.
"Braden's it."
Ian met eyes with Lynch, then slowly turned and shot the same daggers at Carrie. She leaned in and ran with the perfect pass she'd been thrown.
"Easy, Reilly. I'm trying to stop the boy. Right now, you're a hero. No matter how much time you do, you'll be regarded as a saint by your family. When word gets out what happened, the town will forgive you within twenty-four hours.
"But…if Braden succeeds, well, then you're the father of a terrorist. The story will get national coverage. He goes away, basically forever. There isn't a woman in the world that will go near him unless she has a fetish for felons. I, personally, wouldn't trust those genes. Would you?"
The car purred. Warner went back to the top.
"Did you…tell your son…what happened to his mother?"
Something dripped down Ian's cheek. Perhaps a tear; perhaps his regular flop sweat.
"No, but he's a smart kid, and he saw her first."

10. The Station

The exchange bounced back and forth across the table like a casual game of ping pong, each participant trying to out-smug the other. Rick had caught on to Agent Beck's water trick.

Bitch Fibbie drinks from water bottle; punk Fibbie interrupts. Absolute genius.

She fired cliché after sickening cliché.

"You're an intelligent guy, Rick. Put yourself in my place. Gang jacket...gang fight. Two crime scenes...your gang jacket is at one; your little Gordy gofer is at the other. You understand, I've got to make a connection, or I wouldn't be doing my job. And I will. I've got billions of tax dollars at my disposal."

"It wasn't *my* jacket. It was Samuel's. None of us have seen him since last year."

"Is everyone we brought in going to say that, everyone else we dragged in here this morning?"

"They will if they're telling the truth."

"Even Arthur?"

Bullshit.

Arthur never went home after a painting party. He got off on waking up amidst the wreckage.

"Yes ma'am, even Arthur."

The door opened, no knock.

"Agent Beck. You're needed. It's urgent."

Her eyes twitched in the direction of her water bottle before she hopped to her feet. She left without taking it with her.

Rick was correct in his observation. She hadn't taken a sip before the peon agent entered. The interruption was not planned.

11. Amid Chaos

Agent Beck Spoke.

"Stay cool, Ernie. I'm on my way, and I have two specialists that are going to beat me there by five minutes. Take a picture of the trunk and send it to me. Then check his computer. He probably learned how to do this stuff on line."

"I did that already. He cleared his browsing history, and I don't know how to get it back."

252

"Don't worry about it. My guys will suss it out. Was the kid at the confirmation?"

"You mean, do I think he drew the thing on the yellow paper? It's certainly possible."

12. The Station

All four interview rooms were full. Rick was in one. Steven was in another. The remaining two held lesser active members who claimed they hadn't been to a painting party in months. The other three UJ's they were able to track down were under observation in the holding tank. Arthur, Bubbs, Traci, indistinguishable Eric, and, of course, Kelly were not among them.

Things moved quickly.

Officers Truesdell and Simon brought Ian Reilly through the back entrance and right past holding. There were no signs of recognition between Reilly and the UJ's … odd.

One of the two expendables was removed from his interview room and replaced with Reilly. Still considered hostile, his hands were cuffed to the table. Officer Simon offered one last courtesy before leaving the room.

"Can I get you a coffee or soda?"

"Brilliant, genius. How would I drink it?"

"We have straws."

Lynch and Warner entered from the parking garage and crossed the foyer. Boris, the desk sergeant, was just finishing a call. There were three people seated in the station's poor excuse for a waiting area. One of them, Lynch did not recognize. The other two…

Oh no. Not now!

Mrs. Weiss sprung from her chair.

"Detective Lynch, I need to talk to you. You were so nice to my boy last week. I was hoping you could talk some sense into him."

"Ma'am, I…holy cow, Gordy, what happened to you?"

The boy kept his head down.

"Nuthin'"

"Forgive him, detective. He's young. He got beaten up this morning on the way to school, and he won't say by who."

Lynch gave Gordy a hard stare...a detour worth taking? Little doubt, the kid knew the location of the cloister.

Couldn't hurt I suppose.

"Where are they, Gordy?"

The answer came with feigned cluelessness after a twitch of an eye towards his mother.

"I don't know what are you talking about?"

"Yes, Detective Lynch, what on Earth are you talking about?"

Instant dead-end.

He couldn't question Gordy further without a guardian present, which meant the kid would have to admit to his UJ stuff in front of his mother. Was the threat of a bomb enough to make this frightened little fart with a loose grip on reality and low regard for the truth incur that kind of wrath?

Probably not.

It wasn't worth the risk anyway. If Gordy couldn't be broken, or the questioning took too long, Lynch would never hear the end of it from Special Agent Beck.

"You had a whole station loaded with confirmed members of the UJ, and you were questioning who?"

Right.

He would do his best to keep the Weiss's at the station, and *maybe* go to work on Gordy later on if all else failed. In the meantime, perhaps he could throw the kid off balance a bit.

"Look, Mrs. Weiss. I am up to my neck right now with Sergeant Reilly's assault. I have a holding cell filled with witnesses…"

Gordy didn't react. Lynch couldn't even be positive the kid heard him.

"…I promise I will help get to the bottom of whatever it is. Please just take a seat for now."

"No offense, detective, but nothing doing. I'm sick of getting jockeyed around."

"Ma'am…please."

254

Half taken aback and half realizing she didn't have much choice, Mrs. Weiss theatrically returned to her seat with an obstinate plop.

Good. Take a time-out.

The desk sergeant ended his call and waved Lynch to approach.

"What we got, Boris?"

"Ian Reilly is in room four. We've got members of that gang in the other three."

"Any progress?"

A nearby FBI Agent interjected.

"None. What do you locals do to these kids? They'd rather have their dicks stuck in a pencil sharpener than talk to the cops."

Mrs. Weiss gave a disapproving "tsk." Lynch heard nothing after the word "none." Four rooms. Four morons. One of them knew what put a cop in a coma. The other three knew the location of the UJ cloister.

The gang needed to be turned upon itself; Ian Reilly needed to formalize his confession with convictable detail.

Textbook.

Warner sidled up and spoke.

"You take the UJ Fuckheads. You know them better than I do. I'll take care of Reilly."

"Perfect."

Lynch removed his coat.

Not getting me again, coat. No way.

He would be walking in and out of three interview rooms. His brain would be going a hundred miles a minute in a hundred different directions. Under no circumstances could any of those UJ pricks know what was going on in the next room. The wonky latch wasn't going to get the best of him a third time.

"Boris, put this behind the desk for me, would you?"

"Yeah yeah. Oh, Sergeant Warner, there's a…"

And then…

"You missed me, bitch!"

255

Lynch went rigid with his coat in mid-handoff. His eyes flitted about like he was a cat messing with a laser pointer. Was he hearing things?

"You missed me, bitch!"

He spoke to Boris.

"Exactly what the hell was that?"

"A ringtone. One of those gang guys put his cell phone in the bin with his personal effects."

"You missed me, bitch!"

Now that it wasn't associated with the story of a nun's kidnapping, Lynch instantly recognized the line and the voice. It was a sound bite from an Eddie Murphy stand-up routine. The joke involved Eddie's mother hurling a shoe at his dad: a classic. And damned if one of those UJ fools wasn't using it as a ringtone, the same UJ fool that would owe Sister Edwina a great deal in the near future.

"You want to know what room he's in, Jim?"

Outwardly cool as a cucumber, but inwardly doing cartwheels and handstands, the detective rolled up his sleeves and straightened his tie.

"Why yes, Boris…I believe I would."

Detective Warner, who had been observing the curious exchange with zero understanding, lent her voice.

"Everything cool? You need me?"

Lynch breathed a satisfied reply as Boris took his coat.

"Thank you, Sergeant. I do not. I believe this will go much quicker than anticipated."

"Then I'll pretend I get what's going on and…Boris, were you trying to say something to me before?"

The Desk Sergeant had to choke down a partially ingested donut before he could answer.

"Yeah yeah. This fella over here says he knows what went down in the junkyard."

He pointed at the third person in the waiting area. Carrie looked. He was a young, handsome man with a minor head wound. He stood cordially.

"What did he say, exactly?"

"He says he was there when it happened."

And Detective Warner introduced herself to Tony Evans, resident of Franklin Village, and devout member of the Potterford First Baptist Church.

13. The Waiting Area

It had been months since Gordy questioned the point of his own existence.

A school counselor once asked him if he ever thought about killing himself. His response was "No, but I've thought about thinking about killing myself." He was handed a pamphlet and a hot-line phone number both of which he threw away on his way back to class.

The only thing of late that gave him a reason to get up in the morning was the prospect of joining the UJ. Now he was a full member. He ran with a pack. Fifteen (ish) badass brothers and sisters were at his beck and call. For the first time ever, someone had his back. That's what he thought anyway. His present circumstances proved otherwise.

Beck and call? He was given the number of *one cell phone* that may as well have belonged to a dead person for all the good it did him.

Gordy was left alone to deal with the humiliation of walking into school with tear-stained cheeks, a bloody nose, and a limp. He barely made it in the door before one of the teachers saw him and pawned him off on the school nurse. After ten minutes and some rudimentary patching, he was scooted to Vice-Principal Bono's office.

Not once was he asked how he felt. All anyone cared about was whether or not the fight happened on school grounds and who else was involved. He said nothing. Forking over Braden would reveal the reason for the beating. That would lead back to the UJ, and everyone would learn the truth about Gordy's involvement in Detective Reilly's injury.

Or would they? The UJ had his back, right? Right?

Dr. Bono (Dr. Boner to his students) called Gordy's parents. His father was in Virginia that day, but his mother was at his side in a matter of minutes.

The call was clearly placed out of mere obligation. Dr. Boner treated the whole thing with his regular schmucky apathy. He'd have the faculty ask around, but "these things happen" blah blah blah. He probably wouldn't have even done *that* much if Mrs. Weiss hadn't read him the riot act.

The putz was squirming in his blue leather armchair.

Sitting in the police station, Gordy's back was sore. His wrists were sore. He felt like he was going to shit blood, and no one cared.

His mother's cell phone rang.

"Here Pun-pun, your father wants to talk to you."

Great.

"Hi, dad."

"Hey, Gord. Sorry I didn't call earlier. I just spent three hours discussing whether to put polka-dots or stripes on a pair of toddler-sized overalls. I got mom's message. You okay?"

Gordy felt his mother's arm drape over his shoulder.

"Yeah I'm fine. Just a fight."

"Your mom says you're not saying who started it."

Gordy could only say what he'd already said to everyone else.

"It just…it just doesn't matter. Okay?"

"Well, you should, and that's all I'm going to say about it. I'm forty-six years old, and I've never swung a punch or been hit in the face. You've already got one more story to tell than I do."

A puff of a laugh went through Gordy's nose.

"Not much to tell."

"Fair enough. Look, these yahoos want me back in the room. We're moving on to which animal to put on a pair of socks. You call me if there's anything I can do, or if you just want to rap okay? I can be interrupted."

"Yeah…sure."

"Excellent. Bye, son."

Gordy's back was sore. His wrists were sore. He felt like he was going to shit blood, and…no one cared?

He looked at his mother.

No one? That's not true.

That single frame would be evermore etched in Gordy's memory. He wouldn't put a name to it like Father Leo, yet the moment was no less profound than what the good priest experienced at sailing camp. A sense of lifted burden just beyond his full understanding washed over him. He felt the corners of his mouth go up, and the cause wasn't a gang insignia or a new track by The Forever Damned. It was an awesome realization…his first adult thought.

His whole paradigm was messed up. Maybe the trick to an easy life wasn't being a good liar. Maybe the trick was not constantly putting yourself in situations that made the truth an obstacle.

He'd still stay quiet about the UJ, not out of loyalty, but indifference. They could kick him out if they wanted. Fuck 'em. He had something else to care about now.

Would the feeling last? Only time would tell, but it was a damned fine start.

He leaned back and put his head on his mother's shoulder.

In a good way, it surprised them both.

14. The Station

Cock sucker! Son of a bitch! Piece of shit! Motherfucker!

Ian Reilly was not pleased with himself.

Asshole! Asshole! Asshole!
He'd bought into their line, fell for their bluff. As a result, he'd jeopardized the success of his son's first honorable act.

Brainless bastard! Idiot prick!

About his own situation, he was still in denial. He realized they had him dead-to-rights. So what? He'd confess to being the one who delivered the bulk of the beating, and probably the fatal blow to the Jew kid. The cops could twist on the rest.

He wouldn't tell the truth about whom was with him. Petey, his younger brother, and Quentin, his shop assistant, were *not* going down. Ian would swear that he went to the shelter on Hamilton Avenue and paid two homeless guys to put on masks and jump in the back of his truck. Easy peasy. He'd give false descriptions; maybe look at a few line-ups. He'd waffle; he'd stutter; he'd be generally fuzzy about the whole evening. His accomplices would never be found.

In the meantime, he'd go to trial.

Kevin told him how things worked in a courtroom. Jurors could be bought. Fake defense witnesses could be found. Real prosecution witnesses could be defamed. The story could be spun at the Herald. The public could be swayed.

It would all make for an inconvenient year, but Ian wasn't worried. Things would work out.

Goddammit…he was a Reilly.

15. The Station

Someone knocked. Rick felt a cuff button pull out of his cheek as he lifted his head. He'd fallen asleep. They'd let him fall asleep. He hadn't seen the silly FBI chick for a while. His decaf had gone cold.

Another knock…why? Still in a fog, he put his shoddy focus on the door. He wasn't sure what to do. It opened. A detective entered. Rick recognized him from the night all this shit started, but he couldn't remember the guy's name.

"Hi, Rick. Wasn't sure who was in here. I'm Sergeant Lynch. Remember me?"

Rick slurped and rubbed his eyes.

"I do remember you, Sergeant. How's it going?"

Lynch was carrying a random manila folder he'd grabbed from his desk. He also had a pen. Neither item had anything to do with Rick, mere props. He opened the folder exposing some old traffic reports.

"We'll let you out of here soon. We're going a little crazy out here in case you couldn't tell."

Rick yawned and smiled lazily.

"Beats working."

"I hear ya. I just need one thing from you."

"What's that?"

Lynch clicked his pen.

"Stand up and pull up your sleeves."

260

For the first time since Rick entered the station, he became visibly irritated.

"Pull up my sleeves?"

"It's nothing. I just need to eliminate something from my list here. Pull up your sleeves, and I'm out of here. Okay?"

Good God, Rick hated cops.

"I'm not doing anything until you tell me why."

"Fine, if you want it straight between the eyes. I need to make sure you're not a cutter."

"A what? Is it suddenly 2007?'

"The profiler says I gotta check. Come on; call it a favor."

Rick stood and belligerently pulled up his right sleeve...then his left...and felt his favorite oversized watch flop around his wrist. With forced ennui, he answered the detective's question.

"Not a cutter."

Lynch put a sloppy check mark towards the center of the redundant paper and closed the folder.

Left wrist...got it.

"Didn't think so. Give me five minutes."

Rick was, once again, alone. He spoke to the walls.

"Did you enjoy that?"

16. The Station

Lynch took a seat in the hall.

That's the guy. That's the one with a conscience. He's the one that's going to tell me where to find the cloister.

The fastest *legal* extraction method was the only thing left in question.

"Hey, Jim..."

It was Carrie.

"...if you're stuck, I think I can help you out, but I need your help too. It's delicate."

261

They walked to where the hall opened into the squad room. Carrie tipped her head toward her desk and spoke in a hush.

"See that kid?"

Lynch took a glance.

"Doesn't look like much of a *kid*."

"He's younger than he looks. How much would you love me if I told you he led the crew that duked it out with the UJ in the junkyard?"

Lynch's response was a quiet explosion.

"You're fucking kidding me!"

"No, I'm not…"

Lynch did a little dance and started to say something, but Carrie cut him off.

"…Hang on a second, Jim. Hear me out on this."

She told Lynch about Tony Evans's predicament, about the neighborhood watch, and the trouble he would be in if his pastor knew he was in the Industrial Complex that night.

"What are you talking about? I know Pastor Seymour. He'll be pissed off, but he's not going to…"

"I know, I know, but you should have heard Evans talk. There was honest fear in his voice. A guy that big…real *fear*. Bullets probably bounce off of him, and he is scared to death of disappointing his church."

"But Carrie, for crying out…"

"I just want to know if there's a way we can do this without getting him into trouble."

Lynch sized the kid up. He was slumped over in one of the station's cheaply upholstered, city-purchased armchairs. His elbows were on his knees, and his head was hung low.

"You realize that means we can't make it public that he was there that night, right?"

"Right."

Tony wiped his eyes and sniffled.

"Which means we can't use him as a witness."

"Give me a little credit, Jim. Yes, I realize that. Look, if we can't, we can't. But if we can…you know."

This was not a typical request from Sergeant Warner. Lynch put his hands on his hips and tapped his foot. He looked back and forth between the interview rooms and the promising young man at Carrie's desk who only wanted to avoid letting down his pastor.

Yeah, he could make it work.

"Let me talk to him."

17. One Floor Below the Cloister

The situation wasn't optimal. There were three of them (plus a girl), and Braden only brought two devices. Two were all he had time to make; two were all he could carry. He also couldn't bury them like he was supposed to. There wasn't a lick of soft ground in the entire building. So, he put one at the bottom of each flight of stairs leading to the ground floor. The devices were tucked under the lips of their respective steps. Anyone descending wouldn't be able to see them. He would have to trigger them remotely. It was the only way he could ensure the timing was precise. If all of them came down together, he'd blow the bottom one when they reached it. If one of them came down without the other two, he'd blow the bottom one first, and then the top one when the others ran to see what was going on.

He wore gloves which he would destroy later. He realized he'd probably get caught. Still, there was no point in being stupid

It all seemed so easy. They were fast asleep when he got there. It allowed him to get a head count, but he couldn't do what he wanted to while they were lying down. They had to be standing. Better yet, they had to be walking. The girl had passed out on top of her sheets naked and not in the most dignified of positions, so Braden used her cell phone to take a few pictures. The idiot never signed off of any of her social media accounts, so uploading them for the world to see, even while incensed, was easy. Humiliation would be her punishment. As far as his sheltered fifteen-year-old sensibilities knew, she couldn't have done anything to his mother. She would not be dealt with as harshly as the boys.

So, he sat seething in the shadows. To his left was the switch that he'd placed on the ground. To his right was a clear exit.

263

18. The Station

Tony would follow his instructions to the letter. All he had to do was sit the hallway and stare down whomever Detective Lynch let out of the interview room. Under no circumstances was he to speak, and if anyone ever asked him what he was doing in the station, he would claim he was reporting a stolen wallet. Lynch would make sure everyone Tony had spoken to, including Boris, would back him up.

It was show time.

19. The Station

"Okay, Rick, you're free to go."

Rick slapped both hands on the table to put an audible exclamation point on the end of the sentence that was his tedious morning.

"Alright, well, that's that then. Thank you, detective."

"No, thank you, and I'm sorry we hosed a perfectly good Friday morning for you. We've got Cardinal Romero in town this weekend. Everyone, and I mean *everyone,* interviewed in connection with Bishop Ryan's murder is being interviewed again. You got caught up in it, and we apologize."

Rick was dubious, but what could he do? They were letting him go.

"I have enough time to get to work by noon. I'm okay."

He'd taken the day off like he did the day after every painting party. He was looking forward to taking a shower, spending the afternoon watching porn, and catching up with Arthur later on so he could break his nose.

"Your personal effects are behind the front desk. I'll walk you up. I don't know why they took your cell phone. You weren't under arrest."

Lynch opened the door, and Rick breezed by.

"I did that. We have a security check point at my job. It's a habit. Wait a minute, how did you know my cell phone was…"

Rick recognized Tony immediately. His face and voice were permanently burned into Rick's memory along with Arthur's inopportune dropping of the *n* word. The guy was ten or twelve feet away, staring at him, burning a hole in Rick's face with the same intensity he'd summoned during his sermon at the junkyard. Rick clenched his buttocks as a natural reaction to his bowels loosening. For a fat moment, he was frozen in place. He heard the detective's voice.

"Everything okay, Rick?"

The only four words in Rick brain flew out.

"What's he doing here?"

"Who? You mean Tony? I don't know. I think he's here to report a crime or something. Come on. This way."

Rick felt the location of the cloister and every detail of Kevin Reilly's assault get stuck in his throat.

No way you pigs! Not yet.

The next sensation was tunnel vision. The desk sergeant came into view. All else disappeared. All else … except Gordy. He was there with his mother. It finally happened. The little turd had been kicked in the balls one too many times.

And the words that were stuck in Rick's throat completed the journey outward.

"Fuck you, Lynch! The cloister is in the D building at Hallcroft! Get me back in that goddam room! I'll tell you what happened to your asshole jerk-off coma cop too!"

He was in cuffs before the feeling returned to his hands.

Lynch got close.

"I know what you did for Sister Edwina. That's going to help you. Keep your voice down, and when someone in the room offers you food, take it."

He turned to any and all FBI agents within earshot of Rick's confession.

"You heard him, everyone! Program 'Hallcroft Mental Facility' into your GPS's and load up!"

20. Braden's Room

Gomez put his partner on speaker.

"Give me some good news, Jaime."

"The Cloister's at Hallcroft. Do we know what we're dealing with yet?"

Beck spoke.

"The short answer is 'no,'"

Agents Russ Madigan and Paula Grant specialized respectively in explosives and IT. They were charged with determining the specific type and strength of Braden's device. Between the trunk contents and a recovery of his browser history, they were quickly able to narrow it down to seven basic designs. They were, however, coming up short on a blast radius.

"We can tell what materials from the trunk were most recently used, but we can't tell how much. We also don't know what he used for a casing."

"Send me what you've got. We're leaving the station now."

The call ended.

"Ma'am, I may have something here. It's a stretch."

"Stretching is good Paula. Please stretch."

Grant had thoroughly routed Braden's web activity and moved on to his application use. At the top of the list was a movie streaming service called CineChoice. She was lucky to launch it and find that Braden hadn't logged out, so his viewing habits were easy to trace.

There was an anomaly.

"Most of these movies and TV shows are what you'd expect of a boy his age, except this one."

THE BIG RED ONE

"Sounds like porn."

"It's a WWII pic made in 1980. Mark Hamill is in it, you know, Luke Skywalker..."

"Yes, thank you. I know who Mark Hamill is."

"I'm guessing that's how Braden linked to the film, but he didn't just pass it by. He viewed it several times, including this morning. Obviously, there's something in it he likes. Maybe it's where he got inspiration for the design??"

"Maybe. If we run with this, what's next?"

"We'll hit the cinephile blogs and all the plot summaries we can find, but the thing is over two hours long. It would help if someone knew it. I don't."

"I've never heard of it. Have you, Madigan?"

"No."

"Sergeant Gomez?"

"I've heard of it. I haven't seen it."

"Is there anyone we could ask?"

Ernie still had his cell phone out. He tapped it once and put it to his ear. "Let me try something."

21. The Station

Until five years ago, Boris Miller was Potterford's favorite beat cop. A hip replacement put him behind a desk. He'd retire soon to his lake house in the Poconos.

The phone had been ringing non-stop all morning. It rang again.

"Potterford Pol...Hi Ernie...The Big huh?...What's that?...Okay, I'll try."

He pushed two buttons simultaneously to activate the station's PA system, and held his hand set to his mouth like a walkie-talkie.

"Hi, everybody. Pardon the strange question. Does anyone know about a movie called the Big Red One?"

Silence.

"Anyone? Anything at all? Okay, thank you."

He was about to take Gomez off hold, when a single voice was heard. "I do."

Boris looked to the waiting area finding a single hand in the air. The smile on the boy's face represented a combination of trepidation and pride.

"C'meer. The detective on the other end wants to talk to you."

Gordy went to the desk and took the phone. It smelled like chocolate. He was glad to hear Ernie's voice.

"Talk to us, amigo."

"It's a war film. Luke Skywalker is in it. That guy with the big nose is in it. He's in a lot of stuff like that."

The next voice he heard was female.

"Thanks, Gordy, but we know all that. Is there anything in the movie about planting a bomb or making a bomb or revenge or anything like that?"

"No, not really."

"Are there any scenes that are particularly memorable? When you think of the movie, what's the first thing that comes to mind?"

"I see what you're asking. Yes, there is, but I don't like to talk about it out loud. Just thinking about it makes me…"

"What? What Gordy? What is it?"

Gordy pulled the phone from his face and looked into the receiver as if to tell the person on the other end to calm down.

Jeez, it's just a movie.

"There's a scene where a soldier steps on a land mine, only it's not a regular land mine…"

22. The Cloister

Arthur awoke from a fantastic sleep, one of those uninterrupted, dreamless, void of tossing and turning so you wake up with perfect hair kind of sleeps.

What a night.

Sex, drugs, booze, revenge…a hattrick plus one.

The sun hit his face through the skylight, announcing a new day of kicking ass and getting tail.

The room was quiet (the generators having long run empty) except for the occasional tousle and snore.

He'd done it. The Unjudged was finally as Arthur envisioned, pure and animalistic without apology. There was nothing left to do but expand. He'd make more connections. He'd find more muscle. He'd collect more women.

"(Sigh) What a dump."

He'd also locate better accommodations. Access to moonlight? Fuck that. He'd shove the whole thing so far underground the ATF would need trained gophers to find it. The town was for the taking. Someday soon, the tiny piece of the world called Potterford would be his.

In the meantime…breakfast.

He emerged from beneath his toasty comforter, rose to his tiptoes, and stretched donning naught but a pair of brown socks.

He wandered about searching for his clothes, noticing with finite interest who else had spent the night in the ward. Bubbs was asleep on the corner couch. No big surprise; his body clock was on a bouncer's schedule. Indistinguishable, Eric was bundled up and face-down on the cot across from Arthur's. Traci looked as though she had woken up at some point and tried to throw a sheet over her lower half.

Gonna hit that later. Now where the hell are my pants?

Two short buzzes drew his attention.
"There we go."
He'd left his phone in the pocket of his tight, leather, sperm-killing, too-many-zipper-having trousers. He'd received a new text message, but he couldn't tell who sent it.

DUDE I HOPE U GET THIS IN TIME. I'M AT THE PPD. RICK RATTED US OUT. THE PIGS KNOW WHERE U R AND THEYR ON THE WAY. GET OUT!!!!!

"Fuck me! Everybody up!"
There was absolutely no response.
"Wake up, assholes!"
He started picking up debris and throwing it at the cots. Eric was the first to show signs of life.
"What the hell, Artie!?"
"Rick dimed us! This place is going to be tits-deep with cops in about three minutes! Move your ass! Down the stairs and out the back like we practiced!"
As if on cue, sirens from what sounded like 100 police cars fired up in the distance.
A stale beer poured on Bubbs's face got him moving. Arthur tossed Traci's cot, sending her tumbling to the floor, but it didn't seem to affect her sense of urgency.
"Traci! Are you deaf?"
"Hmmm? Where's my dress?"
"It's right under you! I threw it at your empty head!"
Arthur scrambled to get dressed. Eric froze with a combination of fear and information overload. Bubbs brainlessly threw things out the window in an attempt to destroy evidence.
"What the hell are you doing?"

"Fingerprints man!"

"Are you serious!? Get your shoes on! Eric, snap the fuck out of it!"

Traci had managed to put on her thong and pull her dress up as far as her waist. Her bra was proving to be a struggle.

The sirens stopped. The cops were on the grounds.

"Dammit, Traci! Come on!"

The sound of Arthur's untied Doc Martin's slapping heel-toe against the concrete floor filled the room as he dashed for the stairs. Bubbs and Eric followed several feet behind like good little foot soldiers. Traci put herself together as best as she could and got to her feet for a few seconds before blacking out again.

"Wait guys, I'm…"

The back of her head met the edge of her cot. She was unconscious for everything that followed.

23. Hallcroft

For fifty years, Hallcroft was Southeastern Pennsylvania's premier facility for the mentally ill. Lack of state funding caused it to close in the mid-90's. It was a sad, poorly executed state of affairs that left the bulk of the patients in the hands of underqualified volunteer host families. It was a vast property with several now-abandoned buildings. The county paid to have the grass mowed twice a year, but, otherwise, Hallcroft was generally ignored.

Not today.

Every car the Potterford Police Department could spare, along with three black sedans, crashed through the entrance and onto the grounds.

Lynch was on point. The sun blinded him for a moment as the clock tower that topped the D Building came into view.

This was it.

The car came to a screeching halt, followed by all the others, as they formed a wide perimeter around their target. Lynch elbowed into his door and put a foot on the ground just as his cell phone rang.

It was Gomez.

"What'cha got, partner?"

"Go in as tight as you want. The bomb isn't designed to kill; it's designed to…"

270

And before Gomez could say the word "castrate," the first bomb went off.

Then the second.

In the foreboding silence that followed, a voice crackled over someone's walkie-talkie.

"We've got the Reilly kid. He was trying to sneak out the back."

And then the screams started…like nothing Lynch had ever heard or imagined.

24. Clean Up

The aftermath was, as one might guess, not pretty. Braden's pipe bombs, due mostly to the fact that they were constructed at 4:00 in the morning by a fifteen-year-old, didn't perform exactly as intended. The injuries were, nonetheless, brutal. No major arteries were cut.

The victims would live.

Because Arthur took the first blast solo, his damage was the worst. After some intense surgery, he'd be left with one testicle and scar tissue that would render the rest of the area functional, but horribly deformed. Bubbs took his half of the second device's shrapnel up the rectum. It would be a long time before he could ride a motorcycle without bleeding, and pooping would be an issue for the rest of his life. With Bubbs as a cushion, Eric's wounds were primarily on his left leg, with the exception of one bit of metal that went straight through his hand. His souvenirs from the soon-to-be defunct UJ would be a permanent limp and the inability to make a fist.

None of these injuries would serve the three UJs well in prison. Some irrefutable trace evidence, such as the drug in Molly Reilly's system along with the threat of testimony from four reliable witnesses, including Traci, would bring about three puny plea bargains. Arthur, Bubbs, and Eric would spend the powerful years that Wallace Avery spoke of in a cage, a nasty cage, and with qualified use of their lower extremities.

Traci would have her own problems. Legally, she managed to sidestep all the major land mines by, among other things, agreeing to testify. She'd spend six weeks picking up trash along route 422. That was the easy part.

Having no recollection of the morning (she didn't even remember how she got her dress…somewhat…on), she couldn't swear that she wasn't the

271

one who uploaded her naked pictures, even though she obviously wasn't the one who took them. Fairly or unfairly, society had its way with her. The captions that Braden had added with only partial accuracy read "holy fuck am I wasted" and "this was after my second gang bang" and so forth. These paled in comparison to the ensuing comments. It didn't take long for the underwriters she worked for to send her packing using her criminal record as an excuse. The garbage she had to deal with when she left her house made her become more and more reclusive until she finally found it necessary to relocate. For better or worse, she'd start over...wiser for the ware.

25. PMMC

Lynch followed the ambulances to the hospital, but not for the sake of the passengers. The gurneys were rushed into the trauma center. Lynch parked in the visitors' lot, went in the main entrance and made a b line for the elevator which he took to the sixth floor. His partner was waiting for him with coffee in hand.

"Good bust, amigo."

"Yeah, good bust."

A nearby picture window displayed the east end of Main Street as if on a postcard. In contrast to everything the day had so far produced, it was a beautiful afternoon. Both detectives took a moment to breathe and enjoy the view.

Gomez still smelled like Fowler Brew.

"You stink, partner."

"I know."

"How's Molly doing?"

"She's getting looked at downstairs."

"Did Leo get here yet?"

Gomez nodded and motioned toward the ICU with his elbow. Lynch stepped back from the window and took a look down the corridor. June Reilly and Father Leo Pascucci were seated facing each other on one of the sectional couches. They were praying. Lynch spoke to his partner.

"This is your territory, Ernie. What do you think?"

"Is Carrie coming?"

"Not for a while. She's still working on Ian."

"Then we should walk down there, and you should talk to the grieving mother."

Lynch's feet suddenly became very heavy.

"You sure about that? She likes you; she doesn't like me."

"She needs facts, Jaime, and you're closest to the case next to Carrie. Father Leo will take care of the comfort part, and you know I've got your back."

Gomez held out his coffee cup for his partner to "clink." Lynch looked down at it, then forward again.

"You know I'm not doing that."

"Aw, man. I thought we were having a moment there."

"Shut up. Let's do this."

It was a short hallway. Lynch wanted to rehearse what he was going to say, but he only had time to get it started in his head.

Mrs. Reilly, your son, Kevin, was heavily affected by the murder of Bishop Ryan. He acted irrationally and decided to use his resources as a cop and a Reilly to make sure the murderer was appropriately punished. He went to Father O'Rourke to get what proved to be inaccurate information on the killer's whereabouts. Kevin knew he would be missed at the station so he called Ian and asked him to handle it.

I need to be clear that, at this point, there is no proof that Kevin asked his brother to kill anyone, nor is there proof that Ian went to the barn intending to commit murder. It all could have been simple scare tactics. The unfortunate truth, however, is that the action sparked a war between Ian and...

The only two meaningful words he would use from his inner monologue were "unfortunate truth.: When the time came, June Reilly asked one question before giving Lynch a chance to speak.

"What will happen to my son?"

Lynch was a breath away from responding the worst way possible ("Which son do you mean?"), but he caught himself.

"Honestly, I can't offer much comfort on that front. Ian believes being a Reilly in Potterford will spare him the brunt of the regular process. He's admitted to what he did, but he won't help us with his accomplices. He's fed us a far-fetched story about a couple of homeless. There's little chance it will pan out. I'm afraid the unfortunate truth is he's going to wind up taking the rap for Jeremy Sokol's murder all by himself. That will be after a trial that he feels he can beat. He won't. We have a solid witness and blood evidence on the murder weapon. As much as everyone involved will want to let Ian off the hook, it just won't be possible."

Gomez was right. The woman's heart was breaking, but behind the tears, was appreciation for the candor. Lynch swallowed the lump in his throat and continued.

"However...I believe the sympathy and leniency that everyone would have otherwise given your son will be transferred to Braden. Despite the seriousness of what he did, it's obvious that your grandson's plan was neither to kill nor cause any widespread damage. On top of that, all of his victims lived, and *their* crimes will be made *very* public. Braden's actions won't be excused, but they will be understood.

"He'll probably spend significant of time in Youth Corrections, and he'll definitely be required to get some intense counseling. It won't be easy, but his life won't be destroyed, especially with the help of his family and the likes of Father Leo here."

Leo emphasized Lynch's words with a reassuring smile. Gomez brought it all home simply and elegantly as was his talent.

"He's going to be okay, abuela."

There were no hugs. It wasn't a time for hugs. Father Leo would spend the rest of the day in the hospital with Molly, June, and the rest of the family. Lynch and Gomez would go back to the station and help tie as much of a bow on the Sokol case as they could.

So many lives forever changed. It would have been easy to blame whoever shot Bishop Ryan, but the groundwork had been laid long before the killing. Arthur's ambition, Kevin Reilly's sense of privilege, Ian Reilly's ignorance, Gordy's dissatisfaction, Tony's pride, it was all bound to collide one day.

"Where's Julie?"

"She's in Jersey at a convention."

"Want to grab some food and drink later?"

"That sounds fantastic."

"Maggio's sound good?"

"Why do you want to go all the way out there?"

"Figured you'd want to get out of Potterford for a while."

"Nah."

26. Philip's Home Office

BOYBANDH8R's connection all but told Philip to go hump a banister when he was given the specifics of what was needed and when. The last thing he typed before leaving the chat room was "I'll see what I can do, but don't hold your breath."

Nice guy.

Philip considered the possibility that he was over thinking things. Why was he messing around with identity theft? Because two essential parts of his plan required a priest. Or did they? Could he just sneak in? Could the answer be stealth rather than disguise? Probably not. He'd spent all day researching procedures during Mass. The problem was there were too many things that went on behind closed doors, too many chances to bring the plan about too soon. Also, if he didn't know how to behave *all* the time, would assuming the identity of a priest even work?

He felt himself getting fidgety. He closed his eyes and thought back to the first killing, and how he just happened to walk past Ryan in the church when he was telling one of his sheep where he was staying that night. Then he thought about the day he went into the confessional and how his flimsy escape plan went off without a hitch. Then he thought about the second killing and how Fellini was right where he needed him, just as he'd planned within the first day of his perch. He thought about all these things and then realized that he didn't have to worry about stealth versus disguise, or how he was going to get the key he needed from Pastor Karney, or timing, or anything at all. He would just continue what he was doing. He would keep doing his research. He would keep concentrating on these hurdles. He would let the things he'd put in motion take shape. Everything would work. Everything had worked so far; everything would continue to work moving forward.

God approved of what Philip was doing. There was no doubt. A day would be enough to get it all together; of course it would.

He cleansed himself by blowing out a gust of air and shaking his arms to expel any and all residual negative feelings. Then he popped open his search engine and got back to work.

A clerical vest is called a rabbat. Interesting.

27. The Condo

The condo was dark, and Lynch saw no need to turn on the light. The moon was bright enough. He and Gomez had enjoyed two rib-eyes and two tall beers at Angus Heffer's Steak House. A scotch and some sort of visual distraction were in order. He didn't feel like flipping through channels or browsing On-Demand, so he turned his phone into a flashlight and pointed it at his/Julie's Blu-Ray collection. He had two or three go-to movies for when he didn't feel like thinking. He kept them all together. Fellowship of the Ring was too long; he didn't think he could handle the psychedelia of The Big Liebowski; John Wick? ...no. So, it would be Ocean's 11, probably his first choice anyway.

He flipped everything on, popped in the disc, and went for his favorite scotch glass. Before the copyright infringement warning disappeared, Lynch was on his couch. The attire: white t-shirt and boxer briefs; the position: eased back with his feet on the coffee table; his scotch: on the rocks half an arm's length away; the remote: in hand. There was nothing left but to punch the [Okay] button.

"Click."

Ahhhhhhh!

How many crimes had been solved since he walked out of the convent, or, at least *re*solved? Three? Four?

Jeremy Sokol's murder

Kevin Reilly's assault

Molly Reilly's assault

The bomb

Perhaps a couple others that had escaped Lynch's notice...

There was one left, the biggie, and it was no longer his responsibility. There would, of course, be plenty of paperwork to do along with a slew of unpleasant interviews, but it was all tomorrow's problem.

The movie was roughly half over, and Lynch had a good buzz going when Julie got home.

"Hey."

"Hey."

She disappeared into the bedroom and returned having put her jewelry away. She undressed in front of him so they matched and went to the fridge for a Corona to complete the ensemble. Then she nestled up beside him with her feet on the coffee table next to his. They kissed.

"I heard what happened on the news. I'll wait until tomorrow for the story."

"Much appreciated. How was your day?"

"Would you be jealous if I said fantastic?"

"Not at all. Tell me about it."

"Tomorrow."

They drank in unison. Lynch's vowels were starting to run together.

"We really do spend a lot of time in our underwear, don't we?"

"Whatever, it's comfortable."

"Are you cold?"

"No."

An hour later, the heist was a success, Julia Roberts went back to George Clooney, and it was time for bed. Julie got a playful piggyback ride into the bedroom from her boyfriend. She rested her head next to his so her nose was on his shoulder. She loved the smell of a cotton shirt, especially on him. With uninterrupted motion, he put her down, and crawled into bed while she removed her bra and put on a t-shirt with a pair of flannel shorts.

Their eyes closed, and they started to drift off in each other's arms.

"Were you saying something to me as I walked out the door this morning?"

"Tomorrow."

LYNCH'S DREAM

That night, Detective James Lynch had a dream. During his second year at Drexel, he was made to take a Humanities elective outside his major which put him in a teaching theater with Dr. Jon Platt. From Lynch's perspective, Platt was the only Liberal Arts professor at the university that actually enjoyed his job. He was in his sixties and bald with a white macaroni moustache and perpetually ill-fitted clothes. He was known to do things like stand on top of a table when talking about Aristotle and the concept of high-minded men. When he did his lecture on Nietzsche, he spent the first half of the period in seated, uninterested silence just to see how many students would walk out.

His true passion, however, was for surrealist art. If he could have spent the entire school year discussing Salvador Dali and Max Ernst, he would have happily done so. Lynch vividly remembered Platt's take on the surreal and his accompanying theory on the origin of dreams.

"Your conscious and subconscious are behind two separate and differently functioning doors. Your conscious is behind a latch door like you have on your dorm rooms. One of your senses…sight, smell, taste, whatever…centers in on something and your conscious lets it in. It then gets stored in an organized place, like a filing cabinet, and gets recalled when it your conscious chooses.

"Your subconscious lies behind a revolving door. It takes in absolutely everything. When you look into a crowd, your subconscious sees and remembers every face. When you glance at the front page of a newspaper, your subconscious remembers every word.

"While your conscious memories get stored in a filing cabinet, your subconscious memories get piled in a heap. They are recalled while you sleep and fly through the revolving door without control and in no particular order. That's why you see people in dreams that you don't believe you've ever seen before. That's why things continuously morph. That's why, while a dream in its entirety can seem bizarre, the individual pieces…the minutia…often make sense.

"It's also why the most vivid dreams occur in the twilight of your sleep cycle…in that dozing period when you're sort of half asleep and half awake. This is where your conscious and subconscious collide. The dreams are more memorable and easier to recount because the intrusion of the conscious causes them to make more sense."

It was one man's theory, impossible to prove or disprove. Regardless, Platt's take on the "twilight dream" described Lynch's to a T.

He was sitting in a room that he'd never seen before, but, somehow, it was the dining room at his parents' house. His father was sitting at the head of the table as he normally did, but his teeth were metal and sharp like he had a small bear trap in his mouth. His mother was in her regular seat as well, but she kept stabbing her mutated meal with a wooden spoon sending bits of it across the table each time. His sister was there with her husband and their five kids. They had no odd characteristics other than the fact that in real life they only had two.

Lynch told his family that he'd closed a case, and they all cheered. His mother then pointed her wooden spoon at his sister's family. She half-sung and half-spoke.

"Remember what I said about your sister? See? I told you!"

Then one of Lynch's nephew's that didn't exist started to sing like Barry White. A feeling of ascension came over Lynch bringing him out of his dream. He opened his eyes to find himself face to face with his clock radio. It had gone off. WPPO FM was rockin' the Barry White.

...Can't get enough of your love...and I don't know why, don't know why...

Freshly awake, Lynch could remember what the dream version of his mother said to him. Just as Platt asserted, the context didn't make sense, but the words did.

When James's sister and her husband first got married, they got to work on trying to have kids right away. They had a very difficult time with it. They unsuccessfully employed the biblical method for close to two years before seeking the aid of a fertility specialist. Fortunately, there was nothing wrong with either of them medically, so *un*fortunately, there wasn't much the doctor could do. She prescribed them some fertility pills which may as well have been dog suppositories. From there, they took a stab at some new age treatments which yielded nothing. They eventually decided to go in utero.

Her mother was against it.

She spoke to James in confidence, and he remembered every word.

"You watch! They're going to spend all this money, and risk permanent injury, and, in the end, all they need to do is calm down! They are pressurizing themselves! Mark my words, they'll have this first child the idiotic way, and, once the pressure is off…boom! She'll be pregnant again, the *real* way! When you put pressure on yourself, things don't work correctly. You over think; you cramp your brain and the brain controls *everything*!"

Her prediction came true.

Lynch rubbed his forehead and sat up.

Weird…

He looked at Julie who was still asleep despite the dulcet tones of Barry White. He stared at her thoughtfully for a full minute, and then got up to take another look at the photos on his dining room table.

THE CARTOON TEETH, THE GRUMPY SNAKE, THE EIGHT-POINT BUCK, AND THE UPROOTED TREE

Friday

1. Ernie's Apartment

Ernesto Gomez lived alone. For a thousand reasons, he lived alone. His apartment was on the river in a complex that was barely two years old. He was among the first ten to sign a lease, so he got a special rate on a two-bedroom unit. He set up the master bedroom as a gym. When you live alone, you can do things like that. He had just finished his third set of squats when his phone rang.

"Hola."

"Hey, partner. I cleared some lost time with Carrie. Feel like taking a ride?"

"I've got to shower and stuff, but sure, where?"

"I want to head over to the 'Church of Rock.' I had a thought."

"*You* had a thought?"

The dynamics between James and Julie were well known to Ernie.

"Alright, I had some inspiration."

"So, Julie had a thought."

"How soon can you be ready?"

"Give me twenty minutes."

"Cool, meet me along the river bank outside your place, and bring your bathroom scale and a hoodie."

"My what and a what?"

"I'll explain when we get there."

2. Along the Schuylkill

Lynch and Gomez hadn't given the chase and capture of poor Eddie Williams a second thought. A one-legged man wearing a snowshoe could have overtaken the tweaked-out meth head in Eddie's mug shot.

"Okay, amigo. I'm here but I'm not sure why."

"This is a river bank. I thought there'd be rocks."

"By the way, I didn't feel like a friggin' idiot carrying a bathroom scale across my complex, in case you were wondering."

"We need two-and-a-half-pound rocks, about a dozen of them. Best if they don't have sharp edges too, so you don't cut your hand."

"Awesome … still don't know what's going on."

Lynch had always wanted to reenact a crime scene. Cops did it all the time in the movies and on TV. It was one of the things a "uni" envisioned when tossing around the idea of becoming a detective. In Potterford, the opportunity rarely (in Lynch's case, never) arose.

But Julie, filling her role as the perfect muse, got Lynch thinking. In high school, before the drugs took hold, Eddie Williams was an athlete. He was middle linebacker for the football team and ran the hurdles in track. Yes, he was in bad shape the night he put a bullet in a cedar pole fence, but when adrenaline gets pumping, instincts kick in. In a dead sprint, tweaked or not, Eddie would have been fast, most certainly faster than any member of Generation Us.

"What do we need rocks for?"

"A loaded 9-millimeter weighs about two and a half pounds. Guns are expensive. Rocks are free."

"I repeat, what do we need rocks for?"

Lynch shielded his eyes from the sun as he espied a patch of rocky shoreline less than a hundred yards away. He walked and talked.

"Eddie Williams slowed down that night, and I want to know why."

Gomez shrugged and followed.

"Alright, I'm game. It's not like we have a day's worth of paperwork waiting for us at the station or anything."

"You are being uncharacteristically sarcastic today. You know that?"

"Dude, I cut my workout short to put smooth rocks on a bathroom scale. If there was ever a time for sarcasm…"

By mid-morning, the two detectives were back behind the Fellowship Church of Ellisport. They were both still on a high from the day before. It was a strange, manic sort of high born of the conflict between feeling good about themselves and having witnessed the decimation of a family. They spoke naught of it.

Using the police report as a reference, they positioned themselves. Lynch pretended to load an imaginary van, while hoodie-clad Ernie emerged from poor Eddie's hiding place, wielding a smooth two-and-a-half pound rock.

"Hand over your shit, fatso!"

"Okay, okay, meth head freak. Take it easy."

Lynch stomped to signal the moment Pastor Devlin opened the door. Gomez pointed the rock at the bullet hole, doing his best to let the action take place via reactionary momentum rather than controlled muscle movement. The result was a comedic spasm that left Lynch doubled over with laughter.

"Wait, wait, wait, Ernie, wait!"

"What? You didn't dig that?"

"Start over! Without the seizure or whatever that was."

Gomez was laughing too.

"From where?"

"Right before Devlin walks out."

"Got it."

Gomez pointed. Lynch stomped. Gomez skipped the theatrics and aimed with an added sound effect.

"Bang! What would you do next?"

"I'd duck and cover. You?"

"I'd look to see what I hit. Once I realize I only hit the fence, I'd haul ass."

"Sounds good. Do it again…same place."

Point, stomp, aim, bang.

"Hijo de putaaaaaaaa!!!"

And Gomez was off like a shot with Lynch twenty feet behind. When he passed the spot where Chaz saw Eddie toss the gun, Ernie underhanded the rock across his body right-to-left, sending it into the Schuylkill River. When he passed the spot where Eddie was tackled, Lynch was still a good distance back, so they stopped. They were both out of breath, Lynch more so than his partner. Gomez spoke.

"So, what did that prove?"

"I don't know. What was going through your head while you were running?"

"I didn't want you to catch me."

Lynch caught his breath.

"Let's do it again."

Gomez started walking.

"Fine with me, Usain."

They ran the act twice more. The first time yielded identical results. The second time, Gomez first put his head down and spun around several times to make himself dizzy. It disoriented him as planned, but Lynch was still unable to catch him.

"This isn't working, amigo."

"No, it's not. What are the variables?"

Gomez held up the rock.

"This isn't a gun. I'm not high on meth, and you don't weigh 200 pounds."

Lynch, still winded, braced himself on the cedar pole fence, and thought out loud.

"So...guns. Water pistols?"

"Too light."

"We can fill them with something. They'll be close."

"I guess I should get some meth and smoke up then?"

"What do meth heads do? Do they sweat?"

"Anyone who's nervous sweats."

"Cool. Let's go to Wal-Mart."

A pack of eight water pistols cost a cool $4.99 plus tax, which the detectives didn't bother to expense. They returned to their staging area to find the church's front door ajar, as well as most of the first-floor windows.

Lynch spoke.

"Looks like Pastor Dani's here."

He slapped the bag of pistols into his partner's chest.

"Take these apart."

"Where the hell are *you* going?"

"Just being courteous. I'll be right back."

The location of Ellisport Fellowship made structural expansion of the building impossible, so the church had to do what they could with the space they had. The sanctuary was something to behold...real James Bond stuff. The default setting was for Sunday services, but push a button, and the pulpit would disappear into the stage, the floor would retract, ceiling panels would open, hoops and backboards would descend, and...presto change-o...the youth group had a place to play basketball. Press another button, and the congregation had a movie theater; press another, and they

284

had a concert hall for the Battle of the Bands. Only the chairs appeared to require manual set-up, and even they were stacked on motorized dollies.

The coolest fixture in the room, though, was the professional-grade sound console along the back wall. Lynch's eyes and ears were drawn to it instantly.

To him, the gear looked state-of-the-art, but it was actually a couple of generations old. The new stuff wasn't that big. All twenty-four channels of the mixer, plus its custom-made cabinet, stuck out from the wall a little over six feet.

There was someone behind it. Lynch couldn't see the guy, but he could hear him singing to himself…badly.

"I feel like a woman! Bap Baaahh na na na!"

As it was pointless to shout, Lynch moved closer and took a peek behind the cabinet finding the khaki-covered rump of the church custodian.

"Bap Baaahh na na na!"

He was on his hand and knees, scrubbing the floor with industrial strength solution…

"Woooo!"

… and listening to Shania Twain on his iPod. His name was Nate, although the subject of his name never came up.

Lynch gave Nate's foot an apologetic kick. His demeanor gave him away as a local.

"Hi there, sir! Sorry, I didn't hear you. I can't get back here with the buffer. Can I help you with something?"

"I just wanted to ask if was okay to use some of the gravel from your walk way."

"I'm not a member here, but I'm sure it's okay. If they can afford all this stuff, I'm sure they can spare some gravel."

"True enough."

One of the dollies holding twenty or so chairs was parked nearby. A sheet was thrown over the entire stack with a sign on top that read "Hands Off! (signed) Damien."

These are Damien's chairs. No one better touch Damien's chairs. Damien needs to get over himself.

Gomez had two of the guns gutted and separated when his partner returned. The little Craftsman multi-tool from his keychain was poised on a fence post with the Phillips-head screwdriver extended.

"You aren't done with those yet?"

"There are like seventeen screws holding each of these little pieces of shit together."

"Well, if anyone gets pissed at us for using the church's gravel, I'm blaming the cleaning guy."

"How mature of you."

The scheme worked half as well as Lynch had hoped and twice as well as Gomez had expected. The weight was off; the size was off, but at least now the weapon was the right shape.

"Ready?"

"Ready, amigo."

Point, stomp, aim, bang, run, toss, splash…same result.

"Goddammit!"

They heard a door slam on the other side of the church. Nate had moved to a different part of the building.

"Hang on a second, Jaime. I have a thought."

"I hope so, man. All I have right now is a side stitch."

"When Eddie turned tail, it was a survival instinct. The drugs were leaving his body. That's why he was looking for quick cash and stuff to pawn. He needed to score. He was probably having trouble processing more than one thought at a time. That's why he didn't toss the gun until he was way over here. He forgot he had it. Getting away *and* ditching the evidence was too much for him to think about all at once."

Somewhere in the church, the floor buffer whirred up to full blast.

"So, what are you thinking?"

"I'm thinking something distracted him. Something took his mind off of running, so he slowed down."

"Like what?"

"How the fuck should I know? Come on. The endorphins are kicking in. I'm thinking better. I want to get my hand sweaty and run with my eyes closed this time."

They decided to keep at it until the water pistols ran out, regardless of the outcome.

Point, stomp, aim, bang, run, toss, splash.

"Dammit!"

Point, stomp, aim, bang, run, toss, splash.

"Son of a…"

Point, stomp, aim, bang, run, toss, splash.

"I'm getting pissed."

Point, stomp, aim, bang, run, toss.

"…"

They finished the fifth run, the eighth if they counted the three with the rocks. Lynch's lungs burned, his feet were swollen, his hair was sticking to his forehead, and in his hand was a fistful of Eddie's hoodie. He could barely speak through his own wheezing, but the words he managed were those of amazement.

"Dear God, I caught you. What happened?"

Gomez, also fighting for air, made a quarter turn and looked out over the river.

"The tip of my finger hooked around the trigger. Plus, my arm is so tired, I followed through too much, and the gun took a weird arc close to the wall."

"Is that why you slowed down?"

"No …"

With a smile, the handsome Puerto Rican from North Philly slapped his hand over the back of his partner's neck to emphasize the profundity of what just happened.

"…I didn't hear a splash. All the other times I knew I was close to the stopping point when I heard the splash. That was it. Eddie didn't hear one either. His mind switched from running to ditching the gun. He expected to hear a splash, and he didn't. That's why he stopped."

They wearily stumbled to the fence and stuck their heads over the edge. Lynch spoke as he considered regurgitation.

"Where'd it go, then?"

Gomez craned out to follow the arc of his toss.

"Not sure…"

He pointed.

"…there maybe?"

Lynch looked.

"No way."

The church had a dock. They didn't see it on their last visit because it was under the walkway and obscured from view. Tied to the dock, there was a boat. They didn't see it on their last visit because it wasn't there.

The laws of physics disallowed anything thrown from the walkway to hit the dock. Under the boat's port gunnel, however, there lay a cheap, gravel-filled, piece of green plastic from Wal-Mart.

"I'm not bumping your fist."

"I didn't put it up."

"You were thinkin' about it."

A narrow mahogany staircase took the detectives from the church lobby to an area beneath the sanctuary, untouched by gadgetry. The room, complete with a full kitchen, appeared to be used for social events that required food. The floor was hardwood on top of concrete. A beautiful stone fireplace made up the center of the south wall. The middle of the room was barren, except for Nate who was working the floor buffer…

"Any man of mine better be proud of me!"

…and listening to Shania Twain.

The detectives left him oblivious as they exited the building though a pair of French doors on the church's river side. They found themselves standing on a granite slab. When they looked up, they saw the underside of the wooden walkway.

They shared a cheeky grin before strolling to the edge of the slab, and the boat (christened 'Delilah') moored there.

"You guys doing okay?"

Nate passed through the French doors just in time to see Lynch pull a water pistol from Delilah's stern. One would have thought Excalibur had just been freed from the Stone.

"I said…you guys okay?"

Lynch froze and responded with the pistol brandished above his head. "We are incredibly fine, sir."

He twirled and pocketed the plastic weapon while Gomez showed his shield and spoke.

"Mind if we ask you a few questions, sir?"

The custodian defensively swept his pointed finger between the moorings.

"Pastor Dani told me it was okay to dock here while I do the floors. I live just up and across the river. It's easier than driving."

"No, no, no. That's not it at all. This isn't even our jurisdiction. Delilah's yours, then?"

Nate immediately relaxed and went back into Ellisport mode. The boat was, indeed, designed, built, and owned by him. Like every honorable sailor, he named it after his wife.

"Was she moored here during the last BOB?"

"That thing? Naw, I never go to it…"

He held up his iPod so the detectives could see his playlist.

"…country fan. I think the River Tram was here that night though. She's a big 'un. Takes twenty passengers comfortably. Wouldn't surprise me if there were a few other launches tied up too."

Lynch pulled out one of his cards and handed it to Nate.

"Here…if you need anybody shot, give me a call."

The man was still laughing when Lynch and Gomez reached the top of the stairs. They knocked on every door they could find. No one else was in the building. They took a walk around the sanctuary to see if anything new popped; nothing did. Gomez spotted the sheet-covered dolly of chairs.

"Who's this Damien cat?"

"I don't know, but he takes his chairs seriously."

"And how do they get this stuff downstairs? I didn't see an elevator. Did you?"

"Push a button. I'm sure the fireplace spins around or something. All this is easy enough to confirm."

He called the number given to him by Pastor Dani and left a message for her to call him back.

The captain of the River Tram was easy to track down and easier to eliminate as a suspect since he and had been in New Zealand for almost a

289

month. They took a shot at calling him, but it was two o'clock in the morning where he was.

"Feel like lunch?"

"I feel like lunch."

On Julie's texted recommendation, they found their way to a little mom-and-pop hole-in-the-wall called Apron Strings. The walk sobered them. Their shared high wore off as they talked.

"Tell me, Jaime, why are we just finding out about this stuff *now*? Nobody said nuthin' 'bout no River Tram. There should have at least been something in the report."

"I'll tell you why, Ernie. Because they're just like us, only worse. They're small town cops. We do fine with robberies, drug busts, domestic disturbances, lost children…but throw a murder or a shooting at us, and we are way out of our bandwidth!"

"But this wasn't a serious crime. No one even got killed."

"Exactly! No one got killed. If someone *had* gotten killed, they might have handed the thing over to the Feds, just like *we* should have done from the start. No, no. They figured everyone was okay, they caught the shooter red-handed, plus six witnesses saw the gun go into the river. Why spend all the time, money, and energy dredging the Schuylkill when no one got killed."

"So, they let it go."

"They let it the fuck go. Who cares about a weapon when you've got a bullet and a confessed criminal? No one does, of course, until the weapon is used again."

The conversation continued along the same lines all the way through lunch, culminating in one basic truth: even with the Delilah revelation, they weren't that much farther than before. They didn't need to prove that the gun didn't go into the river. Ballistics proved that. They now had an *idea* where the gun *may* have actually gone provided Eddie Williams threw the thing *exactly* the same way Gomez did.

"There is one thing though amigo, and it isn't small change."

"You mean We're All Lazarus?"

Gomez nodded.

"Being on stage during the shooting doesn't alibi them anymore. Anyone at the show could have picked up that nine mil any time before the boat unmoored."

"I'll do you one better. Pastor Devlin's on the list now too."

"Holy shit! I didn't think of that."

"He has lost no love for the Philly Archdiocese. We saw that."

"That's beautiful!"

Lynch looked at his watch.

"We've got a little under two hours of lost time left. I say we start with Devlin."

"Works for me. How's the cheesecake here?"

"Good thing we're not in a hurry."

"*Now* who's being sarcastic, bro?"

3. Beside an Open Window

Philip looked down at the top of his girlfriend's head. This was not intimate sex, the kind that was enhanced by closeness, best executed skin to skin with deep passion and utterances of love. This was the other kind: the kind that filled a primal need for release and nothing more: the kind he usually got in the afternoon.

He'd already done his part. His taking care of her first made it better for both of them.

By design, the kitchen blinds were up. Anyone walking by would have seen him from the waist up smoking a cigarette in profile. Fifteen minutes earlier, they would have seen her sitting on the counter reading a strategically positioned magazine. The feeling of getting away with something, sprinkled with the chance of getting caught, was a mutual turn-on.

He tapped ash into the sink.

She looked up and said the last thing a guy wants to hear when getting his world rocked.

"Everything okay?"

She was right to ask. Nothing was working. Philip was too preoccupied. He hadn't heard anything from his ID guy since their deflating online chat. He had no back-up plan, and time was growing short. The divine guidance he was counting on had yet to come through.

"I need to think."

"What?"

"I need to think...yes...I need to think."

291

As if his girlfriend was invisible, he backed up, got himself together, and left the apartment all the while mumbling to himself.

She was left kneeling on the floor with her bare butt on her heels. He'd done that sort of thing before, not *exactly* that, but things similar. She shrugged and crawled out of the room, lest she give the neighbors an eyeful they didn't deserve.

The thrill was oh so gone.

With a devilish smile, she put on some sweats and decided to take a nap. What did she care? She'd been good to go for ten minutes. He'd let her know when he snapped out of his funk. He always did.

4. About Town

The afternoon's events led Lynch and Gomez to the YMCA, but not before a stop at St. Aloysius. The drive back to Potterford started with a series of irritating phone calls. The first was to Maplewood Evangelical and only made it as far as the church secretary.

"Brother Devlin's appointment book says 'O'Rourke two o'clock'. I don't know what that means. Do you need his cell number?"

They didn't. They had it. They called it. No answer. They called Father O'Rourke. Also no answer. They got through to the secretary at St. Matthews and were told that the St. Al's boys were back in their regular digs. They called St. Al's…no answer.

So, in hopes of tracking down Father O'Rourke, and, in turn, Pastor Devlin, they set a course for Prospect Street.

The church was nearly as they'd last seen it, except the cops were outside rather than in. The guard force was comprised mostly of uniforms that could be spared from other stations in the county. They were to remain on guard "until at least one man wearing a miter made it out of Potterford alive." This was an order, verbatim, from Special Agent Beck.

Lynch and Gomez went in through the side door. There was music: The Dona Nobis Pacem from Bach's Mass in b minor (not that either detective recognized it). It was faint, but followable, and drew them, familiarly, behind the sanctuary.

They found Father Leo in his office. His back was to them, and his CD player was blaring the Bach Mass. The scene was, to say the least, interesting. Leo had cleared his white board of all writing and Post-its and refilled it with a bunch of photographs. He was putting the array under intense scrutiny.

Lynch touched the priest's shoulder, expecting to scare the man out of his rabat, but Leo's reaction was more of embarrassment than shorts-shitting. He picked up a little remote control and paused the Bach Mass mid-nobis.

"Jim! How are you?"

Lynch nodded toward the white board.

"Not bad, actually. This is impressive."

"This? It's just a…it's nothing. Just an experiment."

The pictures were immediately recognizable as being from the confirmation. Lynch remembered Leo mentioning an appeal to his parishioners for photos and whatnot from the service.

"Shouldn't the FBI have all this?"

"They have copies of it all on a flash drive. These came off my photo printer."

The machine was in the office…easily fifteen years old, but, apparently, still worked. Leo continued.

"Really, this is just me playing detective. Ignore it. Did you need something?"

A dry smile came to Lynch's lips. Leo realized he'd chosen the wrong turn of phrase.

"Well, considering how *you'd* probably react if you caught *me* playing priest, I think I'm interested."

Gomez approached.

"Yeah, Father. Whatcha got here?"

Father Leo begrudgingly gave in.

"It's an approximation of Cardinal Romero High School's gym last Saturday. Most of the pictures are worthless…Bishop Ryan … kids … Ryan … kids … backs of heads … kids … kids … Bishop Ryan. That's about it. No one, of course, got any pictures of the congregation from Bishop Ryan's point of view while the Mass was going on."

Leo closed his eyes and inhaled not wanting to continue. He did anyway.

"But look at this."

He pointed to a picture of a very tall boy posing for a photo with Bishop Ryan. On the side, sneaking in some face time, was Constance Henderson.

293

Leo sounded like a man trying to explain to his wife why he didn't wipe his feet.

"One of the things that's been bugging me all week is how the killer knew Ryan was staying at the Marriott. I understand he could have followed him, but if he didn't, someone blabbed. And the biggest blab in the church is (pointing) Constance Henderson. I remember her talking the Bishop's ears off after this picture was taken. I was standing right there, see? I couldn't hear what she was saying, but she was the only one to linger."

He paused, hoping the detectives would stop him and leave. With no such luck, he forged ahead referencing the same photo.

"This guy here...the guy sort of in the foreground...that's Jake Leary, and he's in the line of people walking out, right? That means, anyone hearing the conversation would have been in line behind Jake, which means they would have been *sitting* somewhere behind Jake."

He changed pictures.

"Now, here's Jake sitting down, that's definitely the back of his head. See where the aisles cross? That puts him maybe ten rows from the back."

He drew the detectives' attention to a cluster of photos on the right side of the board.

"All of these were taken from the back of the room. These three over here contain men I can't vouch for. This guy I don't recognize, and these two I can't see very well because the view is blocked by other heads."

By hound-like guidance or dumb luck, Lynch spotted Braden Reilly's unmistakable red hair. The kid was looking down at his yellow confirmation insert, doodling no doubt.

Gomez interjected.

"There are more heads blocked than just those three."

"Yes, but I know all the people who are sitting around the others, so I can pretty well tell who they are by association. It's a confirmation. Just about all of the men in these pictures are family men."

Lynch interrupted.

"You're assuming the crime was committed by someone you don't know."

"That is true...wishful thinking, I guess."

Lynch and Gomez looked at each other, silently acknowledging that they'd just witnessed some damned fine detective work. Lynch put his

294

finger on the white board next to the three pictures containing mystery men.

"May I take these?"

Father Leo folded his arms with an expression of relief and confusion.

"Be my guest. This makes sense, then?"

The detectives beamed.

"Si Padre."

"This is good, Leo, really good."

The priest, caught off-guard, indulged in a moment of pride for which he would later ask forgiveness.

"My old man had a saying. He said it in Italian, but it translates into English roughly as 'know your stuff.' I know my congregation."

Lynch dug out his pad and pencil and asked for a quick rundown of all the people sitting immediately next to the men in question. Leo obliged, while Gomez bagged the pictures for protection. Lynch finished up his scribbling, thanked Father Leo, and started to exit.

Gomez cleared his throat. Lynch spun back. Once again, he'd gotten off track and forgot to ask question number one.

"Any idea where Father O'Rourke might be?"

"He left with his racquet ball gear maybe a half an hour ago, so the YMCA's a strong possibility. He keeps his appointments in plain view on his desk. Take a look there."

There was, indeed, a Star Wars Day-at-a-Time calendar on the corner of Aiden's ink blotter. The entry upon it read 'Devlin two o'clock,' so both he and Devlin knew *that* they were getting together that day, but the specific plans weren't made ahead of time.

"Check this out."

Tucked into the corner of the blotter was a long, narrow piece of paper containing a list:

~~First Baptist~~
~~Torah~~
Xavier Lutheran (?)
Maplewood Evangelical
First Pres
Potterford United Methodist
Masjid Aljamia

SJ Episcopal

Etc.

Something about it, or rather, the way it was written, rang a faint bell somewhere in Lynch's recent memory. It nagged at him for about an hour.

5. The "Y"

The racquetball courts at the YMCA were installed to tournament standards. The floors were hardwood and heavily varnished. The front and side walls were made form a resilient, single-purpose material called FiBERESiN™. The rear walls were all paneled glass with spectator seating beyond.

The match was Aiden's idea, racquetball being the only common ground between him and Devlin. They held their conversation between the slaps and pops of rubber against wood and fibrous plastic.

"Aiden, I don't know what to tell you."

"I'm here against my boss's advice, you know. He told me it was a waste of time talking to you."

"I've said it before, and I'll say it again. I don't have a problem with you, Pascucci, or even Karney. I feel the same about Catholics as Jesus felt about the Jews. Jesus didn't speak out against the Jews. He *was* a Jew. He spoke out against the pharoses. I don't speak out against the Catholics; I speak out against Catholic leadership."

"We're busting at the seams. You get that, right?"

"Yeah, you guys are all about the numbers. That's why you hate homosexuals, birth control, and abortions. They stunt the production of little Catholics."

"You're contradicting yourself now."

"Cheap shot, sorry."

"What I mean is…(grunt)…we need more room. That's the only reason we're building the new church."

"Interesting how your parish spent the biggest chunk of change it ever collected on itself."

"You want to talk money?"

"Okay, point made. Look, if you want me to back off, I'll stop looking for trouble until you break ground on the new church…son of a …!"

Devlin missed his shot, putting things even at a game apiece. They took a water break while he completed his thought.

"…but you know what happens if another kid gets felt up, or anyone does, or says *anything* that resembles defiling Eddie Williams' character."

"Who?"

"Just remember the name. You may hear it again. If you do, leave it alone."

"This conversation just got awfully mafia-like."

"Well, you would know. Serve it."

There was a knock on the glass. Brother Devlin reacted with mute confusion while Father O'Rourke walked over to the door and gave the handle a yank.

"Hi, fellas. Pardon the interruption."

The young priest, fazed by nothing after the week's events, bade his visitors enter. Devlin remained perplexed…more so as the casually-dressed detectives made their way intimidatingly toward him. He pointed at their feet.

"It's a good thing you've got on regulation footwear. The YMCA folks are sticklers about scuff marks. Is this your day off?"

Lynch spoke over his shoulder.

"We need to talk to Brother Devlin alone, Father. Can you occupy yourself for a few minutes?"

Aiden grabbed his towel and stepped out. Lynch lubed his gears for a long, teeth-pulling interview. He would not get one. Devlin spoke.

"Mind if I smack the ball around a little while we talk?"

"I don't have a problem with that. Do *you,* Ernie?"

"No, I'm cool. Go ahead."

"Thwack – pop!"

"So, what's this about, detective?"

"Oh, some new stuff has come to light. I didn't know you and Father O'Rourke were friends."

"Thwack – pop!"

"We're friend-*ly*. I wouldn't exactly call us friends. He's working all of us over."

"Who's 'all of us?'"

"Thwack – pop!"

"All of the religious figures in Potterford. He's…"

"Thwack – pop!"

"…looking to get all us non-Catholic organizations on the side of St. Al's …"

"Thwack – pop!"

"…Someone over there has it in their head that support of that kind will…"

"Thwack – pop!"

"…push back on negative press."
"Do you agree?"

"Thwack – pop!"

"I don't care enough to agree or disagree."
"Do you know who else he's spoken to?"

"Thwack – pop!"

"Rabbi Sager at the synagogue, Pastor Seymour at First Baptist…"

"Thwack – pop!"

"...Reverend Beech over at Extra Large."
"Excuse me? Over at where?"

"Thwack – pop!"

"Xavier Lutheran. Everyone calls it Extra Large: XL, get it?"

Like an approaching locomotive, the distant bell rung by the cryptic list
on O'Rourke's desk blotter grew louder. Lynch closed his eyes and dug.
Dribs and drabs of the past six days came forth as though his brain's
[shuffle] button had been pushed.

*"Yeah ,Jim. Sorry. I'm afraid the 'how' is going to be easier than the
'why' on this one."*

*"You might call them a gang. They don't really call themselves
anything."*

*"We all passed out in the loft like we always do. Next morning, he was
gone."*

"I just wanted to paint some boobies. We create our own truths."

"I left it on a pew in the church."

Lynch opened his eyes, broke into a pace, and started talking to himself.
Ernie had seen it before, but Devlin was clearly creeped-out.

"The band...the day we questioned the band at Maplewood. There was
something else."

He turned to face his partner.

"Ernie, I'm an idiot, a complete, worthless idiot. I'm the one with a
certification in ladder logic programming and a degree in computer science
from Drexel fucking University! You're the one with the street smarts.
You know people. I've got the overactive powers of deduction. That's my
role. If I don't play that role, what good am I? When I'm at a church
clothing drive and I see signs labeled SM, ME, and XL, I think they
indicate sizes. It makes perfect sense that they're sizes; it's a clothing
drive. But when I see other signs in the same room labeled SA, F, and FB,
I dismiss them as something I don't understand. Do I ever think to ask for
clarification? No, because it makes perfect sense that the other signs
indicate sizes, *but they don't!*"

299

Devlin launched another ball…

"Thwack – pop!"

…but Detective Lynch caught it before Devlin could hit it again.

"Pastor Devlin, do you take clothing drive donations from other churches?"

The minister was frozen in mid-swing.

"Yes, several. Why?"

"And the letter codes put up around Community Hall, they aren't sizes. They represent the churches that make the donations. Right?"

"Again, yes. Who said they were sizes?"

"So, XL is hung above the pile from Xavier Lutheran; SM is Saint Matthews; ME is your own pile: Maplewood Evangelical."

"SM is South Methodist, but yes. Could I have my ball back?"

"FB is First Baptist. F I don't know."

"Fellowship…the Church of Rock. It's all the way over in Ellisport, but they live for stuff like…"

"And SA is Saint Aloysius."

Devlin broke eye contact to see why Detective Gomez suddenly slapped the wall. A toothy smile gave the impression that something good just happened.

"St. Al's donates sometimes; not often."

Lynch didn't care about "sometimes." Once was enough: one donation, one black trench coat with a Theban S on the back. Finally…FINALLY…there was a route that an article of clothing could have taken from St. Al's to Maplewood.

"Get Father O'Rourke, would you please, Ernie?"

The chaos surrounding Fellini's assassination had prevented Lynch from discussing Samuel's jacket with Father O'Rourke…until now. This time, the detective wasted no time getting to question number one.

"If someone leaves a personal effect in a pew after a Mass or confession, what happens to it?"

"We have a lost-and-found box in the secretary's office. I don't know what happens to the items that go unclaimed. That's a question for Pastor Karney."

"That's okay. I think I know."

Gomez spoke to Devlin.

"I don't completely understand why you need to know who the donations come from."

Devlin, now engrossed, answered enthusiastically.

"It's something we started doing a couple years ago. It inspires competition between some of the larger churches. There are also some things we can't use, so it's good to know where they came from so we can send them back."

"Give me an example."

"Sometimes we get an item that looks too nice to wind up in a donation box, so we check to make sure it wasn't put there by accident. We also get personalized items like sports jerseys and bowling shirts."

"What happens to that stuff?"

"We put it aside. After that, it gets sent back, or someone from Maplewood finds a use for it."

"Who gets first crack?"

"Anyone helping with the drive. That's not much of a lead for you. A couple o' dozen people volunteer."

Lynch handed his tablet to Devlin, along with a pen. It was time to put the jacket and the gun in the same hands.

"We need a list of all the volunteers who were also at the Battle of the Bands."

Devlin took both with no eagerness.

"Okay, but this will take a while. It's just about all of them."

"Leave out the blue-hairs."

The good pastor's expression said "fine…you asked for it." He scribbled down a couple names and paused.

"Detective Lynch, can you get YouTube on your phone?"

Lynch brought up the app, knowing exactly where Devlin was going.

"Yes, I can."

"While I'm doing this, you might want to search for performances from the Battle of the Bands. I'm sure someone posted something."

For probably the sixth time that day, Lynch felt useless for not thinking of such a thing himself. The posts were easy to find. Most of them were shots of the stage.

No good.

One channel, however, was full of onstage, offstage, and audience footage shot using a mobile device. It was all too dark to be helpful, but it showed that the user took a greater interest in the event than most. The guy probably had many more clips than he'd posted. Lynch checked the YouTuber's name, and, with joy, showed it to his partner.

CHAZ-ROX76

"You took a business card from him, right?"
"That I did, Jaime."

6. Le Chataeu du Chaz

Looking around Charles 'Chaz' Martin's apartment, one might assume he was rich. He was not. Somewhere around the tenth of every month, he would tally the earnings from his day job, along with his gig money. He'd subtract his expenses which amounted to rent, bills, food, and gas. Whatever he had left, he'd spend to the last penny.

"Irresponsible moron" was the general flavor of the name-calling, but such things merely bounced off of Chaz. In his mind, he wasn't broke, he was (quoted verbatim) "happily even." He had neither a mortgage nor a credit card. He paid cash for everything from his collection of concert t-shirts to his Subaru Outback. The man was, unlike everyone who gave him shit, free of debt. True, he was also free of savings, but savings did not concern him. When he got too old to enjoy his stuff, he'd sell it, hand the profits over to the nearest senior living center, and let the government take care of the rest.

The lifestyle was careless and bound for disaster, but also made a twisted bit of sense. That was Chaz. His energy level was the same over the phone as it was in person. Whatever he did for a living, he had no trouble taking off for an hour. He freely offered his apartment as a place to meet.

"Dude! You want to watch these vids, you gotta watch 'em right!"

He purposely chose a corner-basement unit to minimize noise complaints, but it wound up being a non-issue. He could have put a moto-cross track in his living room, and no one would have complained. All of his neighbors (like everyone else) loved him.

302

He'd divided his only bedroom in half using some lead piping and a heavy, black curtain he purchased at cost from a local community theater. He ushered the two detectives into the room, halting them just inside the doorway for full effect. All smiles, the drummer backed up to the curtain and whipped it aside…

"Pa-dow!"

…exposing his bitchin' array of AV gear. To the left was a seventy-eight-inch curved-screen UHD TV mounted four feet off the floor. To the right was Chaz's work station, complete with a captain's chair and the latest Mac Book Pro. Five JBL speakers of varying size and purpose were positioned strategically around the room. Sound proofing concealed the only window.

Chaz made a sweeping gesture toward a duct tape 'X' on the carpet.

"Stand on the mighty X for the optimal sound experience gentlemen. I worked it out specifically for the room. I can drag a La-Z Boy in from the living room if you want. There's room for two in it if you squeeze…"

"We're good, Chaz, thanks."

Lynch, out of both courtesy and curiosity, planted himself on the mighty X. Gomez followed Chaz behind the console. Seconds later, the signature Apple "chime" came forth permeating three of Lynch's five senses.

"Whoah! Optimal sound…you weren't kidding."

"I know, right?"

Ugh!

Chaz held up two remote controls and finished the ritual.

Right hand – "Pyooow!" – the TV went on.

Left hand – "Pyooow!" – the lights went off.

"What would you like to see, gentlemen?"

Lynch answered.

"Any extra footage you took. Anything you shot other than the performances."

"Okay, I don't have that stuff memorized. Here, watch this while I find it."

Before Lynch could protest, Generation Us's opening number from the BOB appeared before him…with optimal sound.

Jesus is just alright with me…Jesus is just alright oh yeah…

By the light of a Mac Book Pro, Gomez was watching a man in his
element. Chaz was bouncing around well-organized folders of raw footage
taking breaks to play air guitar and comment on the music.

"You don't need to change the lyrics to this one!"

Get past the chintz, the boy knew what he was doing.

The tune ended…

"Sorry guys, had to let it finish."

…and he brought up the first of twenty-three crowd clips he'd saved
from the show. Most of the clip was filled with young(ish) women
showing support for their respective praise teams by revealing copious
amounts of leg and cleavage.

Gomez asked the obvious.

"This is a church thing, right?"

"Hey man, rock 'n roll is rock 'n roll."

The drummer held up a fist for Gomez to punch. The detective didn't
leave him hanging. Lynch didn't see it, but he sensed it.

Tool.

"Is this enough, gentlemen? Or do you need to see more?"

Lynch answered.

"What do you have from the We're All Lazarus performance?"

"The question is what *don't* I have from the We're All Lazarus
performance."

With a click of the mouse, the shot changed, and We're All Lazarus
appeared on stage getting ready to call up their first number.

"No no Chaz. Off stage, *off stage!*"

"Oh, right. My bad."

There were a few moments of silence while Chaz found the right clip.
Lynch took advantage.

"So, you had two cameras there."

"I had a camera set on a tripod that I used to shoot the show, and I had
my phone which I kept mobile…ha!…mobile phone…funny!"

The next clip started. It was a long one. We're All Lazarus was blurry
in the background playing to an adoring crowd. People walked into and

out frame bobbing their heads to the music and drinking their non-alcoholic beverages.

Lynch hollered to be heard.

"You're outside at this point loading the van, correct?!"

"Yes! A guy named Rudy has my phone. I didn't want to miss anything."

"Any particular reason you chose that moment to load?"

"We drew the short straw! With that many bands, the event has to stick to a pretty tight load schedule! More than one heavy vehicle back there, and the walkway tumbles into the Schuylkill!"

Lynch went back to the clip. Not much was audible above Rudy's whistles and cheers. When the video hit ten minutes and twenty-one seconds, Lynch spotted what he'd hoped.

"There we go. Chaz, pause it!"

"Paused!"

It was Brother Devlin walking to the back of the hall, and he was on his cell phone. Lynch rubbed his chin.

"Eddie Williams has you guys at gunpoint right now."

"I would say so."

"In a few seconds the gun will go off. Let it run a bit."

They watched the clip to the end. It ran another eight minutes, and as far as Lynch could tell, no one in the church had a clue anything was happening on the walkway. It was consistent with We're All Lazarus's story, but the clip was too shaky and dark to tell for sure.

"Back it up to Devlin again."

"Done."

They watched Devlin cross the screen, yelling into his cell phone.

"What song is this?"

"It's one of their originals. It's called Pity Party."

"Can I see the stage footage of the song?"

"Easier done than said."

Another paused image of the BOB champs appeared.

"Ernie, come up here and give me a second set of eyes."

"What are we looking for?"

"No idea."

Lynch was reminded of an old joke:

A guy is walking around at night and sees another guy looking for something under a streetlamp. The first guy asks, "what are you looking for?" The second guy replies, "I lost my watch over by that fence." The first guy then says, "If you lost it by the fence, why are you looking for it under the streetlamp?" The second guy answers, "Because I can't see a fuckin' thing by the fence."

The band couldn't have seen anything. The church's rear entrance was 150 feet from the stage. Eddie was next door when he tossed the gun. Pile on the light show and the sea of bodies that was the audience, and the exercise turned futile.

But Lynch wanted to see who in the room took notice of Devlin's exit, and only the stage footage (shot from the tripod) was clear enough to examine.

"I think we're ready, Chaz. Go ahead."

"With pleasure, my man!"

The song kicked on in ultra hi-def. The two detectives probed every movement of every musician from the first note to the last. Lynch took the singer and the bass player. Gomez took the guitar player, keyboard player, and drummer. The singer played to the audience for the entire set. The bass player kept his eyes mostly on his left hand. He looked up now and then, but not high or long enough to see anything at the back of the hall. It fit. The bass player is, as a rule, least obligated to put on a show. The guitar player was all over the place. He didn't focus *anywhere* for more than a couple seconds, and never past the front row. The keyboard player didn't look up at all. The drummer was difficult to read for a very specific reason. Gomez waited until the tune was over, and the vid was paused to say something. He pointed to the still image on the screen.

"Yo, Chaz, what's with the sunglasses?"

"Oh, that. I'll tell you, bro if you don't mind an unrelated story."

Gomez prayed that, whatever the story was, Chaz would act it out.

"We don't mind."

"Jerry...that's the drummer's name...he's covering up a black eye. He and Mick, the sound guy, went at it a couple of days before the show."

Chaz had the detectives' instant and undivided attention. Lynch spoke as the two of them gravitated toward the Mac Book.

"Went at it over what?"

"Jerry and I have been friends for a long time. That band kicks ass, but they have serious drama issues. We're talking Fleetwood Mac-level drama."

"So, a love triangle then?"

Chaz nodded.

"Patty, that's the singer, and Mick are married."

"We got that much."

"Cool, well, Patty and Jerry were together first. This was maybe seven years ago."

"Who broke up with whom?"

Gomez rolled his eyes at Lynch's sensitivity to grammar.

306

"Understand man, I only got one side of the story, and Jerry wasn't exactly sober when he told it. Mick is more than the band's sound guy. He does the booking, writes a lot of the music, and writes *most* of the lyrics. He's a talented guy to the bitchin' degree. Pity Party is his. You heard it; the music just flows out of him Amadeus-style.

"But here's where the drama starts. He's not an original member of the group. He wasn't even voted in. He was…and, mind you, this is drunk Jerry talkin'…forced on them by Bro Devlin."

"How'd that happen?"

"I'm shaky on details. Mick joined 'Maplewood E', like I said, about seven years ago. I don't know what drove him there. I get the vibe, just like from his tats and stuff; he was kind of a lost soul. Drunk Jerry says Devlin took the dude under his wing pretty hard. Word has it Mick studied music engineering somewhere, Berklee maybe, I don't know. Bro Devlin put him in charge of running sound during services at Maplewood. Three guesses who lost the job to him…that's right, Jerry. Anyway, cut to a few months later, the band is kicking ass, and everyone is thanking Mick for it."

"So that's a couple of nails in the coffin. How did Mick hook up with Patty?"

"The regular way: alpha male shit."

"You still haven't told me who did the breaking."

It was like talking to Samuel all over again, only with half the attitude and twice the cholesterol.

"Drunk Jerry said *he* did, but I don't really know. Our band played the wedding reception. Damn, I guess that's like six years ago. Doesn't seem like it."

"Six years and these two guys are still scrapping over it?"

"Man, you don't know the half of it. You guys want a beer?"

The detectives politely rejected the offer. Chaz reached under the console and produced a Miller Lite from a camouflaged mini-fridge. With a pop of the tab and an unreturned "cheers," he slammed back the majority of it.

"Anyway, that's not why they were fighting. Not really. You see…"

Chaz belched and set down his beer.

"…Jerry found out that Mick was cheating on Patty."

Lynch's reply was more out of reflex than interest.

"With who?"

Gomez joyfully corrected him.

"With *whom*."

"I don't know the chick. You know the funny thing is…and again…drunk Jerry…I don't think it was the actual cheating that pissed him off the most. I mean, the chick has a kid, and I don't even think *that* was it. Mick got Patty smoking again, and I don't even…Aw, I'm sorry, guys. I'm babbling. You don't need to know this shit."

"No Chaz, it's okay. What do you think pissed him off the most?"

"Look, you've got to understand, they take their beliefs like mondo-seriously over there at Maplewood. Stuff bugs them that doesn't bug us mere mortals."

"Chaz…what?"

The drummer picked up his Miller Lite and took it down to backwash.

"The chick Mick is banging … she's Catholic."

The words hung in the air like a bubble asking to be popped. Lynch thrust his hand in his pocket and yanked out the plastic bag containing the three pictures from Bishop Ryan's last Mass. He spoke as he fiddled with the seal.

"How old is the girlfriend's kid?"

"Whoa dude! Did I say something important?"

"How old!??"

"Okay, man. Chill. I think Jerry said she was ten or eleven. That was a couple years ago so…"

"So, confirmation age then."

"Yeah, I guess."

Lynch rifled through the pictures, trying to find the back of Mick's head, but he couldn't clearly remember what the guy looked like. He slapped the pictures down in front of Chaz.

"Does anyone in any of these pictures look like Mick to you?"

Chaz, wishing he had the theme to Mission Impossible at his fingertips, scooped up the pictures and inspected them one at a time. He went through all three, and then went back to the first.

"This guy could be him. I don't know. Mick changes his hair all the time."

Lynch tossed the empty bag on the floor, then, mumbling to himself, dug for his note pad and cell phone.

"That little jerk-off was in the back of the hall behind the sound board at the BOB too."

Chaz belched again and spoke.

"Mick? Behind the board at Fellowship Church of Ellisport? Damien's Board?? No, he wasn't! Nobody touches Damien's board."

Lynch froze as another piece…as it wound up, a crucial piece…snapped into place.

Damien is the fucking sound man at the Church of Rock; not the chair Nazi!

Lynch recalled the sign … "Hands Off". The sign wasn't referring to the chairs. The sign was from the sound board, as was the sheet. Nate the custodian (must have) moved them from the board to the stack of chairs so he could clean.

"Mick was there though…at the church, right Chaz?"

"Yeah. He was there."

"And he was angry. He was angry because *his* band was competing in front of a full house, and he had to trust their sound to a rival sound man."

"Dude, that's right! I mean, you'd think he'd be used to it. Him and Damien argue about it every…"

"So, he went out for a smoke. You said he got Patty smoking again. That means he smokes. He was pissed off and didn't want to hear someone else mess up *his* band's sound, so he went for a smoke."

"Uuhhhh… I guess he could have."

Gomez was already going through the list of names given to them by Brother Devlin.

"Ernie, if you want to have a smoke to calm your nerves, and you're at Fellowship Church, do you hang out on the street side or the river side?"

"The river side…any day of the year and twice on Easter."

"And you didn't see him on the walkway, did you Chaz?"

"No man. I didn't."

"So, he was *under* the walkway. He was grabbing a butt on the slab when the gun landed in one of the boats. He got the gun from the boat. He got Samuel's trench coat from the reject pile at the clothing drive. He was at St. Al's Saturday because his girlfriend's daughter was getting Confirmed. Say cheese, Mick! We've got you!"

Gomez reluctantly interrupted his crazed partner with a raised finger.

"There's one problem with that Jaime. Mick isn't on the volunteer list."

"That's impossible."

Gomez turned the list around.

"There isn't any 'Mick' on here, partner, I checked it twice."

Chaz had become hypnotized by the exchange. His knuckles were white from clutching the arms of his captain's chair as he waited for his moment to spring up and become a hero. That moment had come.

"Mick's not his real name."

Lynch replied.

"What's that?"

"Mick's a nickname. It's short for McKenzie."

Lynch started to scan the list again.

"His name is McKenzie?"

"His *last* name's McKenzie."

"Well, for fuck's sake, what's his first name?"

"Uh…Phil, I think."

7. The Woods

"Pow – ping!"

Not good.

"Pow – ping!"

"Maybe next time" isn't an option this time around.

"Pow – ping!"

Think, dammit, think!

"Pow – ping!"

No pain; no fear. No pain; no fear. No pain; no fear…

"Pow – ping!"

Philip McKenzie put his eyes on his uncle's shed as he stopped to reload.

"Well…if this whole thing goes pear-shaped, I guess that's *one* positive thing to come out of it."

A feeling Philip hadn't experienced in a long time started to creep up into his guts. The shrink he hadn't seen in seven years called it "anxiety-triggered" something-or-other. Brother Devlin called it demons. Whatever it was, it was helping. His heartbeat slowed. His focus returned. His thoughts started to filter through one at a time in a way that was manageable, and horrible.

"Why am I so worried about collateral damage? I've already killed two people. I killed them as a means to a heroic end. There is no restart. At this point, if I don't see this thing through, I'm not a hero; I'm a murderer. I'm doing God's work. If He hasn't sent me a solution to this by now, then there is no solution. What if three innocent people die, or six, or twelve? If they are truly innocent, God will give them their place in heaven. If not, they deserve the same fate as those before them. I can do this. I just have to change the game plan."

He started to pace.

"What am I going to need? I'll need a…"

His ears twitched. He turned his head toward the distant tree line. A vehicle was approaching, and it wasn't his uncle's truck.

8. Lynch's Car

Three phone calls put them on the right track. The first was to Father Leo.

"We think we know who the girlfriend is."

According to the photos, Leo's info, and Chaz's best guess, at Saturday evening Mass, Philip "Mick" McKenzie had an aisle seat next to a woman named Hesper Laraway.

"Do you have a phone number or an address for her?"

"I can get both, Jim. Hang on."

Lynch would later find out that Hesper lent a hand in the church secretary's office from time to time. For years, she'd been donating St. Al's unclaimed lost-and-found to the Maplewood clothing drive. It was how she met her whacked-out boyfriend. It was also how the last link in this particular chain of evidence hooked into place.

True to his word, Leo found contact information for Ms. Laraway easily enough. Gomez (and the PPD data system) followed in kind with the McKenzies' address, along with the make and model of Philip's car. The detectives arrived at Philip's and Patty's townhouse to find only street parking, and no blue Prius in sight. Knocking on the front door yielded no response.

"This is the police, Mick, open up."

After a mutual go-ahead nod, Ernie raised his right heel, aimed it at the latch, held his pose, and spoke.

"Anything?"

In the absence of a search warrant, the fake break-in ploy (as silly as it was) had a high success rate. If Philip was peeking out a window, a cop's foot in the air should have sent him scrambling. That was the idea anyway.

"Nope. No car. No noise. He's not here. Let's go."

Per Chaz, Patty McKenzie was a caregiver for Potterford's only Hospice. She too would be easy to find.

"Who do you want to call, Jaime? The wife or the girlfriend?"

"Both. You take the wife."

"How about Beck?"

"Not yet."

Things were looking good, but they still hadn't laid eyes or hands on the jacket or the murder weapon. Lynch wasn't going to rally the suits, armed only with what he'd reasoned so far. When he had a solid piece of evidence *literally* in his hands, he would call Agent Beck; not before.

They held their conversations simultaneously as Lynch peeled out from the curb headed down a one-way street.

"Hello this is Detective James Lynch."

"Hello, is Patty McKenzie available? Hi, Patty. This is Detective Ernie Gomez."

"We're looking for Mick. Any idea where his?"

"We have some questions for your husband. Do you know where we might find him?"

"Quit jerkin' me around! I'm not looking to out your relationship to his wife. If I was, I wouldn't be calling; I'd be at your door with the friggin' photographs!"

"Something's come to light, and we're taking another look at the Ellisport shooting."

"We tried his house. He's not there."

"We just need to re-eliminate him as a suspect."

"Give me a good guess then."

"He's not home? Do you have any thoughts as to where else we could try?"

"Do you know where that is?"

"Could I get an address from you?"

"Thank you. Stay on with me until we get there. I don't want you calling him."

"Thank you. Could you stay on the line in case we get lost? Great."

They put their phones to their chests, and Lynch stepped on the gas. Gomez spoke.

"His uncle has a…"

"Patch of property out Pruss Road. I'm on it."

9. The Woods

Philip circled around…

"No…not today. You want to stop me. You don't understand. You don't want me to finish. You want to make me a murderer. I am not a murderer. I am not a murderer."

…and climbed

I am not a murderer.

10. Walter's House

Pruss Road ran north-south, parallel to route 100. The ride was hilly, green, and served as a haven for anyone wanting to avoid the highway during rush hour. The homes visible from the road backed up against thick woodlands, giving the illusion that all the properties ended at the tree line. Some of them did. Others, like Walter's, had gravel or dirt paths that started behind the houses, wound through the woods, and opened onto acres of protected, undeveloped land.

Retired river ranger and former recluse Walter McKenzie spent the majority of his days jarring pickles and meticulously cleaning the sizable gun collection hidden in his basement. With no kids of his own, over the years he'd tried to teach his nephew a thing or two about survival in the wild, but it didn't take. All Philip wanted to do when he visited was ride the dirt bikes, and even that stopped when he got his driver's license. The kid was good with his hands though. His ability to pick through trash and use what he found to fabricate useful little gadgets would allow him to last longer than most when the shit hit the fan.

Had he pegged the two plain-clothed visitors on his porch as cops, he never would have opened the door.

"You want to talk to Phil? Uh…yeah, he went back to the field maybe an hour ago. Follow the path."

"Mind if we take a look inside your house, sir?"

The door to Walter's basement/armory was well-hidden, but not *that* well-hidden.

"I prefer you didn't."

"May I ask why (the fuck) not?"

313

"I don't like visitors. Look, my nephew's right where I told you. Park him in if you don't believe me."

Again…no warrant. Without much choice, they took him at his word.

"Thank you. I guess we'll be in the field then. Back a path you said?"

"Right off the yard towards the woods."

Hands in pockets, Lynch and Gomez descended the wobbly steps and disappeared around the side of the house.

Uncle Walter, having diverted the detectives from his house and the half-ton of illegal firearms under his feet, went into the house, locked the door, took a seat in his living room, and opened a jar of pickles.

"Pigs."

The one-car garage housed an ozone-destroying pick-up with a blue Toyota Prius behind it on the tarmac. Philip evidently decided to get to wherever his uncle was talking about on foot. Some recon revealed the reason.

The path to the field was not naturally formed. It started in the back yard's left corner, snaking left and right so a person had to travel it to see where it led. It was wide enough for a car, but covered in gravel and had at least one mountainous speed bump. One purpose; it offered passage that was neither quick nor quiet.

"Think Mick's armed?"

"To the teeth."

The woods were dense, but not too deep. Foregoing the gravel path, Lynch and Gomez quickly found themselves on the other side of the trees facing a grassy field three football fields deep and too wide to estimate. It ended at another tree line with more woods that stretched beyond the horizon.

Lynch spoke.

"Walk it, or ride it?"

"I'm a little short on Kevlar. I say we take the car."

"We lose the element of surprise."

"We gain the element of Detroit steel and bullet-proof glass."

"Well-observed, except my car doesn't have bullet-proof glass."

Gomez reacted as though he'd been told there was no Santa Claus.

"What???"

"Get the poop out of your ears. My car doesn't have…"

"You mean I've been riding around with you for four years behind non-bullet-proof glass?"

"Can we get back to the task at hand please?"

Gomez crossed himself.

"Dios me salve."

Gravel shot up into the wheel wells as they weaved their way to the field. Upon breaking the tree line, gravel turned into two parallel lines of tire-worn ground that led just about directly to a small grey structure at the far edge of the field.

"How are you feeling, Ernie?"

"Like a sitting duck."

"Me too. Get as low as you can."

"Fucking glass."

The building (a shed) grew closer. There was a thirty-foot gap between it and the tree line. It faced the woods width-wise, making visible the closed barn-style doors that would open away from the woods. The adjacent wall had one small window. The roof was slanted toward them and covered with corrugated steel as was the entire structure.

"You know, we don't even know that he's clocking us."

"I don't care."

Lynch slid the car next to the shed in a cloud of dirt. Both detectives drew their sidearms and shouldered their doors open. They slid out and crouched behind the doors.

"See him?"

"All I see is grass, trees, and a dirty car window that can be shot through."

"Stay there a sec."

Lynch flattened his front softly against the shed and shuffled toward the woods in an effort to get a look around the corner. He grabbed a peek through window on the way. The inside was too dark to see more than silhouettes and a few slivers of sunlight, but he could tell there were no entrances other than the two that were pad-locked from the outside.

"Whatcha got, acho?"

"He isn't in there."

Lynch kept moving. The soft ground allowed him to creep along in silence other than the pounding of his heart. As he neared the corner, a gas can came into view followed by the distinct edge of a portable generator.

315

Otherwise, the area between the shed and the tree line appeared empty, but it was difficult to tell.

"Hey, Jaime, can you see that?"

Lynch looked across the hood of his car to see his partner pointing at the woods. Unable to tell what Ernie was talking about, he shrugged and shook his head "no."

"In the woods, straight ahead of you. Call it fifty feet. It looks like plywood."

Plywood?

It took some doing to lay eyes on it, but Ernie was right. The distant and knotty corner of a piece of weathered plywood stuck out from the foliage about eight inches. It looked like they were going to have to do what they *really, really* didn't want to do. Lynch scurried back around the car door and spoke to his partner across the front seat.

"If we're going in there, it's going to have to be cowboy style."

"Who goes first?"

"I will. You're the better shot."

"You're going to have to check yourself for ticks tonight, you know."

"I'm starting to hope he *is* hiding in there. This isn't exactly going to be a story to tell our grandkids if he isn't."

"I'll count you down."

"Cowboy style" meant "run like hell across an area without cover, and pray you don't get shot." Of the three possible outcomes, obviously the most favorable was that Philip wouldn't have enough reaction time to fire. Failing that, hopefully he would miss and give away his position to the runner's partner. Failing *that*, the afternoon would become academic.

"3...2...1...Go!"

Lynch leapt off his mark. Gomez frantically scanned the trees, readying himself for whatever happened next. Out of the corner of his eye, he saw his partner's blue windbreaker dart across the grass. Five excruciating seconds later, Lynch was on his belly and out of harm's way.

Nothing.

Lynch readied himself. Gomez repeated the countdown to himself and sprinted a corner route putting him twenty-five feet away from his partner.

Again, the trees stayed quiet.

316

They worked their way slowly and separately to the plywood. As long as they stayed low, the trees and undergrowth provided the protection they needed...fingers crossed.

Lynch saw the whole of it first.

"Good Lord."

It was Philip's clearing, his think tank, his war room. He'd spent countless hours of target practice there. He'd invented and constructed his collapsible tree stand there. Three days earlier, he'd climbed above it, and after a chorus of "You Are My Sunshine,", tossed a set of costume false teeth into the surrounding trees.

Lynch was sitting on the ground with his back propped up against a 100-year-old red maple taking it all in. The only things to see were plywood, saw horses, and an assortment of tin cans. The sparseness of the décor made the scene no less eerie.

He noticed something about the cans.

The labels had been torn off, but they weren't blank. One lay less than an arm's length away, so he snagged it for a closer look. Two painted lines formed an 'X' across its center. One was silver; one was gold. He looked for his partner and found him sitting similarly, but facing the opposite direction, across the clearing.

"Hey, Ernie, what do you make of this?"

The can arced across the clearing, landing softly in Ernie's hands. It took a few seconds for him to recognize the symbol formed by the silver and gold brush strokes. Before he could say anything, his partner was shouting to him.

"What are those lines supposed to be? Swords?"

"No...keys. It's a papal symbol."

"A paper symbol??"

"No acho, *papal*! It's a symbol of The Pope."

Lynch's heart rate slowed.

Good enough for me.

He was glad he hadn't left his cell phone in the car.

317

10. Up a Tree

Philip had been watching the entire process from his favorite tree; the one he was sitting in the day before he did the Archbishop.

He had to respect them for tracking him to his uncle's woods, despite their ineffective method of approach. They did some jazz with their car that he couldn't really see, followed by some running that reminded him of the last scene from "Butch Cassidy and the Sundance Kid."

Spoiler alert fellas: They die at the end.

Eventually, their ill-conceived plan had them sitting still.

He braced his shooing arm on a convenient branch. He recognized them from the press conference, and the rehearsal interruption at the church. There was no clear shot at Detective Lynch. He could nick a shoulder at best.

Or perhaps his elbow. What's he doing?

Detective Gomez, however, was facing Philip straight-on. The distance between Philip and the clearing was less than twice the length of the clearing itself. He remembered the bull's-eye he made after throwing the teeth…lucky shot? Maybe, but he did it with little effort and an obstructed view.

He could do this.

No pain; no fear.

As he slowly readied his nine to fire, he visualized the next thirty seconds. He had to fade them out of position. Once the dying cop had them properly distracted, he'd have plenty of time to do what he needed to do.

He'd fired the gun enough times to know its idiosyncrasies. He aimed it directly at Detective Gomez's throat. If his hand jiggled in any direction, it would still be a kill shot.

All he had to do was squeeze the trigger.

He closed his eyes and took a breath.

318

I am not a murderer.

11. The Clearing

"Mierda!!"

Bark exploded over Ernie's left ear, sending him into the weeds.

"You okay, Ernie!"

"I'm okay. Gonna be pickin' splinters out of my skull for a week, but I'm okay!"

"Where'd it come from!?"

"Straight ahead somewhere."

"Stay low!"

"No shit!"

A second shot whistled over Lynch head. The bastard had them pinned.

"Son of a bitch!"

Ernie tried talking to him.

"Hey Philip! You've got…"

A flat rock shattered two feet from Gomez's nose.

"Take it easy, man! I said you've got…"

A fourth bullet ricocheted off the side of stump close enough to Ernie to make him scurry backwards.

"Okay, okay okay! Stop it! I get the point!"

It was a stand-off. Every time the detectives made noise, they gave away position. Every time Philip fired, he did the same. They were keeping themselves concealed for different reasons. Philip didn't want to get caught. The detectives didn't want to get killed.

Lynch worked his way beside a dead, ant-infested old log, and raised his head. He'd lost view of his partner. His phone buzzed…a text. He ignored it. He got up on his elbows and started to crawl on his belly toward the field. His phone buzzed again.

"Jaime! Pull your cabeza out of your culo!"

Ohhhh! Idiot.

He read Ernie's text.

319

THE FIRST BULLET WAS SHOT AT A DOWNWARD ANGLE.
THAT LAST ONE CAME STRAIGHT ACROSS.

The angle of trajectory was decreasing. The shooter had climbed down a tree. He was on the move, but which way? His options were limited. He could head for his car or head deeper into the woods. He could make for the road or make for the wilderness. He could go to the right or go to the left.

Lynch texted back.

TALK TO HIM AGAIN.

"Hey, Philip! Come on, hombre! You can't possibly think you've got a way out of this! Let's talk!"

Silence...Philip wasn't stupid.

"Flush him!"

Both detectives sprang to their feet and emptied their magazines high into the trees before hitting the ground again. For the next five minutes, they lay still, listening for rustling leaves or a snapping twig.

Nothing.

Lynch sent another text.

HOLD TIGHT. I'M GOING TO WORK MY WAY BACK TO THE CAR.

He never hit [send]. The distant "pop" of a pad lock stopped him.

"Fuck! The shed! Go, Ernie, go!"

The two detectives heaved themselves off of their bellies and bobbed and weaved as fast as they could toward the tree line. Lynch emerged first with Gomez a couple of yards behind.

The barn doors had been swung open, but the lock on the side door was still closed. They crouched down and moved as fast as they could, putting Lynch's car between themselves and the window. The tires had been flattened. They ignored the implications and slipped around the back bumper to the near side of the open barn door. They were about to do a three count and storm the shed when they heard a sputter.

The sound was unmistakable.

"Is that...?"

"Shit!"

They darted around the side just in time to hear a second sputter turn into rev and a roar. They tried to raise their pistols, but it was too late.

All they could do was jump out of the way.

12. Racing to the Tree Line

Philip had only one plan: get to his car, and get his ass out of there. The resurrected bike would be no good on his uncle's effed-up gravel path, but he could get close enough to the house to run the rest of the way. Then, he could be on the road heading for one of a thousand hiding places before the cops were half way across the field. He only wished he had his hands free to flip a double-bird behind his back.

He thought he heard gun fire behind him.

"Nice try, guys."

He was too fast and too far away. In thirty years, some kid would find the bullets embedded in the field and wonder how they got there. Perhaps he'd do some research and find out about the showdown in Walter McKenzie's woods. Then they'd read about Philip and how he singlehandedly brought down the whole damned thing. The kid would read about the empire that existed before Philip started his good works and become inspired to rid the world of the remaining evil. Maybe…just maybe.

The bike rumbled under him as he sped across the grass toward his goal. Wonderful memories of a simpler time coupled with a feeling of triumph blended into a new perfect moment. He couldn't help but let out a Howard Dean war cry.

"Yeeeeeaaaaahhhhhh!!! Suck my…"

Uh oh.

The first black sedan burst into view, throwing up gravel as it crossed Philip's path. Three more followed. Eighteen inches of turf went flying as he planted his right foot on the ground, jammed the handlebars to the right, and reversed direction.

He caught a glimpse of the two detectives. They'd stopped running. They'd stopped shooting. They were…just standing there.

"You knew I called Beck, right?"

"I tried to warn the guy, but he kept shooting at me."

It mattered not. He still had one advantage over all of them. He knew his uncle's woods. He knew the old trails. He hadn't ridden them for years, but he knew them. The two idiots on foot were leaving the rest of the chase up to the idiots in the cars, and no car would be able to follow him where he was about to go.

The entrance was invisible to the naked eye. His pursuers would think he was either nuts, or about to dump the bike and run for it. If the driver was good enough, and didn't care too much about the car, he might be able to maneuver through the first 100 feet or so, but there was no way they could take the ravine.

The air changed as he broke onto the trail. The ride was smooth as silk. Branches whipped past his head on either side, welcoming him home. The creek was two minutes away. He hadn't learned as much about survival in the wild as his uncle would have liked, but he knew how to find food and make shelter. It would suffice until he and God could come up with another plan.

He cheered and laughed as the ravine came into view. As the landscape changed, and the trail dipped down between two grassy, rocky, muddy, chest-high ledges, Philip looked over his shoulder for a split second to see if anyone was stupid enough to try and follow him. No one was.

Good bye.

With a satisfied grin, he faced forward just in time to feel the air leave his lungs and see his bike disappear into the distance without him.

His next sensation was blurred vision coming into focus. He was on his back looking up at the sky. He'd taken something like a cannon ball to the chest. The backward fall left him stunned.

When the world stopped spinning enough for him to understand his surroundings, Detective Lynch, Detective Gomez, and Special Agent Beck came into view. Gomez and Beck had weapons drawn; Lynch was twirling a set of handcuffs around his right index finger. In his other hand was the black trench coat he found in the shed.

"Hi Philip...right to remain silent and all that."

13. The Ravine

It had been a crummy summer for storms. The flooding was bad, but the wind was worse. Hundreds of trees were uprooted including one on the edge of Walter McKenzie's ravine.

The wind, however, only loosened the tree at its roots. It didn't actually knock the tree over causing it to wedge itself in another tree across the gap.

An eight-point buck did that.

It had been startled by a snake.

The snake was understandably grumpy. Her nap had been interrupted by a splash. The splash was from a set of disgusting costume false teeth landing in a puddle near her head.

Some people would have called it fate. Others would have called it an exercise in chaos theory. Still others…

14. Father Leo's Office

Leo was having a difficult afternoon. As it usually happened, a series of fleeting, random thoughts put him back in front of Eric Bell's Grand Jury. It crippled him, allowing him to do little more than sit at his desk and stare at the ceiling.

"Based on your years at school with the defendant, do you think he could have done what he is being accused of?"
"No."

His second year at seminary, Leo saw something. There were two students. One was in his year; the other was a year behind. What Leo saw, he saw in silhouette. It could have been something as simple as two men in a consoling embrace. He may have thought nothing of it had they not scurried in opposite directions when he cleared his throat. He recognized them both as they left the shadows. The one, it had been remarked around school, looked young for his age. The other would stand accused of violating Eric Bell thirty-two years later.

"Based on your years at school with the defendant, do you think he could have done what he is being accused of?"

"No."

Presently, he heard a voice.

"Father Leo?"

It was detective Lynch, or, more accurately, it was Jim. It had been a few days since Leo had seen…Jim.

"Did you catch him?"

Lynch nodded with an expression of resolution and relief.

"Come with me, Father."

"Where are we going?"

"I feel like I owe you for the other day. You wanna ride with me or take your own car?"

Leo stood.

"I'll drive myself."

THE INTERROGATION

In the interview room, were Detective Ernesto Gomez and Philip David McKenzie.

In the observation room, were James Lynch, Special Agent Marjorie Beck, the Mayor of Potterford, the P.P.D. Chief of Police, and Father Leonardo Pascucci.

The tape was rolling.

"We need to be perfectly clear about this for the record, Philip. Is it correct that you are waiving your right to have an attorney present?"

"It is."

"Very well, then we'll…"

"Under one condition."

"Alright…you didn't say that before, but I'm listening."

Philip's demeanor was one of concern, but not defeat.

"I am willing to make your job easier by keeping the shysters out of this room, but you have to do the same for me."

"I don't understand."

"I was unable to complete my task."

"I know. I still don't understand."

"Someone will need to complete it for me."

"Can't help you there."

"I don't mean anyone specific. I don't have anyone waiting in the wings, and I certainly don't expect *you* to do it. You're bound by your job. I understand that. No, no…plenty of people will want to see my mission complete when they hear what I have to say, and I need you to facilitate that."

"Philip, I'm sure, in your mind, you're making perfect sense, but I'm still lost. What are you asking me to do?"

"I need you, the Potterford Police Department, or whoever is behind that mirror over there, to make sure my statement is made public…and I mean viral-level public. I want everyone…*everyone* to hear every word.

"Your statement will be part of the public record. That's just a matter of course."

"No one goes looking for that shit. I need you to do more. Take out a page of the Herald, stick in on YouTube, give it to CNN, go on Howard Stern. I don't care how you do it."

"You won't need me, the P.P.D. or anyone behind that mirror to help you with that. No matter what we do, in twelve hours, your story will rival O.J.'s. I hear NBC's already working on the Saturday Night Live sketch."

"That's lovely sentiment, detective, but I'd still like your word that none of what I am about to say will be suppressed."

"Okay…yes…within the boundaries of the law, I can promise that. Fair?"

"Fair."

"Good, are you ready?"

"I am."

Gomez motioned toward the microphone.

"It's all yours."

Philip sat up straight with his fingers interlaced upon the table. This was the end of the line for him. All along, he'd considered the possibility that things might turn out this way. He'd started adjusting his thinking the moment he knew he was caught. Eloquence would have to succeed where planning and action had failed.

It was time.

"When I was living in Boston, going to Berklee, my roommate showed me a video. I don't remember where he got it. It might have been from one of his classes. It was called 'The Evils of Rock and Roll' …not 'Rock 'n Roll', 'Rock *and* Roll' …which already shows that the makers of the video didn't know what the fuck they were doing. Anyway, the writer-slash-director-slash-narrator was some sort of religious figure. I don't think he was a priest. He made big deal out of his Theology degree, that's for sure. Whatever he was, he'd made it his mission in life to abolish rock 'n roll.

"He started by explaining the origin of term. Do you know the origin of the term *rock 'n roll*?"

"Can't say I've given it much thought."

"It's sex. When straight-laced society first heard the music, they considered it lurid, so they gave it nickname to equate it with something they considered just as lurid. The nickname stuck. The same thing happened with 'jazz' and 'bebop.' Makes sense when you think about it. *Rock 'n roll*…there aren't too many activities that call for that action. Stay with me. I'm going somewhere with this. I promise."

"I'm not the least bit worried."

"The guy pontificated a bit, and then moved to examples of bands and solo acts that he deemed particularly demonic. The first few were what you'd expect. Any guesses?"

Gomez didn't flinch.

"Led Zeppelin, AC/DC, Black Sabbath, Alice Cooper, Kiss…"

"Excellent! I tell you, man, when you recognized Bill's guitar as the same instrument Carlos Santana plays, I knew that you knew your shit. But those bands were just a warm-up. The real crux of his spiel had to do with a *second* set of examples. Care to guess again?"

There was a cheek in Philip's tone. Ernie made his guesses accordingly.

"Neil Diamond? The Beatles? The Police? Bon Jovi?"

"Hey! You got one of them. Bon Jovi was there along with Prince, Billy Idol, and Madonna…all of them fairly innocuous compared to the first list wouldn't you say?"

The detective nodded. The killer continued.

"Not according to this guy. Damn! I wish I could remember his name! At any rate, he believed this second list to be worse than the first. Why? Because they all wear symbols of Christianity when they perform. He put a slide show under his narration zooming in on their necklaces and tattoos. You with me so far?"

"Completely."

"Next, the video showed a bottle of poison. You knew it was poison because it had an over-the-top skull and crossbones on the label. The narrator talked about how slim the chances were that someone would pick up the bottle and take a swig since the contents were so overtly deadly.

"Then he said 'however…if the poison is hidden,' and the video cut to a bowl of M & M's. The implication was that the poison was *in* the candy. To drive the point home, four children were shown eating it. Luckily, we were spared the image of four dead kids slumped beside an empty bowl.

"The narrator was a crackpot, but he was completely dead-right about one thing. The Devil is clever, and he hides. His plan is to take over, to undo, to *unmake*. For that, he needs numbers; for that, he needs souls."

He became lost in thought for a minute, and then snapped himself out of it with an expression of disgust.

"People think it's an 'opt in.' Thank you, Hollywood! Everyone pictures the Devil showing up in a time of desperate need and offering some kind of a mystical contract. Too easy. It's like the Devil gets thwarted by just saying 'no;' that's nonsense. Hear me now, Detective Gomez. If the Devil gets you, you won't know it happened until it's too late. That's the sick genius of Satan.

"It's misdirection, just like stupid-ass concept of the Satanic Cult."

He put his index fingers over his head like horns and wagged his tongue back and forth.

"Blaaahh! Satanic cults! What a load of shit...oh, don't get me wrong. I don't deny their existence. They're out there. They eat babies and skin people alive and offer up virgin sacrifices to the Devil and all that crap...but you see...that's Satan's bottle of poison! The horns and the red cape and the hooves and the fire and the fangs and the slick hairdo, that's the over-the-top skull and crossbones. Regular people are naturally repulsed by it. You don't get numbers that way. It's faddish. Almost no one gives a life of devotion to that kind of ridiculousness, and the ones that *do* end up in jail or dead by their own hands.

"The Satanic Cult is a distractive tool, nothing more. And besides..."

He leaned forward.

"...who needs a cult when you have a church?"

Philip cast his eyes about the room, allowing his words to penetrate all who were listening and picturing the millions who would soon also hear.

"That's right, detective. Satan has a church, and it ain't the guy in the goat mask surrounded by a throng of naked disciples jumping around a campfire. That's what Satan wants you to believe his church looks like! You want to find the Devil's church, the one true religion of Satan? Don't look behind the goat mask. Look under the miter. You want to look though history and find Satan's crowning achievement? His pride and joy? It isn't any serial killer's rampage, corporate buggering, or genocide..."

He stabbed his finger into the table.

"...it's Catholicism!"

Lynch looked for a reaction from his partner. There was none.

Attaboy Ernie. Don't give this guy nothin'!

Philip continued, obviously ignorant to the faith of his interviewer.

"You see, detective, it all goes back to the apostle Peter. The Catholics hang their hat on a bible verse in which Jesus says to Peter 'You are the rock upon which I build my church.' They believe Peter started the first and only true church of Church of Jesus Christ. They believe *Peter* was the first Pope. Peter didn't start shit. Peter was a dick and loser. Most of the apostles were losers. They blew just about every test that God threw at them."

An arrogant smile had worked its way onto Philip's lips. Gomez interpreted it correctly and said the killer's next sentence for him.

"But not you."

Philip shook his head slowly.

"I recognize a test when God gives it to me...every time. I pass them all, and I'm rewarded. I embrace His gifts, and I interpret them correctly. So, when I'm grabbing a smoke under Faith Church of Ellisport, thinking about all this stuff like I usually do when I'm alone, and a gun comes down from the heavens, glances off the near gunnel of a rowboat, and lands at my feet, I know what it means."

"That gun came from a meth-head, not the heavens."

Philip laughed.

"I know whose hands were on the weapon before mine. I also know how to interpret a one-in-a-billion shot like that, and I act."

Gomez was tempted to point out that Philip's present situation was proof that he, in fact, *didn't* 'pass all of his tests', but he let it slide. He'd already opened his mouth, and he was kicking himself for it. This was a confession, not a debate.

"Detective, I don't know what hand Peter had in the birth of Catholicism. A part of me believes that he was turned...turned the moment he denied Christ. That's admittedly far-fetched. I won't push it. I'm just saying that...son of a bitch...I lost my train of thought."

"You were talking about the Apostle Peter."

"No. Before that."

"The gun? Passing tests? Satan is the creator of Catholicism?"

"That's the one! Only don't use the word 'create.' Satan distorts, corrupts, ruins, but he doesn't create. He lacks the power to do so. It's one of the things that makes him so jealous of the All Mighty."

Then Gomez did something. He didn't know what it was. No one behind the mirror could tell what it was. Whatever it was, it made Philip show his first signs of frustration.

"You think I'm a nut. Don't you? Okay, let me reel it in a little…try a different angle. Say you want to proliferate a religion, or a political movement, or any kind of an ideology, but you have to do it using a pre-existing system. What do you do first? Think about the Nazi's, or, better yet, think about Leninist Russia: one of the biggest ream jobs in the history of the world. What did the Reds do? They re-interpreted and eventually gutted Russia's constitution to suit their own values.

"So, let's talk about the Ten Commandments here. Let's talk about God's constitution. Do you remember number one?"

Gomez gave the answer quickly and academically.

"Thou shalt have no other God before me."

"And Satan answered with sainthood! Don't pray to God, pray to these guys. And, guess what. If you're cool enough, you can become a saint too, and everyone will pray to you. By the way, you have to be Catholic. Fuck you! It ain't Saint Matthew's Church; it ain't Saint Peter's Church. It's God's Church!

"Number two: no graven images? Go into any Catholic Church and try and find an image of Christ. It'll be in there, hidden among ten-foot statues of Saint Asshole and Saint Pubic Hair…"

Lynch whispered under his breath.

"So much for reeling it in."

"…and none of the images are of the *risen* Christ; they're all of the *dying* Christ. Are you serious!?" He took a moment to catch his breath.

"Three: taking the Lord's name in vain? They've got everyone thinking that means saying 'Goddammit' and 'Jeezuss Christ.' It doesn't. I won't bore you with the Jewish ins and outs of the matter, but the only way we can take The Lord's name in vain is by saying it…by saying Jehovah! That's why we call Him God!

"Four: keep the Sabbath holy? How about we change the day it's on! That'll keep things nice and confusing.

"And all the rest: honor thy father and mother, don't steal, don't kill, don't covet. Apparently, ignoring all that stuff is okay as long as it's in the name of The Lord. Or, better yet, in the name of The Church which is the same thing if you're Catholic, and that's a whole topic unto itself.

"You know something detective? The sermon or the homily or whatever the hell it was that Bishop Ryan gave at Ella's confirmation centered around the topics of wrath and greed. He actually had the nerve to preach against them. How can any bishop, priest, archbishop, cardinal, or whatever preach against wrath and greed with the crusades and the Vatican in their wake!?

"It's devious hypocrisy, the same hypocrisy that got Jesus pissed at the pharoses! Religious leaders are supposed to be teachers. That's all! The word 'rabbi' means teacher. The second they become more than that, the *instant* they are perceived by their congregations as wielders of divine ability, or, even worse, conduits to God, Satan gains the power to usurp. I told you a couple minutes ago that Satan is incapable of creation; he's also incapable of controlling anything divine. Any control he assumes has got to be over things that are of the Earth. Hear me again, detective, when people believe that God and church are one and the same, *literally* all hell breaks loose.

"But all this is background. What I've been talking about is just tilled soil. This is all a way for Satan to access and utterly corrupt the core of God's message."

Gomez couldn't stop himself.

"Which is?"

"Forgiveness and repentance."

Saying the words let the steam out of Philips internal pressure cooker. The veins in his neck smoothed over. His shoulders went down. His face returned to its normal color. His expression turned almost pleasant, but it didn't last long.

"That's the whole thing, Sergeant Gomez. For God so loved the world that he gave his only begotten son. He died so we can live. He took the rap for the world, and over and over God's sons and daughters keep fucking up.

"When Adam and Eve fucked up, God kicked them out of paradise. He took everything they had and exiled them to the desert, cursed them with mortality, bestowed upon them everything that sucks about being human. Did they learn their lesson? No! But, even after one of their kids committed fucking fratricide, God decided to give humanity a chance…a chance that we blew.

"When it came time to do something about it, God decided to only punish those that deserved it. So, he had Noah build an ark. God wiped out everyone but the righteous, hoping Noah's descendants would follow God's will. They didn't. They fucked up again. They murdered each other, fornicated with each other's wives, built shrines to false gods, and even enslaved each other. They undid everything God had accomplished with the great flood.

"God then figured...maybe I've made things too complicated for these idiots. Maybe if I narrow it down to ten simple rules, things will get better, so God chose Moses to free the Jews, and take them to a place where the rules could be explained all in one shot...and on the way there...you guessed it...they fucked up! So, God had them wander for forty years, so the ones that fucked up would die off, leaving their children to pick up the torch.

"That seemed to work...for a while...until the Jews' spiritual leaders, the pharoses, started to get too self-important. Satan heard his dinner bell ring. With him whispering in their ears, the pharoses did deals with the pagan Roman Empire, preached a hierarchy of those deserving God's grace, and as a result, got fat and rich off of God's chosen people. This happened slowly and insidiously over thousands of years. That's the Devil at work, Detective Gomez. That was his first major attempt at taking the world from God...second if you count the snake and apple thing, but that was only two people so...easily handled.

"But I'm getting off point again.

"When it was all on the brink of turning on itself, God came up with a plan, and it was a simple one. He impregnated Mary, and, when the boy born of the divine union was old enough, God went to his subjects and said 'Okay! You see that guy? Do what he does! I can't make it any simpler than that!' and, with the apostles leading the way, we fucked that up too!"

Philip took a sip of water.

"But God loves us so much that he's given us a route back to paradise. All we have to do is acknowledge that we're fuck-ups and atone, all the while doing our best to follow Christ's example.

"Detective Gomez, if someone were to tell you that you could give everyone on Earth a trip to Heaven that they don't deserve, and all you have to do is suffer the most excruciating death imaginable, would you do it?"

Ernie's answer was simple and honest.

"I don't know."

"I would. You bet your ass I would. That's Christianity! It isn't crossing yourself. It isn't taking Communion once a week. It isn't eating fish on Fridays for a couple months out of the year, and certainly isn't wiping your slate clean through the retarded and futile exercise that the Catholics call confession! I kid you not, detective, (finger quotes) 'Confession' is the cherry on top of Satan's sundae.

"You push your grandmother down the stairs, walk into a box, tell a priest about it, then you're given some friendly advice along with a meaningless act of attrition, and you're sent on your way clean of all wrong-doing in God's eyes?? There are no words to describe how messed up that is. Bullshit doesn't cover it; horseshit doesn't cover it; garbage, nonsense, completely fubar; tell me the word, and I'll use it!

"It's a distortion of the worst kind. God's love has, does, and always will manifest itself in His forgiveness. But you have to repent...not 'confess'...repent! You have to throw yourself on God's mercy, take whatever Earthly punishment you are due, do the best you can to right your wrong, and be truly, deeply, honestly sorry for it. 'Confession' requires no remorse; all you have to do is say what you did out loud...to a *priest*. You don't get to confess directly to God, no no no, you confess *to a priest*. You pray to a saint, and you confess to a priest. Are you starting to see it, Detective Gomez?"

Ernie remained still, silent, and expressionless.

"Can you see how Satan wins two ways with this system? One, he makes it easier to sin. Two, his servants know your secrets. Hold on. I'm sorry; 'servant' is too harsh a word. I don't believe lowly priests know what they're doing. They serve The Devil, obliviously. That's pretty obvious. I don't know at what point in their ascension through the ranks they're told the truth. I would guess at some point before they make Cardinal. Lowly priests are just parts of a corrupt system. That's why I've left them alone.

"People get up in arms about molested children and the cover-ups that occur as a result, but there's a bigger picture here. People wonder how the diocese can let a priest stay in the church after such a thing happens. People stare in shock and awe when a violating priest gets relocated instead of kicked out. The diocese has no problem doing that stuff because their messed-up system justifies it! The molester has gone into a box and confessed. His slate is wiped clean. From the Catholic Church's point of view, the bastard gets a reboot. And the law can't do anything about it. Too many police commissioners are Catholic. They've gotten in the *big* box and aired their dirty laundry to the diocese higher-ups. They have blackmail to worry about."

Lynch breathed a small sigh of relief. Philip's wheels were finally coming off.

"The Catholic Church sells secrets told under the protection of the sacrament of confession to the mafia for money or favors. Oh! Catholicism is the *perfect* religion for criminals. It's not so perfect for women though. Have you noticed? Women are a tough nut for Satan to crack I think. They're not nearly as easy to corrupt as men. They're twice as easy to fool, but not as easy to corrupt. Nuns are funny though. They're one of the three 'universal funnies': nuns, farts, and Scottish accents. Think of a nun farting and then excusing herself in a Scottish accent. Then try and think of something funnier. You can't do it."

Philip waited for the laugh. It did not come.

"Aw, come on, detective. How can you...wait a second. I feel really stupid right now. You're of Latin American descent. You're Catholic, aren't you? This is perfect! I compliment you on your knowledge of the bible. I know you've probably never seen the inside of one. This must be very difficult for you to hear."

Not at all. The story of Little Red Riding Hood doesn't faze me either.

"But you see it now. Don't you, detective Gomez? You've been surrounded by it your whole life. You saw the disproportion of ritual to charity, of pageantry to humility. You saw the two faces of the leadership. You saw the Orwellian quality of Mass: 'Stand up, sit down, kneel, cross yourself, eat this, and drink that.' You found it all strange, didn't you? But you couldn't put your finger on why. You couldn't find the one horrible thing that brought it all together in a way that made sense. Now you've met me, and it makes sense, doesn't it?"

"Do you want an answer, or is the question rhetorical?"

Philip chuckled.

"Neither actually. I don't expect you to answer honestly while we're being recorded. With my help you've put it together. I can tell. You see now how the Devil works. He twists God's words and uses them against Him. He pretends to advocate Godly things like family and gift giving

334

when all he's interested in is growing his congregation and building more temples."

He was getting louder with every sentence.

"He dogmatically convinces his priests that salvation is attained through a lifestyle that drives them half-crazy and turns them into perverts. He facilitates sin. He sets up an infrastructure that elects its own members, and goes unquestioned by its congregation for fear of going to hell. And the key to the whole thing…is one guy in charge! One guy that answers to on one. No king, no nation, no one!"

For the first time since the tape started rolling, Lynch turned his head to check on Father Leo.

He was not there.

IT'S THAT BEAUTIFUL

It didn't take much to find him. When Lynch pushed the door open to Frankie and Jimmy's, the light from outside fell on the good priest. He was sitting at the bar staring forward with a full pint of ale in front of him. He'd put the money on the bar. Jimmy hadn't taken it.

"Hey, Jimmy."

"Hey, Sergeant. You on the clock?"

"I am, and I'll have a Lager, thank you."

There was an unoccupied stool next to Father Leo. It made a noise across the hardwood floor as Lynch pulled it back from the bar and hopped on. Tom Petty was playing on the jukebox. For a full minute, it was the only noise in the bar.

"She was an American Girl…"

Then Lynch spoke.

"You missed the best part."

"Did I? What's that?"

"Well, as far as I could follow, Philip believes himself to be a descendant of Judas Iscariot…"

Leo's expression turned inquisitive but did not dignify the statement with a response.

"…I know. That's what I thought. Judas had no kids, and he killed himself, but that's the thing, see. Philip believes that Judas *didn't* kill himself. The proof, he claims, is if he killed himself, no one would know what Jesus said to him in the Garden of Gethsemane.

"He also said that Judas was the only apostle that did what was asked of him, and the others were spiteful because of it. That's how he got the bad rap. Then Philip went back into talking about how the apostles were dicks yadda yadda. Then his eyes glazed over and he started talking about a dream he had, or a vision or some such."

Leo reached for his ale and took the first pull.

"I see. Is everyone going to be safe tomorrow? Did he tell you where the bomb is?"

"It wasn't a bomb; it was a poisoning. The bomb was another thing."

"A poisoning? That sounds complicated."

"He was going to impersonate a priest and access the wine before Mass. The poison was fast-acting stuff. Cardinal Romero would have drunk first and keeled over immediately. Painting it positive, no one else would most likely have been hurt.

"If that didn't work, he was going to take Communion during Mass, *then* add the poison and get Cardinal Romero to drink it somehow. He hadn't completely formulated his backup plan. We got to him too soon."

"That's good."

"Care to hear what he had in mind for the Pope?"

"The Pope was next? I don't know…a grizzly bear?"

"He was going to kidnap him."

"No shit."

"He wasn't about to make the Pope a martyr. He was going to kidnap him, set him up on a webcam, and make him confess 'the truth' to the world. Mind you, he has no idea how he was going to do it, but he knows exactly what he was planning on saying to the Pope once he got him alone."

"Does he realize Pope Gregory doesn't speak English?"

"He didn't say anything about it. Probably not."

Leo sighed.

"Well, as mislaid as it was, you've got to admire the man's ambition. I wear roughly the same uniform as His Holiness and I've never even gotten *close*."

"He wasn't worried about that. He was counting on the Philly diocese to continue working upstream. You replaced a Bishop with an Archbishop; you were about to replace an Archbishop with a Cardinal. You had to bring the Pope to Potterford sooner or later."

"Yeah, we helped him out there, I suppose."

"I'm guessing that never would have happened though."

"Not in a million years."

Both men nipped their beers and watched the golf match that was on the bar television. Neither of them played. The juke box switched to Johnny Cash. Lynch pointed to the five-dollar bill lying flat in front Leo.

"You're not expecting Jimmy to take that, are you?"

The priest gave the money a fleeting glance.

"He will eventually, or I'll just leave it there."

"You'll get it back at Mass."

"That's okay."

The case was over. These were just two guys shooting the shit over a beer. Bon Jovi was next.

"Johnny used to work at the doooock..."

They both smiled to themselves for the same reason. Leo spoke.

"Interesting day, then?"

"Wasn't bad."

Leo's head had been in a bad place most of the day. In just about any other environment, what came out of his mouth next would have come across as a sudden and nutty change of subject. But this was Frankie and Jimmy's at three o'clock on a Friday afternoon. No rules.

"Can I ask you something, Jim?"

"Of course."

"What are you? I mean what religion? I've never asked. I know it's none of my business, but I'm curious."

"I was raised Methodist, but I haven't practiced for a long time."

"Do you still believe in God?"

"Whoa-ho! Livin' on a pra-yer!"

"Do you want the short version or the long version?"

"Give me the short."

"Yes."

"Now give me the long."

"I don't think you'll like it."

"I'll take my chances."

Lynch finished his lager and signaled Jimmy for another.

"If I speak in paragraph form, it's only because I've talked this through several times, to myself, out loud. Keep in mind that my parents were both church-going academics. Whether by nature or nurture, I have spent a lot of my life trying to reconcile religion and science.

"I believe there is a force in the universe that tries to steer all things toward a greater good. I believe this force to be benevolent, and, simply out of habit, I call it God.

"On a daily basis, I am brought face to face with the argument against a world with purpose. People see things like muggings, sexual assaults, child neglect, and drug overdose as evidence of a world set afloat with no rudder. I see the opposite. When I see that stuff, I see pushback. I see collision. I see the friction and the resulting fire that ignites when people act in contrary to God's guidance.

"I'll tell you something else. I've got no problem with science. It's done its job. But nothing has convinced me that science can explain why I feel the way I do about my girlfriend. There's no electrical impulse in my brain that explains why I like creamed herring and Steely Dan."

Jimmy put Lynch's pint on the bar. Lynch nodded thank you, took a foamy gulp, and continued.

"So, yes, I believe in a soul, for lack of a better thing to call it. And the soul is friggin' awesome. It's a good thing that it is too, because the body sucks. The soul is what God speaks to, and the body fights it because the body's time is limited. It's only interested in solutions that are quick, easy, or both.

"A guy is beating up his wife and the neighbors hear it. They should do something. They *know* they should do something. God is *telling* them to do something but they don't. Why? Because the guy might be a psycho, and the body doesn't want to risk injury. Because they may have to serve as witnesses at a trial, and the body would rather watch reruns of Seinfeld. And that, father, I believe to be the actual root of all evil … when the body wins.

"And, yes, I acknowledge that nothing I've said accounts for mental illness. I'm still working on that one.

"My partner was actually talking about this stuff a few days ago (burp) sort of. He was theorizing about the soul being quasi-parasitic."

"I'm sorry. What?"

"Never mind. I'm trying to work my way around to death. I mean, if the soul lacks the limitations of the body, then it must be eternal, right? Death has to be nothing more than the soul leaving this ridiculous, overused vehicle and going on to a plane of existence we can't begin to understand. Is it Heaven? To put a name to it, I suppose so. I find the clouds and angels thing challenging, but I it's got to be free of pain…free of the body…and that's good enough.

"Now, here's the thing. If I'm going to believe there's something out there that can speak directly to the soul, then I have to acknowledge that it's not too far of a leap to believe that such a thing could manifest itself as human and walk among us a bit over 2000 years ago. Does that make me a Christian? If I knew more about Islam or Hinduism, I could probably make the same leap to one of those. So, I guess I don't know.

"How's that for the religious beliefs of a certified ladder logic programmer?"

Leo cracked a smile.

"I've heard worse…"

He turned back to the golf.

"…but you should get yourself to church every once in a while, to nurture that stuff. Religion is a team sport."

"I know. I'd rather sleep in."

Both men laughed. So did Jimmy, who was washing wine glasses and eavesdropping from the end of the bar. Lynch went on.

"My dad had something to say to me once when I gave him a fight about going to church. I was twelve, and I remember saying 'What's the point? How do you even know God exists?'. And my dad looked me square in the eye and said 'I don't. I have no proof; I want no proof. If there were proof of the existence of God, then God's existence would be a fact, and there would be no reason to believe. If there's no reason to believe, then there's no reason to have faith. If there's no reason to have faith, then there's no reason for faith to be tested. And if faith doesn't get tested, then someone has a shit-load of explaining to do.'"

Leo perked up.

"You remember that whole thing from twenty-some-odd years ago?"

"I do, and I'm guessing you have thoughts."

"I have … one thought."

"Hit me."

"I think you just gave evidence that not only God can speak to the soul."

Lynch opened his mouth to respond, but receded into contemplative silence hoping he could match the good priest thought for thought. After 30 seconds, he took his shot.

"Do you find it interesting that my vocation led me to my beliefs, while your beliefs led to you to your vocation."

"Vocation?"

He pointed at his collar.

"…you call this a vocation?"

"Okay, poor word choice. Your calling then. Nuns call it a calling, don't they? I don't know what priests call it."

"Relax, Sergeant I'm kidding…"

Leo did a quarter-turn to face his companion.

"…but, as long as you brought it up, it wasn't my beliefs that made me a priest. It was a series of early life experiences too long and too personal to list."

"Too personal? Didn't you just ask me…"

"Yes, I did. I don't mean they're too personal to share. I mean they're too personal to talk about in a way that I can make coherent. But, if you're interested, I can tell you why I stay; I can tell you what drives me."

Lynch caught Jimmy's eye, and flashed him a three-part hand signal: two fingers like a peace sign, then the index finger and thumb spread vertically about an inch apart and lastly, a thumbs-up.

The translation: two shots of the good stuff.

"You bet your ass I'm interested."

Leo was suddenly twenty-three again, having a cigarette behind the family butcher shop. He saw the old man with the pipe and wondered for the hundredth time what ever happened to the guy.

"Jim…I was in line at the Wawa a couple of weeks ago. The woman in front of me handed the cashier a hundred-dollar bill and said, 'everyone's coffee is on me this morning. Then she left. Is that going to make the evening news?

"All anyone has to do is look around, and they'll see a thousand acts of kindness in a day. People hold open doors. People get things off of shelves for other people. People help people off the ground when they fall. People fix things for other people. People run clothing drives, food drives, clean-outs, walk-a-thons, charity bake sales. It happens *every second of every day.*

"People get so down on the world. We turn on the TV and get pummeled by bad news. We go to work, and see people get shit on by their bosses for eight hours. It's disheartening, and it clouds the truth."

The detective and the priest fired down their shots.

"Whew! The truth, Jim, at least as I see it, is that the bad guys of the world are in a vast minority. It just doesn't seem like it because they make all the fucking noise.

"Good is anonymous; bad is boastful. Good is fair; bad is ruthless. Good only takes what it needs; bad uses thing up and continues to take. Good has its power in millions of little acts of kindness; bad has its power in a few acts of devastation. Good blossoms from a single point like tree; bad spreads like a virus.

"My point is that the world is a good place. I'm a weirdo for saying it, but it's true, and God forgive me, but I consider myself in the majority..."

He took another pull. Somehow, the beer at F & J's never got warm.

"...within the context of the fact that we're all sinners of course, I consider myself in the majority. I consider *you* in the majority. I'm not talking about the diocese or the Potterford P.D. here. I'm talking about people, individual people, God's children. For every diddling priest, there are 1000 Father O'Rourkes. For every Kevin Reilly, there are 1000 Jim Lynches. The organizations need to be taken to task, but it's still just a few assholes ruining it for the rest of us, and when I say 'the rest of us,' I don't mean priests and cops; I mean humanity. I do not believe you to be corrupt. I hope you don't believe I'm a diddler."

"I don't."

"Good. People need to be reminded of that. People need to be reminded that they can look in the face of nearly every other person they meet in a day and say 'I don't think you're a jerk.' And church is, hands down, the best way to do it. You put dozens...hundreds...thousands of like-minded people in one room, and through the sacraments, have them unite under one awesome ideal. That is a church..."

Another pull.

"...and that is why I am a part of it."

His voice hadn't gone above conversation volume. His facial expression had been nothing but pleasant.

Both men needed a breather. Leo needed to rest his diaphragm, and Lynch needed to process everything he'd heard since he walked into the bar. He asked Jimmy for the remote and flipped around until he found a Phillies game.

"You like baseball?"

"Sure."

"Cool. Heads up, Jimmy"

He tossed the remote down the bar. Jimmy nabbed it without looking. Leo spoke.

"So, what else did I miss?"

"I've told you all the details I can remember under the circumstances."

"Thank you for letting me in the room by the way. You didn't have to do that, and I'm sorry I left."

"No, *I'm* sorry. I completely understand. It couldn't have been easy hearing someone accuse the Catholic Church of belonging to the Devil."

"Did he quote Revelations, reference the Seventh Day Adventists, or do any comparisons to Druidic rituals?"

"Not that I remember."

"Then he wasn't thorough. It's all been said before. Every religion on the planet has been persecuted as some point, and Catholicism is no different."

"Yeah, but…"

"Look…Philip doesn't get it. Neither do you for that matter. If you did, you'd be Catholic. Everybody would."

"You think so?"

"With all my heart. Believe me. It's *that* beautiful."

Lynch took his last sip of alcohol for the afternoon.

"Then why did you leave the room?"

Each of them had put down two beers and a shot. That was nothing for Leo…cocktail hour…but he was still feeling the effects.

Archbishop Fellini's face appeared in his mind's eye. He was in the courthouse speaking to Father Leo as he was on his way to testify before Eric Bell's grand jury. Leo heard the Archbishop's words as loudly and clearly as if His Grace was in the room.

Whoosh…

"Because, Jim, for all of Philip McKenzie's psychoses…"

"Just do what you think is…"

"…he was just doing what he thought…"

343

"...right Father."

"…was right."

Lynch was confused. He was sure it was the booze.
"Detective Lynch."
"Yes, Father Pascucci?"
"Prepare yourself for a unique experience."
"How's that?"
"You're about to take a confession from a priest."

EPILOGUE 1

Two and a half minutes from Pastor Devlin's next sermon:

"... with special permission, I was given early access to the transcripts from Mick's arrest interview. They will soon be made public, and I highly recommend that all of you read or listen to them when you can.

"You will be saddened, as I was, to notice several word-for-word similarities between his...statements...and past sermons of mine.

"If I may beg your indulgence, I'd like to bear witness; no...not bear witness. I'm going to drop the religious nomenclature for a minute.

"I put no positive spin on the events of this past week. Admittedly, I initially looked upon the murders of Bishop Ryan and Archbishop Fellini as chickens coming home to roost. The transcripts...well...let's just say *my* chickens certainly came home to roost."

A pause.

"Some of you know Father Aiden O'Rourke from Saint Aloysius Roman Catholic Church. Until two days ago, our relationship was similar to that of two ambassadors. Now he and I find ourselves sobered...humbled...able to reach out a friendly and empathetic hand. I don't know what he thinks of me, but I feel I can call him a friend.

"That's a powerful word: friend. So much can change as the result of a really good conversation with a friend.

"The papers aren't going to be kind to us over the coming weeks. Mick will be painted as a religious fanatic, and they'll spin it as a reflection upon this church. They'll find ways to spin it back on St. Al's as well.

"Please. This is not a time to fight. It's not a time to prove who's the bigger bad guy. If you know anyone from St. Aloysius or anyone else who has been affected by these murders, extend a hand. Have a good conversation. Make a friend.

"You want to thwart Satan? You want to see some good rise from the ashes of Mick's actions? Then do two things: Make a friend...an *unlikely* friend, and learn. Use what the bible tells us, and learn.

"Learn what? That will be too personal to generalize, but I'll give you my take-away.

"A good number of people, including the press, will infer that the lesson to be learned here is religion is dangerous, and they won't be completely wrong. Religion *is* dangerous, but that doesn't make it bad.

"Friends, just like justice, just like freedom, just like honor, just like loyalty, *religion*…or, if you prefer…*belief* is a good thing. And, if the week's events have shown us anything, if there is anything to be learned, it is how dangerous a good thing can be in the wrong hands."

EPILOGUE 2

With the murderer caught, Cardinal Romero thought it best to stay in Batswana. Saturday Mass was turned over to Father Aiden O'Rourke. Here are fifteen seconds of his sermon. This is after a reading of the parable of the Good Samaritan; Luke 10: Verses 25 – 37:

"We find inspiration in Paul's letters. We find solace in the Psalms. We find salvation in eyewitness testimony of the Gospel. But, when we read the words of the Lord, the things that Jesus said himself, what came from the lips of our savior … and, by this, I mean primarily the parables and the Sermon on the Mount. If we read these passages, we find that the vast majority of His teachings deal with how we treat each other. This is as easy to forget as it is important not to forget…"

Few in the congregation understood what he was getting at, but that was good enough.

EPILOGUE 3

Lynch was glad to get back to robberies and drug busts. The McKenzie murders (as they came to be known) made the national news, but James Lynch, to his own delight, did not.

It was six o'clock on a Friday afternoon some months later. Lynch reached the top of the stairs to find Julie staring thoughtfully at her laptop. They'd planned a trip to his sister's house in Savannah, Georgia.

He spoke.

"You packed yet?"

"Yes, and so are you."

"Awesome, thanks. What are you doing?"

"Taking a survey."

346

Lynch laughed.

"A survey!?"

"Shut up. I'll get a ten-dollar gas coupon at the end. That should at least get us to Delaware."

He kissed her neck and rubbed her back. She purred and responded likewise. Hands wandered, breathing deepened.

"How long is your fucking survey going to take?"

"Half hour maybe."

"I can't wait that long. We'll be sleeping in my niece's bedroom for a week."

"My session times out in ten minutes."

He pulled off his tie and kicked off his shoes.

"Piece o' cake."

They launched into each other and maneuvered to the couch.

"Watch the laptop!"

Twelve minutes later, Lynch lay staring at his girlfriend's bare back as she answered questions about her favorite reality TV show. The late afternoon sun put her partially in silhouette.

She looked back and winked.

He thought to himself...

Yeah, I can do this.

EPILOGUE 4

Kevin Reilly came out of his coma four days after his brother's arrest.

In the end, he was allowed to keep his badge, thanks to a strong union delegate and a rally by the other detectives.

After the final hearing, Lynch took Reilly aside and made it very clear that he, Gomez, and Warner went to bat strictly for Braden's sake.

"Your penance will be served behind a desk. Your redemption will be earned by being a role model for your nephew."

Boris retired within the year, and Kevin Reilly took his place.

EPOLOGUE 5

It was early summer on Lake Wallenpaupack. The wind was perfect.

For the sake of his health and sanity, the diocese made Leo take some time off.

When word got to the Bell Family that the case was getting a second look, Eric, now twenty years old, came forward.

Whether faced with the fear of going through it all again, or coming to terms with the stakes having grown a few years, Eric Bell finally told the truth. The boy *had* been molested, but not by a priest (Leo's classmate or otherwise). The actual perpetrator was one of his mother's business partners. The monster convinced Eric that the brokerage would never survive if the truth came out, so the angry and confused boy projected the abuse onto an innocent.

Video from a laptop proved everything; the slime pled no contest.

While in a familial embrace, Eric was assured by his mother that the low percentage loss in clients was well worth the trade-off. The Bells would be okay.

But this wasn't enough for Leo. His whistle had been whetted. He started a crusade against Father Braniff, the bastard priest who took Carl Ingram camping. With help from Lynch, Gomez, Warner, and eventually Special Agent Marjorie Beck, the case got reopened.

Braniff would be found guilty, and there would be no relocation. That, however, was several months off.

Now, Leo skimmed across the choppy waters of Lake Wallenpaupack, one hand on the main sheet, the other on the tiller. Even with the Eric Bell and Carl Ingram cases resolved, or close to resolved, Leo was tortured by the notion that a lot of it could have been prevented if he'd spoken sooner.

How though? Lynch, Beck, the diocese…they all confirmed what I'd hoped: I didn't lie on the stand. The lawyer screwed up. I can't be held responsible for that. Braniff would have done what he did regardless of the trial outcome. But, perhaps he hurt more boys in the interim. Perhaps…I have no proof of that. I have no proof. No proof…no…

"Ahhhh! What a beautiful day."

And Leo finally understood why his father wanted him to learn how to sail.

Made in the USA
Middletown, DE
03 July 2020